PRAISE FOR LORELEI JAMES'S
BLACKTOP COWBOYS® NOVELS

"Takes readers on a satisfying ride. . . . While James is known for erotic interludes, she never forgets to bolster the story with plenty of emotional power."   —*Publishers Weekly*

"No one writes contemporary erotic romance better than Lorelei James. Her sexy cowboys are to die for!"
    —*New York Times* bestselling author Maya Banks

"Lorelei James knows how to write one hot, sexy cowboy."
    —*New York Times* bestselling author Jaci Burton

"The down-and-dirty, rough-and-tumble Blacktop Cowboys kept me up long past my bedtime. Scorchingly hot, wickedly naughty."   —Lacey Alexander, author of *Give In to Me*

"Combining the erotic and family, love and romance with doubt and vulnerabilities, and throwing in some plain old fun always makes her reads favorites of mine every time."
    —The Good, the Bad, and the Unread

"Hang on to your cowboy hats because this book is scorching hot!"   —Romance Junkies

"Lorelei James knows how to write fun, sexy, and hot stories."   —Joyfully Reviewed

"Sexy and highly erotic."   —TwoLips Reviews

"Incredibly hot."   —The Romance Studio

"[A] wild, sexy ride."

ALSO BY LORELEI JAMES

The Mastered Series

Bound
Unwound
Schooled (A Mastered Series Novella)
Unraveled

The Blacktop Cowboys® Series

Corralled
Saddled and Spurred
One Night Rodeo
Turn and Burn
Hillbilly Rockstar

WRANGLED AND TANGLED

A BLACKTOP COWBOYS® NOVEL

LORELEI JAMES

A SIGNET BOOK

SIGNET
Published by the Penguin Group
Penguin Group (USA) LLC, 375 Hudson Street,
New York, New York 10014

USA | Canada | UK | Ireland | Australia | New Zealand | India | South Africa | China
penguin.com
A Penguin Random House Company

Published by Signet, an imprint of New American Library, a division of Penguin
Group (USA) LLC. Previously published in a Signet Eclipse edition.

First Signet Printing, April 2015

ISBN 978-0-451-47312-7

Printed in the United States of America
10 9 8 7 6 5 4 3 2 1

Chapter One

❦

*J*anie Fitzhugh had a new rule: Never make drunken promises at a bachelorette party.

When she'd hit the local honky-tonk for Harper Masterson's big blowout, Harper's former nail clients—all women over the age of seventy—insisted on buying multiple X-rated shots, including a tasty little one called a cowboy cocksucker. She'd lost track of the number she'd consumed and vaguely remembered dancing on the bar with a firecracker of a woman named Garnet. Evidently Janie had a rip-roaring time; too bad she had zero recollection of her actions after the karaoke started. Evidently she'd also promised her ex-husband, Abe Lawson, she'd owe him a favor—any favor—if he took her drunken ass home.

A favor Abe had waited a whole week to collect on.

So that's how Janie found herself driving to the Lawson ranch on a beautiful fall morning, half in disbelief she was returning to the one place she swore she'd never go again.

As she started up the long, winding driveway, past the haystacks, the refueling station, the hopper that released the livestock supplement known as "cake," she expected to see the same old, same old. Most ranchers were averse to any kind of change, which was one of the main issues she'd had with Abe. He maintained the "if it ain't broke don't fix it" attitude in all aspects of his life.

At first, she'd really loved Abe's steadfastness. But eventually that trait had driven them apart.

Not that you're completely blameless. When Abe swept you off your feet, giving you everything you told him that you wanted, how could you fault him for being the man you'd fallen in love with?

So the improvements shocked her. The dull gray house had been repainted a vibrant shade of terra-cotta. The front deck had been revamped with the addition of a sheltered arbor and a wooden porch swing. A new split rail fence separated the yard from the pasture and disappeared around the back of the house.

The outlying areas between the house and outbuildings no longer had piles of busted farm machinery, abandoned vehicles, and stacks of warped lumber. How much of the cleanup had been Hank's wife's doing? The cluttered state had never bothered any of the Lawson siblings when Janie lived here.

The enormous wooden barn had retained the charming, weathered look. It was sandwiched between the machine shed and a new metal structure twice the size of the old one.

She parked behind a 350 Cummins diesel truck caked with mud. Made no sense why she experienced a bout of nerves.

How many times had she come home from a long day of classes to see Abe leaning against the porch rail, waiting for her with a smile on his face? No one had been as happy to see her since. Maybe she was disappointed he wasn't waiting for her like he used to. Shoving aside her melancholy, she climbed out of her car.

Janie admired the new concrete walkway crafted to resemble a cobblestone path. She resisted smoothing her hair or adjusting her clothes after she knocked on the door.

The door swung inward. Abe smiled at her. "Hey. Come on in."

Wasn't it grossly unfair he looked better now than he had when she'd married him almost eleven years ago?

Maybe it's poetic justice since you left him.

His gaze moved over her, head to toe, as sensual as a full-body caress. "You look great even when you're fixin' to clean the basement. I always admired that about you."

"You're kidding, right?"

"Nope. I say what I mean, Janie. You know that about me."

Maybe it's time you *stop kidding yourself you're immune to his attempts to lure you into his lair for a little mattress dancing.*

Hah. Janie wasn't immune to him. Not even freakin' close.

And the hell of it was, his damn cowboy charm was weakening her resolve not to get mixed up with him again. They'd been divorced eight years. She was over him. She'd been over him a long time.

Hadn't she?

"Janie?"

Meeting his gaze, she swallowed a purely feminine moan. Abe Lawson had the most beautiful eyes—silvery-gray offset by long, thick black eyelashes. Yet he hadn't mastered the art of masking his feelings. They'd always been right there, bold and unapologetic. Like now.

Intent. Fortitude. Amusement. Lust.

Then he violated her personal space, moving close enough she caught a whiff of his cologne. Not the *Chaps* scent she remembered but a woodsy, skin-warmed aroma that encouraged her traitorous brain to purr, *what are you waiting for? Hot man, hot skin, hot damn.*

"Cat got your tongue, cupcake?" he drawled.

"No. Seems a little weird to be here." Janie stepped around him and into the entryway. Boxes of ceramic tile were piled next to the wall and new mortarboard spread to the edge of the carpet.

"Watch your step. It's a mess. I hope to get back to it this week."

"I didn't know you could tile, Abe."

"I didn't either. Not until we started putting the finishing touches on Hank and Lainie's house. Found out it ain't as hard as I thought."

"I'm sure it'll look great when you're done. Can I see the tile?"

Abe pulled out a square from the top box. "Nothin' fancy."

The tile was swirled with brown and rust in a random pattern, but wasn't plain. "I like it."

"Thanks." Abe set the tile back and gestured for her to precede him past the wall separating the entryway from the living room.

Now this room had sustained major improvements. The frayed orange and brown sofa patterned with horses? Gone. As were the matching tangerine-colored corduroy side chairs. Abe's late mother's knickknacks no longer adorned all available shelf space. The room was typical bachelor, puffy tan couches with built-in recliners. A ginormous TV. A sturdy wooden coffee table piled with remotes. The only reminders of his parents were the family picture on the wall and the crocheted afghan draped over the back of the couch.

"I know it ain't up to the decorating standards of the Split Rock."

Ooh. Snap. Janie bristled. "I wasn't comparing, if that's what you're getting at. I was trying to remember what it used to look like."

The tense lines around his mouth relaxed. "I'd think you'd remember in detail, since I pretty much forbid you from making any changes after we got married, didn't I?"

"Probably. But I was moving into your home with your family, so I didn't push it."

"I shoulda tried harder to make it our home." Abe rubbed the back of his neck. "I did some dumb things, Janie. You can't know how sorry I am."

As thoughtful as his apology was, she waved him off.

Playing the blame game now was pointless. "You said those boxes were downstairs?" She cut through the kitchen to the door that led into the basement.

"Careful you don't trip," he said as he followed her.

The lights were already on. This room hadn't changed a bit. Wood-paneled walls. Floral curtains covering the small windows. Beanbag chairs held together with duct tape. Olive green shag carpeting. *Reader's Digest* condensed books filled shelves. Along with board games she'd remembered: Life, Battleship, Mouse Trap, Chinese checkers. She and Celia had spent hours challenging each other, since Abe and Hank had been too busy or they believed it too juvenile to play board games with their little sister. Somehow in the bitterness of her marriage ending, she'd forgotten those happy times spent with Celia, munching popcorn, listening to the country tunes on the boom box.

Janie focused on the stacks of boxes rather than the memories. "Remind me again where you got all of this stuff?"

"My ex-girlfriend Nancy. She had so many boxes in her garage she had no place to park her car. I swear the whole reason she was dating me was to get rid of all this crap."

"Oh, I'm sure there were other reasons." One nine-inch reason in particular popped into her head.

Not productive. Think of something else.

How about his muscled chest spattered with just the right amount of dark hair? Or those perfect buns, tight and muscular from years in the saddle? Or those wonderfully callused hands? Or that heated look Abe got in his eye when he—

"Janie?"

She jumped. What was wrong with her? She wasn't supposed to be imagining her ex-husband naked. "Sorry. I'm just trying to figure out a starting point." She ducked her head to hide the blush and opened the closest box. "First we should determine what to do with the clothing I don't want."

"I'm tempted to throw it all in the garbage. But that seems wasteful, don't it?"

"Yes. Especially after keeping it all this time." Janie peered up at Abe. "How long *has* this stuff been down here?"

"Since last Christmas." He winced. "I have to pass by it when I use the laundry room. Every time I think I'll take care of it next week. And then I never do."

"Because you don't want to let go of Nancy?"

He snorted. "Not even close."

Outdated, matronly styles filled the first box and wouldn't fit the hip, retro theme of the resort's Western store, Wild West Clothiers. If all the boxes contained these types of clothes, they'd be done lickety-split. "Let's put the stuff I'm not taking in garbage bags."

"I'll grab some." Abe disappeared up the stairs.

The next box had two funky vintage Western shirts and a denim skirt that went into the keep pile.

By the time Abe returned with a roll of garbage bags, she'd cleared another box. "Look at you go."

"I'm a woman on a mission." She scrutinized a paisley scarf. If Harper couldn't sell it she'd probably craft a headband out of it. The woman had a knack for recycling old pieces into new and had an eye for style, which was why she and Renner had hired her to run the store.

A heavy male sigh echoed. "I'm standing here doin' nothin'."

"That's because I want you to rest up all those big muscles. I'll use you later." Janie glanced over at him. "You okay with that?"

"Ah. Sure." He tugged on the collar of his shirt. "Is it getting hot in here, or is it just me?"

"Must just be you." She shook out a floral sweater and caught a glimpse of Abe as he unbuttoned his cuffs.

Oh no. He wasn't stripping—*yep*—off went his gray shirt, leaving him in a white wife beater. Ow wow. Had his chest always been that broad? Had his biceps always been that big? Had his forearms always bulged with ropy muscle? Had his stomach always been that flat?

"Lemme bring these to you." Abe dragged the boxes

closer, which seemed to strain his back muscles until those strong, tight cords of flesh rippled beautifully beneath his skin. He stood fewer than two feet away from her, breathing hard.

Wowza. He wasn't the only one breathing hard. Something about seeing the man in heavy work mode had always tripped her trigger.

You'll get eyestrain if you keep gawking at him like that.

They worked in silence. Although Janie feigned the utmost concentration on unpacking, she was hyperaware of Abe's every move. Of his every toiling muscle. Of his every labored breath. "Were you serious about wanting to redo the basement?"

"Nah. I just wanted to lure you down here so we could relive the washing machine episode." He paused and peeped at her from beneath those absurdly long eyelashes. "Do you remember?"

A wave of heat blasted her. They'd been out checking cattle on the ATV and it'd started to pour. By the time they returned home, their clothes were soaked. She'd insisted they strip in the entryway and she'd carried the sopping bundle down to the laundry room, expecting Abe would take his shower first. But he'd followed her. After the washer lid had slammed, he'd been on her. Dropping to his knees and making her come with his mouth, before stretching her across the washer and taking her from behind as the machine kicked into the spin cycle. It'd been a sizzling encounter because it was so out of character for Abe—and out of the norm for them. Living with two other people—his younger brother and sister—restricted their amorous activities to the bedroom.

She lifted her gaze to his. Her heart sped up witnessing the fire in his eyes. "Of course I remember. It was one of the few times we were . . ."

Abe inched closer. "We were what?"

"Alone. Sexually spontaneous."

"Sad state of our marriage, doncha think?"

"It was what it was."

"You can't know how that eats at me." He reached out to touch her, but dropped his hand at the last second. "I wasn't aware of the mistakes I'd made with you until Hank and Lainie got married."

"Abe—"

"I'm sorry. So goddamned sorry. If I could go back . . ."

"You can't. It wouldn't change anything. We both made mistakes."

His gray eyes searched hers carefully. "Are you saying it was a mistake when you left me?"

The last thing she needed was to justify why she'd left him. The mistakes hadn't been all his, but she would've suffocated if she'd stayed here. There was no way she could tell Abe that without revisiting the pain they'd caused each other when she'd walked out. She smiled at him softly. "I'm saying we have a lot more boxes to get through. Let's not dwell on stuff that doesn't matter now."

Abe didn't argue. After a bit, he said, "I did ask you here for your professional advice. I don't want to spiff up the downstairs for Celia. I want to do it for me."

"That's surprising."

"Why?"

It'd dredge up the past they were tiptoeing around if she pointed out how rarely Abe had done things for himself. His efforts had been ranch or family focused. "You considered the basement Celia's domain."

"I ain't kiddin' myself that Celia will ever live here again for any length of time."

Janie smoothed the wrinkles out of a sleeveless red and white checked blouse. "If she finds her dream guy will she inherit a chunk of Lawson land to build her own place so she can be close to family?"

"I guess we'll see. Something's changed in her. She always was a little naïve and I blame me'n Hank for that. We overprotected her. Set down ultimatums—which is something I was good at, huh?"

"You've had your moments."

"Like I said, I have changed. So has Celia. Now she's quick to leave a situation if it riles her in some way."

"Meaning what?"

"Meaning the Celia we raised never backed down from a confrontation with me or Hank or any of the guys she's been around her whole life. Now she walks away."

"You don't see that as a sign she's grown up? Grown out of her mouthy ways?" After the words tumbled free, Janie wished she'd kept her trap shut. Abe had always leapt to Celia's defense—no matter what. It'd been another sticking point in their marriage.

Abe shook his head. "I'm guessing life on the road shocked her more than she'd imagined. Anytime I've tried to talk to her about it, she clams up. Anyway, I don't need her approval for the changes I intend to make to my house. Especially after sharing it for so many years and taking what everyone else wanted into account."

"Whole basement remodel or just one room?" At his confused look, she clarified, "If you want to update the bathroom or the bedrooms, the time to do it is when the place is ripped to shreds. Not two or three years down the road."

Abe's gaze encompassed the space. "Does it need that?"

In lieu of answering, she lobbed a hideous mustard yellow sweater at the throw pile.

"Come on, Janie," he cajoled. "Tell me what you'd do to set up my man cave in style."

"I'd knock down the walls of Celia's bedroom, adding space onto this room and turning that area into a bar. Then I'd take out the tub/shower combo in the bathroom and install a walk-in glass-walled shower. Building a small half wall would hide the toilet and allow for a double sink vanity. I'd have the décor in the guest bedroom be something fun and funky and totally unexpected." Janie glanced up when Abe stayed quiet. "What? Sound too extreme?"

"No. It sounds exactly like what I want."

"Really?"

"Yep. Any chance you could get goin' on this soon? Granted, I'll need time to dig up the coffee cans in the backyard to pay for it."

She balled up a polka-dotted turtleneck and threw it at him. "Smart-ass."

He grinned and threw the shirt right back at her. "I am serious. Holt's crew is almost done with Bran and Harper's remodel. I'd like to get him booked for this project before someone else snaps him up."

"He's your friend. Why don't you call him up and book him?"

Abe shifted his stance. "Because I'm not sure he'd believe me since I've always done the construction around here myself. If you tell him I hired you to design the space and I want him to construct it, it'll sound more official."

"And it won't give you an opportunity to back out."

He nodded. "That'll also let him know you think he's a worthy contractor."

Janie stilled. "Why would it matter to him what *I* think?"

"Not you personally. But with all the construction up at the Split Rock, it's been sticking in his craw he wasn't hired for any of it. Especially after Renner made such a big deal about wanting to hire locally."

"Wait a second. That was not our fault. The reason we didn't hire Holt was because Bran hired him first. Exclusively. We couldn't come close to paying him what Bran did."

"Holt earned every penny too. Man, they gutted that house. Everything is new from the plumbing to the electrical to the ceilings and walls. It's really something." He stared at her thoughtfully. "Did you help Harper with the interior design?"

"Some. But she has a great eye. Both she and Bran knew exactly what they wanted in their home."

"Hank and Lainie were the same way. They'd started planning for their house the second they moved in here."

Such a wistful tone. Was he lonely living by himself for the first time in his life? Why did that make her so sad?

The next hour they spoke very little. When Janie reached the last stack of boxes, Abe started hauling them upstairs. She'd ended up with nine boxes of resalable goods—a prosperous haul considering it was free.

After four quick trips, Abe leaned against the wall next to her to catch his breath.

Her fingers tightened on the box top as the musky fragrance of his skin rolled over her. Male sweat wasn't supposed to create the urge to bury her face into the damp spot on his chest and just breathe him in. She shifted slightly, hoping physical distance would clear her thoughts and her senses of him.

"Sorry. I probably reek."

No, you smell divine. But again, she redirected. "All those boxes won't fit in my car."

"I'll bring the rest in my truck."

"Oh. Thanks." She lifted the box and turned.

But Abe removed the box from her arms. "You're using me, remember?"

She stood on the porch, watching him haul boxes up, and shove them in her backseat, until the car was crammed full. When he ambled over, she intended to grumble about his underappreciation of her physical abilities, but his gaze zoomed to the lower left side of her face.

His fingers tenderly brushed the spot his eyes had marked. "How is it you haven't aged a single day in the last eight years?"

"How long has it been since you've had your eyes checked?"

Abe chuckled and opened the driver's-side door for her. "You're full up on this tin can tryin' to pass itself off as a car."

"Just because my car isn't a monster gas guzzler like yours doesn't give you the right to insult it," she retorted.

"Cupcake, it's a Prius. Callin' it a car at all is insulting to all other cars on the road."

She huffed out an annoyed breath. After she started the engine, Abe rapped on the window. "What?"

"Watch the lead foot."

Janie had to use her side mirrors to back up since the boxes were stacked too high to see out of her rearview mirror. And yeah, when she purposely spun a little gravel just to be ornery, she swore she heard Abe's deep laughter.

She absentmindedly tapped her fingers on her steering wheel, trying not to focus on thoughts about Abe and their convoluted past. She'd gone about ten miles on the shortcut to the highway, when her car lurched. Janie automatically glanced in the rearview mirror. Before she could curse the boxes blocking her view, she was hit from behind again.

The jolt sent her upper body forward and her seat belt snapped her back, jerking her hands free from the steering wheel. Just as her hands reconnected with it, she felt another hit from behind. She slammed on the brakes and the back end of the car fishtailed on the gravel. Attempting to keep the car on the road, she overcorrected and cranked the steering wheel too hard. The last thing she remembered was screaming as her car headed for the ditch.

Chapter Two

*A*be found himself whistling as he tossed the last box in the bed of his truck. Things had gone better today than he'd hoped.

Over the past five months, he'd stopped being angry his ex-wife had breezed back into Wyoming without a care of how it'd affect his life. After she'd left, he'd been forced to deal with pitying looks and conversations that ended when he entered a room. As the years passed so did people's memories.

Until she returned, looking beautiful and confident. All practiced charm and sweet fire, completely polished, acting nothing like the shy, plain woman he'd married. Now he wanted her with an ache that defied reason.

He suspected she hung out at Buckeye Joe's for the same reason he did. Loneliness. He'd started to flirt with this new, charismatic Janie. Nothing big. Buying her a drink. Asking her to dance.

Dropping hints about the warmth of his bed.

She'd laughed him off, not meanly, but in the same way the old Janie did—using deflection to hide her interest. Her mouth might've been saying no, but her body had been saying *hell yes*.

He'd seen the appreciative glances she'd sent him last night at the wedding. And again today he'd caught her eyeballing his chest—so he'd obliged her need to ogle him by removing his shirt.

And ogle him she had.

Abe knew his physical appearance had changed. His rangy build became bulky after Hank quit bullfighting and they'd started lifting weights together. Those hours sweating and pumping iron had definitely been worth it, seeing the heated lust in Janie's eyes. It was only a matter of time—and his patience—before teasing words and hot looks wouldn't be enough.

He hung a left on the gravel road, suspecting Janie had taken the shortcut to the highway, which didn't shave off more than thirty extra seconds from the paved road. Not that she ever believed him.

He'd driven this stretch so many times he usually let his mind wander. But he noticed fresh skid marks in the gravel immediately. Then his gaze snagged on the ass end of a car sticking out of the ditch.

Not just any car. Janie's car.

Everything went into slow motion.

He jammed both feet on the brakes until his rig shuddered to a stop. While the voice in his head screamed *no no no, not Janie*, he threw the gearshift in park and half ran/half slid down the dry grass covering the embankment. He reached for his phone and dialed 911. Somehow he remained calm as he stood beside the mangled car and explained the situation. The voice on the other end of the phone assured him the ambulance and sheriff's deputy had been dispatched. Major problem with living in rural Wyoming: they were a long way from medical treatment facilities.

Don't look, man. Just stay the hell away and wait.

But he couldn't. When he crouched down, he saw the air bag had deployed. *Thank you, Jesus.* Janie was slumped across it, her head turned the opposite direction—but not at an unnatural angle. The windshield had shattered, scattering glass everywhere.

He had half a mind to wrench the door free and extract her himself. But deep down, he knew that might cause more harm to her body. The last thing he'd ever do was cause her more pain. Feeling helpless and heartsick, he dialed his brother, hoping Lainie was home and could offer medical insight.

Hank answered on the first ring. "Abe. What's up?"

"The wheels on Janie's car. Is Lainie around?"

"No. She's workin' second shift." Pause. "What do you mean *the wheels on Janie's car?*" After Abe rattled off an explanation, Hank said, "I'm on my way."

Abe's answering, "You don't have to—" was lost in the dial tone.

He talked to Janie. Making promises. Telling her every sappy, sexy, sassy thing he'd noticed about her since she'd returned to Muddy Gap on the off chance she was conscious.

The spray of gravel dragged his attention to the road. Abe glanced up as Hank started down the incline with Celia close on his heels.

"Is she okay?" were the first words out of Celia's mouth.

"I don't know. I haven't even opened the damn car door."

Celia ran her palm down Abe's forearm and squeezed his hand. "Hard as that may be, you've done the right thing."

"Well, looks to me like she's still breathin' or else I might've done something rash."

"Understandable," Hank said. "How long ago did this happen?"

"She came out to get some boxes for Harper. I left the ranch about twenty minutes after she did. I figured she'd take the short cut and this is what I came upon."

As the three of them looked into the window, Janie stirred.

"Janie." Abe's heart kicked hard and he placed his palm

against the glass, wishing he could reach through and touch her. "Don't move. We're gonna get you outta there."

Her head lifted and then it fell back.

No one spoke. Abe remained crouched, staring inside the vehicle, willing her to show more signs of consciousness as Hank and Celia walked the perimeter of the car. Willing her to be all right. Trying like hell not to burst into tears or scream his rage and frustration. He breathed slowly, knowing he'd freak out his family if he gave in to those impulses. Abe Lawson had a reputation for being cool, calm and collected, no matter what the situation.

He sure as fuck didn't feel that way now. He felt like the bottom had dropped out of his world.

Wailing sirens became louder. Abe stepped aside when the EMTs scrambled down the embankment with a gurney. One guy pried open the door and began examining Janie, tossing off comments and medical lingo to the other EMT.

Footsteps shuffled next to him and he looked into Deputy TJ McConnell's face. "Lawson."

"Deputy."

"Did I hear right? The woman in this car is your ex-wife?"

"Yep."

"You have a friendly relationship with her?"

Weird question. "Yeah."

"How'd you happen to run across her vehicle?"

"She left my place and I was meeting her at the Split Rock to drop off the rest of the boxes in the back of my truck."

"So you've no reason to want her harmed or dead?"

"Hell no. Why?"

McConnell sidled in front of Abe, blocking his view of the paramedics. "She was struck from behind. Repeatedly. I'm guessing it was a truck of some kind."

Abe's eyes narrowed. "You askin' me if *I* ran Janie off the road?"

"Did you?" He pointed to Abe's truck. "A pickup that size could do some damage."

"But my truck would show damage if I'd purposely rammed another vehicle?"

"Yes, it would."

"Then go ahead and check my truck, Deputy. Take pictures. Do whatever you have to. Match up the damages from Janie's car because you'll see I didn't do this. I'd never . . ." His voice broke.

Hank and Celia flanked Abe and faced down McConnell. "Abe didn't do this," Celia retorted hotly.

When Abe realized Janie was out of the car, he stepped around the deputy and raced beside the EMT. His stomach knotted. God. She looked so pale. So tiny. So helpless. He was afraid to touch her but couldn't stop from enclosing her small fingers in his large hand. "Janie?"

Her eyes opened but held a blank look of shock. "Abe? What's—?"

"Don't try to talk. You were in an accident. They're takin' you to the hospital in Rawlins."

"Will you—"

"Yes. I'll be right behind them. I promise."

Janie swallowed. "Okay. Will you call Renner?"

"Don't worry about that now."

She tried to pull him closer. "No. I'm serious. You have to call Renner. Right away."

"Why? He can find someone to cover for you tomorrow, Janie."

She blinked at him. "Please. Will you just call him as soon as possible?"

Jealousy and anger consumed him but he managed a curt, "Fine. What's his number?"

"It's in my cell phone. In my purse. It was on the front seat. Just . . . bring it to the hospital."

Abe reluctantly tore his gaze away from her and grilled the EMT. "How bad are her injuries?"

"Bumps and bruises mostly. She's lucky she wore a seat belt and the air bag deployed. They'll run more tests at the hospital."

Janie shivered and they whisked her away.

He hated he didn't have the right to ride in the ambulance with her. To comfort her. To give himself peace of mind that she wasn't dealing with this alone. He stuck his head inside the driver's-side door and spied Janie's purse on the floor.

Deputy McConnell glared at him. "What exactly do you think you're doing, Lawson?"

"Takin' her purse to the hospital. She needs it for insurance. Is my truck cleared to go?"

"It wasn't involved in the accident as far as I can tell."

Abe looked at Janie's crumpled car, then back at the deputy. "Lemme know as soon as you're done doin' whatever you need to do and we'll get this towed outta here."

"Do you need someone to ride into Rawlins with you?" Celia asked after the deputy wandered away.

"Nah." He blew out an impatient breath. "Thanks for coming. I'll keep in touch." He climbed into his truck and took off, his thoughts a jumbled mess. He didn't remember he was supposed to contact Renner Jackson until he'd parked in the hospital parking lot. Her command "call Renner right away" didn't sit well with him, but he shoved his annoyance aside and scrolled through Janie's contact list.

Chapter Three

❧

*H*ome at last.

Inside her modular log cabin, Tierney Pratt pressed her back against the door and inhaled a deep breath. Although it was tiny compared to her Chicago apartment, she loved the coziness of the space. She loved that it was one hundred percent hers.

Daddy had to buy you a brand-new house? You too good to live in a used trailer, brainiac?

Once again she'd allowed Renner's rude opinion to intrude on her thoughts. The man was everywhere. She'd run into him while buying groceries. Granted, Muddy Gap had only one store, but his smug comment irritated her—how it must be a real hardship she couldn't find caviar and lobster rolls at the C-Mart.

How little the man knew about her. How much he assumed.

Tierney remembered the tipping point last night at Harper and Bran's wedding reception as she silently reeled from the insufferable man's incendiary comments. On impulse, she threw her martini in Renner's face, and secretly basked in his total surprise as the vodka dripped off his stubborn chin. She'd sidestepped him and headed to the bar. No one had intercepted her, but plenty of curious eyes had followed her across the room. Sometimes she felt like a character in a Clint Eastwood movie—an unwelcome stranger in a small Western town.

Dwelling on it won't change anything because you're here for the duration.

Faced with a boring Sunday, Tierney opened the Sudoku program on her computer. When her cell phone rang ten minutes later, she answered, "Hello," without checking the caller ID.

"Tierney. How are you?"

Great. Now she'd have to hide her sour mood from her father. Then again, it was doubtful he'd notice. Forcing a chipper note in her voice, she said, "I'm fine. And you?"

"Can't complain. The stock market is up. The weather has been decent. Now the reason I called is . . ."

Of course you have a specific reason to call. You'd never ring me up to shoot the breeze or ask what's been going on in my life besides work.

There was a situation of her own making—her life had revolved around work, work and more work for the past four years. Slaving in front of a hot computer seventy plus hours a week hadn't done a bit of good when push came to shove; her father had passed her over for a promotion again. In a rare show of backbone, she'd handed in her resignation and escaped the Windy City for the windswept Wyoming prairie.

But Gene Pratt, CFO, CEO and world-class SOB, was treating her defection as a "sabbatical" after she'd invoked the obscure clause in her upper level employment contract that allowed her six months of hands-on management training at the PFG property of her choosing. A clause her father couldn't argue with, since he'd been enforcing it for years whenever he needed to divest his company of troublesome managers. His response had been predictably businesslike.

Why are you wasting your skills in some backwater burg?

This isn't an acting-out episode like I'm suffering through with your sister, is it?

Acting out. As if. But she'd never gone against the grain. Never bucked the system. Never argued with her father.

Never stepped out on her own.

After she first arrived at the Split Rock Ranch and Resort, she worried Renner Jackson would call her father to send her packing because of her obvious lack of people management skills. But she soon realized Renner was swamped doing ten billion other things, including running his stock contracting business, so he turned the accounting over to her entirely.

It'd almost been too easy to slip into the role of ball-busting bottom-line financier. But it gave her a once-in-a-lifetime opportunity: she'd recreate herself. Shake off the remnants of boring, brainy, geeky, reserved Tierney Pratt and find out who she really was when she wasn't her father's *yes* woman. Find a new direction for her life. Because the truth was, most of the time for the past two years, she'd felt more than a little lost.

". . . plans for Thanksgiving."

Tierney grabbed the aspirin bottle on her desk—guaranteed she'd have a headache after this conversation—shaking out two pills and knocking them back with a swallow of coffee. "I'm staying at the Split Rock, since we have a full booking that week. What are your plans?"

"Since Europeans don't celebrate Thanksgiving, it's the perfect time to go to Barcelona to check out a property that's nearly bankrupt."

No surprise her father had figured out a way to operate during the holiday. Official holidays had always been just another day to him, or worse, an inconvenience that interrupted his work. "Are they searching for a buyer?"

"No. But when has that ever stopped me?"

A short bark of laughter escaped. "You are unstoppable when you get your mind set on something and you don't see anything except the bottom line."

The phone line iced over with stony silence. "And what exactly is that supposed to mean?"

Crap. Rewind. The last thing she needed was to antagonize him so he hauled ass here and messed everything up. "Nothing. Only that I hope you allow free time to enjoy yourself. I've always wanted to go to Barcelona."

"I'll take you with me if you come back to Chicago where you belong."

She retorted sweetly, "Maybe you should take your newly promoted right-hand man, Steven the wonder boy, to Barcelona."

Petulant much, Tierney?

A weary sigh. "When will you stop this nonsense?"

So he thought it was nonsense that he'd passed her over for promotion again? "I'll stop when you understand that calling my career *nonsense* only strengthens my determination not to come back to work for you. Ever." So much for not antagonizing him. But she felt . . . freer for saying it.

"Sometimes I do not understand you at all." Another impatient paternal sigh. "Very well. Have your little adventure. You'll tire of it soon enough. I'll touch base with you in a few weeks and we'll see if you've come to your senses."

Tierney said, "Nice talking to you too, Dad," to dead air. She tossed the phone on a pile of books.

Distracted, she stared out the bay window beside her desk. No snow had fallen yet, but heavy gray storm clouds hung in the distance. Before moving to Wyoming she'd never noticed how the time of year affected the color of the sky and the shape of the clouds. After spending hours gazing in wonder at the wide-open space where rugged, unforgiving land met endless horizon, she could discern some differences in impending weather. But it'd take a lifetime to catch the nuances. That prospect appealed to her more than she'd ever imagined.

Bang bang bang pulled her out of her musings.

Only one person knocked with that much authority. And

arrogance. Mr. Tenacious would keep banging until she answered.

She took her time crossing the room. Wouldn't want him to think she jumped when he beckoned. She peeked out the blinds to find those vivid blue eyes peering back at her. Eyes the same beautiful hue as the Wyoming sky on a hot summer day.

"Dammit, Tierney, let me in."

Sighing, she flipped the locks.

Renner rushed over the threshold. "We need to talk."

"How about in the office tomorrow morning?"

He stopped wiping his boots on her rug, peeking at her from beneath the brim of his black cowboy hat. "Why not now?"

"Because it's my day off."

"Hate to break it to you, sweetheart, but there are no days off in the ranch business."

"Hate to break it to you, *sweetheart*, but this isn't a working ranch—I've yet to see a single cow. And last night you put me in my place as far as the horses are concerned. Since we won't have guests checking in until tomorrow, I'd like one day this week without a confrontation with you."

"*You* threw the drink in *my* face, remember?"

"You deserved it, remember?"

A scowl twisted his full lips. "Believe it or not, I don't get off on fightin' with you."

She resisted the urge to retort, *Coulda fooled me.*

"You gonna move and let me off your rug, or what?"

Say no. "Fine." Tierney headed for the kitchen, where they'd have to stand, to keep this talk short. "What's on your mind?"

"It occurred to me when I saw you at the store today that we didn't discuss your role in helping out at the Split Rock until Harper gets back from her honeymoon."

"Helping out how?"

"Hands-on help with the guests and employees instead of hiding in the office."

Her cheeks heated. "I don't hide. There's actual work done in my half of the office." Sort of. For the first time in her working life, she had little to do and all sorts of time to kill. She stretched out her accounting duties, but they still took less than half of her workday. In the last month, she learned to look busy, disguising her online chess games and closing her e-books whenever he blew into the room like an angry bull.

"We're shorthanded on opening week, so I'll need you acting as Split Rock hostess for the guests."

"No."

He cocked his head like he'd misunderstood. "Come again?"

"I said no. Now, was that all?"

It pissed her off that Renner stalked her until her back hit the edge of the counter. It really pissed her off she allowed him to force her retreat.

"What? Think you're too good to mingle with the common folk?"

No. I'm too awkward. I'll embarrass the resort and myself with my obvious lack of social graces.

Not that she could tell him that because the shrewd man would lord her insecurity over her forever.

At her nonresponse, he goaded her. "Don't want to get your manicured hands dirty? You feel it's beneath your lofty position as financial whip cracker?"

Rather than lashing out, Tierney said, "You really have me pegged. I'm a stuck-up bitch who has no place in the hospitality business. I can't imagine why you'd want a snob like me hanging around making our guests feel uncomfortable, so I'll pass on your charming request. Now please leave my house."

"Like hell."

The man remained as solid as a stone wall in front of her, but he sure threw off a lot of heat. Tierney kept her face aimed at the floor, her arms folded over her chest. Her posture screamed "back off," but apparently Renner was deaf because he kept trying to provoke her.

"Is this some new tactic?" he demanded. "Insulting yourself, then giving me the silent treatment? Hoping I'll get confused and fed up and go away? Guess what, it won't work."

"It's worth a try."

He laughed abrasively. "You don't give an inch, do you?"

"Not usually."

Another laugh. Softer. "I don't like talkin' to your hair. Can you look at me?"

"Even if my eyes shoot fireballs at you and you spontaneously combust?"

"I'll take my chances." Her pulse leapt when his rough fingers slipped beneath her chin and tipped her face up. "Gotta flash them pretty browns if you want to start my hair on fire."

Pretty browns? What was he up to, complimenting her? When she met his gaze, the compassion in his eyes stunned her. As did his gentle, "Ah darlin', what's really goin' on?"

Tierney blurted, "I stay in the office because I'm good with numbers. I'm not good with people. I'm not charming like Janie or sly and sweet like Harper. The Split Rock would be better off having *no* hostess than having me acting all fake and shit."

That'd shocked him. "Why didn't you just tell me that?"

"Because you jumped in and told me why I said no. Why should I explain myself to you when you've already made the worst assumptions about me, my character and my business acumen?"

Renner's too blue eyes searched hers intently. "Tierney—"

"You can't claim you didn't do that, because you did exactly that."

"I know. I'm an asshole sometimes."

"No argument from me."

He smiled. A wide, gap-toothed smile packed with pure roguish charm and damn if she didn't catch herself smiling back. He touched the left side of her mouth. "Whoa. Lookit that. You've got dimples. Never noticed those before. Is this really the first time you've ever smiled at me?"

"Probably."

His phone rang and he backed away to fish it out of his front pocket. "Jackson."

Tierney watched the blood drain from Renner's face.

"Where is she? Is she all right?"

"What happened?"

He snapped, "Hush for a second," and turned away. "I'll be there as soon as I can." Renner hung up and booked it to the door.

But Tierney grabbed the back of his coat. "You can't just leave without telling me what's going on!"

"Janie's been in a car accident. Abe's at the hospital with her in Rawlins."

"I'm coming with you."

He whirled around. "Now why would you do that?"

Instead of saying, *because I'm worried and I might be useful for a change*, she tossed her head and retorted, "Because you need someone to keep you from driving like an idiot."

Renner snorted. "I've driven that road in my sleep."

"But—"

"No buts. And no way will I listen to you nagging me all the way to Rawlins. Jesus. That's my worst nightmare." He leaned in until they were nose to nose. "I go. You stay. End of discussion." Then he hustled out the door.

Right. Like she'd start listening to him now.

Tierney waited until she heard the roar of his truck; then she grabbed her keys, her coat and followed him.

Chapter Four

≈

*R*enner put the pedal to the metal. Christ. Poor Janie. After what that woman had been through in the last three years . . . and now this? If she'd been sentient enough to insist Abe call him, he felt encouraged her injuries weren't life threatening. Given Janie's past, he couldn't help but wonder if this had been an accident.

Think of something else or you'll go crazy with worry and drive like an idiot.

He glanced at the speedometer. Ninety-five. He eased up on the gas, but his hands still white-knuckled the steering wheel. He tried to focus on practical matters. His thoughts kept circling around the question: What was he going to do without Janie on opening week?

She was an integral part of his operation. She'd helped him with the concept for a ranch and resort. A place where he could feed his social nature and share his love of the Western lifestyle. The process hadn't been as easy as he'd imagined—and now he worried he'd devoted the last two years to creating something with no guarantee it'd ever truly belong to him.

As much crap as he'd taken from his buddies in the rodeo world about the Split Rock being a resort, he intended it to be as much a working ranch as an upscale hunting lodge and retreat.

Hunting. Right. His brain raced a million directions. With Janie possibly being out of commission, good thing he'd already planned for the week ahead. Hunting permits had been secured. He'd laid in an extra supply of ammo. The ATVs were tuned up. The hunting guides were ready to switch off.

Since Renner wasn't much of a hunter, he'd hired two ranchers familiar with the lay of the land. The guys loved hunting so much they'd been happy to serve as guides in exchange for unlimited hunting rights. That'd been a cheap solution in the scheme of getting the Split Rock up and running.

The only cheap thing so far. The land hadn't been that pricey. He'd saved enough cash to purchase an additional two thousand acres alongside the first parcel. He would've been in good financial shape to fund this entire enterprise himself had the stock market not crashed and wiped him out. At that time he'd already had the building plans drawn up. Paid the hefty retainer for the specialized contractors that were scheduled a year out. Hell, he'd even had the building sites leveled and concrete footings poured.

Then financial disaster struck.

He didn't remember where he'd initially gotten the name of Pratt Financial Group. Gene Pratt owned a variety of small businesses in the hospitality industry, as well as a finance company loosely tied to his interests. It hadn't occurred to Renner until too late that the reason Pratt owned so many companies was because those businesses had defaulted on loan repayment. Pratt Financial Group—PFG— boasted enough equity that Renner was surprised when Gene Pratt agreed to meet with him personally in Kansas City.

If Pratt had played coy or spun tales of instant financial security Renner would've walked away. But Pratt set him straight; chances of obtaining the funds from a traditional source, such as a bank, were less than five percent. He'd gone on to explain the real estate market was in the toilet, especially in the areas of luxury homes and private retreats. But Pratt admitted the potential of the Wyoming property interested him and he was willing to lend Renner the money—with a few conditions, which would be spelled out in the contract.

A contract Gene Pratt just happened to have with him.

PFG number crunchers projected a fifty percent chance of success and a ten percent return on investment if the resort could capitalize on hunting season, the holiday season and ski season. So PFG's stipulation for lending Renner the money? The Split Rock Ranch and Resort had to be fully constructed, fully operational and fully staffed by October first.

Renner knew meeting the criteria was a Herculean task, but he was so damn desperate for the capital he'd signed on the dotted line. After construction was under way, Tierney Pratt called on her father's behalf, announcing she'd be on-site as PFG representative to ensure the resort opened on time.

In the past few months the woman had dug in her high heels like an Old West homesteader with the promise of free land in exchange for proving fortitude. Since she was Gene Pratt's daughter, Renner's hands were tied. She'd invaded half his office space, a clear indication she wasn't leaving anytime soon. And she'd gotten under his skin like a sand burr. It was more than her snippy attitude when she questioned him on every damn thing under the sun. It was more than the mesmerizing way her ass swayed in body-hugging skirts as she haughtily flitted away from him.

She annoyed him. Frustrated him. Challenged him.

Turned him on.

How fucked up was it that the uptight woman did it for him in a bad way? He'd been stupid enough to fall for a rich daddy's girl once; he had no intention of repeating that mistake.

Keep telling yourself that.

Renner continued to brood about Tierney because it kept him from thinking about Janie. Tierney had garnered his interest so completely he'd barely paid attention to Harper and Bran's wedding last night; he'd been too busy watching her. Expecting to see boredom or derision, signs to remind him that she was a privileged, overeducated pain in the ass who'd look down on a small country wedding.

But she'd blown that perception all to hell with her tears.

His thoughts backtracked to the moment the minister had pronounced the couple husband and wife. Bran had said, "Finally," before kissing Harper with such tenderness and wonder, Renner felt a little choked up. He'd glanced over to see Tierney crying hard enough to fog up her sexy smart-girl glasses. He'd never pegged her as the sentimental type. And that fascinated the hell out of him.

So he'd kept up his covert study of her during the reception. Tierney might not know how to work a room, but she sure knew how to rock a suit. Damn. He'd considered slathering her with compliments in case flattery would thaw the frosty void between them. But when she'd railed on him at the wedding reception about empty stalls and full haystacks, which weren't her concern, he'd lashed out at her. And what had he found out? The woman's aim was as sharp as her tongue.

A fact she'd proven again today. Yet, there'd been a couple of moments when she'd actually seemed sweet. Shy. Wanting to reach out to him, but unsure how he'd respond. Maybe it was an assholish thing to do, refusing to let her accompany him to the hospital. Being enclosed in his truck with her would be hell. Not because they'd argue the entire time, but because he'd lose his train of thought whenever he caught a whiff of that sweet fragrance she wore.

No, he had to be a jerk to her to make her stay put at the Split Rock. He'd apologize later.

A flash behind him caught his attention and Renner

glanced in the rearview mirror just as a car signaled to pass. A familiar car.

Tierney's car.

Sonuvabitch.

She gave him a little finger wave as her Land Rover sailed past him.

So much for her staying put.

Chapter Five

~

Abe's sister-in-law broke off her conversation with the elderly lady manning the desk at the hospital when he entered the emergency room doors.

From the back, Lainie didn't look pregnant at all. But from the front, she definitely had a baby bulge under her scrubs.

"Abe. Your wife"—she stressed the *wife* part and her eyes begged him to follow her lead—"is about finished with the CT scan. I'll take you to where you can wait." Lainie led him down the hallway to a room with a curtain that bisected one space into two.

As soon as they passed the patient on the left side, Abe said, "Is Janie all right?"

"Enough to insist she was fine and didn't need anything but a couple of aspirin."

"She's a little headstrong."

"Ya think?"

"So what's up with the *your wife* lie, Nurse Lawson?"

Lainie's mouth quirked. "Not a lie. She *was* your wife. She's just not your wife now."

Abe's gaze dropped to her hand stroking her belly. "How're you feelin', Mama?"

"Like there's a bowling ball jumping on my bladder."

"Is my brother takin' good care of you?"

"He'd wrap me in cotton batting if I let him. But yeah"— she smiled a bit dreamily—"Hank is beyond awesome."

He knew how much Hank worried about Lainie working the last three months of her pregnancy. But Hank's constant overprotectiveness didn't dim Lainie's glow when she spoke of him and the baby. "He worries because he adores you. And he's gonna be just as bad with baby Lawson. Worse than ever, probably."

She smirked. "I know. I'll check back later."

Abe stared out the hospital window. The town and the landscape became a blur as he tried to rein in his jumbled thoughts. Who'd run Janie off the road? Why hadn't the person stuck around to help her out? He turned it over and over in his mind, but it didn't make sense.

Finally the *squeak squeak* of rubber on linoleum alerted him to a nurse wheeling Janie into the room.

Christ. She looked about fifteen years old, wearing an oversized hospital gown and an ill-tempered scowl. But he was damn glad to see her feisty instead of frightened. "Why can't I go home now?"

"That'll depend on the CT scan results," the nurse said. "You might as well rest. Once you get settled, you can ask for something to help you sleep."

A sour look distorted Janie's face. "No drugs."

When Abe took a step closer, Janie held up her hand. "Stay right there, buster. Turn around. This gown doesn't cover my rear."

"I'm sure your husband won't mind," the nurse soothed.

"But he's not—"

"At all put off by seein' those delectable bare buns," Abe inserted with a sly grin. "In fact, since my *wife* is a little shy, I'll help her into bed if you have someplace else to be."

"Knock yourself out." Then the nurse was gone.

"I cannot believe you lied and told her you were my husband, Abe Lawson."

"Hey, I'm just following Lainie's murky logic that I *was* your husband, not that I *am* your husband." He held his hands out. "Up you go."

Janie batted away his offer of help. "I'm not an invalid. Turn around so I can climb on the bed."

"So damn stubborn." Abe faced the curtain and muttered, "Ain't like I haven't seen it before."

The bed frame clanked and rattled as she wiggled to get comfortable. Just as he was about to suggest she swallow her pride and let him help her, a commotion stirred the curtain and Renner stormed to Janie's side.

How had he gotten here so damn fast?

"Jesus. Are you okay?"

"Banged up. Mad. But yeah, I'm okay."

An unspoken communication passed between them.

The dark-haired woman Renner called the tyrant leaned against the wall.

Janie stared at her. "What are you doing here?"

"Me'n Tierney were chatting when you called," Renner answered. "And because she never listens to a fucking thing I tell her, she opted to follow me instead of staying put and handling resort issues, like I asked."

"If you call the ear-blistering diatribe you treated me to a chat, I shudder to think how an actual conversation with you might go. And you didn't *ask* me a damn thing. You commanded. Big difference."

Renner sniped. Tierney sniped back. Abe wondered how much of Janie's job entailed refereeing.

A guy in a white coat entered the room. He flicked the arguing visitors a perfunctory glance and they both shut up. He tapped on his clipboard. "You're cleared to leave. No signs of head trauma or internal bleeding. You'll have a nasty headache and body aches, but the pain meds should make it bearable." He looked up at her. "Any questions?"

Janie shook her head.

"Got someone who can stay with you tonight?"

"She'll stay with me," Abe and Renner said simultaneously.

Tension distorted the air.

"Sort it out. She doesn't leave until it's decided, understood?" The doctor ducked out of the room.

Abe tried to reiterate his point as Renner talked over him.

Janie whistled loudly. "Someone just get me back to my place."

"I'll take you," Tierney offered. "I'll stay with you too."

"You?" Renner scoffed. "You'd give up the mini princess palace to cool your heels in a trailer? I don't think so."

Tierney drilled her index finger into Renner's chest. "You don't think at all, which is your problem. I'm staying with Janie tonight. Period. So why don't you trot your smarmy cowboy self back to the Split Rock to handle any issues that might've come up in your absence?"

Renner's lips flattened into a thin line.

Abe would've enjoyed Renner getting his comeuppance if not for Tierney directing her attention to him next. "You can take off too."

"But—"

"Save it." Tierney grabbed the pile of clothes on the dresser and pointed to the door. "Move it. Both of you. Leave her be. She needs to rest and won't get any if you two are peeing circles around her. I'm perfectly capable of taking care of her."

"Tierney—"

She gave Janie the stink eye. "No negotiation." Then her face softened. "I want to help out, okay?"

Janie nodded. And seemed relieved.

Neither man spoke until they stood outside the emergency room doors.

"She's a tough little thing," Renner said.

"Janie? Yeah. At least on the outside." Abe rubbed his jaw. "Just so you know, Deputy McConnell said this wasn't an accident. Someone hit her car from behind a couple of times. Any idea why anyone would wanna run her off the road?"

Renner's face remained blank. Too blank. Then his gaze shifted to the back of Abe's truck. "Are those the boxes Janie was picking up at your place?"

Not a subtle segue and it left Abe uneasy. "Yeah. I was on my way to drop them off when I saw . . ." He cleared the lump from his throat. He doubted he'd ever get that image out of his mind and his immediate, almost paralyzing bone-deep fear he'd lost her. "I need to unload because I have other stuff to haul tomorrow."

Renner scowled. "I don't even wanna think about tomorrow being the opening day of the Split Rock and Janie being out of commission."

No wonder the man was in such a piss-poor mood. "I assume you have keys to the store?" Abe sent Renner a sly look. "Or do you need to ask Tierney for them?"

"Fuck off. I don't answer to Tierney. Let's go."

Chapter Six

❧

The opening day of the Split Rock Ranch and Resort was a total clusterfuck.

They'd forgotten to designate a baggage handler, so Renner was stuck schlepping luggage.

The ice machine went crazy and shot out every cube of ice like a baseball-pitching machine. Then it gave up the ghost entirely in a wire-sizzling pop.

The damper hadn't been opened in the stone fireplace and the main area of the lodge filled with smoke, forcing the guests to evacuate for two hours.

The second day? Worse. Way worse.

The power went out due to a freak electrical storm.

It began pouring before dawn. It rained so hard the hunting party was called off and the guests were trapped inside the lodge. With nothing to do but drink, play pool, and drink.

Which meant they ran out of beer. And whiskey.

But the awful part? The food. It'd been a nightmare watching the guests' faces as they were subjected to another lousy evening meal: overcooked roast beef, lumpy mashed potatoes, salty gravy, and undercooked root vegetables.

After the disgruntled guests adjourned to the main room, Tierney sagged against the wall inside the kitchen. Willie and Denise finished cleaning up quickly and got the heck outta Dodge, not that she blamed them. She wished she could retreat to her cabin, because she hadn't slept in her own bed for two nights.

Renner approached and opened his mouth—probably to growl a command at her—but she held up a hand, warning him off. He rested his shoulders on the wall right next to her. After a few beats of silence, he said, "How's Janie?"

Janie, for all her bravado at the hospital, took a turn for the worse after she'd returned to her trailer. She'd been downing painkillers and sleeping nearly round the clock to deal with the trauma to her body. So in addition to slapping on a happy face as a hostess and dealing with the shit storm at the Split Rock, Tierney had been playing nursemaid, checking on Janie every couple of hours. Talk about exhausting. "Better, but not ready to come to work yet."

"Does she know about the last two days?"

Tierney shook her head.

"Good."

"Are the guests ready to run for the hills yet?"

He rubbed his jaw, in what she recognized as a frustrated move. "Damn close. There's part of me that's happy we're not full on opening week."

"Well, I hate to bring it up, but Dodie burned the pies. I've never seen an apple pie with a black crust."

"I have. My first wife broiled a frozen pie once. We're talkin' flames. Hell, we had to buy a new oven."

First wife meant he'd been married more than once. No stunner Renner had taken a trip or two down the aisle, but Tierney wasn't bowled over by the fact he was divorced.

"Any suggestions on what we can offer as dessert?"

"I'm hoping they're so traumatized by the horrendous meal they won't want dessert."

"Or maybe they're starved and hoping something sweet

will fill up the empty spot in their gullets from the shitty supper," he countered.

"Damn. This sucks."

"No kiddin'." He bumped her with his hip. "Come on, brainiac. The food service part is outta my area of expertise."

It was out of hers too, but someone had to fix it. And since there was no one else to step up, it was trial by fire time. Literally. Tierney checked her watch. "How much time do we have?"

"About an hour."

She had exactly one dish in her cooking repertoire. "I saw boxes of brownies in the pantry when I was looking for ..."

"What?"

Tempting to lie, but enough half-truths existed between them. "A hiding place," she admitted sheepishly.

Renner laughed in that deep, sexy way that made her want to press her mouth to his throat and feel the vibration on her lips.

"Brownies are easy. Add some ice cream and whipped cream, and voila, brownie sundaes."

He sent her a sidelong glance. "What? No sprinkles?"

"I can run to my place and get a jar of sprinkles," she offered.

"You have your own jar of sprinkles?"

"I have two jars. Everything in life is better with sprinkles." She peered at him over the top of her glasses. "If you ask if I store my sprinkles next to the rainbows and butterflies in my cupboard, I'll leave you here all by your smartass self to dish up blackened apple pie."

"Shutting up now."

Tierney smirked and pushed off the wall.

After she'd mixed, poured, and shoved the pans in the oven, she grabbed the sprinkles from her cabin. While the vanilla ice cream softened, she lined up twelve bowls and dusted them with powdered sugar. *Hah! Take that, Dad. I can too think on my feet.*

By the time Renner returned to the kitchen, she was sliding warm brownies into the bowls. "That looks fantastic. Almost like we planned it."

"We did plan it. Late planning still counts." She gestured with the can of whipped cream. "Start carrying those out before they melt."

"Bossy, much?" He frowned. "You're short a couple.".

"Twelve guests, twelve plates."

"What about me? Don't I get to sample your wares?"

Heat stained her cheeks. But she doubted he'd meant that as a sexually suggestive comment, especially toward her. "Got a sweet tooth?"

"Like you wouldn't believe." He lifted the first two bowls and winked at her on his way out the door.

Once the guests were served, Renner positioned himself against the steel prep counter with his black cowboy boots crossed at the ankle. He should've looked ridiculous, holding the delicate gold-rimmed dessert plate with his large, scarred hands, but he was completely at ease. "You got raves out there." He took a bite, chewing slowly and thoughtfully. "I prefer my brownies more cakelike than chewy. And you were awful damn stingy with my sprinkles, but besides that, it's not bad."

"Not bad?" she repeated.

He offered her a roguish grin. "Just funnin' with ya, Tierney. I'm afraid if Dodie doesn't pull her head out of her"—he stopped and amended—"if Dodie can't pull off consistently good cooking, you might be called in for KP duty."

"It's a one-time-only offer."

Renner scrutinized her face and set down his plate.

"What?" she said testily.

"Lickin' the bowl, were you?"

When he reached out to touch her cheek, she flinched.

"For Christsake. I'm not gonna punch you. Hold still. There's brownie batter on your face." Renner curled his fingers around her neck and rubbed her jawline with the pad of his thumb.

Her heart rate spiked. His fingers were so warm, so rough against her damp skin. His tender touch sent a shiver through her. Was it pure insanity to imagine Renner replacing his thumb with his mouth as he slowly, thoroughly licked the brownie batter away and grazed his lips down her jawbone to capture her lips with his?

Yes, it is insanity. You don't like this man. Do not close your eyes and pretend you're enjoying this.

But she did relish his attention. She raised her gaze to his, but his focus was entirely on her mouth. When Tierney moistened her lips, he dropped his hand and scrambled back.

"Ah. I think I got it all, but you might wanna check."

"Will do." Tierney needed to escape from his über-masculine presence, so she snatched the suit jacket she'd draped on the prep stool and headed to the door. "I'll see you tomorrow."

He called out, "Tierney. Wait," when her hand gripped the door handle.

She turned and Renner was a foot away.

"Thanks for pitching in the past two days. We would've been screwed without your help. I know we have our differences, but it'll take all of us pulling together to make this place work."

"I agree."

Renner flashed that swoon-worthy smile. "So, how about a . . . truce?"

"Truce." She smiled as cagily as he did. "At least until you piss me off."

Chapter Seven

❦

$\mathcal{T}$he truce lasted all of thirty-six hours.

Tierney froze in the doorway of the office—an office that'd been tidy when she'd left it the previous evening. Now the space looked as if it'd been ransacked by raccoons.

Papers strewn across the coffee table. A disemboweled printer, the spent ink cartridge next to a pair of greasy pliers and a screwdriver, teetered on the edge of the table.

She crossed to the sitting area, picking up a fleece blanket. Beneath it was a decorative tasseled pillow from the guest sofa downstairs. She studied the paisley pattern. Was it her imagination or was there a drool stain? She sniffed it. Smelled like coffee. Better than bourbon, she supposed.

Renner had left his laptop charging, a fact she'd discovered after tripping over the cord in the middle of the floor. A pair of gray athletic socks peeked out of a gap in the cushions—cushions that were askew indicating he'd slept here last night.

He'd made himself coffee, evidenced by the grounds scattered all over the coffee station. Also evidenced by the Styrofoam cups everywhere—next to the fax machine, her printer, her computer. Her eyes narrowed. Hey. Wait a second. What had he been doing in her private area? Were those . . . boot prints on the edge of her desk?

She stalked over and scrutinized them. Yes, indeed, those were boot prints. Muddy boot prints. And he'd taped something to her monitor. She bent down to read it. Squinted at it because she couldn't believe her eyes. A to-do list.

The man had made her a to-do list.

That was the last straw.

Infuriated, Tierney barreled down the stairs and out the side door that led to the barns. When the pavement ended, she was forced to traverse the rocky path to the back of the corrals.

Wooden planks ringed the perimeter of the fence. A dozen men hung on the corrals on the opposite side. One guy was inside the corral, but he kept throwing looks over his shoulder to the chutes.

Her gaze followed his to where a couple of cowboys stood on the upper ledge. A sound of something hard, like a hoof or a horn striking metal echoed and the entire enclosure shook. The bull jumped again, throwing the rider in the air.

Two things happened simultaneously: the rider vigorously nodded his hatted head and the gate burst open.

A whitish-gray bull leapt from captivity with its hind legs in the air. The cowboy kept one arm high above his head, as his other arm, somehow attached to the bull, was jerked every which way as the animal whirled and kicked. What a display of power, man versus beast. How strong the man's leg muscles must be. How beefy his biceps and forearms must be. How agile he must be.

What an idiot he must be to climb on the back of a bull in the first place.

When the bull twisted toward her, Tierney caught a glimpse of the rider beneath the cowboy hat. Every bit of breath stalled in her lungs.

The idiot rider hanging on to that beast was Renner.

Fear, anger, and more anger surfaced. Surely he could've forced another cowboy to exhibit this dangerous behavior. But as that thought popped into her head, she knew Renner wasn't the type to pass the buck. Or the type to pass up a chance to buck, apparently.

A loud buzzer sounded. Renner freed his hand and sailed off the bull. Clapping and wolf whistles exploded from the peanut gallery as he landed on his feet with grace and ease.

The bull, seeing his nemesis unharmed, charged.

The other guy in the ring shouted for Renner's attention—or maybe he was shouting at the bull. Renner turned, lost his footing and slipped beneath the bull's stomping hooves.

Tierney shrieked.

Renner rolled away before a hoof connected with his body. Then he was up, the fringe on his chaps making a *flap flap* sound as he raced toward the fence . . . straight toward her.

She tried to scramble away from the man and the beast giving chase. Her heels slipped off the edge of the wooden plank, her arms pinwheeled and she fell on her butt. Right in the muck. Then Renner was throwing himself over the top of the fence beside her.

The bull's gigantic body distorted at the last second before it plowed into the fence. The substance on the hooves sprayed over them in a wet splatter.

Renner reached for her hands to drag her out of the mud. "Are you all right?"

"No!" She looked at her clothing with disgust. Her pink tweed skirt was speckled with brown. As was her beige silk shirt. The sleeves of her matching pink tweed suit coat had brown smears from elbow to wrist. Although she couldn't see her backside, she felt cold dampness of mud seeping through. But witnessing the state of her shoes, her beautiful pink suede pumps, caused the most distress. They were ruined. She'd worn them one time.

"Where are you hurt?" Renner placed his mud-caked gloved hand on her right forearm.

"I'm not hurt." She knocked his hand away. "I'm mad." Mad and humiliated and the person who'd caused this distress was right in front of her, so she pushed him.

He staggered back a step before his eyes turned icy. "What the hell is wrong with you?"

"What is wrong with *me*?" Tierney pushed him again, but this time he didn't budge. "What is wrong with you? Did you even know what you were doing, getting on a bull?"

"Yes, I knew what I was doin'. In case you forgot, I own a stock contracting company. I know how to load bulls in the chute and I sure as shit know how to ride them. So I don't know where you get off—"

"Where *I* get off?" she repeated. "You got off right in front of me! Straight over the fence like some high jumper on meth. I thought you and the bull were going to trample me!" She did a sweeping gesture over her clothes. "Now you've ruined my suit, not to mention my shoes—"

"Which is your own goddamn fault." He gave her feet a derisive look, sneering, "No woman in her right mind would ever wear a pair of shoes like that to the barn and corrals. You come out here in the real world you should expect to get dirty, understand?"

"I cannot believe I'm coated in mud and manure and God knows what else." She removed her glasses, which were almost impossible to see through because of the splatters. She jerked her blouse out of the waistband of her skirt, using the clean corner to wipe her lenses. She shoved them back on her face and glared at him.

"Is there a reason you came down here? Or was it just to chew my ass in front of a bunch of guests?"

Tierney glanced over at the chutes. The bull was gone from the arena and the guys were waiting for something— Renner the bull-riding stud, probably. She dropped her voice. "Yes, I came down here looking for you."

"What for?"

"To ask why you trashed my office. It did not look like that when I shut the lights off last night."

He angled closer, keeping his voice low. "It's my freakin' office too."

"Well, it's not your bedroom and I don't appreciate that you slept in there last night." A new thought crossed her mind. "Oh. My. God. You didn't bring a woman into my office and screw her on my couch, did you?"

"Fuck no. But if I had it would've been the first time that couch had seen any action, 'cause God knows *you* haven't put it to good use since you've been here."

She gasped, even when she hated that she'd gasped like some affronted maiden. Which she was. Holy buckets. Could he tell? Her face burned as red and hot as a pepper.

"Sorry. Shit. That was a low blow and totally out of line." His sheepish eyes roamed over every inch of her flaming face. "I . . . I have stuff to do right now. Can we talk about this later?"

"As far as I'm concerned, we're done talking now." Tierney spun on the toe of her pump and started walking the plank.

"Tierney, wait."

She faced him. "What?"

"You have a streak on your face that looks like . . . ah, hell, just c'mere." Yanking off his glove, he reached out, exactly as he had the other night, curling his hand around the side of her neck, using his thumb to rub on her jawline. "Sorry if I'm pressing too hard."

"What is it?" She shuddered, but she wasn't entirely sure her response wasn't from Renner's tender touch. "Maybe I don't want to know."

"It sorta looks like brownie batter, but it don't smell near as sweet."

"Eww."

"I'm pretty sure it's mud, but I wanted to make sure it wasn't blood. Or a bruise."

"Blood. Great."

His thumb slowly arced over her jaw. "It's not blood. If it had been I'da felt guiltier yet."

"Really?"

"Uh-huh. However the level of guilt would've been dependent on if it was your blood or mine."

That was a sweetly insightful, yet somewhat bizarre statement. "And if it would've been a bruise?" How had that come out sounding so breathless?

"Maybe I would've offered to kiss it and make it better." He grinned. "More's the pity it's just a smudge of dirt."

Damn you, Renner Jackson, don't be nice to me now. Now that I'm publicly covered in shit and humiliation. Be an asshole so I can stay mad at you.

Then he turned abruptly, scaled the fence and raced across the arena toward the chutes without looking back at her.

∞

Jesus. Telling Tierney he'd like to kiss it and make it better. What kind of pussy says shit like that?

Him, apparently.

His recriminations ended when the group of guys all started talking at once.

But Hank Lawson took him aside. "You all right?"

"Yeah. That bull is a mean son of a bitch, ain't he?"

"No offense, but if you managed to stay on him eight seconds? He ain't gonna be much of a challenge for the pros. Although he's perfect for amateurs." Hank knew his stuff. He'd walked away from the world of pro rodeo at the top of his game as a world-class bullfighter. As much as Hank loved being a rancher, he also loved going head to head with the rankest stock around, so Renner was glad Hank agreed to share his skills at the Split Rock and protect the guests who wanted to try their luck on the back of a bull.

"So any of these guys ready to give bull ridin' a whirl?"

"Probably. You made it look awful damn easy." Hank grinned. "What's up with that landing? You nailed it like an Olympic gymnast."

Renner shrugged. "No clue."

"You weren't showin' off for Tierney?"

"I didn't even know she was here until I heard her scream." That'd shocked him. Seeing her scared to death, leaning against the fence in a fucking pink suit. Pink. Christ. She might've just as well waved a red goddamn cape at the bull.

"Thought maybe for a second there I'd have to send Abe over to referee."

"Nah, I set her straight." Renner hopped up on the second rung of the metal fence and looked at each one of his guests. "So who's next?"

∾

After watching eight guys eat dirt within two seconds of the bull exiting the chute, and two other guests managing to hit the three second mark, the last two guys decided to skip bull riding. Renner needed a shower in a bad way, but he had to talk to Janie on her first day back after the car accident.

He unhooked his chaps, ditched his vest and kicked off his boots and spurs before entering the lodge's laundry area. At the industrial-sized steel sink, he scrubbed his hands with water as hot as he could stand.

When he raised his head, a towel appeared in his peripheral vision. Mopping his face, he met Janie's curious gaze.

"Should I ask?"

"No." He dried his hands. "But lemme ask you something. Did you and the tyrant have a conversation about Dodie today?"

"No. I haven't seen Tierney yet."

Damn woman probably ignored the to-do list he'd left her.

"But I had a long talk with Dodie this morning," Janie said. "We went over a few basics, and she confessed nerves got the best of her. Cooking in a new place, new expectations. She asked if she could bring her pans and stuff from home to cook with here."

"Really? That seems like an excuse."

Janie shrugged. "Most cooks I've dealt with have preferences for everything from knives to ramekin sizes. I told her to use whatever she needed to better do her job." She tossed a look over her shoulder. "I emphasized the word *job*, to remind her that this gig is more serious than whipping up appetizers for a bridge party. She picked up her utensils after breakfast. I sampled what she's been working on. It's fantastic."

As she spoke, Renner studied her. Her face was still puffy in spots, but she'd covered up the bruises with enough makeup that he wouldn't have known they were there if he hadn't seen them with his own eyes.

"What? You're staring at me."

"Just wondering if you're up to the challenge of managing the staff as well as bein' the chipper hostess with the mostest for the guests tonight?"

"I'm fine. The thought of being stuck in my trailer with my own miserable company for another day drove me bonkers."

"I ain't gonna lie. The last three days have sucked. I'm damn glad to have you back. I don't think I can run this place without you, to be real honest."

Her eyes softened. "Ren, this is temporary."

"I know, so don't get any ideas about hittin' me up for a raise because the tyrant would have my neck measured for a noose." He loomed over her. "That said, if you think your accident might've had something to do with—"

"It doesn't," she said too quickly. She snatched the towel from his hands and snapped him in the butt. "Get cleaned up or I'll hose you down myself. You smell."

He bent down and bussed her forehead. "Aw, listen to you. A few months back in Wyoming and you're talkin' cowgirl tough, makin' threats and shit. Next thing, you'll be chewin' tobacco." Renner ducked her snapping towel and scaled the stairs to the office, half afraid, half looking forward to going at it with the tyrant again. That woman fired his blood in more ways than he'd thought possible.

It didn't take long to straighten his mess, but he could see why it'd gotten Tierney's panties in a twist. She was such a neatnik. Her personal items didn't take up much room. No photos on the desk or bookshelves. No live plants or quirky desk objects like his pooping cow jellybean dispenser. Every item had a specific purpose and a specific place.

However, she'd left her mark in the bathroom. The shower curtain was printed with rubber duckies. Some wore funky hats—cowboy hats, bowler hats, stocking caps, trucker caps. And if that wasn't bad enough, the rest of the shower curtain was dotted with pirate duckies. Devil duckies. Angel duckies. And his personal favorite, psychotic-looking clown duckies. He couldn't imagine any kid wanting this shower curtain in the bathroom—it was as scary as it was embarrassing.

Renner stripped and kicked his clothes aside, thinking about Tierney. The woman defined contradictory. Shrewd financial mind but limited managerial skills, almost bordering on . . . shyness. She wore classy, sexy tailored suits, but she had a weakness for colored sprinkles, ducky-printed shower curtains, girlie shoes with bows, ribbons and flowers, and romance novels. He'd noticed the jam-packed bookshelves in her cabin. Not a newsflash the woman was a bookworm, but he would've pegged her as the type to read self-help books. Not novels with titles like *Take Me, Barbarian*, and *Slave To His Rough Touch*, and *Seduced Against Her Will*.

He cranked on the shower and climbed in, letting the hot water flow down his face and body. God, it was almost better than an orgasm.

Man, it has been a long time if you're comparing getting wet to getting off.

He squirted the gel in his hand and created lather. Tempting, to jack off, as a reminder of the pleasures of the flesh, even if that pleasure was brought about by his own hand. But given how his day had gone, it'd be his luck to literally get caught fucking off.

What would Tierney do if she caught him with his hand on his cock? Back away with embarrassment, stammering and blushing? Roll her eyes and remind him to clean his come off the wall when he finished? Would she watch him with those liquid brown eyes? Or would she lend a hand?

Right. Might as well keep up that fantasy, bub, 'cause her hand and your cock ain't ever happening.

Sighing, Renner ignored his hard-on and finished sloughing off the mud. As he dried his chest, he realized he hadn't grabbed clean clothes from the closet. Securing the towel around his waist, he opened the bathroom door and strolled out.

Naturally, Tierney walked into the office at that exact same time.

Naturally, the end of his towel snagged on the edge of her desk.

Naturally, the towel hit the floor.

Tierney's jaw hit the floor too, seeing him naked as a fucking jaybird, sporting a hard-on that'd make any man proud.

Hell, he'd've been proud of it if the circumstances had been different.

And she sure wasn't helping matters, acting as if she'd never seen an erect cock before.

The more she stared, the happier his dick was to swell with pride, doing a stellar flagpole imitation.

About a year later, Tierney dragged her gaze away from his groin and looked him in the eye. "This is why I was against casual Thursdays. There's always that one person who takes it too far."

"You're fuckin' hilarious." He set his hands on his hips. "I'm thinking we need a cabinet in the bathroom for clothes."

"Maybe you should put it on your to-do list," she suggested sweetly.

The woman was such a smart-ass. "Did you even look at it?" he demanded.

Silence.

Her gaze lowered to his groin again and then zoomed back up to his eyes. "Yes, I looked at it. Do you want an assessment of its length?"

Well, hell, that'd been the wrong thing to say. He blushed. Goddammit, he never blushed. "We are talkin' about the list, right?"

"Of course. What did you think we were talking about?" She sashayed past him. Close enough the end of her ponytail tickled his collarbone. Close enough he swore the silky fabric of her skirt brushed the tip of his cock. Close enough to bend over and pick up his towel. "I believe you dropped this." She tossed it to him and slid behind her massive desk.

Damn her. Mostly damn her cool reaction to him standing in front of her buck-ass nekkid. Renner wasn't a guy who strutted around shirtless like some gym rat, but he knew his body appealed to women. All women.

All women except for Tierney Pratt.

Maybe she was gay.

Maybe you're a sorry son of a bitch for thinking she has to be gay to not be attracted to you, asshole.

Just to be ornery, Renner slung the towel over his shoulder. He opened the closet and reached for his clothing. When he turned around, he caught Miz An-Erect-Naked-Man-Doesn't-Faze-Me . . . eyeballing his ass. Big-time.

Okay. So Tierney definitely wasn't gay.

For some reason, that made him happy. So happy in fact, that he whistled as he nonchalantly strolled back to the bathroom. As much as he wanted to stop at her desk and ask a question, he didn't.

That'd be over the top.

Chapter Eight

❧

Tierney wouldn't be dreading this meeting if she hadn't seen Renner Jackson naked yesterday. Totally naked. Right in front of her. All rough-skinned, scarred, muscled, and aroused masculine excellence.

God. How had she managed not to stare at his penis— his fully erect penis—longer than she had? Her feigned bored expression? An Oscar-worthy performance for sure. Even if she *had* gotten busted two seconds later for ogling his butt.

After Renner meandered back to the bathroom Tierney had to drop her head between her knees to keep from hyperventilating. She'd seen naked men in movies. In magazines. She'd even attended a nude, all-male revue in Las Vegas. But having a hunky man with that buff body so close to her? First time ever.

And it was also the first time she'd experienced overpowering lust. A need to put her hands all over those incredibly toned muscles. A need to put her mouth on his as she touched him. An urge unlike any she'd ever felt. A longing to wrap her fingers around his girth, watching his eyes burn with lust as she learned how to drive him wild with her hands. With her mouth. Any way he wanted. Any time. Any place.

It'd shocked her.

It'd annoyed her.

Flustered, she'd fled the office in an attempt to convince herself it was far better to be repelled by Renner than to be captivated by him.

The smarmy part of her brain taunted, *too late for that*, when the door opened and Mr. Captivating himself moseyed on in.

"You summoned me?" he drawled.

"Yes. I wanted to go over a few things."

"Is this a fortify myself with whiskey conversation? Or a fortify myself with coffee conversation?"

"Coffee. I just made a fresh pot. Help yourself."

He poured a cup and wandered to the seating area. "Can we do this over here? Sitting in front of your desk makes me feel like a naughty kid who's been sent to the principal's office."

"You would know all about that, I imagine."

He laughed. "Nice shot at me first thing."

"I meant it to be funny." She sat on the opposite end of the couch since he'd put his boots on the coffee table.

"Your sense of humor needs work."

Tierney pushed her glasses up her nose. "Now who's taking potshots?"

He flashed that naughty-boy grin. "Sorry. What's up?"

"Now that we've been open a few days, I've drafted a list of what's working and what needs improvement." She knew enough about management to start with the positive aspects and gradually segue into the negative aspects. "I compiled the final financial data for the construction. The cost overruns were expected, but I have to admit, comparing the initial blueprints to the revised ones, I believe the additional building costs were justified."

Renner's mug stopped halfway to his mouth. "Come again?"

"Connecting the four separate buildings made sense, given the Wyoming winters. And it creates the illusion of a bigger resort."

"It was a pain in the ass leveling the area and pouring more footings. We didn't add much in material costs since I'd purchased in bulk, but our labor costs were higher."

She tapped the building plans in front of her. "The overall flow, the main lodge and guest areas at the center, separate dining and entertainment area to the left, and the retail section to the right, is easier for guests and employees to navigate. The additional square footage for the dining area makes a difference in terms of retaining the open feeling."

He rubbed the back of his neck. "That addition was pricier, because for some reason we'd forgotten to add laundry facilities to the initial plans. Luckily we had room to expand rearward. Relocating the bar and game room away from the lodge keeps it a place to relax."

"I haven't heard any more complaints about the food."

"Janie dealt with Dodie."

"Where did you find the rest of the employees?" Tierney didn't ask if he'd requested references, and if he had, if he'd actually checked them.

"I have no idea. Janie handled the employee hiring."

"All of it? Without your input?"

"No. When she found someone to fill a position she ran it by me. I trust her gut and she trusts mine."

"Which works, but the bottom line is we don't have all of the advertised services up and running, so we need to make some hard decisions about those services."

His eyes challenged hers. "Ain't that why Daddy sent you here? To make those types of financial decisions? I'm surprised you're even giving me an option."

She'd promised herself she wouldn't take his bait today, no matter how juicy it was or how close he dangled it. "Whose idea was the spa?"

"Mine. I thought it'd be a nice draw for guys who wanna

bring women here. Give the ladies something to do while the men are out doin' their thing."

"What constitutes a spa in your opinion?"

He scratched his chin. "Fuck if I know. A place for women to hang out."

"You constructed an entire building around this concept," she chided. "You have to be more specific."

"A place for a woman to get her fingernails and toenails painted. A place to get some of that organic goop slopped on her face. Then she's got her choice between soaking in a deep tub with herbs and shit thrown in or having a massage. Then we'd serve girlie food for lunch and lots of fruity alcoholic drinks with umbrellas." He flashed his captivating smile. "Did I pass?"

"No. It's not sustainable. Why is the building an empty shell and construction stopped?"

"It wasn't a priority after we added to the original building plans. The main areas needed finishing first according to the specific timeline in your father's contract."

Another jab she left unanswered. "It's a good thing the spa aspect wasn't realized."

"And why's that?"

"Spas require specialized employees. Most spas boast a variety of services—manicures, pedicures, hot wax treatments, aromatherapy, as well as massages. No one has hired a single qualified employee to handle any of these specific beauty-related services." Tierney cocked her head, looking at him curiously. "Unless *you* intend on painting toenails and slopping face gunk on female guests?"

She sensed Renner wanted to tell her to deal with the luxury spa idea, since the high-end idea was right up her daddy's little rich-girl alley, but he didn't. "Everyone has fuckups."

"Renner. This is not a simple fuckup. This is a fatal flaw."

"On a financial level?"

"Not yet. And I want to keep it from becoming one."

He crossed those muscular arms over that muscular chest and stared at her coolly. "How?"

"By eliminating the spa concept entirely." Tierney stopped his interruption. "I've scoured the reservations for the next six months. From what I've gathered, exactly two female guests are interested in spa services. What does that tell you?"

"Our marketing plan is a piece of shit?"

"Partially. But it means we can cut out this spa option without losing our ass or without pissing off existing customers. It'll take little more than a Web site change. We'll delete any reference to the word *spa* and luckily the brochures just feature the lodge."

Renner looked at her pensively.

"Go ahead and tell me I'm wrong."

"That's the thing, Tierney. You're not wrong. I won't argue with you on this just for the sake of arguing."

She was pretty sure her jaw hit the coffee table.

"Between us? Some of these hospitality things weren't well planned. I take full responsibility for it. The Split Rock shouldn't try and be all things to all people. We'd be better off focusing on the Western element. Hunting, fishing, hiking, trail rides. I'd still like to get men and women here, but I don't want this place to get a reputation as a romantic couples retreat."

"Because calling it such wouldn't make it more appealing to women at all," Tierney said wryly.

"Very funny. If you noticed I didn't call it a dude ranch either."

"Again, dude ranch implies hot cowboys. What woman isn't all over that concept?"

Renner leaned forward to bestow a sinful grin. "Are *you* all over the concept of hot cowboys?"

Only if you're the hot cowboy who'd be all over me.

Tierney tossed off, "Of course. Since moving to Wyoming I understand the appeal of men who exist in Wranglers, chaps, hats and boots, real men who make their living in the great outdoors. I never did before."

"I think that's the most honest thing you've ever said to me."

"Other things I've said have been just as honest—you just didn't want to hear them."

"You may be right. As long as we're bein' honest, can I ask you something?"

Do I want to see you naked again? Absolutely. "Sure."

"How much experience do you have with on-site management?"

"None. However, I will qualify that by saying I've been financial overseer for several PFG properties for the last two years. So I'm very good at cost analysis. I lack hands-on experience on the management end. As you've pointed out. Repeatedly."

Renner gave her a hangdog look.

"I'm here to learn. Not to spy."

"Why didn't you tell me that from the start?"

"We're not exactly friends." She studied him quizzically. "How much experience do *you* have within the hospitality industry?"

No answer. Several long moments passed.

Guess her honesty didn't guarantee his. She shuffled the papers together. "I think—"

"Tierney. Look at me."

She raised her head to meet his gaze and melted a little seeing the softness and sweetness of his smile.

Damn his charming cowboy hide. The man was getting to her.

Chapter Nine

❧

"**I**'m no stranger to management. I'm used to workin' with men. I'm the boss, they do what they're told and don't question it." Renner's least favorite part of owning the Split Rock was dealing with employees. He had no problem barking orders at his stock manager, Hugh Pritchett, or at half a dozen cowboys and stock handlers, but bossing the women on staff . . . didn't feel right.

You've got no issue bossing Tierney.

That was different.

You don't hold any real power over her anyway.

True. Maybe that's why he was always pissy around her.

No, you're flustered because the woman riles you up in ways you've long forgotten.

"Something else on your mind?" she asked.

He frowned and swigged the coffee that'd gone cold. "You know them pens I've been workin' on? We had the blowup last week about wasting my time on building livestock containment areas? Especially when those containment areas remained empty?"

"Then you snapped that Jackson Stock Contracting was

footing the bill. I seem to recall you blowing a gasket about me questioning you."

He wouldn't apologize for that dispute. Little Miz Spreadsheet had been out of line. "I always intended to move the rough stock up here."

"I know. But why?"

"I'd rather be based out of Wyoming. Kansas ain't my home." It never had been. After his father and Boz died, he would've been happy never seeing another wheat field.

"And Wyoming is your home?"

"Right after I bought the land, before I ever scraped away a shovelful of dirt to set the footings for the buildings, this was where I wanted to be." Maybe it was foolish, telling her how much this chunk of rock and dirt meant to him when it provided ammo to use against him. So he backtracked. "Then again, I didn't spring for the sweet setup you've got. Bet that cabin set your daddy back a pretty penny." Another example of the many differences between them. She wouldn't make do if she didn't have to.

Tierney's eyes flashed a warning but she held her tongue for a change.

Rather than snipe at her for the silver spoon in her mouth, he continued brusquely, "The problem is I haven't moved the stock up here yet, but that doesn't change the rodeo schedules I've committed to. I'm taking off after supper tonight because I'm needed at a rodeo in Nebraska tomorrow. I'll be back late Sunday."

"Excellent timing. You're gone. Harper's gone. Janie's limping around. I'm stuck dealing with Dodie, Lisa, Denise, LouLou and that groundskeeper guy . . . what's his name?"

"Willie. Groundskeeper Willie."

Tierney didn't crack a smile at *The Simpsons* reference. "What am I supposed to do?"

"You wanted hands-on management experience, darlin', looks like you've got it."

∞

Renner's phone rang at four a.m. Never a good sign. He picked it up from the passenger seat and said, "Jackson."

"Ren? It's Hugh. Look, we just got to the fairgrounds and were getting ready to unload the steers and . . . Shit, no easy way to say this. They're all dead."

"What the fuck? All of 'em?"

"Yeah. It's the goddamndest thing. I have no idea what happened."

"Which one of our trucks did you use to haul them?"

Pritchett sighed. "That's the problem. It ain't one of our trailers. We were short a truck so we rented from the stockyard. Had to've been something inside, 'cause all the livestock ate outta the same load of hay as the bulls and none of them are sick."

"Fuck." Renner cracked open his last can of Red Bull. "I assume you've isolated the load?"

"Right away."

"Here's what you do." Renner rattled off the options. It wasn't the first time something like this had happened, but it was the first time it'd happened at this particular rodeo.

"Thanks, boss. I hated to bother you."

"The joys of bein' an owner," he said without humor. "I'm just damn glad you hadn't put the bulls in that truck." That would've been a huge financial blow.

"I hear ya there. Where are you?"

"Still about two hours out. Which means I'm close enough to stop and see if O'Hara has extra steers we can use, as well as a trailer." He hated to ask for help, but he didn't have a choice. Maybe he'd catch O'Hara in a rare good mood.

Pritchett whistled. "Wish there was another option. You know O'Hara is gonna jack the cost. Especially when he sees you're desperate."

"Need to come up with something to sweeten the pot. And rodeo tickets ain't gonna do it this time. So if you have suggestions beyond offering him a share in BB, I'm all ears." BB was short for Broken Bones, Jackson Stock Contracting's prize bull. He'd been named Bull of the Year two years running on the Midwest CRA circuit and the Brahman Charolais cross was just getting meaner. Which moved BB closer to being picked for one of the coveted spots in the AFR finals.

"Hey, I've got it. O'Hara's a big hunter. Offer him and the missus a weekend at the Split Rock. I'll bet he'd jump at the chance to kill some stuff. Hell, he might even throw in use of the trailer for nothin'."

Renner snorted. "I doubt that, but good thinkin'."

"That's why you pay me the big bucks."

"That's why I need you in Wyoming, Hugh."

Another sigh. "There's enough shit to deal with without bringing this up now, Ren."

"I was hopin' to catch you at a weak moment," Renner joked.

"No such thing. Good luck with O'Hara and I'll keep you up to date on the shit storm here."

The Red Bull pepped him up, but he couldn't help but consider what else could go wrong. His company had built a solid reputation over the last decade. He'd opted to concentrate strictly on the animal end of the rodeo business. Quite a few stock contractors provided the whole shebang for a rodeo event—the livestock, the personnel, from the bullfighters to the judging officials to the announcers to the entertainers. They also arranged for and set up the venue, dealt with promoting the event, handled the sponsors, the payouts and the behind-the-scenes stuff that'd drive Renner fucking insane. He had a hard enough time keeping four guys on the payroll. He couldn't imagine dealing with more people.

As much as he loved his part in bringing rodeo action to the fans, life on the road tired him out. Burned him out. His business had more potential than just hauling animals from event to event. He wanted to beef up his breeding programs. Invest in heartier stock—a necessity in the colder climes of Wyoming. But none of that business potential could be realized if he was hanging off the chutes every weekend, spending his life behind a steering wheel.

He spied the turnoff to O'Hara's house and forced his thoughts away from dead steers, crappy contracts, his key employee bailing on him, and losing what mattered to him most.

A bear of a man barreled down the steps. "Renner Jackson. What are you doin' in my driveway at five o'clock in the damn morning?"

"Nice to see you too, O'Hara."

"I'd say the same, but I'm barely awake. I'm hoping you're a dream and I'm still in bed snuggled up to my wife."

"Can't help you there. But as long as you are up and dosing yourself on vitamin caffeine, we need to talk."

"Talk? Don't you mean you're gonna try and sweet-talk me outta something?" he grumbled. "Get to the point, boy, I got cattle to feed."

"I do need something. But this time I have a sweet deal. And all it's gonna cost you is a few steers and use of one of your livestock-haulin' trucks for a couple days."

O'Hara laughed. "This had better be good."

"It is. And for your trouble . . . how would you like to hunt in Wyoming?"

Chapter Ten

⧖

Janie had panicked a little the first time Renner left the Split Rock to deal with his stock contracting business. Luckily, everything had gone smoothly and he'd been around the last two weeks, spending most of his time working outside, dealing with the property management issues, which was problematic today since she needed his approval on pricing for a group package, from people that he'd personally referenced.

She hadn't heard the office door slam so Renner and Tierney weren't barking at each other. Those two drove her insane. Bicker bicker bicker. About nothing. About everything. Sheesh. Half the time she feared she'd burst into their office and find them circling each other, wielding machetes.

Over the past three weeks the rest of the staff had really stepped up. Dodie deserved kudos for creating rustic, satisfying meals. LouLou served breakfast and lunch, and assisted Dodie as a prep cook. Lisa handled guest housekeeping and laundry, also filling in as a bartender. Denise served the evening meal and staffed the private bar until ten o'clock or when the guests retired for the evening—whichever came first. Willie was their jack-of-all-trades: dishwasher, bellhop, groundskeeper and building maintenance. If Renner was in a bind, Willie helped him out with the livestock he'd recently bought. Janie knew Renner needed another full-time employee to deal with the ranch end, but so far he'd refused to bring it up with Tierney and for the life of her, she couldn't figure out why.

She wandered through the building. The lodge and dining room were both quiet this time of day, with the guests either outdoors or relaxing in their rooms until cocktail hour. In the past three weeks, Janie had realized the guests didn't want—or need—a hostess every night. In fact, her presence annoyed those who'd arrived as a group, so she'd ended up with free time in the evenings.

Wild West Clothiers remained busy all week. Harper had hit the ground running after returning from her honeymoon, which hadn't allowed much time for them to catch up. Janie missed that connection with another female. Besides the nights Tierney had played nursemaid after Janie's car accident, their daily dealings revolved around business issues.

Abe's concern for her well-being had continued for two weeks after her car accident. He'd tracked her down at the lodge compound. Chatted with her. Flirted with her. Dropped all sorts of sexual innuendos regardless of who was around. But in the last week? Nada. She hadn't seen hide nor hair of him, although she heard he'd been at the barn and corrals working with Renner and Hank.

So it'd shocked the crap out of her when Abe had ambled up this morning and planted a steamy kiss on her. A hot, wet, tongue-thrusting, pelvis-grinding kiss that'd make a porn star blush. Then he'd whispered, "Soon," in that sexy rasp and ambled away.

Which begged the question: why was he screwing with her? Hot. Then cold. Then hotter yet. She wouldn't have pegged Abe as the vengeful type, but there were times when she wondered if she underestimated his bitterness about her leaving him. Had he created a scheme to get even with her? Seducing her, making her want him and then walking away?

But he'd have to actually be in her physical presence to screw with her. Unless he was screwing with her right now by keeping her off balance. By making her want him. Because there was no doubt: Janie wanted her ex in a bad way.

So if she just happened to run across Abe when she was looking for Renner at the barn . . . she'd give the man a dose of his own medicine. Kiss him and run. Maybe she'd kick up the challenge a notch and blow him and run. That'd shock the hell out of him.

Buoyed by that possibility, Janie grabbed her down-filled jacket, which Harper had christened Little Red Riding Hood because the coat was the color of fresh blood. She kicked off her heels and slipped her feet into a pair of Uggs.

With her hood pulled tight to keep the wind from whistling in her ears, she started down the rocky path to the barn. Jamming her hands in her pockets, she focused on her footing. As she slowly picked her way down the slope, she decided they had to fix this treacherous path or someone would get hurt.

Almost as if she'd willed it, the ground rushed up to meet her face with a brain-jarring thump. Without the use of her hands to brace herself, she hit hard and the impact knocked the wind from her lungs. She rolled down the rock-strewn incline like a runaway log as she fought to breathe, but it was a losing battle when she smacked her head and the lights went out.

When Janie returned to consciousness, Willie was nearly nose to nose with her. Startled, she twitched, wincing at the sharp pain in her skull.

"Miz Janie? You all right?"

She moved her lips, but wasn't sure if any sound came out.

"You're bleedin'."

She attempted to get up.

"Whoa there. Sit tight. Miz Tierney went to fetch Mr. Jackson."

Now she hoped Abe wasn't around. He would freak out. *What about you? Are you freaked out? Will you finally admit these accidents are familiar?*

Dread weighted her stomach like she'd swallowed a boulder. Fear crawled up her throat. She turned her head and dry heaved. Sweat broke out on her brow and mixed with blood dripping down the side of her face. The throbbing ache increased her dizziness and she cried out of sheer frustration.

Willie's glove-clad hand awkwardly patted her shoulder. "It's okay. You took quite a tumble. You oughta be more careful out here. It's easy to lose your footing."

Tumble? She hadn't been clumsy . . . had she? It would have taken a violent push for her body to pound the cold ground like that.

Janie must've passed out again, because the next thing she knew, Renner was hoisting her into his arms, amidst Tierney's admonishment to call an ambulance.

"If it looks like she broke something, then we'll take her to the ER in Rawlins."

Tierney tossed out a comment about worker's compensation, which set off another argument between them.

Too bad she couldn't pass out at will.

Janie felt the employees' stares when Renner carried her through the kitchen. When their entourage reached the hallway, she said, "Stop. I can walk from here."

"You are so damn stubborn."

"I will not have you carrying me through the main room of the lodge and spooking our guests, Renner. Put me down."

Seemed to take two hours to climb the stairs and reach the office. Renner settled her on the couch. While he checked her injuries, Tierney brought a warm washcloth and wiped Janie's blood-caked face. "The cut on your forehead stopped bleeding. Hold still. I'm putting on a bandage.

Although, I warn you, it is a Tweety Bird bandage from my personal stash."

"Thanks."

"You're welcome."

She said, "You tired of taking care of me yet?" to Tierney.

"You tired of my subpar caretaker skills yet?" she countered. "Because I'm thinking Renner is about to double-check my bandage application skills."

Janie attempted a smile at Tierney's taunting comment.

Tierney fussed with adjusting the collar of Janie's shirt. "Anything else you need? A glass of water? Aspirin?"

"No. I'm fine." But she wasn't really. Neither was Renner. His frustration fairly pulsed through the room.

He didn't move from her side when he addressed Willie. "What were you doin' when you noticed her?"

Willie twisted his hat in his big hands. "I was takin' the garbage out to the Dumpster. I saw something red on the ground, didn't know what it was and went over to check. That's when I found her."

"Did you see anyone else around?"

"Why are you giving him the third degree?" Tierney asked sharply.

Renner shot Tierney a dark look. "I'm just tryin' to get to the bottom of this. Figure out how long she laid out there before . . ." He sighed, obviously frustrated with the situation. "Look. I'm not accusing anybody of nothin'."

"I know that, Mr. Jackson," Willie said evenly. "But weren't no one around but her. I forgot my walkie-talkie in the kitchen so I ran back up the hill and the first person I saw was Miz Tierney. She went to get you."

Janie cleared her throat. "Thanks for keeping out an eagle eye around here, Willie."

"No problem, Miz Janie. If you don't need nothin' else, I still got stuff to finish up."

"Check in before you leave for the day, all right?"

Willie nodded. "I know you folks don't cotton to some of

the mystical stuff we Crow Indians do, but I gotta say, there's bad spirits around here. Might consider doin' something about it."

That was . . . cryptic. And a little freaky. She shivered.

After the door shut behind Willie, Renner was in her face. "Bad spirits my ass. I cannot believe you . . . Christ, Janie. Was it him again?"

"I don't know."

"The car accident. Now this." Those normally twinkling blue eyes turned accusatory. "What else has happened to you since the car crash that you haven't told me about?"

"Nothing."

"Tell me what is going on," Tierney said.

Renner stood. "Janie will explain everything, but you'll have to wait until Abe gets here so she only has to tell it once."

"You called Abe?" Janie asked.

"Yes. You should've told him the truth after the damn car accident."

Her stomach roiled. Now the shit would really hit the fan.

∞

Abe's heart pounded with his every footstep down the hallway. He blew inside the office at the Split Rock and barked, "What the hell happened?"

Janie said, "Abe. Calm down."

"The fuck I will." He glared at Renner, then Tierney. "What's goin' on around here?"

Tierney gave Renner a frigid glare before focusing on Abe. "I'm as much in the dark as you are. They've both promised full disclosure."

He ignored the *both* portion of her statement and demanded, "Full disclosure? Of what?"

"We'll explain if you'll just sit down—"

"I'll stand." He pointed at Janie. "Start talkin'."

But Janie glanced at Renner. Her haunted look put ice in his soul. Abe crouched beside her, taking her hand, trying to find calmness, if only for her, because obviously she needed it. He softened his voice and kissed her knuckle. "Come on, cupcake. It's killin' me to see you like this."

"I think killing me is the point."

Abe froze. "What?"

She patted the sofa. "Please. Sit."

He sat in the middle of the couch, draping her legs over his lap, needing to touch her to reassure himself, for the second time in so many weeks, that she was all right. He scrutinized her face. The big, square bandage on her forehead was printed with cartoon characters, but the scene before him was far from funny.

Renner spoke before Janie had a chance. "We think someone might've pushed Janie down the path to the barn today."

"On purpose?"

Renner nodded.

"Who?"

"We're not one hundred percent sure, but we have an idea."

"Have you called the sheriff?" he demanded of Renner.

"No. And before you go off on me, Abe, you need to hear the whole story."

"Then somebody had better start talkin'. Now."

Janie's troubled eyes searched Abe's and his stomach lurched. "I was hoping you'd never have to hear this. It still sounds ridiculous to say out loud." She swallowed. "About four years ago I dated a guy who seemed normal enough, but little things set off my alarm bells, so I broke it off after six months. Stupid me. I didn't want to text him or leave a voice mail, so we met face-to-face. But he wouldn't accept it was over. He said I didn't know him. I hadn't given him a chance to prove how well he knew me and how much he loved me."

Jealousy that another man had confessed love for Janie—*his* Janie—set Abe's possessive instinct into high gear. But he managed a cool, "He said he loved you?"

She nodded. "So he began to follow me. Sometimes he'd let me see him. But even if I couldn't see him, I knew he was out there, watching me. Within a month of the breakup, watching wasn't enough. He approached me in public places, forcing me to acknowledge him. I said nasty things, hoping to piss him off, but he wasn't deterred."

"Things escalated. Partially my fault," Renner said.

"No, you helped me. Dave cornered me in the parking lot of a ranch supply store that'd hired me for an interior redesign, spouting his usual undying love for me bullshit. Renner just happened to see Dave push me against my car. He tried to intervene. So I pretended he was my new boyfriend who'd shown up to tell Dave to leave me alone. Luckily Renner played along."

"And this stalker, this Dave guy just accepted your relationship with Renner?"

"God no. But Renner did get me out of there in one piece. Dave's feelings for me turned from adoration to hatred. His actions became violent—not that we could ever prove he was responsible."

"What type of violence?" Abe asked tightly.

"He slashed my tires. The next time he busted out the windows on my car. Then he whacked off the heads of my flowers, followed by smashing all my planters. The incidents were spread out. I never knew when he'd strike next. Finally he . . ." Janie squeezed her eyes shut.

"He what? Janie, you've gotta tell me all of it," Abe said gently.

"That psycho fucker broke into my condo and cut out the crotch of every pair of my panties. Then he used the string of my desecrated underwear to hang one of those sex toys, a blow-up doll, from the ceiling above my bed. He'd put a black wig on her, and wrote 'Die Whore Bitch' across the chest, after X-ing out the eyes."

Beyond horrified, Abe watched helplessly as tears rolled down Janie's face.

"At that point, I did call the cops. They took photos and

my statement. They even brought Dave in for questioning. Whatever story Dave told the cops . . . they bought it."

"Where did this happen?"

"Kansas City," Renner said. "Right after that, I helped Janie get a job with a buddy of mine who manages a hotel chain."

"I changed my whole life because of that psycho fucker. I became an employee trainer in the hospitality industry. I never stayed at a hotel property longer than a month." Janie wiped her wet cheeks with her fingers. "I thought it was over because about a year ago I lost track of him."

Abe couldn't form a noise, let alone a sentence with his tongue stuck to the roof of his dry mouth. Rage such as he'd never felt consumed him. He'd protect her whether she wanted it or not.

"Janie, do you think Dave has been tracking you all along?"

"Jesus, Tierney," Renner snapped at her, "how is a question like that helping this situation?"

"It's a legitimate question. If you and Janie have stayed in touch over the years, it'd be easy enough for Dave to track Janie through you. Jackson Stock Contracting isn't exactly on the down low. Dave has always known who and where you are."

Renner crossed his arms over his chest. "You'd be right, except that Janie and I purposely had a very public breakup while she was packing her U-Haul a month after the police interviewed Dave."

"How can you be sure Dave knew about it?"

"He knew," Janie said softly.

"So Dave also knew you'd lived in Muddy Gap when you were married to me?" Abe asked.

She shook her head. "I never told him or anyone else I'd been married. In fact, I let him believe I was from Colorado since that's where I finished college."

Janie glanced at Renner. "There's part of me that doesn't think Dave is responsible for any of this. That's not me being naïve. It just feels different."

"How so?"

"I can't explain it."

"I'm sorry this happened to you, Janie," Tierney said. "I can't imagine what you've been through." She came over and squeezed Janie's hand. "It's obvious you can't stay by yourself. To be totally up front with you, I'd prefer you didn't live on the property."

Renner got right in Tierney's face. "What in the hell is wrong with you? Don't you care about her at all? We're just supposed to turn her out when that fuckin' psycho is after her again? Fuck that."

"As usual, you've made a wrong assumption about me and the situation. Yes, I do care about her, so quit being a jackass and making me look like a cold, hard bitch. I'm not suggesting we turn her out into the Wyoming wilderness, Renner. I'm suggesting for her safety, as well as the safety of our resort guests, that she finds a more secure place to live than those unprotected trailers when she's off the clock."

"Which works out fine," Abe said, "because Janie is comin' to the ranch with me. I've got a personal security system and no one can get to her without goin' through me first."

"What kind of personal security system?"

"A twelve gauge, a twenty-two caliber and a forty-five."

The eruption of arguments after his mention of guns didn't surprise Abe. Renner and Tierney were nose to nose, loudly locked in battle. Janie was gesturing wildly and trying to talk over them. Abe tried to listen but he didn't give a shit about anything except securing Janie's safety.

A shrill whistle cut through the din and silence ensued.

Harper leaned against the door. "Thank heaven. I could hear you all the way downstairs."

Abe watched Janie, Renner and Tierney exchange sheepish looks—no one had heard Harper come in, which wasn't good.

Tierney recovered first. "Thanks, Harper."

"No problem. I couldn't help but overhear. I came up here to tell you there's a guy wanting a drink at the bar. I would've gone ahead and served him, but after hearing this? I'm not sure if he's even a guest."

Renner made a beeline for the door and would've knocked Harper over if she hadn't moved quickly. Tierney was right on Renner's heels.

"Think it's him?" Abe murmured to Janie.

"No. I don't think he's anywhere around here. So, while the offer of your ranch is appreciated—"

"It's nonnegotiable. You can't live at the Split Rock. Rentals are damn hard to come by in Muddy Gap. You'll be safer at the ranch."

"I'll also be really goddamned isolated," she snapped.

Although she was lashing out because she was scared, her poor opinion of the ranch sliced him to the bone. Not to mention her embarrassment and lack of disclosure about their marriage. But he would not dwell on his feelings because this was about her. Making sure Janie was safe. He'd give the sheriff a heads-up and see what information he could track down.

Harper moved beside the couch to peek at Janie's bandage. "Ouch. How bad did you injure your head?"

"Why?"

"The pain must be blocking the logic center of your brain if you're considering saying no to Abe's generous offer to let you hole up at the Lawson ranch."

Abe bit his cheek to keep from smiling. Harper might look the quintessential beauty queen, but she didn't pull punches. And she did it with total charm.

"Harper, you don't understand."

"Yes, I do. You're being stubborn. Get over it because there's one thing you haven't considered."

Janie's pointed chin lifted a notch. "What?"

"If this Dave guy is targeting you, he'll probably be targeting Abe too, because it's common knowledge around here Abe is your ex-husband. Can you imagine how pissed he'll be that you didn't disclose that to him before?"

With the way Janie's eyes widened, that hadn't occurred to her.

Harper kept going. "If Dave found out where you are, do you really want to be alone, not knowing where he is? And do you really want to leave Abe alone?"

Abe didn't remind Harper he could take care of himself, because Harper driving home Janie's guilt would get Janie right where he wanted her: in his house and in his bed.

Janie smiled weakly. "Oh, girlfriend, you are good."

Harper buffed her nails on her chest. "Thank you. The other benefit of you living at the ranch besides your safety? We'll be neighbors! We can carpool to work. And you guys can come over for dinner. We can do all that fun couple stuff that I've been looking forward to doing as a newlywed."

"You've convinced me. But don't get your hopes up about the couple stuff, because this is a temporary situation."

Abe didn't quite mask his smug *that's what you think* look from Harper and she grinned.

Janie sighed. "Don't you have a store to run?"

"Nope. It's quitting time and I'm heading home to my adoring husband." Harper disappeared with a swish of her denim skirt.

"Not a word, Abe Lawson," Janie warned, rolling away from him to put her feet on the floor. "Just take me to the trailer so I can pack up my stuff."

"Sure. One other thing."

She faced him. "What?"

"This." Abe wrapped his hand around the back of her neck to hold her in place as he kissed her. A kiss brimming with gratefulness that she was all right. A kiss flooded with tenderness for her suffering. A kiss packed with heat, with remembrance of the past, with promise of things to come. When she clung to him, he murmured, "Want me to carry you to my truck, cupcake? Just like old times?"

Janie looked him in the eye. "No dice, cowboy. But I will let you fetch and carry my bags."

Chapter Eleven

❧

*J*anie went nearly comatose in his truck and Abe ended up carrying her into his house. She hadn't stirred when he slipped off her coat and shoes and placed her on the bed in the spare bedroom. He covered her with a quilt and watched her sleep for several long minutes, wishing so much she was in his bed. But he wouldn't push. Not after what she'd been through.

After a quick cattle check, he unloaded Janie's three suitcases. Damn things were bigger than her. But with a pang of sadness he realized everything she owned was probably in those suitcases. With a stalker after her and her frequent job changes, no wonder she was ready to leave at the drop of a hat.

He popped the top on a bottle of Bud and chopped carrots and celery for chicken noodle soup. He'd have to use canned chicken on such short notice, but his version would still be better than cracking open a can of Campbell's.

Would his adeptness in the kitchen surprise Janie? She'd prepared meals for the whole family during their marriage, and at the time, Abe had no desire to learn to cook. That mind-set had changed after Janie left. So he, Hank and Celia had learned together. They'd concocted some truly awful dishes. His memories weren't of the food, but how the three of them had reconnected over a hot stove.

As he tossed the veggies into the chicken stock, his cell phone buzzed. He swiped it off the table and checked the caller ID. "Hey, little sis, I was just thinkin' about you."

"At least somebody gives a shit about me."

"What's wrong?"

"Everything. God. I never thought my life could suck this bad."

He sipped his beer. "Got some examples of the supreme suckage of your life?"

"Didja ever get the feelin' you were just a hostage to your own desires?"

Pretty deep conversation for four in the afternoon. "I've felt like that at one time or another. Why?"

"'Cause I've passed the *held hostage by my own desires* stage and I'm smack in the middle of the *what the fuck am I doing with my life* stage."

The sound of liquid sloshing echoed through the earpiece. Great. Celia was drinking. "How bad was your run today?"

"We tipped over two barrels so I finished last. Again." She swallowed loudly. "I'm foolin' myself, aren't I?"

"Foolin' yourself that you'll make it to the AFR? Honey, you've only been at this a couple years. You're young. There's time to prove yourself."

"It's not what I thought it'd be, Abe. *I'm* not who I thought I'd be."

"And who is that?"

"Who knows? I just don't want Mickey to be the only person who loves me."

"First off, Celia, I love you. Second, Mickey is not a person; Mickey is a horse."

"You know what I meant." She sniffed again. "I miss Murray."

"Murray lived a good life. Twelve years is a long time for

a cattle dog to survive." And two years was a long time to be mourning her dog, but he'd never say that to her.

"Know what's sad? I felt less lonely in the middle of the Wyoming prairie than I do in an arena full of people."

His concern grew because Celia was rarely morose. "Tell me what'll get you outta this funk. Want me to share my screwed-up day to make yours feel normal?"

"Yeah, right. What bad happened to you today, Honest Abe? Forget to brush your teeth so you called your dentist and apologized?"

"No. Someone pushed Janie at the Split Rock and she took a helluva tumble. Remember the hit and run? Come to find out none of this bad shit is a coincidence because Janie had a stalker a few years ago. She can't stay at the Split Rock, so she's here in Hank's old room." Why did he feel the need to tack on that disclaimer?

A pause. Then Celia laughed. "Okay, you got me. That was a great joke. A bit twisted, because dude, a stalker? In Muddy Gap? No freakin' way."

"It's no joke. I'm dead-ass serious."

"Holy cow. Is Janie okay?"

"Banged up. Not happy about bein' forced to live with me in isolation on the ranch again."

He heard the click of a lighter and a swift intake of air. He hated that Celia smoked, but he didn't harp on it, which was damn difficult to do. Yes, Celia was an adult woman. But part of him would always see her in pigtails.

"How long is Janie gonna be workin' up at the Split Rock?"

"She hasn't said. I don't think she knows. Maybe until she's convinced that Renner and Tierney ain't gonna kill one another."

"Still that bad, huh?"

"Yeah. Reminds me of—" *You and Kyle.* He didn't voice the comparison because that was another taboo subject for his prickly sister. "Never mind. So did the story of me playin' the hero, ridin' into town in my white pickup truck to save the damsel in distress provide a distraction from your funk?"

"That's the thing. It's not just a funk. That's not the Jim Beam talkin' either." She sighed. "Although, the booze has loosened my tongue enough to talk about it at all."

The Lawson siblings were closemouthed when it came to sharing their feelings, so he wasn't surprised this was the first he'd heard of it. "You haven't said nothin' to Harper or Lainie about this?"

"No. Harper's a nauseatingly happy newlywed, and Lainie is positively glowing with pregnancy. They both deserve to revel in happiness, not be subjected to my piss-poor outlook on life. Which just seems to be getting worse every damn day."

"Come home," he urged. "We'll get this figured out. Just you and me. Just like old times."

"God, Abe, you're so damn sweet beneath that gruff exterior. I love you. I really do. You know that, right?" Celia's voice broke. "But I don't belong there. I don't belong here. I'm beginning to think I don't belong anywhere."

She was breaking his heart. A level of alarm set in. "Where are you? I'll get in my truck and drive to wherever you are right now."

"No. You have a life too. You have a chance to make it right with Janie."

"Celia, that's not why—"

"You never got over her. I feel guilty Hank and I had a part in breakin' up your marriage." The phone rattled and beeped twice. "Sorry. My cell is about to die. I'll be fine. It probably is the Jim Beam talkin'. Thanks for listening. You really are the greatest. I'm lucky to have you."

The line went dead.

"Goddammit." He redialed her number. It immediately kicked over to voice mail. Maybe her battery had crapped out, but he wasn't taking any chances. Abe dialed and counted the rings while he paced in the kitchen.

Kyle finally answered with, "What have I done to merit a phone call from Abe Lawson?"

"I need your help. Are you and Celia at the same CRA event?"

"Yeah, we're in Taos. Why?"

"Because she just called me. She's drunk, crying, depressed, her phone died and I've no way to get in touch with her. So I need you to track her down."

Silence.

"Kyle?"

"Look, Abe, sending me ain't the best idea."

"Why the fuck not? I know you and Celia have your differences, but this is serious."

"So am I. I suspect I'm the reason she's actin' this way."

"What the hell? I don't have time for cryptic bullshit. Explain that."

Kyle sighed. "Without pissing you off . . . I don't know if I can."

"Try," Abe snarled.

"Celia and I . . . fuck, we had a big goddamn fight earlier today, okay? It's the second time this week we've gotten into it. She warned me if I show my face anywhere near her truck she'll aim that shotgun she keeps under the seat at me and blow me straight to hell."

"That's a chance I'm willin' to take."

"Not me. Besides, I'm not your sister's keeper."

"If you're partially responsible for her acting this way, then you better find her, Kyle, before I find you. And if you don't get back to me within the hour, I'll call the cops in Taos and have them track you both down. Hear me?"

"Loud and clear."

Abe tossed his phone and braced his hands on the counter, trying not to panic.

"What's going on with Celia?" Janie said behind him.

He whirled around. "Ah. Nothin'. I'm handling it."

"Not very well." Janie shuffled closer. She'd wrapped herself in his old terrycloth bathrobe. Something loosened in his chest. He'd forgotten how she used to slip on his shirts and steal his socks and how much he'd loved it. "Talk to me, Abe."

Janie had always complained that Celia was a drama queen, and Abe wouldn't put his sister in a bad light when she was so obviously hurting. "I was talkin' to Celia, we got cut off and I called Kyle, who's on the CRA tour with her, to check on her. He was a little reluctant. I insisted."

"I heard. Is Celia still following him around like a puppy?"

Abe frowned. "What makes you say that?"

"Oh come on. You had to've noticed. The way Celia was always chasing after Kyle. She adored him."

"I never noticed. All's I remember is them fightin' like crazy. Drove us all nuts."

"It was one-sided. Kyle never gave Celia a second glance. To add insult to injury, he treated her like a pesky little sister just like you and Hank did."

"Well, it's a good damn thing he didn't act on her signals or I'da strung Kyle up, family friend or not. He's too goddamn old for Celia."

Janie lifted a brow in that annoying, imperious way of hers. "Seven years is a gap when she was eleven and he was eighteen. But now that she's twenty-four and he's thirty-one? Not such a big age difference." She stood on her tiptoes and tried to peer into the big soup pot. "Whatcha cooking?"

"Chicken noodle soup."

"Homemade?"

"Yeah." Abe dumped the noodles into a strainer in the sink. "Bet you thought I'd never learn to cook."

"I figured you'd marry a proper ranch wife, who'd gladly whip up hearty meals for you three times a day and you'd never have to learn."

"How long did you give me before I remarried?" he asked lightly.

"Six months."

He shook the noodles with extra force. "I must've been a real asshole if you believed I'd need so little time to mourn our marriage, Janie."

"At the time, I didn't think either of us would mourn the end of it."

You were wrong. I mourned that loss longer than I did the loss of my parents. Not that he'd admit such a thing to her or anyone else. He said, "Watch out," and carried the noodles to the soup pot. "We'll be ready to eat in about five."

"I'll set the table. Where are you keeping bowls these days?"

"Middle cupboard."

"I knew you'd change things back to the way your mother had arranged them after I left," she accused.

"Another thing you're wrong about. Lainie made changes when she moved in. I've never cared where the dishes were just as long as I could find them."

She set the bowls on the woven placemats. "Were these Lainie's?"

"The placemats? No, those are mine. Couldn't stand the frilly ones so I bought some that weren't so damn girly." He plopped the pot in the middle of the table next to a box of crackers. His cell vibrated on the counter and he snatched it, growling, "You'd better have good news for me, Gilchrist."

"I found her."

Abe sagged into the chair. "Thank you. How is she?"

"Besides drunk as a damn skunk? Now she's mad as hell too. She took a swing at me."

"I hope you ducked."

"Her aim is a little off, but she wasn't exactly aiming for my face."

Considering the snarl in Kyle's tone, Abe held back his chuckle. Then he heard Celia in the background. "Is that Abe?"

Kyle said, "Yeah. Didja wanna talk to him?"

"Abe, you fucking bastard," Celia yelled loud enough that Abe had to hold the phone away from his ear. "You called *Kyle*? I trusted you and you turned me over to this smarmy douche bag who can't keep his dick in his pants! Do you know what he said to me?" The line crackled and Celia's voice sounded farther away. "Omigod, Kyle Gilchrist you fuckin' pervert, put me down right fuckin' now or I swear to God I will kick your balls into your throat as soon as I've sobered up!"

"Try it, baby cakes, and I'll give you another spanking."

Another spanking? What the fuck did that mean?

The phone clunked again and Kyle snarled, "You owe me, Abe. Big time. Celia is so shitfaced I can't leave her alone so I'm takin' her to my hotel. But since she ditched Mickey at the community barn after the event, now I gotta deal with that temperamental goddamn horse of hers too. Fuck."

"Call me tomorrow and let me know how the night went."

"I'll tell you right now how it's gonna go. She's a pain in my ass and I'll probably end up in jail for killin' her. I don't give a shit if she is your sister. You assholes better bail me outta jail if that happens." Kyle hung up.

Janie stared at the phone. "Wow."

"Yeah. Like I said, no love lost between Kyle and Celia. But at least I know she ain't passed out somewhere alone."

He filled the bowls and they tucked in.

"This is really good, Abe."

"Thanks."

"So Celia's been barrel racing professionally for ... ?"

"Three years. Not that me'n Hank had a freakin' clue about that part of her life. She hid it from us." His gaze zoomed to hers. "Did you know she'd kept up with her training?"

Janie shook her head. "But Celia didn't confide in me much anyway. Is she any good?"

He shrugged. "Some natural talent. She works hard and ended up with a great horse. She's gone a lot, which took some getting used to. Now me'n Hank are her biggest supporters, but when we found out about her deception . . ." Something jogged his memory. When it solidified, a niggling feeling of guilt surfaced. "Wait a second. The last time you contacted me before you came back to Muddy Gap was three years ago."

"So?"

"So . . . was that the same time the incidents with this Dave guy escalated? Was that why you called me and asked if we could meet?"

"I don't remember."

Liar. "Janie."

"What?"

"Look at me and tell me the truth."

Her purple-hued irises flashed frustration. "Yes, that's partially why I called you, okay? I was scared to death and I thought seeing you, hearing you say 'pull yourself up by your bootstraps, Janie, and handle it like an adult' would give me courage."

"So you didn't tell me what was really goin' on that day we had lunch in Cheyenne. You acted like your life was perfect. In fact, you sort of rubbed it in my face. How happy and successful you were." *Without me* went unsaid. It'd sliced him to the quick, hearing from her after years of no contact. Believing he'd heard longing in her voice over the phone had been the only reason he'd agreed to see her. He'd felt like a fool afterward, but seeing her had allowed him to make much needed changes in his own life.

"I lied about my life because I didn't want you to think I needed saving again," she said softly.

Instead of saying, *I've always wanted to be there to save you*, he snapped, "But it was perfectly okay for Renner to come to your rescue, like in the version you told me earlier?"

"Please. Can we just drop it?"

Back to the same old, same old within a couple of hours. Only the clanking of spoons filled the silence.

She delicately broke a cracker and scattered the chunks

in her bowl. "What are your after-dinner plans? Wanna veg out and watch a movie with me?"

"You're more than welcome to watch whatever you'd like. There's a ton of ranch bookwork to catch up on, so I'll be workin' in my office all night."

"Oh. Okay." She hid her disappointment and focused on stirring her soggy crackers. "I'm staying in Hank's old room?"

"Unless you'd rather be downstairs in Celia's room so you have your own bathroom."

"I don't mind sharing a bathroom with you."

He checked the time. "Do you need anything else before I get to work?"

"I'm sure if my stalker tosses a Molotov cocktail through the living room window, you'll hear it."

"Funny. The doors are locked. I don't have to warn you not to go outside, do I?"

She shook her head.

"See you in a couple hours." He snagged a Coke and retreated to his office, locking the door behind him. While he waited for his computer to load, he unlocked the filing cabinet and took out his notebooks. He flipped through the loose papers until he found the assignment he'd finished after the last online class. Thank God he was only nine credits short of finishing his bachelor of science degree in agricultural business. Abe knew such stealth was ridiculous. But he'd been doing it for so long it'd become second nature. It was a miracle he'd kept his academic pursuits hidden from Celia, as well as Hank and Lainie while they'd lived here with him.

Abe had known at an early age his main responsibility would always be to the ranch, but he'd intended to go to college part time. Following his parents' unexpected deaths, dreams of higher education became just that. He and Hank were left to raise Celia. To earn cash to keep them afloat, Hank had started bullfighting. Hank's travel demands meant better money, but it also meant more work for Abe.

With the weight of his ranch responsibilities, by the time he was twenty-three, he'd felt like an old man.

His friends always teased him about being so serious, working too hard. Heeding his brother's advice to cut loose, he'd spent the weekend in Casper visiting his buddy Max. They'd gone to a fraternity dance, scoffing at the pirate theme, opting to wear normal clothes—jeans, boots and hats. The frat boys weren't happy the ladies were clustered around the pair of cowboys, not the surplus of pirates, and tossed them out. Literally. Abe's face had connected with several fists before his ass had met the pavement. A scrap of a woman, dressed as a serving wench, helped him to his feet, and fussed over him like she'd been personally responsible for his airborne ejection from the party.

It'd been years since he'd been the sole focus of a woman's tender care and concern. He liked it more than he wanted to admit—and he milked it as much as he could. It wasn't Janie's unadorned physical appearance that'd immediately captivated him, although she masked her petite curvy body in formless clothes and hid her beautiful smile behind long straight black hair. Her thoughtful nature had drawn him in after she'd taken him to her efficiency apartment and patched him up. Those amazingly expressive purple-hued eyes and the hungry way she kissed him, and the no-holds-barred way she wanted him were just icing on the cake.

He'd hung out with the introverted, oddly compelling woman all weekend. And every weekend after that. He and Janie were inseparable, as inseparable as a couple could be, with him living in Muddy Gap and her living in Casper. The more he got to know her, the more he adored her. He wanted to spend his life taking care of her. He was so happy he'd found a woman who understood his ties to the ranch and his family. A woman who wanted the same things he did.

Or so he thought.

He proposed to her within two weeks of that first meeting. But Janie held him off for four months before agreeing to become his wife. She moved to the ranch, but continued to drive to the college campus to work on her degree. The first year they were happy. But as months went on, so did Abe's frustration with Janie's disillusionment about the life she'd signed on for with him. Why wasn't being married to him and living the same type of life his parents had enough for her?

Eventually, the no-win argument culminated in her leaving him.

In the aftermath, Abe wondered if he'd mistaken her shyness for malleability. There was little resemblance in the Janie of old, to the new Janie. Now she was sophisticated, with her chic short haircut and trendy wardrobe. She exuded confidence in all social situations, using her charm and deeply dimpled smile to enchant both men and women.

Still, Janie's departure from his life had prompted his enrollment in college. He'd never felt smart enough for her. But after his first year of classes, earning a degree became something Abe wanted to do for himself, if for no other reason than to prove he could.

He had the chance to confess about his secret academic life when Hank busted Celia for keeping her barrel-racing career a secret. But he hadn't come clean. It'd become a point of pride that if he failed, no one would know but him.

Abe logged into his student account, mentally preparing himself for a two-hour lecture on the "Analysis of Sustainable Agriculture in the Global Marketplace." He plugged in his headphones, grabbed a pencil and settled down to work. Thoughts of seducing his ex-wife were lost in ag projections and corporate farming practices.

∞

Abe was not acting at all like the Abe that Janie remembered.

He wasn't hovering and fussing over her.

He definitely wasn't coddling and soothing her.

He'd cooked comfort food for her.

Then he'd left her to her own devices. For three hours.

Last night when he'd emerged from his office, he'd double-checked the locks, sweetly kissed her on the forehead and retired to his room.

Janie expected things to be different tonight. She'd spent all day by herself while he was doing mysterious, never-ending ranch stuff. So after he returned from finishing chores, she intended to complain about her aches and pains, expecting he'd offer to rub her neck. Or massage her back. Or put his face between her thighs and use that wickedly talented mouth to make her come.

But he'd not done any of that. He'd cooked, cleaned up, and vanished into his office again. Which indicated the man had no plans to seduce her tonight.

So proposition him.

Right. She already felt crappy, and if Abe turned her down ... she'd be even more mortified. She shuffled to the bathroom and popped two ibuprofen. While scrubbing her teeth, she scrutinized her appearance in the mirror. Pasty white skin, black circles beneath her eyes ... terrific zombie imitation. No wonder Abe hadn't sweet-talked his way into her panties.

Janie stopped in the hallway outside of Abe's room, debating on whether to bother him. The door opened so fast she almost believed he'd been waiting for her.

"Is everything all right?"

Holy hell, no, everything was *not* all right, she was about to have heart failure. The man wasn't wearing a shirt. And check out those exquisitely formed pectorals—firm, chiseled bands of muscle. Her eyes followed the sexy line of dark hair bisecting his well-defined chest, down past his ribcage to abs of steel. Talk about a lip-smacking six-pack. As her gaze drifted farther south to the waistband of his camo boxers, Abe cleared his throat.

Guiltily, she met his eyes. "Sorry. It's just a shock to see you."

"Really? Because *you* knocked on my bedroom door."

"I did?" She stared at her knuckles as if they had a mind of their own because she didn't remember knocking. "Umm . . . I didn't mean it was a shock to see you as much as I meant it is a shock to see you half-naked."

"I'm getting ready for bed. Something you need?"

Dammit. Conjuring a plausible excuse on the fly wasn't her strong suit. "Ah, I just wondered"—*when you got into such fantastic shape*—"what time you were getting up?"

"Around five. Same as I always do. Why? You want me to get you up?"

"No. In fact, I might sleep with a gun under my pillow in case you decide to try." Abe's tendency to adhere to a rigid schedule, especially so freakin' early in the morning, had been a major annoyance during their marriage. He'd always wanted her to tag along when he did his first round of feeding, which never made sense to her because she wasn't much help, but he'd always nagged the point. "I wondered if you were taking me to the Split Rock, or if I could borrow a vehicle. I need to be there around eight."

"I'll take you. I oughta have the first round of feedin' done by then."

"Well, thanks. Good night."

"Night, Janie. Sweet dreams."

They'd be a lot sweeter if you curled your banging body around mine.

"You sure you're all right?"

Janie caught the mirth in his eyes, as if he knew exactly what she was thinking. "I'm fine."

Put your eyeballs back in your head. Turn around. Go to bed.

And somehow, Janie did just that.

Chapter Twelve

No surprise things had come to a head with Renner. Not because Tierney had been pestering him with endless questions. His fury had come from jealousy and disbelief that employees had been approaching *her* with operation questions—not him—while Janie was recuperating.

So maybe she had acted a little smug. But that hadn't given him the right to insult her.

Maybe you should've thrown another drink in his face to cool him down.

No. He definitely wouldn't have stood for that. Renner was deceptively laid back, but underneath his calm façade was a man coiled tight, ready to spring. They'd circled each other, boxers in the ring, words carelessly flying like fists. And when his final punch had hit too close to home . . . she hadn't fought back. She ran.

Unfortunately, there weren't a lot of places to run to in Muddy Gap. She'd cruised past the churches and the lone restaurant, tempted to pray for patience or comfort herself with chocolate cake. On a whim, she'd decided to stop at the local hair salon.

The entire clientele of Bernice's Beauty Barn stopped

talking when Tierney walked in. Four ladies in various stages of beauty treatments loitered in a waiting area straight out of a 1950s beauty shop. Tierney glanced at the salon chair, where a robust woman snipped tiny gray tufts from her client's head.

Immediately the redheaded hairdresser boomed, "Don't look so darn scared. I ain't started cutting your hair yet. That's when you're entitled to get the deer in the headlights look."

Everyone laughed. One woman piped up, "You're so ornery, Bernice."

Tierney's gaze flicked to the lounging ladies and then back to Bernice, wielding the scissors. "It appears you're booked today. I'll come back another time—"

"Nonsense," Bernice said. "Have a seat. I'll squeeze you in between Garnet and Pearl. You want a haircut? Or something more?"

"Just a . . . trim, but I wouldn't want to impose and take someone else's spot."

"Oh, pooh." The lady with rollers in her hair scooted over and patted the empty spot next to her. "There's plenty of room. I'm Pearl Tschetter."

"Tierney Pratt."

"I don't mind if you go ahead of me. I'd probably sit here and gab for a couple of hours anyway, after Bernice fixes me up proper. This is the only time of the week I get to gossip."

Two of Pearl's cohorts snorted. One rolled her eyes.

Tierney perched on the edge of the Danish modern sofa, set her handbag next to her left thigh before she folded her hands in her lap.

Still actin' so prim and proper. You need to loosen up.

Shut up. Your voice has no business in my head, Renner Jackson.

"So, are you the big cheese up at the Split Rock?" came from across the coffee table. Hard not to ogle the woman whose orange hair clashed with the sleek silver jumpsuit from the disco era. The high-topped tie-dyed sneakers were an unusual touch, as was the rainbow-striped scarf she'd jauntily looped around her neck. The woman was eighty, if she was a day.

Before Tierney could respond, a grandmotherly type whapped the disco escapee on the knee with a steno pad. "Garnet Evans, behave." She offered Tierney a sweet smile. "I'm Maybelle Linberg, reporter for the *Muddy Gap Gazette,* and I'm so very pleased to officially meet you."

"Me too," the woman getting a haircut piped up. "I'm Tilda O'Toole. We're all friends of Harper's."

Garnet leaned forward, resting her forearms on her knees. "I notice you didn't answer my question. Who's in charge up there?"

Good question. "I work for the financial management company that invested money in the resort."

The youngest of the group, a distinction Tierney made because the woman in question wore a short denim miniskirt, said, "So you *are* the big boss," as she continued to flip through a fashion magazine.

"One would be hard-pressed to boss Renner Jackson around in any capacity." Tierney almost clapped her hand over her mouth. What on earth had possessed her to blurt that out to total strangers?

"I wouldn't mind being pressed hard against Renner Jackson," Garnet said with a soft *rowr*. "He's a sexy hunk of real man. Have you seen him in chaps?"

"Garnet, are you tryin' to make Tierney run outta here on her very first visit?" Bernice tossed over her shoulder.

"What? The girl's got eyes, don't she? Surely she's let them wander over that hunkalicious bod a time or two?"

You have no idea how many times I've eyeballed that man's ass. And his abs. And his chest. And his arms.

A gasp. A throaty laugh. Then silence.

Tierney glanced at Garnet's self-satisfied expression. "What?"

"Bet you didn't mean to say that out loud."

Her face flamed and she stuttered, "N-no. I didn't."

"Don't make it less true," Pearl said.

"I can believe that man don't like to be bossed around. But I bet he does plenty of bossing in the boudoir."

"Oh, don't be too sure, some of those macho men prefer a woman with a firm hand and a soft whip. Or so I've read," Maybelle said.

Pearl and Garnet laughed.

The miniskirt woman lifted her head and crossed her long legs. Tierney reassessed her earlier age assumption. With spiky auburn hair, vivid green eyes, killer bone structure and flawless makeup, the woman could've passed for fifty, but the truth was, she was probably closer to seventy. She held her hand out to Tierney and smiled. "I'm Vivien Edwards."

"Vivien's got a date tomorrow night," Tilda announced.

"It's just coffee," Vivien demurred.

Garnet patted Vivien's knee. "It's a start, sweetie."

"I know. It's just . . . I haven't done this for so many years." She sipped from a can of V8 juice and looked at Tierney. "What the gossip girls here haven't said, is I've been widowed for five years. I spent the first three years traveling to the exotic places all over the world Bill and I never did. The next year and a half I bounced between our kids' houses until I drove them and my grandbabies insane. I decided I was ready to come home to Muddy Gap last month."

"And she's already got a date! Can you believe it?"

Tilda seemed really impressed with Vivien's date. Tierney wondered how long it'd been since Tilda had a date.

Maybe you should think about how long it's been since you've *had a date.*

"At least somebody's dating. I don't remember the last time I saw a live penis," Garnet complained.

Maybelle whapped Garnet on the knee again. "You saw several last week when we went to the 'Crash with the Past' all-male revue in Casper, smarty." Maybelle confessed in a loud whisper, "It was research for an article I'm writing for the *Gazette*."

Tierney grinned.

"Oh, them penises don't count," Garnet scoffed. "Them penises were in captivity. I was guaranteed to see at least one when we shelled out for the show. That's not like finding a penis out there in the wild. Where at the end of the night when that zipper comes down you discover if he's hung like a horse or just dangling a worm."

"I'll bet Tierney dates a lot," Pearl said, interrupting Garnet's musings on penises.

"Not a single date in the time I've been here."

"But you've been asked out, right?" Maybelle pressed.

She shook her head.

Silence. Exchanged looks. More silence.

Great. These seventy- and eighty-something women pitied her. *Her*. A woman in the prime of her dating life. A woman who'd seen exactly one live penis out of captivity in her twenty-six years—and only recently by accident.

Now she pitied herself too.

"Girl, *you* oughta start askin' guys out. Hit Buckeye Joe's. Flirt a little. Dance a little. Drink a little. Have some fun!"

Vivien squeezed Tierney's knee. "Don't put off living the life you want, waiting for the 'right time'—the right time is now."

Garnet added, "I bet if you loosened up you'd get to see a lot of different penises."

"Garnet, can you head to the dryers?" Bernice called out.

Tilda tottered by, snagging a silver fox fur coat from a rack that'd been fashioned out of animal horns. After Tilda paid and admired her hairdo in the big mirror behind the cash register, she turned and addressed Pearl, Maybelle and Vivien. "You're coming over at five?"

"Wouldn't miss it for nothin'," Pearl replied. "Don't forget the nondairy whipped cream for the pie. Milk gives me gas."

Bernice shut the cash drawer and stopped in front of Tierney. "You're next."

"But what about her?" Garnet's mouth hung open and she appeared to already be asleep beneath the hair dryer. "Is she okay?"

"The white noise resets her brain, and after the penis discussion, we all needed our brains reset."

Tierney ditched her glasses and followed Bernice to the rinse bowl, allowing herself to relax as her head was massaged.

Back in the chair, Bernice combed out her wet locks. "So just a trim?"

"Yes, please."

Bernice paused. "Look, Tierney, I don't know you, and maybe it's none of my business, but how long have you worn your hair in this style?"

"Since . . . well, since always. Why? Do I have split ends?"

"No, sugar, you have such pretty hair. Usually this beautiful sable color only comes out of a bottle. I'd like to showcase it in a style that is more age appropriate."

She didn't know what to say. Her hair was brown. It'd always been . . . just boring brown. "But I don't have time to fuss with my hair. I keep it one length because it's easy."

"If I could give you a style that's easy, but will make you look like the hot young executive you are, would you be willing to try it?"

"It'd still need to be long enough to pull back in a ponytail."

"I was thinking long layers."

"Nothing I'd have to straighten or curl?" she asked skeptically.

"I have a cut in mind that'll allow you to go right from the shower, to putting product in, to a little finger fluffing and . . . hello gorgeous."

Tierney squinted at herself in the mirror, not that she could see anything without her glasses. It was only hair, right? And if Bernice did a hack job, well, she could wear it back and no one would probably notice. She inhaled a deep breath. "Let's do it."

Snip snip snip. Chunks of dark hair started to fall around her. She closed her eyes and mentally chanted, *it's just hair*.

An eternity later, Bernice said, "Put your glasses on and have a look-see."

Quelling her nerves, Tierney slowly lifted her head. Her mouth dropped open. Holy cow. The person staring back at her in the mirror . . . looked like her. But a better version of her. Hipper. Younger, yet more polished.

"Well? You like it?" Bernice prompted.

"I love it!" She angled her face side to side. Her hair was so swingy. So shiny. So . . . cool.

"Check out the back." Bernice spun her and handed her a small mirror.

It even looked great from behind. "It's perfect. Thank you so much!"

"My pleasure. I will caution you this type of precision cut requires maintenance. You'll need to come in for a trim every four weeks."

"On top of being a magician, you're a shrewd business woman. I admire that."

Bernice grinned. "I haven't even pitched the styling products you'll need yet."

"I'll buy them all if I can look this good every day."

As soon as Bernice swept up the hair, Vivien, Pearl, and Maybelle surrounded her.

"You look fabulous," Vivien gushed.

"Sophisticated," Maybelle added. "Perfect for a financial overseer."

"Girl, you look hot," Garnet yelled. "You'd better slip on sexy duds to match your smokin' new look, because when the men in this town get an eyeful of you? You'll have more penises to choose from than you can shake a stick at."

Tierney laughed. "And to think I'm finally getting what I always wanted—a plethora of penises."

She decided to take their advice as soon as she got back

to her cabin, taking her time to get ready and playing with her new look.

Her eyes watered like a fountain and she blinked repeatedly at the reminder of why she rarely wore contact lenses. She smudged black eyeliner along her top and bottom lashes. A shiny berry-colored stain gave her lips the illusion of plumpness. A darker shade of blush emphasized her cheekbones. She used concealer to cover up the dents on her nose from her glasses. She adjusted the low-cut peasant blouse with swirls of orange and brown. Harper insisted the vivid pattern would showcase Tierney's coloring, and once again, she'd been dead on. Turning sideways, she scrutinized her new Western jeans. The dark denim was tighter than she normally wore. Hopefully she could hook a cowboy and entice him into taking her for a ride.

Don't you mean take you on your maiden voyage?

Tierney shoved that niggling thought aside, refusing to put pressure on herself tonight. It'd happen when it happened. Still, she checked the expiration date on her unopened box of condoms just in case. She slipped on the four-inch lace-up half boots, grabbed her keys, and went honky-tonking.

Whatever that meant.

Chapter Thirteen

❧

*R*enner flicked a glance at the brunette as she breezed past him. He'd hidden in the corner at Buckeye Joe's with a Crown and water, which sat mostly untouched. Not in the mood to drink, he'd just needed a break from the resort for a little while.

He snorted. Resort. Even he'd started calling it that, instead of the term "ranch" he preferred.

Just another thing he blamed on Tierney.

Her perfectly polite smackdown still stung. *Dividing is not conquering, Renner. All we're doing is pitting our employees against each other by expecting them to choose sides between you and me. Can't we just try to get along for the greater good? Managerial infighting isn't the way to do that.*

And what words of wisdom had he lobbed back at her?

He'd insulted her. Talk about mature. Now here he was, brooding in the corner. He let his hat shadow his face, trying to look like just another anonymous cowboy drowning his sorrows.

His wishful thinking lasted about five minutes.

"Jackson? What're you doin' here?"

Sheriff Bullard's belt was at Renner's eye level. He glanced at the sidearm strapped on the right side, and his eyes traveled up Bullard's rotund torso. The gray-haired man had been the law around here for over twenty years and had that "fess up" vibe down pat. "You cruising through hopin' to bust underage drinkers?"

"Yep. Susan is good at tossing them sneaky suckers out, but she don't got eyes in the back of her head. I'm just doin' a run-through 'fore I get on home."

"I'll buy you a drink if you're off the clock."

Bullard waggled the Styrofoam coffee cup. "Got mine right here. But I'll join ya for a bit, if you don't mind."

"Not at all. Have a seat."

The sheriff pulled out the chair, tossed his hat on the table and swallowed a slug of coffee before he spoke. "How're things up at the Split Rock?"

Renner shrugged. "Good. I'd be happier if all the rooms were full every night, but we still don't have the staff to handle that, so I'm grateful for what we've got."

"Slow and steady wins the race, eh?"

"I suppose so." Renner sipped his drink. "Any complaints from the locals?"

"Nah. You must have a good crew 'cause I've heard no grumbling at all."

"That would be Janie Fitzhugh's doing."

Bullard frowned again. "She's Abe Lawson's ex-wife."

Renner knew that term grated on Janie. "Any new information on the vehicle that ran her off the road?"

"None. It's the damndest thing. Stuff like that don't happen around here."

"Unless it was someone who'd been drinking and didn't wanna face the music."

The sheriff harrumphed. "Abe's just damn lucky he came upon the accident so fast on that remote section of road. Coulda been a whole lot worse."

"True." Rather than make idle chitchat, Renner seized the opportunity to talk to Bullard without an audience. "When I was talkin' to Abe last year, he mentioned something about the tract of land I purchased bein' bad luck land."

"You're talkin' about the section that used to belong to your grandparents?"

Renner nodded. "Without sounding all woo-woo and shit, Janie's accident happened alongside that land. And Willie, our jack-of-all-trades, says he gets a bad vibe."

"And?"

"And I understand some nasty stuff has gone down with people who've bought that land over the years. It's changed hands, what, half a dozen times since my grandparents owned it?"

"Yeah. So?"

"So, no one in my family has ever told me what happened when my grandfather died. I've heard 'accident' and the subject was changed. I understand them not telling me the truth when I was a boy, but them days are long gone."

Bullard eased back and stretched his arm along the back of the chair beside him. "You asking me what happened?"

Renner met the man's hard gaze head on. "Yes. I am."

"Why don't you tell me what your family has told you."

"Grandpa was out checking cattle. His horse threw him, and he broke his neck. By the time Grandma found him, he was dead." He paused. "No disrespect to my late grandma, but the hushed tone whenever this was brought up, gave me the feeling family members suspected she'd somehow . . . killed him."

Bullard's frown morphed into a smile. "Son, is that what's been eatin' at you? The fear that sweet Rona Harking might've offed her husband?"

"Maybe."

"We had considered that angle, given the circumstances. But I suspect your family didn't talk about it simply because it upset your grandma. She got a mite . . . hysterical after she found your granddad. Took a tranq to calm her down after we loaded the body for transport. Anyway, the coroner ruled it 'death by misadventure' which comes back to your original question of it bein' bad luck land."

"Do you believe it is?"

"Yep. But I'm Crow Indian, so I believe a lot of stuff others don't."

Almost word for word what Willie had said, but neither had given him a concrete way to deal with it. "Great. I don't suppose you have any Crow Indian good luck charms I could borrow to ward off bad juju?"

"Nope. But there are options when you're ready to hear them." Bullard jammed his hat on his head and stood. Pointed at Renner's drink. "I don't gotta remind you about finding a DD if you decide to have more of those, do I?"

"No, sir."

"Good enough. See ya around, Jackson."

Renner was melancholy after Sheriff Bullard left. Lost in thoughts about destiny. Loneliness. Luck. Signs. Family.

The summer he and his dad moved to Kansas, Renner had started working for his dad's oldest friend, Bostwick "Boz" Sheffield, as a hired hand in Boz's livestock business. Renner had been a scrawny twelve-year-old, a wannabe cowboy who'd honed his charm simply because he knew it worked on girls, teachers, coaches, friends.

Charm hadn't impressed Boz Sheffield. Hard work did. So Renner set out to impress the man. Took nine years, but his dedication to the cattle business paid off when Boz offered to sell it to him after Renner's divorce financial windfall. Boz claimed he wanted to retire, but Renner suspected the sale was Boz's way of ensuring Renner didn't blow the cash and his future. Although Boz had never married, never had a kid, Renner was the closest thing he had to a son and he wanted to pass his legacy on to someone he trusted. In some ways, Boz had been the most influential man in Renner's life.

Renner couldn't pinpoint exactly when he figured out that his father and Boz were more than friends. Probably always had been. Tim Jackson joined the service, married, fathered a child, lost his wife, traveled the country and after retiring from the air force, he'd returned to his Kansas hometown to face the man—and the feelings—he'd run from. But both Tim and Boz were old school, firmly in the closet, content to let the world see them only as best buds who did everything together.

Those two strong men had raised him to do the right thing, to be respectable, honest, hardworking. It pained him to watch them maintain the lie. They lived in separate houses. They took hunting trips, sometimes just the two of them, sometimes in a group. Three years after Renner bought Boz's business, Boz and his father were killed in a plane crash coming back from Alaska. Renner's only comfort was that they'd been together. With the last of his family gone, he'd thrown himself into work. But no matter how hard he worked, he'd always felt as if something in his life was missing.

Catcalls bounced to him in the lonely corner he'd chosen, and he shook off the memory. The crowd had grown and he was debating on whether to order another drink or leave, when he saw the brunette. A dude in a cheap brown Stetson knockoff stepped aside and Renner's gaze locked on the woman's profile. She turned and Renner's eyes nearly bugged out of his head. He recognized that smirk. Although little else was recognizable about her.

Gone was the straitlaced, straight-faced tyrant he dealt with every day. Tierney looked . . . hot as fire. Her hair, a gorgeous mix of mahogany and mink hues, shone even in the dim bar light. She continued to smile, and damn if his breath didn't catch. Her cheeks were pinkened. Her mouth looked as soft and lush as a rose petal. Her eyes were dancing with delight . . . wait. Where the hell were those maddeningly sexy smart-girl glasses she always wore?

That brought Renner out of his seat. He watched as the happy-handed cowboy's touches veered dangerously close to inappropriate and Tierney didn't notice.

He stealthily bellied up to the bar behind her and lifted

his hand to Susan, who nodded and slid a Crown and water across the bar top. He said, "Evenin', Tierney," and gulped a drink.

She whirled around on her barstool so fast her hair slapped him in the face.

Oh, fuck him. Not only did she sport a fancy-ass new hairdo, but her shiny tresses smelled like flowers. With the musky undertones of sex. And because he hadn't gotten laid in a coon's age, that alluring fragrance made his dick stir.

"What are you doing here?" she asked with unrestrained hostility.

"Same thing as you are. Winding down after a rough week." He toasted her. "You are one ball-bustin' boss lady, but I'll admit, you do get the job done."

The heat from Tierney's eyes could've scorched his eyebrows.

The young bucks glowered, puffing up their scrawny chests. "Who are you?" brown hat demanded.

"Name's Renner Jackson. I see you've already met the woman who cracks the whip on my ass every day."

"I didn't crack it hard enough if it didn't keep you where you belong," Tierney snapped. "Don't you have other people to annoy?"

He laughed. "Nope."

Brown hat said, "Don't seem like she wants you here annoying her, so why don't you buzz off?"

"Yeah, we were here first," his buddy interjected and took a menacing step closer.

Renner's humor fled. "You punks don't know anything about handling a woman like her." Placing his hand on the back of Tierney's chair, he got right in the kid's face. "So why don't *you* take a hike and stick to the high school girls who prefer ball-less wonders such as yourselves and leave her to a real man."

The cowboys exchanged a look and backed off. "Uh . . . She's all yours."

Goddamn right she is.

Then all five foot five inches of pissed-off Tierney was crowding him. Except her hooker boots added a good four inches to her height, putting her mouth in direct line with . . . holy hell, since when did she have such sweet tits?

"Handle me?" she repeated. "What makes you think *you* can handle me?"

Somehow Renner dragged his eyes up to hers. Christ. Her eyes were potent, a rich cherry brown. But when she was angry, which frankly was all the time around him, the reddish tint gave her a demonic look. And damn if that didn't make him crazy hot for her too. "I was only trying to help."

"Help?"

In his peripheral vision, he noticed the glass clutched in her hand. He curled his fingers around her wrist and squeezed, forcing her to let go. "Tossing another drink in my face, sweetheart, is a big no-no."

"Too bad I'm not armed like the rest of the people in Wyoming. I'd just shoot you and put you out of my misery."

He laughed and dropped a ten on the bar. Then he grabbed her coat off the barstool and headed for the door.

∞

Tierney didn't catch Renner until they reached the end of the entryway. She jerked her coat from him. "Give me that."

"Put it on. Then we're out of here. This is not the place for someone like you."

"Someone like me? Meaning what?"

Renner's gaze tracked her body as she covered it with her long wool coat. "Look at yourself. All tarted up to troll for losers."

"Tarted up? Who even uses that archaic phrase? My God. You are such a Neanderthal."

"Where are your glasses? Could you even see them low-class yahoos were tryin' to feel you up?"

"Did you ever consider I *wanted* those yahoos to feel me up?"

That retort got a surprised look from him.

"But no, you didn't care what I wanted. You bulled your way in, scaring them off with the macho bullshit about me being your boss—as if anybody could ever tell the almighty Renner Jackson what to do—and then you announced what a total ballbuster I am . . ." Tierney froze as something occurred to her.

Renner pointed at her. "See? You know I'm right."

"First, you're *never* right. Second, I finally get it."

"Get what? Why I'm dragging you outta there?"

"No, now I know what that term means."

"What what term means?" he demanded with exasperation.

"Cock blocker. You were a cock blocker tonight. I had two potential cocks on the line and you came in swinging your dick to prove yours was bigger."

Renner's mouth fell open.

Tierney's satisfaction at stunning him boosted her courage to punctuate each word with a finger poke to his hard chest. "I. Don't. Need. Another. Man. In. My. Personal. Business."

When his eyes narrowed in that familiar way, indicating he was about to lash out, she muttered, "Screw this. And screw you." She hightailed it out the main bar door. Her boot heels clicked as she crossed the asphalt parking lot.

Before she disengaged the locks, she was spun around. With her back against her car, Renner was in her face, crowding her body with his.

"You have no fuckin' idea how sexy that bitchy little attitude of yours is, do you?"

Was he drunk?

"No, I'm not drunk. I'm frustrated as hell and the screw you comment was a little out of character for you."

"Oh, so you *can* hear me mutter? But you ignore me when I talk directly to you?"

Renner flashed his teeth. "I listen to you when it warrants it."

"Then listen up. Move."

"No. Fucking. Way."

"What is your problem?"

"My problem?" He laughed derisively. "You. I see you every goddamned day in those high-dollar, high-collar professional business suits. Then add those brainy-girl glasses to cement the 'she's out of your league' impression you convey to me at every opportunity."

Tierney couldn't believe her ears. Was that a compliment? Or an insult?

"Tell me how I'm supposed to react when the Tierney I see off the clock is not the Tierney I know from work."

His mouth was so near hers that his every angry breath puffed across her lips. "You don't know me because you've preferred to judge me on the surface."

"So I should've knocked you off your damn high horse to get to this 'real' Tierney months ago?"

Tierney rolled her eyes. "Does every phrase you use have to contain a barnyard animal reference?"

"God. You piss me off to no appreciable end."

"The feeling is mutual."

"Oh yeah? What about this? Is this mutual too?"

The man was babbling. "Is what mutual?" she demanded.

"This." Renner crushed his mouth to hers. His rough hands were on her cheeks, holding her in place as he kissed her.

Dear God, did the man know how to kiss. Soft and then hard. Wet and hungry. He took what he wanted. Kissing her with passion laced with provocation. Building one kiss upon another, and another, until they were both short of breath and had to break free in order to suck air into their oxygen-deprived lungs.

But Renner didn't push away from her. He pressed his damp mouth into the section of skin in front of her ear. Then his lips moved up the side of her face. Slowly. Like he was savoring the moment.

As Tierney felt him vibrating against her, she knew his reaction had shaken him to the core. Because it was so totally unexpected. Or because it was unwanted?

The next thought immediately cooled her libido; Renner hadn't acted on his supposed attraction to her until she looked nothing like herself. She shoved him away.

"Hey, what are you doin'?"

"Getting out of this screwed-up situation and going home." She held up her hand when he started to protest. "I get it, okay? You thought if I didn't look like the woman you'd called *daddy's pet monkey* earlier today, then maybe I'd act differently too. Well, guess what? I'm exactly the same." She swung the car door open so fast it would've clipped his stupid head if he hadn't moved.

"Now wait just a damn minute, Tierney—"

"No. It's over and done with. Go away, Renner, and leave me alone."

"Fine. I'll drop it for now. But this ain't over."

Chapter Fourteen

❧

"Come on, cupcake. Time to get up."

Janie rolled to her back, trying to get closer to her husband's low, sexy rasp.

The bed dipped as he sat next to her hip. "You're going to be late."

She stretched her arms above her head. "Crawl back in here and we'll play hooky. Surely Hank can handle chores so you can spend time with your wife?"

No response. But she felt Abe tense beside her.

Janie opened her eyes. She wasn't in the bedroom she'd shared with Abe. He wasn't waking her up so she could drive to Casper. Abe wasn't her husband.

Talk about déjà vu.

Or maybe wishful thinking?

The sheet had dropped, exposing her upper body from neck to hips. Abe's eyes weren't on her face. His focus was on her nipples. "Glad to see you still sleep in the buff."

She yanked the covers up. "What are you doing in here?"

"You eyeballed my chest last night, so I figured turnabout is fair play."

Janie smacked him with a pillow. "Scram so I can get dressed so I'm not late for work."

Conversation was minimal on the ride to the Split Rock. Janie opened the truck door, but Abe was right there, helping her out of his monster rig.

"Thanks for the ride."

"Call me when you're done tonight and I'll come get you." Abe ran his finger down her jaw, and she shivered discreetly from his unexpected caress. "I wish you'd take another day to rest."

"I'm fine." She danced a little jig to prove it. "See?"

"Just be careful and watchful. I don't want nothin' bad happening to you."

Because his concern flustered her, and comforted her, she fiddled with the top button on his shearling coat when she asked the question that was on both their minds. "What does me living with you again mean for us?"

Abe tilted her face up and looked into her eyes. He brushed his lips over hers. "It means we're not done. We never were. See you later, cupcake."

❧

And Janie's day just got weirder from there.

Tierney waltzed in sporting a sexy new hairstyle.

Renner showed up late, in a lousy mood, which Janie attributed . . . to Tierney's new rockin' hairstyle for some odd reason.

Lisa, hired to clean rooms and fill in as needed, broke a stack of plates. Twenty custom-ordered, gold-rimmed dinner plates, smashed to smithereens at Janie's feet. When Lisa had burst into tears, Janie assured her she wouldn't dock her paycheck for the breakage. Which somehow opened Lisa's conduit to God. The woman almost started speaking in tongues—she freaked Janie out.

Two reservations were cancelled.

Willie kept mumbling about bad spirits.

Her computer froze up. Twice.

Her cell phone died even when it'd been fully charged when she'd left the house.

Then Renner demanded she stay late to serve as hostess for the guests, after she'd spent the day catching up on all the work that'd piled up.

Luckily Harper had stayed late too so Janie didn't have to call Abe for a ride home. But Harper was distracted or pissed off—Janie never could tell with her—and she barely said two words to her on the trip home to the Lawson ranch.

Janie paused on the porch steps and dug out the house key Abe had given her. First thing she'd do after kicking off the four-inch heels murdering her arches? Pour herself a generous drink.

Shoes off, coat off, she padded from the entryway into the silent living room. Abe brooded on the sofa, holding a lowball glass filled with amber-colored liquid.

"Looks like your day went like mine. I'm desperate for a stiff one myself." In the kitchen she spied a bottle of bourbon on the counter and reached into the china hutch for a glass. When she turned around, Abe was there, right there, crowding her against the wall. "Abe? What are you doing?"

"Where in the hell have you been?"

"At work. I had no choice but to stay late. I'm sorry. I know I should've called, but—"

"Damn right you should've called. Especially after all that's been goin' on. I tried your cell and you didn't answer. I tried the resort but no one answered. The only thing that stopped me from racing there straightaway and ripping the place apart lookin' for you, was that Bran called as I was on my way out the door and mentioned Harper was giving you a ride home." He rested his forehead to hers and sighed heavily. "You have no idea how crazy it makes me to imagine you hurt again. No fuckin' idea what it was like for me to see you in that wreck. And then to see you scraped up, bloody and bruised. It rips me apart."

"Abe—"

"Ssh. Just let me . . . calm down."

But when he lifted his head and looked at her, he didn't look calm at all. His worry had been replaced by hunger. Immediately her mouth went bone dry from the lust raging in Abe. His eyes. His body. Even his sinful mouth was primed.

"I'm sorry."

"I know you are. I also know how you can make it up to me."

"Oh no," she breathed, when she really meant *oh please, yes please, right now.*

"Oh yes." He put his lips by her ear. "And listen to you, askin' me so nicely."

Holy crap. She'd said that out loud?

Abe pried the empty glass from her death grip and set it aside. Then he slapped his hands on the wall by her head. "Isn't it fortunate that in making it up to me, you'll get the stiff one you wanted?"

Her response was lost as Abe's mouth crashed down on hers in a ferocious kiss.

∾

He'd been waiting months—no, years—for this. Sweet, delectable Janie pressed against him. He'd given her no chance to overthink the situation. None of that "can I touch you" bullshit that defined their married sex life. He'd have her. And he'd have her now.

Not that Janie was protesting.

Abe thrust his tongue between her parted lips, forcing her mouth open to accept more of his ravenous kiss. The way she kissed him back was familiar . . . yet new. A potent combination that kicked his need up another level.

His lips slid across the plump moistness of hers, as he changed the angle of his head. Her hands yanked his hips closer and she moaned greedy noises that reverberated straight to his dick.

Abe kept his hands on the wall. Letting the heat and the need between them build.

But Janie had other ideas. She broke the seal of her lips

to scatter kisses down his throat to where her fingers fumbled with the buttons on his shirt. "Abe. Please. Touch me."

He whispered kisses over her jaw. "You oughta know I'm not interested in foreplay."

That admission seemed to send a shudder through her. "Oh, God, me neither."

"I want it hard. Fast. And now."

She moaned. "Yes."

He stepped back. "Ditch your nylons."

Her shaking hands rolled up her skirt. She peeled the nylons down her legs and kicked them off.

When she looked at him, her purple irises glazed with lust, Abe covered her mouth with his. Clamping his hands on her ass, he lifted her, turned, and placed her on the counter.

She gasped, "Oh wow, that is cold on my butt."

"Friction will warm it right up." Unbuckled, unbuttoned and unzipped, he reached for a condom before he dropped his Wranglers.

She stared at his cock as he rolled on the condom. "This isn't a dream? It's really happening? You're gonna fuck me right here in the kitchen?"

"Yep." He palmed her hips and said, "C'mere," tugging her closer.

Her fingernails scored the back of his neck when she pulled him down for an openmouthed kiss. Abe's thumb traced the wet seam of her sex before he aligned his cock to the opening and eased just the head in. Slamming home on the first stroke wasn't an option, no matter how tempting. Janie was small and he . . . well, he wasn't small.

She stiffened slightly as he pushed inside.

He teased her clit, keeping his left hand spread across her lower back, slowly urging her forward. Her shirt was blocking access to the warm softness of her skin. As soon as he was fully seated inside her, he murmured, "Lose the shirt."

Janie lifted the formfitting sweater over her head. Her

bra was a black push-up number that highlighted her curves. He groaned, pressing his mouth to the mounded flesh.

She released a throaty sigh and arched into him. "This day is getting better. Oh yeah, tons better. Do that again. Harder."

"Been waiting a long time to hear you say that."

Each thrust picked up speed to the point any finesse he'd planned had vanished. His mouth cruised over every dip and hollow of her throat. Tasting. Teasing. Remembering. Wanting her as absorbed in the moment as he. A moment he'd been waiting for, for eight long years.

Her breath came in short puffs of air and her belly tensed against his. That sexy purr started and her thighs squeezed his hips as she gasped and came undone.

Janie's orgasm unleashed his. A wash of white-hot pleasure that made his eyes roll back in his head with each body-shaking pulse. Spent, he dropped his head on her smooth shoulder. "Damn. Guess we'll call that one the speed round."

She nuzzled his ear. "What's the next round called?"

Pecking her quickly on the mouth, he withdrew and ditched his clothes completely. Then he slid his hands around her hips, warning, "Hold on," and carried her out of the kitchen.

"Abe!"

She seemed surprised he entered the bathroom, not his bedroom. He set her on her feet, gesturing to her bra and skirt. "This is the water round. So take 'em off unless you want them wet." After tossing the condom, he turned and Janie was naked. "Such a petite package. You still pack a powerful punch for me, cupcake."

Janie smirked.

Cranking the shower on, he slid the glass door open. "Beautiful, sexy ladies first."

"Flattery? *After* you've already fucked me? You have changed." As she stepped into the tub, he smacked her luscious ass and followed her inside the enclosure.

He squirted shampoo into his hand and scrubbed his hair. When he faced the showerhead to rinse, she plastered her slick body against his. Her hands flowed with the soapy water down his chest and abdomen. Circling his cock. Goose bumps followed in the wake of her questing fingers.

She whispered, "This big, buff body of yours still bowls me over."

Abe turned, dragging kisses down her chest. Feasting on her nipples until she thrashed and cried out. Yep. She still loved nipple play. He lapped the water from her skin as he lowered to his knees. Arcing his mouth across the delicate sweep of skin of her lower belly, he lifted her left foot and set it on the lip of the tub. Oh hell yeah. That gave him total access to the sweet and tasty flesh between her thighs.

The first swipe of his tongue across her slit had them both groaning. But one lick wasn't enough and he settled in to take as much of her in his mouth as possible. He growled every time he elicited a gasp. A moan. A whimper. A plea. His thumbs opened her cunt like a flower and he burrowed his tongue deep, licking away every drop of her sweet juice. Over and over.

"Abe. Are you testing the strength of my knees? Because they're about to give out."

He pulled the soft skin of her mound away from that pouting pearl. "Hold it like this. I wanna see every inch."

Janie's hands shook as they replaced his. Her plump bottom lip was trapped between her teeth. Her cheeks were damp from the steam. He plunged his thumb into her channel the same time he suctioned his mouth to her clit. Sucking ruthlessly, sliding his thumb up to where his mouth worked her and back down into the opening of her sex.

She moaned his name, her body trembling as her clit pulsed beneath his dancing tongue.

He loved this part. Loved to feel every intimate muscle pull tight as she unraveled against his mouth. Her knees did start to give out and he laughed as he caught her. Then he licked the moisture from her skin on his way back up to her ear. "Turn around. Brace your hands on the wall."

She made a murmur of assent.

Abe was so ready for her, so damn hard, that as soon as she waggled her ass at him, he slipped inside her to the hilt.

Her head fell back. "God. That's so good."

"Damn straight."

Slapping sounds of skin on skin surrounded them. He kept hold of her hips, focusing on the visual of his cock disappearing into her body as he tried to stave off his orgasm.

His balls drew up and he rammed into her harder, the slick heat of her flesh gliding on his. Had it ever felt this good?

Then it hit him why it felt so great.

"Shit. No condom."

"But—"

"I can't stop," Abe panted and pulled out. He stroked his shaft against the cleft of her ass. He was about to blow— then heat shot up his cock and he groaned as he shot his seed all over her back.

Soon as he caught his breath, he kissed her shoulder and stepped aside to let the water rinse her.

"Ooh, that's getting cold."

"We need a bigger water heater if we're gonna play water games." He shut off the tap and reached outside for the towels hanging on the towel bar. As he wrapped the bath sheet around her, he kissed her. The way she clung to him made him believe this was the start of something. Was he a fool for feeling a twinge of hope?

Maybe. Because once they were out of the shower, Abe felt her staring at him. Sensed the change in her. Thinking. Planning. Backtracking. He knew his response to whatever she was about to say would set the course for what happened next.

Abe knew exactly what he wanted: a second chance. But he wouldn't coerce her. He wanted her to come to the same conclusion of her own accord. In the past he'd made all the decisions and expected her to fall in line. This time he'd woo her differently, in a way she'd never expect, but he'd pull out all the stops to convince her they belonged together. "You all right?"

"Yes. I'm great. Thanks for . . . blowing my mind."

"It was my pleasure."

"Look, this happened so fast and we didn't talk about what it means." She vigorously towel dried her hair. "We agree this is just sex?"

Oh, cupcake, you're running again. Setting parameters. And that just won't do.

He'd let her have that little delusion for now, that their connection was just physical, even when deep down inside she knew better. She'd soon learn something new about him: that he had no parameters when it came to sex. That oughta shock her more than the fact he could cook.

"Abe?"

"Uh, yeah. No worries."

"Glad we're on the same page."

Same page? Hell, they weren't even in the same book. But they would be. Keeping the towel wrapped around his waist, Abe moved to the mirror to brush his teeth.

Janie leaned against the wall and watched him. "You caught me by surprise, not that I'm complaining, because it was freakin' awesome, but I'm hungry. Would you like me to fix us something for supper?"

He rinsed and spit. "Fix yourself whatever you want. I'm not sure when I'll be back."

By the way her spine stiffened, she hadn't expected that answer. By the anticipatory look on her face, she probably assumed Honest Abe would do the gentlemanly thing and invite her along.

He didn't.

His research trip could wait another couple of days, but Abe had the perverse need to be unavailable to her for the rest of the night.

Then they'd see how long her "just sex" attitude lasted.

Abe was gone when Janie got ready for work the next morning. The man confused the hell out of her and she was relieved not to have to face him, because it bothered her that he'd just taken off, while she was still naked, for Christsake, without letting her know where he was going.

You surprised? After your comment about it being "just sex" between you?

Then to add insult to injury, he hadn't invited her into his bed. She'd lain awake in the guest bedroom after he'd come home, waiting for him to sneak in, scoop her up and drag her into his room for round three.

He hadn't.

In fact, she was half afraid the click she'd heard was Abe locking his bedroom door.

Locking her out.

So she was trying to figure out this "new" sexually confident, sexually aggressive, but oddly ambiguous Abe.

Not that Abe had been a slouch in the bedroom during the time they were together. His passion for her was evident from the night they met. He'd made love to her so sweetly, so tenderly that first time she'd felt cherished. She'd fallen a little bit in love with him right away, even when she berated herself the next morning for sleeping with a dropdead gorgeous cowboy hours after she'd brought him to her apartment. When he kept coming back, she'd known frequent sex was part of her appeal, but she'd also known they brought something to each other neither had found in previous relationships: comfort.

So maybe Abe hadn't been the most inventive lover, but he'd always satisfied her. He always wanted her. Even when things were bad between them at the end, he'd reach for her in the middle of the night. Loving her with everything he had. But in the morning, he'd revert to the same gruff Abe. The sexy, sweet side he showed her in the dead of night hadn't been enough to convince her to stay.

Would more of that smokin' hot sex be enough to get you to stick around now?

Who knew? Focusing her mental energy on this situation allowed her to put the stalking issue on the back burner. She knew from past experience that obsessing over something she couldn't control, could completely control her life. Besides, it'd take some mental fortitude to unravel the mystery of this new Abe. And she couldn't wait to find out what she discovered next.

Since her car was still in the repair shop, Harper picked her up for work. And again Harper seemed distracted.

"Don't feel obligated to drag me to the Split Rock every day just because I'm your boss," Janie said offhandedly.

"It's not that." Harper sighed. "I'm sorry I wasn't good company last night either. I've just been preoccupied."

"Anything you want to talk about?"

"This is gonna sound weird, but yesterday? I was waiting outside the office. The door was open and I heard Tierney . . ."

Please. Not another complaint about Renner and Tierney fighting. "You heard Tierney what?"

"On the phone, talking to Celia."

Janie looked at Harper. "Celia? Really? I didn't know they were friends."

"I didn't either."

"But now that you mention it, they did hang out at your wedding reception after you and Bran left."

"I figured as much. Here's the really stupid thing. I was jealous. Celia has friends on the circuit. Heck, she has lots of other friends in Muddy Gap. But ever since Bran and I got engaged, even when I sort of figured out she'd set it up and was happy for us, I've felt her pulling away. It bugs me. After you and Abe were married, did your single friends decide since you were part of a couple you didn't need them? Or did you end up having new friends? Couple friends?"

"I don't remember." At that time none of Abe's friends were married. He and Max had always been tight but Max had taken a job out of state right after their wedding. Abe

and Hank's other pals—Bran, Kyle, Eli, Ike, Devin, Fletch—
were around sporadically. Although she had female college
classmates she saw weekly, Janie had felt isolated from
everyone living on the ranch. She didn't think it was wise to
tell Harper the closest thing she had to a friend during that
time had been Harper's husband.

"Since Tierney lives here, same as me, I know Celia pulling away from me can't be a location thing. Is it because
they're both single? What do they have in common?"

"I imagine people said the same about you and Celia,"
Janie pointed out.

"True." Harper smiled. "Now some of my best pals are
the retired ladies who hang out at Bernice's Beauty Barn."

"Really? Them throwing you a bachelorette party wasn't
a farewell?"

"No. I miss the regulars who used to be my nail clients.
Maybelle, Garnet, Pearl, Tilda and Bernice have me over
for lunch every couple of weeks." Harper looked at her
oddly. "You *do* still get your hair cut at Bernice's?"

"Yes. But I go in at the end of the day when there's no-
body there. It's faster."

"But you miss out on all the good gossip."

"That's exactly why I don't go. I avoided anything resembling gossip when I lived here before." Hadn't that been one
of Abe's complaints? She acted as if she was too good for
the locals?

"It's weird. I thought since Tierney's from the big city
she'd feel the same way about that small town type of stuff.
But according to my sources, Tierney has fit right in."

"Tierney? Seriously? Surprises me she doesn't go to
Casper for her beauty fix."

Harper's gaze turned sharp. "Don't you like her?"

"Actually, that came out sounding snottier than I meant.
I do like her. Quite a bit. But my first loyalty is to Renner
and Tierney knows that."

Harper became quiet again.

"That's not all that's on your mind, is it?"

"No. But I don't know how to say this to you because you're my boss."

It stung a bit that Harper didn't consider her a friend, even after they'd lived together for a couple of weeks when Harper had signed on to work at the Split Rock.

But you haven't gone out of your way to befriend anyone since you've been here. You're holding yourself off, just like you always do.

Like that was news. Every job she'd had in the last two years had been temporary. Getting close to people knowing she'd never see them again was pointless and that mind-set wasn't easy to shake.

Maybe it's time you actually tried to make a change.

The reason for Harper's reluctance hit her. "This is about Abe."

Harper nodded. "Everyone is concerned you'll hurt him again."

"Everyone?" she asked with a bitter edge. "Meaning … Bran, Hank, and Lainie?" She fought the urge to lash out and managed to keep her tone even. "Remind them that *Abe* insisted I move out to the ranch. Yes, Abe and I have a past. Not a volatile past, but there were plenty of things left unfinished between us." She snorted softly. "Know the irony in all of this? Everyone had an opinion on our marriage back then. Living with other people, we were subjected to input we didn't want or need, and yes, it affected us. But what 'everyone' is forgetting? Abe and I loved each other. But unfortunately, at that point in our lives, love wasn't enough." Janie's eyes blurred with tears. "So you can tell everyone to back off. What goes on between us now is no one's business."

Harper didn't speak until she parked in the employee lot. "I'm sorry. You're right. I hope the fact I was coerced into bringing this up won't affect our friendship."

Janie was appeased Harper admitted they were friends. It drove home the point that she wanted to be the warm and affectionate type of friend. Not only with Harper, but also with others. What if she didn't know how? How did she admit that failing? How long would it take her to become the person she'd always longed to be? To put herself out there? To be the first to offer her trust?

No time like the present to take a chance and just do it.

"Keep in mind any time you want to talk, Janie, I am here for you. I know you've got a lone wolf attitude, but you really helped me sort things out when everything was so confusing with Bran."

"Thanks." Janie looped her arm through Harper's. "Now didn't you say something about inviting me'n Abe over for supper and cards? 'Cause I'm thinking a casserole and canasta sounds like a helluva good time."

Chapter Fifteen

❧

ierney had successfully avoided Renner all day.
Or has he avoided you?

Like a total chickenshit, the morning after the kiss in the parking lot, she'd left instructions not to be disturbed in her office, claiming she had rush projects to finish for PFG. When in truth, she'd caught up with her two best friends in Chicago. When Celia called, she'd offered financial advice, because God knew, relationship advice was out of her realm of expertise. After sending Harlow funny, bizarre Web site links that played on their childhood inside jokes, she'd browsed the Zappos Web site and ordered two new pairs of funky shoes.

She'd been bored out of her freakin' mind all day and a little disappointed in herself that she'd reverted to avoidance behavior instead of acting bold. Her night hadn't been any better; she'd dreamt of one pain in the butt cowboy whose full lips redefined kissable.

Yawning, slurping coffee, determined to do something productive, she'd just started plugging her monthly expenses into a spreadsheet when the door opened and slammed shut. Before she looked up she knew Renner would be looming over her desk.

And loom he did. All six feet two inches of him. His black hat cast a shadow over his eyes. She suspected his menacing posture meant his baby blues would be snapping fire.

Petty, but Tierney let him cool his boots for a minute before she glanced up with a prissy, "Yes?"

"We need to talk."

"I'm busy."

"Now."

After releasing a long-suffering sigh, she said, "Fine. I've run across a couple of items I'm not sure how to categorize—"

"Tierney." His hand enveloped hers as she restlessly rolled the mouse over the mouse pad. "Please."

The softly spoken *please* brought her gaze back to his. No anger darkened his face, just unease. "What?"

"I wanna talk about what happened the other night at Buckeye Joe's."

"I don't want to talk about it. Ever."

"Tough."

"Look, I'm sure you're here to apologize—"

"That's the thing. I'm not here to apologize."

Tierney went very still. "Excuse me?"

"I'm not sorry I kissed you." He paced to the seating area and back. "I'm not sorry you kissed me back. And before you go getting that superior look, can we be honest with each other just one goddamn time and admit this attraction between us ain't gonna go away?"

She wanted to act cool and sophisticated but she blushed ten shades of red.

His eyes roved over every inch of her flaming face. "You are hell on my intention never to get mixed up with another woman like you."

She didn't own the confidence to toss off a brash *there is no other woman like me, baby*. Heck, she just stared at him because he was looking at her like he wanted to eat her alive and she was seriously tempted to let him.

"You denying you feel this pull?" he asked softly.

"No."

He closed his eyes and exhaled. "Good. That's . . . good."

"So while I'm obviously not immune to your cowboy charm, I'm also not an idiot. Why else are you here?"

"Am I that easy to read?"

No. You confuse me more than any man I've ever met. Tierney shifted in her chair. "Yes."

"Oh yeah? So what am I thinking about right now?"

"Bulls?"

He rolled his eyes. "Wrong. Try again."

She gave him a considering look. "Horses?"

"Nope."

"I give up."

His smile disappeared. "I need access to the money in the escrow account."

Of course this was about money. She masked her disappointment that their banter had led straight back to business, even when she was the one who'd steered it in that direction. "For what?"

"Material for fences. And for wages to hire a guy to help me build the fences. Before you ask, this doesn't have anything to do with my stock contracting business. The hunting guides pointed out sections where the fence needs fixing." He scratched his head. "A lot of fences in the outlying areas need to be ripped out and reinstalled. Not for aesthetic reasons but for guest safety. I wanna do it while the weather is holding and the local building supply has fencing supplies twenty-five percent off this week."

She forced a bland expression to keep her worry from showing. Renner had used up the money in the building escrow account last month. She couldn't transfer funds from the operating costs account because they were barely squeaking by since the resort hadn't regularly hit full capacity yet. But if she told him no, he might call her father and ask for an extended line of credit. In her opinion, Renner was already overextended and the last thing she wanted was for him to be even more indebted to her father and PFG.

Doesn't that make you a traitor to the company? Considering giving the advantage to the lendee and taking it away from the lendor? The lendor that's allowing you to be in Wyoming?

No. This situation was different. The more time Tierney spent at the resort and with the people who wholeheartedly believed in it, the more she wanted to see it succeed. Plus, she didn't feel she was here on PFG's behalf, since technically, they weren't paying her. So she had to do whatever it took to keep the Split Rock afloat until the place could survive on its own income. "How much are we talking?"

"Fifty thousand. That's cash up front when I place the order."

"After the discount?"

He nodded.

She whistled. That was a lot of money. Way more than she expected.

But not more than you have . . .

Her personal account could cover the cost, but that'd bleed her cash reserves dry.

What else were you planning to do with the money anyway? If you really believe in this place, for once put your money where your mouth is.

Could she really do this? Go against everything she'd been taught? Purposely put herself at financial risk?

Yes. Because in some ways, if the Split Rock failed, she'd feel like she failed too.

Mind made up, she opened a couple of files, hoping he didn't peer over her shoulder. "That will drain your escrow account completely. You'll have less than five hundred dollars remaining."

Renner's eyebrows rose. "That's it?"

"Yes. So this has to be the last expense. No exceptions."

He paced in front of the door. Stopped and said tersely, "Do it. I don't have a choice. It'll cost me less now than if I wait a few months."

Relief allowed her constricted lungs to fill with air again. If she played this right, no one would know she was bucking company policy and personally investing in a business under contract to PFG. Renner would have a shit fit if he ever found out she was personally lending him the money—even temporarily, so she'd have to keep it on the down low. "I'll make the transfer today, but the money won't appear in the operating account until tomorrow morning. In fact, why don't I close the escrow account completely?"

"That'll work. I'll get the order set up and swing by tomorrow to pay for it." He rubbed the stubble on his jaw. "Thanks for takin' care of this, Tierney."

"You're welcome. But it's my job."

"True. And I appreciate you bein' up front and on top of everything with tne finances. I'd be lying if I said I understood half that money jargon."

And isn't it lucky for you that Renner had that attitude?

He leaned forward, completely invading her space. "Now that business is out of the way, can we please talk about what happened the other night and what happens next?"

The phone rang. Tierney picked up the receiver midring. "Split Rock Ranch and Resort." She met Renner's eyes. "Hey, Dad. No. That's okay. Strangely enough, we were just talking about you."

Renner's lips flattened into a grim line.

She said, "Can you hang on for just a second?" and hit the HOLD button.

But Renner already had the door open. "I won't keep you." Then he was gone.

Tierney sighed and took the caller off hold. "Sorry for the confusion, I thought you were someone else. What can I help you with today?"

After she ended the call, she removed her glasses and rubbed her temples to stave off another headache. No wonder she always told the truth. One little white lie on top of another and everything snowballed.

She called the bank and made the transfer. That left her less than two hundred dollars in her bank account. Not a lot to live on for the next few months without moving investments. But she could take on some of the freelance jobs the PFG accounting department had offered when she left.

Do it. Swallow your pride. It is honest work.

Before Tierney lost her nerve she made the call. Three rings. Four. Then, "This is Jennifer."

"Hey, Jen, it's Tierney."

"Please tell me you called because you're coming back to work at PFG."

"In a manner of speaking. Remember when you told me about being backlogged on small projects? Anything I can help with?"

"I have four refinances staring me in the face that you could do in your sleep." Jennifer paused. "Does this mean . . . ?"

"Yes, I'll do them. Send them to me FedEx. Three a week is my max, and I'll need you to give me access to our usual financial data Web sites and to rush my billing statement through accounts payable, listing me as an outside consultant."

"Will do," Jen said. "I still can't believe you gave up your salary for six months for a training position. Doesn't make economic sense."

Tierney laughed that Jen had tossed her favorite phrase back at her. If Jen only knew what she'd just done. "It's been a learning experience, that's for sure. Oh, and since I'm already in the system I won't have to wait the standard sixty days for payment, will I?"

"No. You'll be back on the regular payroll schedule. And can I just say thank you? You are totally saving our bacon, T."

"You're welcome. One other thing? My father is not to know anything about this, okay?" Wishful thinking, but at least it was worth a try.

"Okay. But it'd be remiss of me not to point out I'm glad

you're back on the team—even in a freelance capacity. It hasn't been the same without you."

Surprisingly touched, Tierney smiled. "It's good to be missed."

∞

Abe opted to pick Janie up at the Split Rock, rather than waiting for her to catch a ride home with Harper.

He poked his head inside her tiny office but she wasn't around. He wandered to Wild West Clothiers and found it closed for the day. He bypassed the main guest lounge area and discovered it and the bar were empty.

Where was everyone?

Then he heard voices drifting from the dining room. When he reached the doorway he saw Janie, Renner, and Tierney standing in front of the group. Some sort of staff meeting. He leaned against the wall and waited. Listening to Janie do her thing.

"While everything has been running at top efficiency, and we have all of you to thank for that," Janie said, "we need to stay on top of the little things."

"Like what?" Harper asked.

Abe heard a rustle of paper and envisioned Janie whipping out a list. "I've broken it down by department."

When murmured discussions broke out, Abe peeked around the corner, noticing Tierney and Renner were off to the side in an intense discussion.

He walked in and set his hands on Janie's shoulders. "Hey, do you have a minute?"

"I'm in a meeting."

"Sorry. It looked like it was over."

"It is now," Renner drawled.

Awkward laughter followed. But Janie wasn't amused. She dismissed the staff. Then she wheeled around.

Abe followed her. When she attempted to slam the door in his face, he laughed and bulled his way inside her domain.

The instant they were alone, she slapped her hands on his

chest and pushed him against the door. "Why the hell would you come in and interrupt my meeting? Do I ever demand your attention when you're doing cow stuff?"

"Cow stuff?" he repeated.

"You know what I mean. I've never interfered with you doing your job running the ranch and I expect the same courtesy from you while I'm working."

"I'm sorry."

"You should be."

Abe watched her eyes, those striking purple irises, sparking outrage. He hauled her to the toes of her sexy boots and he couldn't help but inhale her. Suck down the passion she disguised in a haughty attitude, letting her fire consume him. It was like heaven to kiss her again, whenever he wanted, however he wanted. But kissing wasn't enough. He needed her squirming against him, her breath panting in his ear as her body clamped around his. He soothed her with sweet kisses, shaken to the very core by the power this woman still wielded over him.

"Abe—"

"I want you. So fucking much. Do you have any idea how goddamn hot you look when you're in charge? How unbelievably sexy you are to watch taking control of the room with your fire and sweetness? It's a side of you I've never seen. It's a side that makes me burn hotter than ever for you."

Her face softened. "You and that damn silver tongue. Please take me home."

He wasn't so far gone with lust not to recognize that she'd called his house home. His spirit soared even as it cemented his intentions to show her he'd changed. "Doesn't that make you feel powerful? Knowing you got me all kinds of worked up with your bossy ways?"

Abe turned her around, suctioning his mouth to the sexy sweep of her shoulder. He'd never seen the appeal of short hair on a woman until now. Having all that sexy, sensitive skin right out in the open, easily accessible was a temptation he couldn't resist.

As soon as she sighed, and angled her head to rub her cheek to his, he murmured, "Is that a proper apology for breaking up your meeting?"

"No. Because when I apologized to you for forgetting to call, we had hot sex. So you can pay me back when we get home?"

"We'll see."

He wanted more than sex with her. So it was damn ironic he had to hold off . . . to get it.

∞

Abe was not getting away with ignoring her another night.

On the way home he'd suddenly remembered something urgent he had to do. In Rawlins. Alone. He'd dropped her off and hadn't returned until after eleven o'clock. Once again she thought she'd heard the click of his bedroom door lock.

She had a plan that guaranteed she wouldn't need a lock pick to gain entrance into his lair.

Janie played it cool during supper. As soon as she heard Abe head down the hallway to his bedroom following his long shower, she made her move.

His eyes widened when he saw her sauntering toward him naked. "Ah. What're you doin'?"

"Paying you back." She stalked him until his spine met the closet door and then dropped to her knees.

"You don't have to pay me back right now. But . . . Oh holy hell."

She'd stuffed his entire cock in her mouth, loving when that dangling man flesh was still soft and unsuspecting. Loving the feel of it growing bigger, until it no longer fit in her mouth.

Abe's cock didn't seem to be on the same time frame as Abe's brain. In fact, Abe's cock thought right now was the perfect time for payback as it rapidly became erect.

Smiling, she bent her head and brought both his balls

into the wet heat of her mouth. Rolling them over her tongue. Then she closed her lips around the sac and sucked.

"Jesus, Janie." Funny, he didn't seem all that insistent to push her away now.

"Tell me you don't want this." She rubbed her lips across the top of his quivering quad. "Tell me you don't want to see your cock buried in my throat as I swallow every drop of your seed. Tell me no and I'll leave."

A millisecond later his hand was fisted in her hair and he pulled her head back to meet his lust-filled gaze. "Do it."

Janie didn't intend to draw this encounter out; serious power existed in getting a man off quickly. She hadn't realized how spoiled she'd been by Abe's exceptional dick size until she'd wound up with men who weren't as well endowed. She wrapped her fingers around the base and jacked his shaft as she suckled the cockhead. With each wet pull of her mouth, she brought him deeper. Closing her lips around the root, she breathed through her nose and opened her throat, taking him fully.

"Sweet Jesus, swallow like that again."

Her thoughts entered the fuzzy zone where she was lost in the silken push and pull of that male hardness against her tongue. Her head bobbed and she slipped her hand between his thighs. Feeling his balls hard and tight, she let his cock slide free and stared up at him. "Makes me wet to touch you like this."

He murmured, "Prove it," and stroked her cheekbone.

She followed the contour of her belly past her pubic hair. Keeping her eyes on Abe's, she inserted two fingers, fucking herself with them so he could hear the wet, sucking sounds of her pussy. Then she showed him her moisture-coated fingers.

"What are you gonna do with those?"

"Watch." Janie reached between his legs and rubbed her wet finger across his anus. She said, "Don't clench," and sucked his cock in deep again.

As soon as she slipped her finger in his ass and stroked

his prostate, he started to come. His hands cradled her head and his hips bumped into her face. "Fuck. Oh fuck. Yes. Christ."

She swallowed the salty heat filling her mouth, the familiar taste throwing her into the past. When the pulses stopped, she pulled back, placing kisses on his hips, watching that sexy six-pack ripple with aftershocks.

Abe slumped against the door.

Janie stood, adding an extra wiggle in her ass as she crossed the room. At the doorway, she peered at him over her shoulder. "Oh, and a couple things I wanted to mention."

"Uh. Okay."

"When you're done with your mysterious nighttime errands, or finished locking yourself in your office, be aware I'll be sleeping in here, with you, not in the guest bedroom."

"Uh. Okay."

"And I'm on the pill so we can skip the condoms from here on out."

"Uh. Okay."

"See you."

"Uh. Okay." Then, "Wait."

"What?"

"I don't know who taught you how to suck cock like that, but I feel like sending the dude a thank-you note."

Weird compliment, but she'd take it. Her self-satisfied grin was entirely justified as she sailed out of the room.

And she wasn't the least bit surprised when fifteen seconds later Abe scooped her into his arms and finally took her to his bed.

Chapter Sixteen

⦿

"**A**re you a real cowboy?"

Startled, Renner turned away from the fireplace and faced a small girl dressed in glittery pink sweatpants dotted with sparkly unicorns. "Yes, I am. Something you need?"

She nodded and her blond pigtails bobbed. "Can you take me on a pony ride?"

His gaze turned sharp. "Where is your mama?"

"Napping. She's got a bad headache. She said bouncing on a pony would make it badder." Her chocolate-stained chin notched up an inch. "So can *you* take me to ride a pony?"

"Not without permission from your mama."

"Oh." She jammed her hands in her pockets and twisted the toe of her orange and turquoise sneaker into the carpet.

Such a defeated posture. She couldn't be more than seven years old. He crouched down. "What's your name?"

"Marisol."

"Well, Marisol, even if your mama didn't have a headache, we're shorthanded this week and the trail rides have been cancelled."

Marisol peered at him balefully, her enormous brown eyes swimming with tears. "Know what? I even got cowgirl boots before we came here. Sparkly red ones. How can I ever be a real cowgirl if I don't ever get to ride a real pony?"

Shit. Now her lip was wobbling. The waterworks were about four seconds away and he was absolutely paralyzed.

"Marisol!" echoed from the hallway an instant before a woman ran toward them. "I told you not to leave the room."

Marisol focused on the toe of her shoe. "Sorry."

"I'm Joelle Mackenzie," the woman said to Renner. "I'm sorry if Marisol's been a bother. This high altitude gives me a violent headache, so she's been spending a lot of time by herself since her daddy has been off enjoying himself."

"I'm sorry you're not havin' as good a time as your husband is," Renner said.

"I bet *Daddy* gets to ride a pony, huh?" Marisol inserted with a huff.

"Now, honey, we've talked about that. You know I'd go with you if I didn't feel so lousy."

"But he said"—Marisol jerked a thumb at Renner—"that if I got a permission from you I could go." She blinked those puppy dog eyes at him. "Didn't you?"

Yes. But he hadn't meant it.

"If you could take her on a pony ride, I'd be so grateful," Joelle replied. "My husband wanted this Wild West adventure for us. But so far I've been sick and Denny's been hunting and poor Marisol has been left to watch TV."

"Please, Mr. Cowboy, sir? Please take me on a pony ride. I'll be really good, I promise."

Another doe-eyed look.

And right then Renner knew he was going to say yes.

"Okay." He tugged on Marisol's pigtail. "I have to get a couple of things together first, but go to your room with your mama and stay there—no more sneaking out—and I'll come get you, all right?"

She smiled, revealing two gaps in her front teeth. "Yay!

Thanks, Mr. Cowboy, sir. I'm gonna go get my new boots on." She raced up off like a flash.

Hell. Now he'd done it. Renner raced up the stairs two at a time and burst into the office with, "You have to help me."

Tierney adjusted her eyeglasses and frowned. "Help you do what?"

"All she had to do was look at me and I was toast. After I said yes I started thinkin' of all the reasons I shoulda said no and now I have to find someone else to go with us because I cannot take a seven-year-old girl on a trail ride alone."

"You know, if you took a breath, maybe I could understand what you were babbling about."

He inhaled. Exhaled. Pushed his hat back to rub his forehead and resettled it on his head. "Here's the deal. Marisol has her heart set on a trail ride. But her mother isn't feeling well, so the little sneak cornered me, asking if I was a real cowboy, and as soon as I said yes, bam! She begged me to take her. I said no, and then found myself saying yes, but after I did, I realized it'd be inappropriate for a thirty-one-year-old guy to go out alone with her on the trail."

"And you're telling me all this . . . why?"

He angled across her desk, the picture of earnestness. "Because I need you to go with me."

"No."

"Please. I'll never ask—"

"I said no."

"You really want to disappoint that little girl after what she's been through this week? Sittin' alone in her room while her daddy's off havin' fun and her mama's been sick?"

Tierney's eyes tapered to fine points. "Don't guilt me."

"You didn't have to see her tiny lip quivering and the look of defeat and sadness on her sweet face."

"Renner—"

"Did I mention her puppy dog eyes? And how I was utterly heartbroken when those enormous brown eyes shimmered with tears? Real tears, Tierney."

"Stop."

But he couldn't. He slanted even closer to drive home his point. "Do you know who she reminded me of?"

"I mean it, Renner Jackson, stop it this instant."

"You. With those big gorgeous brown eyes. I imagined you as a small girl, trying so hard not to break down, to be strong in the face of disappointment."

"Low blow," she hissed.

"You have to help me out. I've got no one else."

"But I'm the worst possible candidate for moseying along the dusty trail because I'm not a good rider."

"It don't matter because I am a good rider. And I'll bet she'll last about an hour." He paused, and cajoled, "Please? Pretty pretty please with rainbow sprinkles on top?"

Her lips curled into a smile. "Fine. But you will owe me."

"Anything you want." He grinned. "Thanks. You never know, you might even have fun."

Tierney rounded the desk. "I'll need to change."

Which was a damn cryin' shame. His eyes almost hurt from all the stealthy glances he'd sent her way today, seeing her in a fluffy peach-colored angora sweater that rivaled her skin for softness. And like a fuckin' pervert, he'd purposely brushed against her twice, just to feel the heat of her body next to his, just to catch a whiff of her hair. She'd worn another one of those damn distracting skirts, tight enough to hug her hips and ass, short enough to show off a generous section of toned leg. Normally he didn't notice women's shoes, but Tierney's were peep-toe pumps, in some swanky mix of gray fabric and black leather with peach piping that matched her outfit and the heel height also did eye-popping things for her calves. He imagined her in those sexy shoes, a pair of black bikini panties that let the bottom slice of her sweet ass hang out, and nothing else.

"Renner? Did you hear me?"

He raised his guilty eyes to hers. "Ah no. I'm sorry. What did you say?"

"I asked if I should meet you at the barn?"

"That'll work. I'll fetch Marisol."

"See you in ten." She shoved her arms into a trench coat that covered her to her ankles, which ruined his chance to watch her hips swing as she strutted away in those fantasy-invoking shoes.

Renner stopped at the Mackenzies' room, but Marisol's mother had rallied enough to promise she'd walk Marisol to the barn. He was relieved the woman wasn't turning over her young daughter to some strange guy.

He slipped on a pair of chinks and spurs before he readied the horses. A few weeks ago he'd compromised with Tierney as far as keeping a couple of older horses on hand for impromptu trail rides, and he wondered if she'd be smug and point out that she had been right.

Somehow, he didn't think so. The more he got to know her, the more he realized she was a team player. It hadn't been apparent to him at first, mostly because he'd been suspicious of her motives—he still was to some extent—but Tierney really did put what was best for the Split Rock first.

Then other surprising things about her surfaced. Thoughtful things, like when she'd tracked down a bottle of almond oil when he complained the skin on his hands started cracking. Sweet things, like when she'd given him a bag of chocolate-flavored jellybeans for his jellybean dispenser. Funny things, like when she'd found a picture of a naked guy wearing a cowboy hat, holding a towel and asked if he had a brother.

He adjusted the stirrups on the saddle for Marisol, and his mind wandered to the night he'd kissed Tierney in Buckeye Joe's parking lot.

Immediately after the kiss ended and she'd lambasted him with harsh words, he'd formulated a plan to seduce her. To use her. So if Daddy Dearest tried to fuck with him regarding his decisions about the Split Rock, versus Tierney's recommendations, Renner could point out that since he'd been banging Pratt's daughter, then Tierney's opinions might be based on emotion, not business acumen.

But after he'd cooled off, he knew he'd never follow through with such a cruel plan—no matter how much the thought of seducing Tierney appealed to him. And did it ever appeal to him. If—no, *when*—he and Tierney became lovers it'd be for no ulterior motive beyond acting on their sizzling attraction.

He'd tied off all the horses when Tierney appeared. In jeans. The type of skintight jeans he'd seen on cowgirls, but never expected he'd see on her. She wore a thermal shirt, a flannel shirt and a puffy ski vest. A vivid purple snow hat sat atop her head and she'd tucked matching gloves in the outside vest pocket. Her boots were heeled, but they were narrow enough to fit in the stirrups, and sexy enough to send him straight back to nekkid fantasyland.

She froze, realizing he was gawking at her. "What?"

"That's a much better outfit than the one you had on the last time you were down here."

"The last time I was down here I wasn't expecting to ride," she retorted.

"Coulda fooled me by the way you rode my ass," he muttered.

"What did you say?"

"Nothin'." He pointed to the horse he'd picked for her. "That's yours."

"He looks mean."

"*She*," Renner corrected, "is about twenty years old and is almost as gentle as the horse I chose for Marisol. She's used to bein' the pack leader, so that means you'll be on the trail first."

Tierney approached the horse on the left side and patted her neck. "What's her name?"

"Billie Jo."

Marisol shouted, "Hey, Mr. Cowboy, sir, here I am!"

He looked at her and grinned. Not only was Marisol wearing a straw cowboy hat and her brand-new red cowgirl boots; she'd donned a pair of pink chaps with silver fringe. "Well, lookit you. You sure are cowgirl material, little lady."

She giggled and ran to hug Tierney. "Are you coming with us?"

"Yes sirree, Bob."

"Yay!" She giggled again. "But my name's not Bob."

"Right. Your name rhymes with . . . something to do with rain." Tierney snapped her fingers. "I've got it. Umbrella. Your name is Cruella!"

"No."

"Druzilla?"

"No. It's Marisol."

"Marisol . . . Rhymes with parasol. Now I remember."

"I see you two have met."

"Uh-huh. Miz Tierney has been coloring pictures with me in the dining room after lunch."

Renner quirked an eyebrow at Tierney. She took time out of her day to color with a lonely little girl? That was unexpected. And more than a little sweet.

Then Marisol spied the horse and her eyes went as big as pie plates. "Is that my pony?"

"Yes, ma'am."

"Is her name Starfire?"

Jesus. "No. Her name is Pumpkin."

" 'Cause she's really orange, huh?"

"That'd be my guess."

Marisol's gaze zoomed back to Tierney, "How come you didn't tell me you're a real cowgirl?"

"Because I'm not a cowgirl."

"What are you?"

Tierney sighed. "You know, that's what I'm in Wyoming to figure out."

Renner frowned. What did that mean?

Joelle put her hands on her daughter's shoulders. "You sure she'll be safe?"

"Pumpkin is an even-tempered horse. Since it's Marisol's first time in the saddle we'll only be gone an hour."

"See ya, Mom!"

"Hang on. I want to get some pictures."

Renner boosted Marisol onto her horse and held the reins while pictures were snapped. Millions of pictures. Finally he said, "We gotta go. We're losin' daylight."

After they mounted up, Renner went through the basic instructions of reining. He told Tierney to head for the main road. As soon as they were walking the horses three abreast on the gravel road, Marisol started asking questions.

Were he and Tierney married?

Why not?

Did they have a dog?

Why not?

Did they ride horses every day?

Why not?

Why didn't Tierney wear a cowgirl hat?

Why was Renner's cowboy hat black?

Why couldn't she make her horse—which she'd insisted on calling Starfire—go faster?

On and on.

Renner sidled up to Tierney and said in a low voice, "I think I know the source of Marisol's mother's migraine."

Tierney gave him a stern look, but he saw her amusement beneath it. He also knew she was having more fun on the trail ride than she'd admit.

He also realized they hadn't argued once.

∞

Tierney volunteered to take Marisol back to her mother, leaving him to finish chores before dark.

The Mackenzie family opted to take supper in their room since they were the only guests. Renner could've gone to bed early, but he'd built a fire and was relaxing when he heard the office door open. He glanced at the mantel. Nine o'clock. Seemed Tierney had been working late again.

She descended the stairs and wandered to the fireplace to warm her hands. "Quiet night." She half turned, taking in his sprawled posture on the couch. "You look comfy."

He shrugged. "Thought I'd stick around until the embers died down."

"Watching out for the safety of the guests, are you?"

"Hell no. The lodge is a lot nicer than my trailer. There's just something about sittin' in front of a fire at the end of the day that speaks to me. Clears my head. If you ain't in a hurry, pull up a chair." He expected she'd decline. But to his surprise, she eased down on the sofa next to him. *Eased* being the word. He looked at her sharply. "You sore from ridin' today?"

Her cheeks flooded with color. "Yes. My inner thighs are screaming. And I won't go into detail about how my butt feels."

I wish you would. I could feel it for you, if you want a second opinion.

The flames crackled. Tierney's head fell back on the cushions and she sighed. "This is nice. Really nice. Know what would make it perfect?"

If we were rolling around nekkid in front of the fire?

He cleared his libido from his throat. "What?"

"If I had a glass of wine. But the thought of getting up and walking to the bar? I believe my legs might revolt and let me fall on my face just to remind me who's in charge."

Renner laughed. "You really do have a strange sense of humor sometimes, Tierney. I like it."

"You'd be the only one."

"I'll admit my tastes have always been . . . eclectic."

"What eclectic trait attracted you to your first wife?" Right after she said it, she said, "Sorry. That is none of my business."

So she was curious about his marital past. He'd wondered. "I don't mind. My first wife had no sense of humor at all."

"Why did you marry her?"

Money. "She had other attributes I believed would make up for it. Turns out I was wrong."

"How old were you when you married her?"

"Nineteen."

"That's awful young."

"Yeah, well, we thought we were in love and all that bull-shit and her daddy didn't want us living together, so we snuck off and got hitched."

"How long were you married?"

"About eighteen months. But man, did it seem like eigh-teen years."

"And the second time?" she asked.

"About eighteen minutes."

Tierney looked at him with shock. "Seriously?"

He hated telling this story. Made him look like a dumbass. "Actually it was about eighteen days. I was in Ve-gas, helping with my buddy's stock for the AFR, and a bunch of us found a strip club off Fremont Street. The first night I met a stripper who had a thing for cowboys. I was flattered as hell because she was ten kinds of gorgeous and about ten levels outta my league. She gave me the impres-sion she wanted to ditch the stripper lifestyle and settle down. So late one night, a week after we met, after way too many shots of Patron, I married her at some tacky Vegas chapel. I should've known she wasn't serious when she didn't immediately quit her stripping job. The finals ended and I was ready to go home. She didn't understand I had no intention of living in Vegas and I expected she'd move to Kansas with me." He chuckled. "She couldn't get to the courthouse to file the divorce papers fast enough."

"I've never met anyone who has a real-life 'what hap-pens in Vegas' story."

"Which is why I avoid sin city whenever possible."

"Because you were madly in love with a stripper with a heart of gold who broke your little Midwestern heart?"

Renner bumped her knee with his. "No, smart-ass. I didn't love Kandy."

"Kandy?" Tierney snickered. "Her name was Kandy? Please tell me her last name wasn't Cane."

"It was Kandy Land, which ain't much better," he said dryly. "And now that you've had a good laugh at my ex-pense, I fully expect you'll regale me about your dates with the Winstons, Harringtons, and other blue bloods you rub elbows with in the Windy City."

"Sorry to disappoint you, but my dating tales are woefully inadequate compared to yours. To anyone's actually. I'm not much of a dater." Tierney sat up. "I'd better start walking."

Renner put his hand on her shoulder, stopping her retreat. "Hey. What did I say?"

"Nothing. I just realized how late it is."

"Bullshit. You're runnin' from this conversation. And darlin', whatever is in your past can't be half as bad as getting hitched to a stripper named Kandy Land, for Christsake."

She laughed softly. "That's true."

He slipped his hand up her arm. "Talk to me."

"I don't have any crazy stories like yours. I've been all over the place, but it's always for a business-related trip. I'm all work and no play. I'm boring. God. It's embarrassing. I wish I had an ex-stripper in my life because that'd indicate I'd actually lived my life instead of just stumbling through it."

"Tierney—"

"Don't feel sorry for me, Renner. I couldn't stand it."

"You know what I can't stand? The fact I've been feelin' sorry for myself because I've been dyin' to kiss you all damn day."

Tierney blinked at him distrustfully.

He moved in and cupped his hands around her face. "I've wanted to kiss you again since that night I kissed you at Buckeye Joe's."

She went very still. Watchful. Silent.

"Well? Aren't you gonna tell me I can kiss your ass? Tell me I'm not your type?"

"You aren't my type. But I'm beginning to think that's not such a bad thing." She angled her head to press her mouth to the inside of his wrist.

That innocent kiss was far sexier than it had a right to be.

Before he could smother her lips with his, Tierney crawled onto his lap, wrapping her arms around his neck. Blowing his mind with a kiss packed with raging desire and sweet heat.

At first he was so stunned he didn't touch her at all. Then he was tempted to touch her everywhere at once. So he settled for curling his hands around her hips, letting his thumbs sweep the bared section of skin above the waistband of her pants.

The initial burst of passion or whatever had led Tierney to make the first move, ebbed, and the kiss slowed. Sweetened. She gave him a lingering smooch, resting her forehead to his.

He managed a husky, "What?"

"I really should've taken my glasses off first."

"Keep kissin' me like that, I promise to clean the smudges and steam when we're done," he offered.

She slid her hands to his shoulders. "Even when a spoiled daddy's girl isn't your type?"

"I'm beginning to think that ain't such a bad thing." Renner bent forward to place an openmouthed kiss on the side of her neck. "I wish you'd forget I ever said that."

"Keep kissing me like that and I'll probably forget my own name."

He paused. "Speaking of names . . . how did you end up with a name like Tierney?"

"Like Renner is common," she pointed out.

"Renner was my granddad's mother's maiden name. Now spill it."

She fiddled with the top button on his shirt. "Because my father's name is Gene and my mother's name was Jean, they had this brilliant idea to pass the 'Gene and Jean' theme along to their offspring. So they named me Tierney, after Gene Tierney, and my sister Harlow, after Jean Harlow."

"That is kinda wacky. But the name suits you perfectly."

Her nose wrinkled. "How's that?"

"Gene Tierney was a smart-mouthed, dark-haired bomb-shell. You're just like her."

"You really think so?"

"I know so." Renner teased her neck with soft-lipped kisses. Her sexy little moan instantly made him hard. "I want you."

He felt her smile against his cheek. "You do have a certain economy of words, Renner."

"And I'm hopin' to get a firsthand demonstration of your other oral skills, Tierney." He brushed his mouth across the shell of her ear until she shivered in his arms. "Soon."

"Soon enough, but not tonight."

He sighed. "Damn. I'd rather you were sore from ridin' me, not a horse."

"I'm sure you'll live." She kissed the tip of his nose.

This time he didn't try to stop her when she moved off the couch and stood by the hearth.

"The fire's almost out."

He didn't bother to bank the heat in his eyes. "Not all of them."

Tierney studied him. "I'll see you in the morning?"

"You probably won't. I've gotta help Abe and Hank move cattle tomorrow. It'll take all day. By the time I get the cow shit scraped offa me, it'll be time to mingle with the guests."

"Then I guess I'll see you when I see you." She ducked out of view, but not before he caught her strange look of determination.

Chapter Seventeen

~

rue to his word, Tierney hadn't seen Renner all day.
It'd taken an hour to pep talk herself into attempting an impromptu seduction—which just proved how
not spontaneous she was, having to plan to be impulsive.

Her gaze stayed on him as she entered the main lodge
area. Surrounded by a group of men, Renner was spinning
some yarn, keeping them enthralled. The man had a way
with people, any age, shape, size, nationality that produced
a spark of envy.

Correction: just looking at him in his cowboy gear—jeans,
boots, a Western pearl-snap shirt, black hat—caused a spark
of lust to supplant the envy.

Janie chatted with a couple of the men's wives, and Tierney ignored her attempt to grab her attention.

*Starting a fight to get the man to kiss you, Tierney? Pa-
thetic.*

But she wanted to feel Renner's mouth on hers. God,
how she wanted it. Craved it. Another taste of that explo-
sion of passion she'd never experienced. The hum of desire
he triggered just by staring at her so hotly with those intense blue eyes.

Eyes, which were wary as she approached. Did Renner know what she was up to? And the question was: if so, would he play along?

"Tierney," he drawled when she stopped before him, "you've got that look in your eye that means I'm in trouble."

The men in his group laughed.

"Am I in trouble?" he prompted.

"It depends. Anything you want to confess? Something you've done wrong lately to save me the bother of guessing?"

Renner smirked. "So you're narrowing the list to what I've done wrong *lately*? Hell, in that case . . . nope. It's still gonna be a fairly long list."

Another round of chuckles.

"I figured you might say that." Tierney glanced at each male guest and smiled. "Gentlemen, I need to have a few words with Mr. Jackson, if you don't mind."

"I'm expecting they'll be pretty choice words, Miz Pratt," Renner drawled again. "But duty calls. Enjoy the rest of the evening. Remember, your huntin' guides are gonna be at the lodge at five a.m."

"Guess we'll be calling it a night soon," said the brawny biker with a Santa Claus beard.

"Good luck tomorrow." Renner placed his hand in the small of Tierney's back and steered her toward the curved staircase.

The heat from his palm seemed to sear a hole through her clothes, straight into her skin. Desire zinged up her spine. Every nerve ending in her body flared with anticipation. Halfway up the stairs, she turned and looked at him. His jaw was clamped together so tightly his lips had nearly vanished in the hard set of his mouth. "Renner—"

"Not a fuckin' word until we're in the office."

Maybe he thought this was real. She'd never done a covert seduction, or any kind of seduction before. What if she'd hosed it up? "But—"

He bit off, "Not. Another. Fucking. Word. So help me

God if you look at me like that again I will not be responsible for my actions. And that will not bode well for either of us, especially given where we are, understand?"

She swallowed. Managed to nod. Purposely added distance between them as they ambled down the hallway. With the open floor plan, everyone on the lodge's main floor could see them from the waist up.

When they reached the office door, she unclipped the lanyard from the belt loop on her trousers. Her hand shook so much she couldn't insert the key in the lock.

Renner swore and took the key from her, without touching her hand at all, and angrily jammed it into the keyhole. He pushed the door open and said tersely, "After you."

Tierney marched past him, head held high. Two seconds later the door slammed. Hard. She had no idea how she'd heard him engaging the dead bolts above the hammering of her heart.

Before she uttered a sound, she was spun around and her back hit the door. Any protest was lost in Renner's mouth as he plastered his body to hers and kissed her wildly.

No sweet kisses. No tender touches. Just raw hunger.

He tasted different than he had last night. A heady mix of male need and a hint of bourbon.

She kissed him back with equal ferocity. Wanting more. Wanting everything this man could give her. Could show her. Could do to her.

His rough-skinned fingers braceleted her wrists, forcing her arms by her sides as he inhaled her. Wordlessly proving he was in control, whether or not she liked it.

Oh, she liked it all right. She'd imagined his fiery passion but she'd failed to factor in one teeny detail in her girlish fantasies.

Renner Jackson under the influence of lust was not the Renner Jackson she'd ever seen before. It didn't matter she was sexually inexperienced. She knew, without a shadow of a doubt, being intimate with him, even one time, would change her forever.

He ripped his lips from hers to softly snarl, "Damn you." Then his mouth savaged hers with powerful kisses and she whimpered when he stopped. "How can I want you this fucking much?" More, hard, deep, passionate kisses followed, giving her no chance to answer his question.

If it even was a question.

The plastic pieces from her glasses dug into the sides of her nose when Renner changed the angle of the kiss. She gasped at the sharp pain and he pulled away. "What?"

"I need to take my glasses off."

His hands traveled up her arms, over her shoulders and neck to cup her face. He very carefully slipped her glasses off and set them on the ledge below the light switch.

The brightness from the outside sodium lights cast a soft orange glow through the window. Or maybe the glow started inside her, as this man was filling her with so much heat she feared she'd combust.

Renner muttered, "Sassy mouth of yours drives me insane," and returned to burning her up with hot, wet kisses.

Since he'd freed her hands, she touched him across the breadth of his wide shoulders. Dragging her fingertips down his spine. Dipping below the waistband of his jeans to mold his butt cheeks in her hands. Oh, he had a firm ass. She remembered just how drool-worthy his ass had looked framed in a pair of fringed chaps.

She brought her palms around his hips to his lower abdomen, feeling powerful as the rock-hard muscle rippled beneath her touch. Her greedy hands followed the plane of his long torso, caressing his pectorals hidden under his shirt. Her fingers slid sideways to squeeze his biceps. Not the bulging type from hours spent pumping iron in a gym, but steel bands forged from hours expending physical labor required to run a livestock operation.

Renner's hands remained flat on the door by her head throughout her all too brief exploration of his body.

Wanting more body-to-body contact, Tierney twined her arms around his neck, spearing her fingers through his hair, amazed the wiry-looking gold and light brown strands were so baby soft and carried a deliciously male scent.

That's when he changed the pace of the kiss, morphing from an openmouthed inferno into an erotic tease. She gasped softly when the very tip of his tongue stroked the roof of her mouth, never imagining such a simple touch had the power to make her entire body tingle. His bottom lip traced the inside line of her upper lip, and again, the simple changeup had butterflies taking wing in her belly.

Renner eased back until their lips were barely touching. His breath as choppy as her own.

"Want to touch you," he whispered. "Now."

"Yes."

Her head buzzed as his thick fingers circled her wrists. Her limbs nearly floated to land beside her hips and he flattened her palms to the coolness of the wooden door.

"Keep them right there."

Then his hands were at her waist, tugging her blouse from her pants, unbuttoning her shirt from the bottom up. He nibbled along her jawline to her ear: hot breath and hotter kisses. He peeled her shirt back.

She would've expected him to go straight for her breasts, but Renner let his tongue track the line of her collarbone from the hollow of her throat to the dip in her shoulder.

Every wet flick of his tongue, every heated pass of his mouth sent her spiraling into pleasure. She was so focused on absorbing every nuance of his seduction that she didn't feel him messing with the front clasp of her bra until it popped open.

Tierney fought the urge to cover her small breasts.

When he growled, "Damn, you're perfect everywhere," and hungrily closed his mouth around her nipple, paranoid thoughts of her unimpressive cup size vanished completely.

Once he ascertained what she liked—not a hard task since she liked it all—he used his lips and tongue to ensure she squirmed. Whimpered. Grew so moist and hot at her core she couldn't help but move her legs together restlessly, looking to assuage this new ache.

Renner lifted his head from her nipple and looked at her. His eyes were dark with want. Then he bent his mouth to her other nipple and repeated the delicious process.

His hands went from cupping and stroking her breasts to a featherlight caress of his thumb on the sweep of skin below her belly button. Tierney knew his next move would be to unhook her pants.

Much as she wanted that intimate touch, she understood if he slipped even a single finger into her, he'd suspect her innocence. She needed to turn the tables and doubted he'd stop her explorations once her hand connected with his cock.

Tierney shifted free of his kiss. "It's my turn to touch you."

"Bossy thing."

"But I didn't hear you say no." Her lips grazed his earlobe.

Renner groaned. "And you won't because in cases like this, I don't mind bein' bossed around."

In a smooth move that defied her usual clumsiness, she reversed their positions, pushing Renner's back flush with the door.

"Whoa. You're serious about this."

"Yes, I am." She attacked the freshly shaven skin of his throat with persistent kisses, demanding, "Unbuckle your belt."

The pulse in his neck leapt beneath her lips. Her fingers made quick work of his shirt snaps as he unfastened his belt.

Tierney was determined not to let her nerves get the better of her, praying her enthusiasm would make up for her lack of expertise.

Since that day he'd dropped the towel she'd wondered how his shaft would feel in her hands. How it would feel gliding across her tongue.

When the weight of his belt dragged his jeans to the tops of his boots, Tierney awkwardly dropped to her knees.

Up close, the cockhead was purplish-red. The vein running up the underside pulsed, almost angrily. A clear bead trickled from the tiny slit. Curious about the taste and texture, her tongue darted out and she licked it.

Sticky. A little salty. She circled her fingers around the base, leaning closer to take just the head into her mouth.

Renner groaned, "Sweet Jesus."

She moved her lips down his shaft, swallowing him an inch at a time, fighting her gag reflex when the tip reached the back of her tongue.

He rasped, "Stop. Look at me, but keep that hot fuckin' mouth right where it is."

Tierney raised her gaze to his, her heart pounding with the fear she'd done something wrong.

But he touched her face reverently. "Lookit you, sexy girl, on your knees, with your lips wrapped around my dick. You have no idea how many times I've imagined this." He paused and seemed strangely conflicted. "But there's something missing."

With her mouth full of him, she couldn't ask what.

Renner reached over and grabbed her glasses. "This is gonna sound weird as hell, but I want you to wear these while you're blowin' me because in my fantasies, you've always got them on. Hold still." Once they were in place, he murmured, "Better. Now it's really you."

His admission that he'd fantasized about her knocked her for a loop. She wanted to make his reality better than the fantasy. She circled her index finger and thumb at the root of his cock, sliding them up his length as she suckled the head, using fast flicks of her tongue on the rim below the slit.

As much as this was about pushing Renner to the edge of ecstasy, this was also about Tierney pleasing herself. Learning the taste, the feel, and the scent of him. Her heart sped up, her nipples tightened from contact with the coarse hair on his thighs. His every sexy grunt, his every muttered curse, every impatient bump of his hips fired her blood. She never imagined doing this would make *her* body so hot and eager—the *how to please a man in bed* books she'd boned up on had definitely left that part out.

"More. Faster. So good I'm already there."

Her hand increased the speed. Any fear that she pulled too much was lost in Renner's guttural sounds. Keeping the head of his cock balanced in the middle of her tongue, she sucked harder, stroked harder with her hand and swore she felt his cock get harder.

"Like that. Yes. Almost . . . Fuck. Yes!"

His cock pulsed in her mouth. She didn't pull back, even when it appeared Renner expected her to. Instead she matched her sucking motions to the contractions traveling up his shaft and swallowed each hot burst.

After the last pulse, Tierney was curious to see if she could fit his entire length in her mouth. She removed her hand and slid her lips down his shaft until the hair tickled her nose. She swallowed, just to see what'd happen. When she did it again, Renner palmed the top of her head.

"Christ," he panted. "You're killin' me. Tierney. Stop. Please."

She savored the sensation of the separation of his hot flesh skimming her tongue and teeth as he pulled out. She licked her lips. They were fuller than normal. Smoother than normal too.

A clank from his belt buckle hitting the door sounded as he jerked up his jeans, zipping and buckling faster than she'd ever imagined possible.

Renner hauled her to her feet and kissed her wildly, his hands fisting her hair, then trailing down her throat, squeezing her breasts, spreading his palms down her rib cage and stopping to span her waist.

"Goddamn, I wanna put my mouth on you."

That wet ache between her thighs became more pronounced. "Yes."

He fell to his knees and unhooked the clasp on her trousers. Tugging the zipper down, he parted the material to reveal her black and white zebra-print thong.

His breath fanned the damp skin of her belly and she shivered. When he licked the sheen of sweat from that same section of skin, more slowly, more thoroughly, she shivered again and closed her eyes.

"Huh-uh. Watch me."

His penetrating blue gaze fastened on hers as he planted kisses down the rise of her mound over her panties.

Three sharp knocks on the door vibrated against her back. By some miracle Tierney didn't jump and knock Renner on his butt.

Renner left his mouth right where it was and his eyes burned into hers with a hot challenge.

"Tierney? Renner?" Janie's voice sounded through the cracks. "Did you guys kill each other?"

Maybe if they ignored her she'd get the hint and go away.

"I swear to God if you don't open this door and prove to me you're not in the midst of a bloodbath I will kick it in."

"Answer her," Renner hissed.

"We're hashing things out, Janie," Tierney said loudly. "No blood spatters on the wall."

"Prove it. Open the door. Now. Guests are staring at me."

"I don't fuckin' believe this." After Renner zipped and hooked her pants, he rolled to his feet and snapped his own shirt.

Tierney's fingers weren't cooperating. He took over with a whispered, "Let me, okay?" and she could only nod in response.

He kissed her sweetly, murmuring, "We'll pick this up later. For now, follow my lead. Go stand by the windows and pretend you're so mad you can't even look at me."

She blinked at the brightness of the overhead lights when Renner turned them on. The lock disengaged and he opened the door.

"Took you long enough," Janie complained.

"We were in the middle of something."

"What?"

"Not your concern. From now on if the door is shut and locked, that's a big hint to stay the fuck out, understand?"

"Sheesh. All right. But in my own defense, I've gotten used to running interference between you two, so don't blame me for worrying I'd come up here and find bloody entrails on the floor."

"That's in the past. We're tryin' a new approach."

"Fine. I will let you two kill each other from here on out," Janie retorted. "But I wouldn't have interrupted if it wasn't important. I'm taking tomorrow off, remember? One of the hunting guides can't make it and he wondered if his son could fill in."

Renner frowned. "Who's his son? Did he leave a number?"

"The son's name is Tobin Hale. He's downstairs. He wants to talk to you."

"Now?"

"Yes, now."

He gave Tierney a smoldering look that Janie didn't see. "This'll take about five minutes, and I'll be right back so we can finish our previous discussion."

Tempted as she was to sneak off to her cabin, Tierney stayed in her office. If Renner just happened to come back . . . she'd be ready.

But two hours passed and there was no sign of the hunky cowboy who'd turned her world upside down. She worked until she couldn't keep her eyes open and then stumbled to her cabin.

∞

The next morning she found a note on her desk. Renner had been called away to deal with a livestock issue at a rodeo and wouldn't return for two days. Which left her more nervous than disappointed. Because with Janie gone, it also left her in charge.

Chapter Eighteen

✺

"**W**hat time is Holt supposed to be here?" Janie asked as she stripped the bedding.

Abe lounged in the bedroom doorway, wearing his light-weight coveralls. He'd already fed cattle, and probably constructed a new windmill. The man was almost too efficient. "He didn't say. Happy as I am with the work he does when he's here, I hate how them construction guys run on their own damn time frames. Christ. It's almost noon."

"I imagine that drives someone like you crazy."

His dark eyebrows lifted. "Someone like me?"

"Yes." She tucked the bundle of sheets under her arm and stood on tiptoe to kiss him. "Someone who doesn't waste daylight. Who makes hay while the sun shines. Who doesn't like to be beholden to anyone's schedule but his own."

He crowded her against the doorframe, rubbing his lips over hers with flirty kisses. "You oughta talk. I can't believe you're really takin' today off."

"I am. I deserve it."

"That's why I let you sleep in. I kept you up kinda late last night."

Abe had locked himself in his office doing mysterious "paperwork" until past midnight. Then he'd woken her and rocked her world. "The late hours and the tangled sheets were well worth it."

"Such a stroke to my ego. But I'll take it. What are your plans for today?"

"Laundry."

Abe frowned. "Janie. I already told you I don't expect you to wash my clothes."

"I don't mind." She ducked around him. For all the complaints she'd lodged during the last few months of their marriage about her household tasks, everything was different now. Abe didn't expect her to do those things. Washing laundry and dishes, fixing meals and mopping floors wasn't all she did—wasn't all she was to him. Abe appreciated her efforts, which gave her a sense of satisfaction and accomplishment.

Her inner feminist jeered.

But she'd refused to listen to a voice that she'd discovered wasn't hers.

"Need me to come down and help you stuff that in?" he yelled from the hallway.

"Funny."

When she returned upstairs, Abe loitered in the kitchen.

"Since it's so gorgeous out, I think I'll hang the clothes on the clothesline."

"Great. Now I'll have a hard-on all damn day."

"Why?"

"I catch a glimpse of white cotton flapping in the wind, and I'll think about all the dirty things I wanna do to you between those clean sheets tonight."

Janie smirked. "Go do your manly ranching stuff, Abe."

"You'll be here when I get back?"

"I plan on it."

He dropped another peck on her lips. "Good. As much as I love the smokin'-hot sex, I'm glad you can finally admit that's not all there is between us."

Last night, after a particularly intense moment, she'd whispered how much she liked being with him, regardless if they were naked. And Abe, being Abe, pushed the point until she confessed it'd been about more than sex with them from the start. Rather than feeling trapped by the admission, she'd felt . . . liberated. In control of her destiny for the first time in years.

The day was unseasonably warm for November, allowing her to leave the doors open to air out the house. She hung up the sheets and several pairs of Abe's jeans, feeling like a total sap when she found herself humming while she worked. She'd started doing that a lot. Truth was, she was happy. Happier than she'd been in a long time.

She loved when evening rolled around and they chatted about their workdays. Cooking together. Snuggling on the couch after they'd loaded the dishwasher. No more of Abe plopping himself on the easy chair to watch TV after supper while she cleaned up the kitchen. Abe didn't help because it was expected. He helped because he liked to spend time with her. No matter if they were cooking, or washing dishes, or fucking each other silly.

Their couple status meant they'd been invited to Hank and Lainie's for supper a few times. And to Bran and Harper's for dessert and poker. It was all so nauseatingly normal.

Yet, it wasn't. New and improved didn't begin to describe the changes in each of them individually and when they were together. It made her long for things she'd feared she could never have. Especially not with this man.

She swept the front deck with an old broom. She boiled potatoes for supper. Cranked the music while she vacuumed. Blissfully lost track of time. She'd wandered among the building debris downstairs, debating on whether Abe would ever consider masculine wallpaper instead of just paint.

The front door slammed. Then the back door slammed. Abe bellowed, "Janie? Where are you?"

"Down here."

Thump thump thump down the stairs. Abe rushed her, wrapping her in a bear hug that actually lifted her feet off the floor. He held her so tenaciously she felt his entire body vibrating.

"Abe? What's going on?"

"I need you to come outside with me." He leaned back and studied her, those serious gray eyes never wavering from hers.

Her heart raced. Since she'd moved in with Abe, there'd been no more incidents that could be attributed to her stalker and she hoped to heaven that wasn't about to change. "Should I be worried?"

"No. Come on." He took her hand, led her up the stairs and out the front door.

Sheriff Bullard leaned against his patrol car next to a scrawny boy and another man. He acknowledged her with a curt, "Janie," and a nod of his head.

Janie gripped Abe's hand tightly. "Sheriff. Is something wrong?"

He jerked his chin to the boy whose red face nearly matched the color of his hair. "This is Bobby Callan, Junior. Bobby has something to say to you." The sheriff motioned for Bobby to move closer.

Bobby shuffled forward and swallowed nervously. He dropped his chin to his chest, shoving his hands in the front pockets of his baggy jeans.

"Look her in the eye, boy," the other man prompted.

He lifted his head and blurted, "I'm the one who caused your car crash. And I'm so sorry. It was an accident, I swear! I came up on you fast and didn't know what to do after the first time I hit you. I meant to step on the brake but I was so scared I accidentally stepped on the gas and hit you again. Then you swerved just as I was about to pass you, the corner of my truck hit the back end of your car and it headed for the ditch. And I—I didn't stick around to see if you were o-k-kay. I'm so sorry." The rest of his words were lost in his stuttering sobs.

Janie seemed to be frozen in place as she stared at the sobbing kid. He was barely big enough to see over the steering wheel. How had he gotten ahold of a vehicle? She looked at the man she assumed was the boy's father.

The guy ambled up to stand beside the kid, but didn't offer to comfort him. He nodded at Abe like he knew him. "I can't believe my son stupidly decided he'd steal my old feed truck and take it for a joyride when his mom and I weren't home. I hadn't paid much attention until I went out two days ago to switch out the battery and noticed the crumpled right front quarter panel. I looked closer at the scrapes around the cattle guard, imbedded with flecks of paint, so I knew there was only one explanation: someone had driven it and been in an accident. I asked Junior about it and he came clean." He shot the kid a dark look, then locked his gaze to Janie's. "There ain't no excuse for what he did, causing an accident and then just takin' off. I'm more embarrassed and sorry than you can ever know. We raised him better than that. It's . . ." His voice broke. "I'm grateful that Abe came upon the accident as soon as he did or this would be an entirely different conversation."

"I ain't gonna lie, Bobby, I'm upset because Janie was seriously hurt," Abe said to the man. "But I've known you for a few years and you ain't the type to pass the buck, so I appreciate you comin' here and telling us in person."

"We wanted to let you know that we're filing an insurance claim to reimburse you for the car repairs and the medical costs. What the insurance don't cover, we'll repay. Junior is gonna be working for a long goddamn time to pay us back. And I suspect he'll be lucky if he's allowed to drive before he's eighteen."

Bobby Junior wiped his arm across his face and looked at Janie. "I'm sorry. I really am."

Janie couldn't seem to make her mouth work, so she merely nodded.

Sheriff Bullard opened the rear door of the patrol car for Bobby and his son. Then he walked to Janie. "I'm sorry about all this. Not a good way to welcome you back to Muddy Gap, huh?"

"No. I'm just relieved that . . ." She couldn't finish.

Abe's arm came around her shoulder and he pulled her against his body. "Thanks for staying on top of this, Sheriff."

"I wish I could take credit. The unfortunate thing is this would still be an open case if not for Bobby Senior bringing it to us. Sad fact is a lot of parents around here wouldn't have."

"I know that only too well."

The sheriff shifted his weight and addressed Abe. "About that other thing you asked me to check on? Took some doin', but I found out why the guy that was . . . ah, harassing Miz Fitzhugh, disappeared. He died. Massive stroke. No family, so no obituary, but I had the death records checked and it was confirmed." He patted Abe's arm. "Take care, Lawson."

As soon as the patrol car was out of sight, Janie's knees buckled. Abe caught her, scooped her into his arms and carried her into the house.

Janie knew it was stupid to fall apart now, but she couldn't help it. Was it really over? She could scarcely wrap her head around what it meant. She curled into Abe so tightly she was practically inside his clothing. He held her, soothed her, proved he knew what she needed and gave it to her without hesitation or restriction.

God, she loved him. As much as she wanted to look in his beautiful gray eyes and tell him how she felt, she held back. It was too much too soon. Abe might believe her confession was a knee-jerk reaction to the truth about the accident and the final chapter in that nasty part of her past.

Her thoughts backtracked to the first time she'd told him she loved him after they'd started dating. Abe had sort of patted her on the head, mumbling about it being too soon to make declarations. She hadn't the guts to say it to him again until after she knew he felt the same way.

Abe loosened her arms, eased her back to wipe her tears and tenderly kiss her lips. "Better?"

"Yes. Thank you."

"I'm sorry. If you hadn't been out here that morning, you might've avoided this."

"If I hadn't been out here that morning, I wouldn't be here right now."

He smiled softly. "Well. There is that." He swept his knuckles down her cheek. "So does this put an end to your fears about that Dave guy finding you?"

She nodded. "Why did you ask the sheriff to look into it?"

"I couldn't sit around and do nothin'. I felt so goddamn helpless. Happy as I am that he's not a threat to you anymore, part of me wishes I could tear that son of a bitch apart, limb by limb."

Of course Abe would push for answers, even if he had to hide it from her. He defined tenacious and protective.

He peered into her eyes. "You don't seem happy."

"I am. But I still don't know who pushed me."

"Is it possible when you started to trip the wind came up, making it seem like you were pushed? I've been knocked on my ass by Wyoming wind a time or two."

Janie smoothed her hand across his ruggedly handsome face. "Maybe. Or we could go with Willie's explanation that I somehow pissed off the bad spirits around the Split Rock."

He didn't say anything.

"What?"

"If those bad spirits are still gunning for you, it'd probably be best you stay here with me instead of returning to the resort. For your own protection."

For her own protection. Right. Abe doing his duty. God forbid he'd admit he wanted her here for himself. She smiled, taking the coward's way out, reminding him of her temporary position. "Beats crashing in that crappy trailer at the Split Rock for however long I end up working there." She disentangled herself from his arms. "Are you ready for supper?"

Chapter Nineteen

❧

Two whirlwind days of dealing with a new venue took its toll. Renner made no promises to the promoters that Jackson Stock Contracting would be involved the following year. But that stress and the long drive was all behind him as he knocked on Tierney's door.

She twisted the shade to peer out the window. Her smile was a thing of beauty. The locks clicked and the door swung inward. "When did you get back?"

Not cool to admit being so eager to see her that he'd showered, shaved and raced out of his trailer a mere ten minutes after he'd parked his truck. "A while ago." He waggled a bottle of zinfandel at her. "I hoped you'd have a nightcap with me." His gaze started at her sock-clad feet, and moved up the black and white checked pajamas straight out of a 1930s movie.

Tierney hugged herself against the blast of cold air. "I don't know—"

Crowding her into the wall, he kept her arms immobilized as he fed her soft-lipped kisses. While the blow job had been great, outstanding really, he wasn't about to take a backseat to Tierney when it came to sex. He'd been planning this seduction all damn day.

Renner kissed the curves of her lips, her cheeks, the section of skin in front of her ears, between her eyebrows, until she emitted a sexy sigh. "You wanna get some glasses? Or we giving in to my redneck side and drinkin' it straight outta the bottle?"

"Glasses. Definitely."

He toed off his boots, hung up his coat and made sure the condoms were accessible. The entire house was visible from where he stood. Only the bedroom and the bathroom had doors that closed. The wide-open space retained a coziness he found appealing.

Tierney set the glasses on the coffee table and poured. "What really brings you by tonight?"

"I oughta be hurt that you suspect I have ulterior motives."

"You oughta be used to me questioning you on everything by now," she volleyed back.

He laughed. "True."

Sitting next to him on her overstuffed couch, Tierney clinked her glass to his. "Cheers."

"Cheers." He drank most of his in one gulp. "What've you been doin' tonight?"

"Catching up on projects."

"What kind of projects?"

"Quarterly reports for companies on the chopping block. I'm trying to sort through nine months of P&Ls to ascertain whether pumping more money into them would change the long-term financial gain or if we'd be better off selling them, or closing them outright."

"Sounds . . . interesting."

"If you like picking apart every blasted expense and weighing it against past, current and projected income. It's tedious."

He faced her, gently pushing a stray strand of hair behind her ear. "Why do it?"

She shrugged. "I'm good at it. I'm not good at a lot of things, so I stick with what I know." She swallowed a healthy gulp of burgundy liquid. "This is a great zin. Where'd you find it?"

"At the bar at the lodge. I figured if we planned to serve it in the dining room, we oughta at least know firsthand if it tastes like vinegar." Renner smooched her, murmuring, "I like this wine. But I like it best when I'm tasting it from your lips."

"Sweet-talker. Kiss me."

"Maybe I'm waiting for you to kiss me."

And kiss him she did. Steadily. Impatiently. She'd only allow their lips to part to take another breath before she sought his mouth again. He handed over the reins to see how far she'd take them.

But he didn't touch her beyond the gentle stroking of his thumb on the base of her neck. A buzzing sound echoed to him and he knew it wasn't his cell, since he'd left his phone in his trailer. He glided his damp lips across hers. "Your phone is buzzing."

"I thought it was my head buzzing from the wine. Or from you."

"Now who's the sweet-talker?"

"Be right back." She scooted off the couch.

Renner topped off their glasses. When he glanced at her, she wore that cute wrinkle on her forehead as she poked buttons on her BlackBerry.

"Something wrong?"

"No. Just a text from my sister. She'll be out of phone range for a week and didn't want me to worry."

"Where's she gonna be that they don't have cell service? Wyoming?"

"Ha ha. No, she'll be in the Amazon rain forest." She picked up her wineglass and took a long sip. "Love my baby sister, but we are total opposites. She's a free-spirited, tree-hugging, Sierra Club, PETA-supporting vegan. Drives our father insane."

"I'll bet." Renner touched her jaw. "You okay?"

"I worry. Harlow travels to crazy places across the globe being a do-gooder because she has this theory all people are basically good."

"You don't believe that?"

"Numbers have always made more sense to me than people." She squinted at the wine bottle. "Holy crap. We drank that much?"

"Uh-huh. Which is a ringing endorsement for this vintage, if you ask me." He set his glass aside and pulled Tierney onto his lap to restart his seduction. Letting his hand map the outside curve of her thigh to her hip. Twining his fingers in her hair, releasing that intoxicating scent of sex and flowers. Pressing her body closer to his.

Tierney wiggled until he released her. "Hang on. That angle gives me a crick in my neck. And I get that plenty from being bent over my desk all the time."

I'd like to bend you over your desk all the time.

She placed her eyeglasses on the coffee table and repositioned herself on his lap with her knees tucked by his hips. Her brown eyes were nearly as black as her pupils. Her lips were as plump as berries from their kisses and as cherry red as the wine. "Much better."

His cock hardened, feeling the heat from Tierney's groin bearing down on his. Renner's fingers traced her spine from the dimples above her butt to her nape. When his fingertips connected with the elastic band taming her hair, he slipped it off, freeing the silken tresses.

He tilted her head back to blaze a path of kisses down the column of her throat. While eking sexy coos and moans from her, his fingers worked the buttons on her pajama top, until the silky fabric separated, revealing her pearly skin. His hands circled her waist, sliding to cup the sweet mounds of her breasts. He flicked the tip of his tongue across the rigid point of her nipple.

When Tierney arched her back and thrust her fingers through his hair to hold him in place, he couldn't wait to see her reaction when he went down on her. He switched to her left nipple, raking the tip with his teeth.

She rocked her pelvis, her hands gripping the couch cushions behind his shoulders. The friction of her ass grinding over his cock practically had him shooting in his Wranglers.

"Bed. Now." Renner clutched her lower back, bowing her backward as he scooted to the edge of the couch. Balancing her body weight on his knees, he stood and clamped his hands on her ass as his mouth swallowed her surprised cry.

He moved them into the bedroom so fast he accidentally smacked into the wall, and Tierney broke their kiss with an, "Ouch."

"Sorry." Out of habit he slammed the door shut behind them. Her bedroom was a black hole. But he'd gone beyond caring. He'd spend time paying her naked body proper homage after he had her once.

The front of his shins hit the foot of the bed and they fell on the mattress. Somehow he managed not to crush her. Somehow he kept kissing her even as he fought to get his shirt off. He palmed a condom after he unzipped his jeans. Next he yanked her pajama bottoms until her smooth, bare skin rubbed against his. When he kissed her knee and let his lips follow the curve of her quad, Tierney shrieked and scooted across the bed away from him.

He laughed. "It's a little late to play hard to get, doncha think?" He balanced on his haunches and put on the condom. Then he was trying to read her body position in the pitch dark. Ah. There she was. The warm, soft, female part of her.

His fingers gently traced her slit as he scattered kisses up her torso. "I wanna flip on the lights and look my fill of you." He licked the indent of her solar plexus and nibbled the bottom curve of her breast. "Take my time and taste you everywhere. But I'm too damn impatient. Been waiting for this for so long, Tierney."

"Me too."

He growled. "I wanna fuck you. Feel you wrapped around me. Inside and out."

She made a soft noise, which he took as a sign that she wanted the same thing.

Renner nuzzled her chest, her neck, her jawline. So soft. So sweet-smelling. So fucking desperate to have her now, he layered his body atop hers, parting her thighs with his hips.

But Tierney's entire body instantly went board stiff beneath him. Legs clenched, her arms woodenlike by her side, her head turned away from his questing lips.

"Sweetheart?" he whispered, wishing he could see her eyes. "What's wrong?"

"Just go slow, okay?"

"Sure. Anything you want."

The tip of his cock nudged her entrance. She didn't cant her pelvis or circle her legs around his waist. Renner began to push inside her. Although she was wet, she was extremely tight. That, coupled with the motionless way she lay there, tensed from head to toe, barely breathing, not touching him at all, gave him the impression she'd never done this before.

Don't be ridiculous. She's got experience. She sure as hell didn't blow you like a woman unfamiliar with a cock.

Sexual pep talk aside, he forged inside her channel inch by inch, gritting his teeth against the temptation to thrust hard and fast and as deep as he could.

Jesus. She was so snug. And hot. And slick.

And not moving. At all.

Renner lowered his head and kissed the first piece of flesh his lips connected with, the skin below her ear. He murmured, "Sweetheart, help me out here," and eased inside her to the hilt.

She gasped.

A groan left his throat. He counted to sixty. Then he rubbed his cheek over hers. The moisture on her face could've been from sweat, but he started to suspect another source. As he moved his mouth down, he felt the dampness on her jawline, the cool skin beneath his lips and the taste of salt. Not Tierney's sweat. Tears.

He froze.

What the fuck?

Renner wanted the lights on right goddamn now. Wanted to know why in the hell she was crying while they were having sex, for fucksake.

Just as he was about to pull out and scramble off her, she turned her head, pressing her face into his throat, almost as if she were trying to disappear into his skin. "Sorry. I just didn't know it'd hurt this much. It's sort of obvious I don't know what to do."

"Darlin', you're confusing me. What do you mean you don't know what to do?"

Her nonanswer was his answer.

No. This couldn't be. "Do you mean this is the first time in a long time you've had sex?"

"If by a long time you mean ever, then yes."

"Ever," he said slowly, "as in . . ."

"The dreaded V word. Yes. I'm one of those. Or, I was one of those until a few moments ago."

Renner was so shocked he couldn't think of a blasted thing to say.

"Please. Can we talk about this later? After . . . ?"

"After what, Tierney? After you get this over with?" What the hell kind of game was she playing?

"No. After you teach me what to do." Her fingers tentatively moved up his arm. "I don't have any hands-on experience in this either."

"Why didn't you tell me—"

"Because I didn't want it to be like this. It's not about me; it's about us, being together as lovers. Show me how to be your lover. Please. Don't stop, Renner. I want you or I wouldn't be here. I just need a little . . . direction. And probably some patience. Lots of patience."

Tierney's bewilderment coupled with her curiosity did him in. He commanded, "Put your hands on me. Touch me."

"Where?"

"Everywhere."

Her fingertips arced over the dip of his shoulder and slid down the length of his back. She paused; then her hands squeezed his ass.

Gooseflesh rippled up his back. "I love that. Now, I'm gonna move."

"Move . . . how?"

Renner smiled at the panicked note in her voice. So Miz Brainiac was the play-by-play type. He pulled out halfway, then thrust home again. "Like that."

"Oh."

He paused, waiting for her signal. Damn, damn, damn, she was tight. Sweat beaded in his hairline and he gritted his teeth against the temptation to plow into her.

"Do it again," she whispered.

He did it again. And again. "Angle your hips, baby. Rock into me like you did on the couch."

Tierney gasped when that angle forced a direct connection to her clit. "I like that."

"Thought you might." He picked up the pace. The good thing about her being a virgin? She had no comparison for how long this was supposed to last.

Her hands roved over his body, making him tremble. She buried her face in his throat, kissing, licking and God— *biting*, holding on as his hips pumped faster.

Then he was in that suspended moment where his balls emptied as he thrust, harder, deeper, each spurt shooting out of his dick hotter, better and more intense than the last pulse, until he was wrung out and panting for his next breath.

As soon as he reclaimed his senses, he kissed her forehead. "Where is the closest light?"

"There's a lamp on the nightstand to your right. But I think—"

"Don't move." It was a stretch, but he managed to find the button and click it on.

A dim glow erupted. They blinked at each other.

Framing her face in his hands, Renner bestowed a long kiss, then another. And another. Pulling back to ask, "A twenty-six-year-old virgin, huh? How the hell did that happen?"

Tierney squirmed. "You really want to do this right now?"

"Yep."

"Get off me."

"Nope." He pressed his nose to hers. "The truth, Tierney. Now."

∞

How weird was it to be as close as humanly possible to Renner but also feel miles away from him? He wasn't exactly a lightweight. He was sort of squishing her.

You like it. You've waited a long time to be squished beneath a man's body.

"It ain't exactly a hardship having you beneath me, but you oughta know I'm not goin' nowhere until you talk to me."

"I know." Her shyness resurfaced when she thought of confessing her relationship ineptitude to this gorgeous, virile man who'd probably never had a problem connecting with the opposite sex.

He whispered, "Come on, sweetheart. Please. You must trust me on some level, because you trusted me enough to be the first man in your bed."

Tierney blurted, "I stayed a virgin because I'm not exactly a guy magnet."

"Darlin', you couldn't be more wrong." He kissed her. "Keep goin.'"

"I never thought about it much when I was in my teens because I went to a private all girls' school. A lot of my friends were still virgins our senior year—we were all academically motivated, not boy crazy. Then I went to college and focused on my bachelor's degrees. And my master's degrees. The club scene in Chicago just drove home the point I'm socially awkward. I'm not all that comfortable carrying on conversations with guys I don't know. I can't dance very well. I'm not spontaneous. I don't have many hot, single girlfriends, so there was no reason for guys to look at me."

"Are all men in Illinois blind and stupid?"

Her face burned. "You're kinda smashing me."

"Hang on." He rolled until they were lying face-to-face. Renner kept their bodies close enough they might as well still be joined. He kept touching her. It didn't soothe her though because it wasn't a comforting caress, but a very possessive one. "So tell me, was it your big brain that kept guys away? Or did your daddy carry a big club?"

"A bit of both. I tend to stick with friends I've had for a long time, which limits meeting new people."

"None of the douche bags you went to college with ever asked you out?"

How sweet that he was concerned that she hadn't ever been properly pursued. "A few did. I went on dates. But I never got to the point I saw myself getting naked with any of them."

Renner didn't say anything. He didn't look away, either. He just continued the gentle, erotic stroking from her bare shoulder to her wrist. "You weren't keeping yourself chaste for religious reasons?"

Tierney shook her head.

"You weren't abused at some point and have issues with sex?"

"Not at all."

"You don't fantasize about women instead of men, and thought if you hooked up with a studly cowboy I'd cure you?"

She laughed. "God, no."

He smiled. "This didn't happen just because I was handy and you wanted to get it over with?"

"You seduced me tonight, remember?"

"True." He brushed his lips over hers. "Sweetheart, I gotta admit I'm confused by all this."

"Why? It might sound strange in your world of cowboy studliness and uninhibited cowgirls chasing after you, but in my world, the opportunity for sex is limited. The longer I waited the weirder it got. So it morphed into this gigantic thing. At a conference in Vegas last year I mustered the guts to pick up a brochure for a male escort service, figuring a pro wouldn't think my virginity was laugh-worthy. When I started to make the call . . . my father knocked on my hotel room door."

"You're shitting me."

"No. I worried I'd become the female *40-Year-Old Virgin*. After I moved here, I tried to remedy that . . ." She dropped her gaze to the sculpted muscles on Renner's chest. Goodness. These differences between male and female bodies amazed her. And she was so glad she'd picked this sexy man as her foray into sex because he was a prime example of masculine perfection.

Insistent fingers tipped her face up. Renner's eyes blazed. "That's what you were doin' that night in Buckeye Joe's when I first kissed you. Picking out a cherry-poppin' guy?"

Tierney blushed. "Yes. Not that it happened."

"Goddamn good thing." Then Renner's mouth swooped down, commanding hers with molten kisses that set her whole body aflame. He rolled her to her back, batting aside pillows so he could pin her arms above her head. He hung above her on all fours. "Well, sweetness, I will teach you everything you ever wanted to know about bein' my lover and then some."

"So this isn't a onetime thing?"

"No. But we are gonna set some ground rules." He beamed a cocky smile. "Oh sugar, by the mutinous look on your face, you don't like that one little bit, do you?"

"Like *you're* a big rule follower, Renner Jackson."

Still grinning, he kissed her. "Rule one—you don't get to tell Daddy nothin' about what goes on between us."

Like that would pose a challenge since she and her father currently weren't speaking. "Done. Is that it?"

Renner shook his head. "Rule two—same deal for the Split Rock employees. All of them. Complete discretion. Everyone knows your father gave me the financing for this place and I don't wanna give anyone the chance to whisper that I'm with you for any reason besides I wanna be with you."

"That's sweet. But I so wanted you to nail me on a dining room table during breakfast," she cooed.

"Smart-ass. But I do have a whole host of ideas on how we can christen your desk."

She lightly bit his chin and let her tongue trace the indent near the tip. She recited, "Rule three—same goes for the guests. Rule four—same for the people in Muddy Gap. I get it. Now can we move on to the teaching me about sex part? Because I have lots of—"

He fused his mouth to hers, devastating her with a kiss that proved she had a lot to learn about having this man as her lover. When he pulled his lips away to peer into her eyes, she was so dizzy and wanting she couldn't speak.

"I've figured out a way to shut you up," he murmured.

She arched, rocking her hips into him. "Do that again. Please."

"In a second. Two other things. What happens between us on a personal level won't affect our business dealings."

"So if you do something asinine regarding the Split Rock, and I demand an explanation, and we have a big blowup, you won't use that as an excuse to withhold sex from me?"

"I oughta take offense to the word *asinine*. But I'm trying to stay focused even though you are nekkid." His finger followed the curve of her neck to the hollow of her throat. "You're so pretty right here. We haven't been at each other's throats nearly as much in the last month. Why is that?"

Because I might go broke trying to do my part to keep this place afloat and now I have loads of work to do strictly for cash. I don't have time to dissect everything you do or obsess over potential mistakes. "Umm . . . because we realized we have a common goal?"

"Maybe. But I'm glad we ain't snapping at each other all the time." Renner kissed her forehead. "Last thing, if we're together, then there's no one else. You wanna break it off with me, fine. Do it. But I won't stand for cheating."

She outlined the rugged angles of his face, committing to memory his bone structure. "How could any woman ever cheat on you? You're so good looking. And you have this magnetism." Her eyes searched his. "I'm jealous. You don't know what it's like to be shy. Or to be the least interesting person in the room."

"Sweetheart, you're so wrong. You've had my interest since the day you stepped your high heels at the Split Rock and glared at me from behind them sexy glasses."

A blush stained her cheeks. "I'm not fishing for return compliments. I'm just . . . pretty stunned that you're attracted to me at all." She traced the twin slashes of his dark eyebrows. "We're complete opposites."

"In some ways. But in other ways"—Renner touched his lips to the hollow of her throat—"we fit together so well."

He slid down her body. Placing a kiss on her breastbone. Her sternum. Her belly button. Then her bikini line. His eyes danced with mischief. "Ever had a man's mouth down here?"

She shook her head.

He moved south until his face was level with her groin. He dragged his tongue from hipbone to hipbone. Once. Twice. Three times.

Her belly muscles rippled, inside and out. "I—I . . ."

At the first swipe of his wet, soft, hot, determined tongue, Tierney decided she'd died and gone to heaven. He licked. Sucked. Tortured her with his mouth until her body nearly vibrated off the bed. Then he really unleashed all his oral tricks. She cried out when the vortex of pleasure dragged her in and spun her around, upside down, inside out, until she couldn't breathe.

As she floated down from an orgasmic high, Renner was back on her. In her. Watching her eyes as he fucked her. Gauging her reaction to every little thing he did to her. Fast. Slow. Long. Shallow. Hard. Teasing. It didn't take much for that thundering need to build again. Pulse hammering, hips slapping, sweat-slicked arms and legs fought for purchase on the slippery sheets as she detonated again.

As she came to, Renner stopped and pulled out quickly. He panted, "Dammit, no condom," spilling his liquid heat on her belly.

Tierney never imagined the proof of his passion cooling on her skin would be such a turn-on. She arched, forcing their lower torsos to glide together in the sticky wetness.

"Sorry," he murmured. "Won't happen again."

"I liked it. It was sexy." She pressed her lips to his Adam's apple. "Umm . . . is this where I tell you I take shots so I only get my period four times a year, but it also covers us for birth control, so you don't have to pull out?"

He lifted his head. Smiled. Kissed her crazily. "Yes, this is the perfect time because I freakin' hate condoms."

"You do? But you've used them? You're . . . safe?"

"I haven't been with anyone for months, Tierney. And I've always been vigilant."

"Good." She studied him, debating on whether to say something possibly very dorky, or to let it go.

"What?"

"Thank you. This has been beyond what I ever expected. You were . . . this was perfect."

He smooched her nose. "We're just getting started. And I intend to give you a whole new definition for the term 'all-nighter.'"

Tierney traced the shape of his smiling mouth. "I can't wait. Let's start now."

Renner laughed. "Insatiable. I like that. But come on, let's get cleaned up first."

"Why can't we stay here like this?"

"Because we're sticky. Plus, I'm dying to see what crazy kinda shower curtain you picked for your bathroom."

Chapter Twenty

❧

*W*hen Renner saw Tierney meandering toward him, he hid in the shadows. She carried a clipboard, absorbed in flipping through the pages. Each time she inserted the pen in her mouth and pursed her lips around it, his dick pulsed into his zipper.

He'd intended to stay away from her last night and allow her body recovery time. He hadn't been rough the first night, but he'd been thorough. Very thorough. That good intention had been blown to hell when he'd found himself at her front door and Tierney pounced on him. Pawing at his clothes. Begging him to touch her everywhere in a husky female whisper that fired a primal need. He'd obliged her, since it was a total rush to be on the receiving end of such unbridled lust.

They hadn't made it to her bedroom. Renner stripped her, pinned her to the floor and used his mouth to get her off. Driving her higher until she gasped his name as she exploded against his tongue. Then he'd stretched out, bringing her on top to ride him. She had no hesitation at trying whatever he suggested or he demanded. When he focused on her nipples, while manipulating her clit, another powerful climax rocked her, and he got off just watching the surprise of ecstasy on her face. As soon as he stopped coming, her mouth was all over him. Sucking his nipples, mapping every dip and hollow of his body—throat, chest, arms, rib cage, abs, hips, quads—all while verbally marveling at his musculature.

The woman made him feel like a sex god.

So it didn't sit well that Tierney might be embarrassed to face him. Or worse—had regrets for her uninhibited response to him.

Lost in concentration, she didn't notice him until he moved in, curling his hands around her hips. "Hey. Are you avoiding me, Miz Pratt?"

"Stop it," she hissed. "Discretion. Remember? Someone might see us."

"Fine." He herded her into an alcove that housed a janitor's supply closet. Since she'd worn her hair up, his mouth automatically zeroed in to taste that tempting nape. "God, you smell good. I haven't seen you today."

Tierney clutched the clipboard to her chest. "Well, I've seen you."

He stopped kissing the section of her hairline above her ear. "When?"

"At the corrals. Almost getting your melon trounced by fifteen hundred pounds of pissed-off bull."

"You saw that?"

"Yes. And after you were tossed on your butt, you hopped on the back of a bucking bronc without a saddle."

"I was ridin' bareback. Saddles are for saddle bronc ridin.'" His thumbs caressed the lower curve of her back. "You chewing me out? I didn't get hurt." He noticed her breathing had changed. "Tierney? How long did you watch me?"

"Long enough to get all . . . hot and bothered. Highly distracting seeing you strutting around in those chaps. Then I couldn't tear my eyes away as you rode." She shivered. "Such control. Such strength. Such determination. Such concentration. Reminded me of last night."

A possessive growl broke free. He needed to stake his claim on her again. Right. Fucking. Now.

"I had to stay away from you today. I tried to focus on doing my job, but all I can think about is doing *you*. I've never been the type to go overboard on anything. I don't overeat. I don't overspend. But now that I know firsthand how intense a physical relationship with you is? All I can think about is going overboard on you. You and me naked. All that delicious friction of interlocking body parts as you're kissing me stupid."

"Jesus, Tierney, you want me to drag you into the janitor's closet and fuck you like an animal?"

"I'd rather you fucked me like an animal in our office where the door locks." She turned that liquid gaze on him and he couldn't help but capture her mouth in a savage kiss. Finally, he released her lips and softly snarled, "Go. I'm right behind you."

Renner remained in the alcove, despite the temptation to watch her ass sway in that swishy black skirt. He waited five excruciatingly long minutes before he strolled down the hallway.

No one lurked in the main lodge but he cautioned himself not to take the stairs at a dead run. Not to act like he'd rip into anyone who stood between him and the paradise that waited behind his office door. He'd reached the third tread when he heard, "Renner?"

Never fucking failed.

He turned to look at Janie. "What?"

"Do you have a minute? I have a couple of questions—"

"Can it wait?"

She eyed him suspiciously. "I guess. But what's going on? You're acting awful tense."

"I'm tense because Tierney summoned me to the office."

"Want me to go with you and run interference?"

Fuck no. "Nah. I can handle it. Just keep everyone away."

Renner didn't wait for Janie's response. He blew into the office. Shut the door. Locked it.

Tierney had pushed her chair aside and leaned over her desk.

Oh hell yeah. Welcome to his biggest fantasy. And she even wore those four-inch black and white polka-dotted stilettos.

He unbuckled his belt as he crossed the room. "Stay like that." Then he was behind her, inserting his foot between hers, with a terse, "Spread 'em wider. If you don't want this, say so now."

"I want it. I want you. Makes me crazy how much I want you."

His heart pounded. Every inch of his skin was stretched tight. He yanked his jeans and boxers down. Letting his fingers trace the backs of her thighs, past the sweet curve of her ass, he pulled aside that inconsequential thong and slid his index finger inside her. His brain registered wet, hot, ready. Renner flipped her skirt up. Spread her pussy open as he sited his cock and sank into her.

Tierney arched with a drawn-out, "Yes." She squeezed her cunt muscles and threw her pelvis back.

That movement unleashed the beast. He wrapped his fingers around her hips and slammed into her. Hot as hell, seeing his cock disappearing into her pussy with his every powerful thrust. Next time he took her from behind he'd pull her butt cheeks apart, watching the rosebud of her ass clench as he fucked her.

He hammered into her, lost to everything but the sound of his flesh meeting hers. Of her heat and scent and need. Of her grunts competing with his.

"That feels . . . I'm so close."

Renner changed the angle, allowing for deeper penetration.

"That's it. Yes!"

Her voice had escalated with each word. Hopefully no one lingered outside the door because Tierney didn't hold back when she started to come. And he'd never tell her to tone down her passion. Never. Made him cocky to know he was the only man who knew this passionate side of her. Her sexual greed and curiosity equaled his. Who would believe the brainiac city girl and the crude cowboy were so well matched?

One. Two. Three thrusts and she exploded. She didn't scream; the noise was more of a wail, punctuated with *yes yes yes.* But it was loud. It was hot as sin.

The unrestrained sound of her pleasure, seeing her half-dressed, stretched over her desk—it was too much. He pounded into her snug pussy, coming so strongly the orgasm rocked him from his heels to his eyelashes.

He slumped over her, bracing his palms on the desk next to hers, gasping for air. As he nuzzled the back of her head, the scent of sex and flowers returned him to reality.

"Was there an earthquake?" she panted. "Or did we just shake the rafters?"

"You definitely shook me." He slipped his cock free and turned Tierney into his arms. "Thank you for takin' the edge off, but sweetheart, I'm not nearly done with you today. You . . ." *Consume me.* "Are too much temptation for me to resist."

"Will I see you later?"

Not needy. Not expectant. Not accusatory. Just a simple question. "Yep."

"After you chat up the guests. I could . . . cook." She seemed very focused on the buttons on his shirt.

Renner tilted her face up. He loved the soft way she looked after she'd gotten off. "Want me to bring anything?"

"Just yourself." Her kiss was sweet, but firm. "Now shoo. Since you've handled my distraction problem I might be able to get some work done."

∞

How hard could it be to throw a couple of pork chops in a pan?

Plenty hard, she found out.

She burned them to a crisp. While she was tending that fiasco, the potatoes boiled all over the stove. The only part of dinner she hadn't managed to ruin? The salad. Simply because even she could rip open a bag of lettuce.

So Renner looked a little perplexed seeing her shivering on the living room floor, polishing off a bottle of cabernet.

"Tierney? Why are all the windows and doors open? It's twenty degrees outside."

She waved distractedly with the bottle. "The smoke detectors were beeping. I thought it'd clear the air faster since the wind blows so freakin' hard in Wyoming. The smoke is mostly gone now."

"Smoke from what?"

Tierney squinted at him. "Did you know that pork chops can actually catch fire?"

That factoid seemed to startle him.

"The potatoes . . . let's just say burned cheesy potatoes could be used as tile grout." She swigged directly from the bottle. "Or what's that stuff they slap on the outside of houses?"

"Adobe?"

"That. Except it'd be yellowish orange instead of red. Or in the case of my potatoes—black." Tierney closed her eyes in total mortification. "I hope the burned-food thing doesn't remind you of your ex-wife."

"That's what worries you?"

"Maybe. If you haven't guessed by now, my attempt at dinner was monumentally fucked." She hiccupped. "Bet you thought after I whipped up the brownies and saved the day I'd be an excellent cook."

"You can't cook?"

"No, I cannot. The brownies were a fluke."

"So you lied to me?"

Without looking at him, Tierney held her thumb and index finger apart about two inches. "I just stretched the truth a tad." And wasn't that a true statement on more levels than was wise to contemplate when she'd been hitting the bottle.

Renner's fingers caressed her cheek. "Why?"

"Because I didn't want you to think I'm a dork who can't

cook a simple meal. But the truth is: I am a dork. I can decipher financials from ten companies at one time, but I cannot follow one recipe card." She opened her eyes. "I'm sorry. Not only did I flambé dinner, I drank all the wine to calm my nerves after I had to throw my smoking pans in the snow and now I'm a little tipsy."

He smiled. "So you are human. Good to know."

"What's that supposed to mean?"

"Tierney, darlin', you're intimidating as hell. You rarely make mistakes. You seem to know everything. It's sweet that you wanted to impress me. It's even sweeter yet that you failed. Hell, I'm impressed that you even bothered to try." He adjusted her glasses. "And I like you tipsy. I bet you're cuddly as a kitten."

"You confuse me."

"Good."

That statement confused her even more.

"I'll shut the windows so we don't freeze to death." Then he took her hands and pulled her to her feet. "You hungry?"

"Why? Can you cook?"

"Not worth a damn."

"Oh." They stared at each other. It wasn't a particularly comfortable moment.

He gently asked, "I see the wheels churning in that big brain. What's going through your pretty head?"

"I don't know how to do this."

"I know. To be honest, it's been a while since I've done this too."

Her eyes narrowed. "You do know I'm not talking about cooking, right?"

"Yes, I caught that." Renner grinned. "You get more literal when you've been drinking too. It's cute." He traced her lips with his thumb. "No pressure. Let's just hang out."

Tierney flattened her palm on his chest. Then both palms. Would she ever quit marveling at his hunky, muscle-bound body? Probably not. Now that they were lovers, would Renner just let her touch him however she wanted? Actually, when she really thought about it, he'd been a little stingy giving her equal opportunity touching time.

"If you don't quit lookin' at me like that, I'm dragging you to bed."

"Okay. Can I take your shirt off this time? Slowly? And kiss you all over? Because I really really like your body. A lot. A whole lot. I could spend days touching you."

Renner groaned. "How about if you hold that thought and we snuggle up on the couch? It's still damn cold in here."

Once she and the big cowboy were cuddled together beneath a fleece blanket, his chest to her back, their legs entwined, she sighed. "This is toasty."

His warm breath stirred her hair. "Wanna take bets on how long before you're snoring in my arms?"

"I could think of a couple of ways you could keep me awake," she purred.

"I'll take it under advisement for later."

"So what are we supposed to do? Just lie here and think happy thoughts?"

He chuckled. "You don't have much downtime in your life, do you?"

"More here than I did in Chicago." Tierney brought his knuckles to her lips for a kiss. "Although, I do find myself watching the sky change and drinking in my surroundings in ways I never have before since I moved here."

"The way you say *moved here* almost sounds permanent."

I wish. "Why did you move here? Was it really just owning your grandparents' land that brought you to Wyoming?"

"Initially. I had great memories. Didn't know what it was at the time, but I felt such a sense of community."

"I get that too. Weird, isn't it?"

"Didn't get that growing up in the big city?"

"It was hard to get to know your neighbors when fences and security systems surrounded each house. I'm not boohooing my childhood as a poor little rich girl."

Renner caressed her arm. "Were you happy?"

"I guess. I didn't know any differently. My mother died when I was four and my sister Harlow was two months old. My father remarried when I was eight. By my ninth birthday I was at boarding school. Spent summers at camp. Between the ages of thirteen and fourteen . . . I didn't see my father at all." Her stomach still turned queasy when she remembered the blank look on his face because he hadn't recognized her.

"My mom died when I was young." He stroked her hair. "Do you ever wonder what your life would be like if your mother hadn't died?"

"I used to. Those thoughts mostly cross my mind when people accuse me of being detached. I wonder how different I would've turned out if I'd had someone in my life showing me affection." She cringed.

"Didn't mean to make you feel bad, Tierney."

"You didn't. It makes me realize I want more than just sex with you." When Renner stiffened, she rolled over to face him. "Not a wedding ring. More meaning . . . I want to be able to touch you, hug you, kiss you when we're alone. Like this."

His too-blue eyes were as tender as his smile. "Just when I'm sure I've figured you out, you throw me a curveball. I'm tryin' to say this in the least sexual way possible, but any time, any way you wanna touch me, feel free." He teased her mouth with his, each gentle smooch becoming longer. "I like bein' with you, Tierney. You truly are something special."

Despite the clichés and the internal warnings not to moon over him, the first man she'd slept with, at that moment, Tierney couldn't help it. She fell a little in love with him.

Chapter Twenty-one

❦

*T*he night was glacial and Janie was so glad to be cuddled against Abe, hating that he'd had to go out in this nasty weather, especially after he'd nearly frozen to death a week ago.

Abe hadn't come home after doing a cattle check during which snowfall had turned into a full-blown blizzard. Unable to reach him on his cell, she panicked, calling Hank. He'd tried to get her to stay put while he checked for his brother, but Janie insisted on going along.

After two hours of inching through pastures and over snowdrift-covered fences, they found Abe. He'd high-centered his pickup. Both the battery in his truck and his cell phone were dead. Abe knew not to battle the elements, remaining sheltered in the cab of his truck. He'd dressed warmly, but subzero temperatures for six hours had chilled him to the bone. Hank had to carry Abe out of the cab and to his truck.

They returned to Hank's house so Lainie could determine if Abe needed medical attention. The storm became so bad the roads were closed and Janie and Abe ended up spending the night at Hank and Lainie's. Took hours before Abe thawed out. Janie never left his side. She held him through the teeth-chattering shivers and the pain when his limbs warmed. When he'd finally fallen asleep and she realized he was going to be okay, without permanent damage, she let her tears fall.

Yet even the scare wouldn't change anything. Cattlemen were a breed apart, more concerned for the lives of the animals they cared for than for their own safety. He wouldn't stay safe inside when the wind was raging and the snow flying. Abe's compassion was one of the things she loved most about him.

But since that incident, life with Abe in the Lawson household had changed. She knew the reason for Abe's change from casual to possessive—when she admitted she feared for his life and understood how helpless he'd felt after the car accident. That brutal honesty opened the door to his true unrestrained affection. Even when neither spoke of how long they'd continue to play house without promises.

Still, Janie felt Abe was holding something back from her. And because she loved this new openness, she wouldn't let her questions go unaddressed another day.

"Abe?"

"Mmm?"

"You asleep?"

"Uh-huh."

She elbowed him. "I'm serious."

"Janie. I'm whupped. You wore me out."

"So if I said I was ready for another round of rambunctious sex? Would that wake you up?"

They were spooned together so she felt his dick twitch against her backside. "Okay. Now you've got my interest. What's up?"

"I want to know what really happened between you and Nancy."

Abe groaned. "You really want to talk about this *now*?"

No better time than when they were curled together, satisfied from a bout of good lovin' and drifting off to sleep in each other's arms. "Yes. You demanded the down and dirty details about how I ended up with a loser like Dave. I told you. It's been a couple of weeks since I brought this up. Don't think I've forgotten you haven't told me anything about her."

The way his body went on full alert Janie wondered if she'd just opened a big old can of worms.

"How detailed you want me to get?" His breath tickled her ear. "Because I can tell you stuff that'll make you look at me in a whole different light."

He had to be bluffing. She scoffed, "Doubtful. But take your best shot."

His rumbled, "Remember you said that," sent the hair on the back of her neck on end in a deliciously powerful shiver.

"For a long time after you left I wasn't interested in any relationship. If I wanted to get laid I did. I drove to Casper. Or Rawlins. Trolled in the bars of the rodeo towns if I was with Hank. Got off and got gone."

Janie had a hard time believing that. "No woman around these parts piqued your interest? You didn't look at someone like Harper and think, damn, she'd make a helluva ranch wife?"

Abe slid his leg between hers. "Single suited me fine until Hank and Lainie got married. I wasn't unhappy, just floating along. Then I met Nancy."

"What was the attraction? From the grumbling I've heard, she didn't have a fantastic personality. She wasn't rich. Her father didn't own a liquor store. Did she have pistol grip ears?"

Abe snickered at their old "perfect woman" joke. "She was opinionated; she didn't care if she pissed people off, including my family and friends. She preferred to do things her way. She complained. A lot."

"Still not seeing her appeal, Abe."

"You wouldn't."

Indignant, she said, "It's not because I'm jealous."

"Of course you're not," he said smoothly. "But Nancy's appeal? She'd do anything in bed. And I mean anything."

Janie froze.

"Shocked?" he murmured, sending gooseflesh cascading down her spine.

"Doesn't seem like a trait that would matter to you."

"But see, cupcake, that's where you're wrong. I had the normal marriage where the most exciting place we fucked was the laundry room. Where the sex between us wasn't awful, but it wasn't honest either. It was perfunctory. Occasionally great. But pretty straightforward. When I started racking up bedroom miles, I learned a whole slew of new tricks. And I figured out I like sex. A lot of sex. Add a little kink to it, put me in charge and I was a new man."

A funny tickle started low in her belly.

"Women who prefer one-night stands are game to try anything. I'd likely never see them again, right? Made it easier to tell them to do things I'd never dream of askin' my sweet wife to do."

"I don't recall you asking me to do much in the bedroom," she retorted. "So how could I've known what you wanted?"

"You couldn't have. I wasn't honest with you, Janie, because at the time, I hadn't accepted that side of myself. My first date with Nancy? Boring. I'd decided no second date, because she had some really fucking annoying qualities. But she showed up at the ranch the next day, in the middle of the afternoon. Freaked me out, especially when she claimed I was the type of man she'd been lookin' for."

"What kind of man was that?"

"Uninhibited. Forceful. To prove it she sucked me off in the goddamn barn. She got herself off in front of me with a vibrator she just happened to bring along." His voice rumbled in her ear. "That's a serious turn-on for me, watching a woman get herself off. After she finished I bent her over the bench and fucked her."

Holy shit. What was she supposed to say?

"I couldn't tell my friends Nancy was fulfilling my every

raunchy fantasy. Except Ike had an idea after he joined us for a few threesomes."

Janie blurted, "You had more than one?"

"Shocked yet?"

"Uh. Yeah."

Abe brushed his warm, soft mouth over the same spot behind her ear. The goose bumps would appear, then recede and appear again with every unerring sweep of his lips.

"Ever been in a threesome?"

"No."

"Oh, sweet Janie. It's a thing of beauty watching a woman give herself over to the whims of two men. Imagine one man sucking on your nipples while the other man sucks between your legs? Jacking off two guys and watching their come splat all over your body? Sucking one dick while the other dick is rammed up your pussy? Blowing one guy while the other guy's cock is reaming your ass?" His voice dropped an octave. "Tell me . . . have you ever been to that line between pleasure and pain? Where one little nudge either way . . . and you explode?"

The way he'd described it? Janie was jealous of Nancy—because she'd elicited such a strong response from Abe. Like most women, Janie had wondered how it'd feel to have two sets of hands touching her skin, two hungry male mouths on her body. But it'd always remained in the realm of fantasy. "Was this a regular thing with you, Nancy and Ike?"

"Happened a couple of times. Nancy was really into it. Ike was into it. About that time, you blew back into town."

"And threw a wrench into everything. What would've happened if I hadn't taken the temporary job at the Split Rock and disrupted your life? Would you be twirling Nancy on a pleasure swing in here while you flog her ass and confess your love?"

His voice was fierce. "I didn't love her. I had no intention of loving her. But I'd reached the point in my life where hot sex was enough. It was more important than love."

He hadn't denied wanting kinky stuff on a permanent

basis, just denied the emotional attachment to it. Had she done this to him when she'd left him? Rendered him incapable of loving?

"Surprised?" he murmured in a silken drawl.

Janie snapped, "No," a little too quickly.

"Or are you surprised that I admitted it?"

"I'm surprised you're bragging about it."

Abe didn't give her the angry, defensive response she expected. Instead, he laughed. "I ain't one to brag, but I've never had any complaints about my demands or my performance in bed."

Luckily she didn't have to look him in the eyes when she asked the next question. "Did you reveal this side of yourself because you think I'm incapable of letting loose? Is this a warning that sex has been boring? I'm somehow holding you back from being Abe, master of kink?"

Abe rolled her over to face him. "No. It's been great."

Janie let her fingers trace the shape of his mouth. "Not exactly a ringing endorsement."

He didn't deny it.

She knew what she had to do. What she'd wanted to do since the moment he'd taken her on the kitchen counter. "Will you show me what you want me to be in bed?"

"Teasing me isn't smart."

"I'm not teasing. I'm serious."

His eyes glittered with a look she'd never seen before. A look that made her nervous. And very very hot. "Prove it."

"How?" As if she didn't know.

"By doin' anything I tell you to do. Without question."

Could she?

Yes.

"I'll do it. But no pain."

"You don't get to decide that. I'd never beat on you or make you bleed, but if you haven't experienced the bite of pain that comes from pleasure games, how can you know whether or not you'll like them?"

"You'll stop if I tell you to?"

Abe stared at her steadily. "You either trust me, or you don't. Choose."

Wow. He wasn't giving an inch.

That was really forceful. Fierce. Sexy.

She said, "Okay," so quietly she wondered if he'd heard her.

But he did. Abe didn't pounce, but gave her a very thorough kiss before he moved to rummage in his dresser.

Would he come back with a paddle? Or something kinky she'd never seen before? She'd browsed in sex toy stores, but she'd mostly stayed in the vibrator section.

When Abe turned around, she couldn't tell what was in his hands. He sat on the edge of the bed. "Stand." As soon as she was in front of him, he said, "Close your eyes and keep them closed until I say otherwise."

His mouth latched on to her right nipple and he suckled strongly. Used his teeth to tug the tip into a rigid point. She loved the way he just knew how far he could push her. One last hard suck and she felt a sharp pinch. Then he focused that same precise attention on her other nipple, and again she experienced a pinching sensation.

Abe kissed the top of each breast and murmured, "You can open your eyes."

Janie glanced down and saw a small rubber tube attached to each of her nipples. He pinched the ends. She gasped at the sensation—like two mouths.

"I knew these'd be perfect for you." He pinched them again. "And no, I never used these on anyone else. I got these specifically for you in the hopes . . ."

"That I'd come around?"

"Oh, make no mistake, darlin', I would've *brought* you around."

Gulp.

"This is a part of who I am. You understand that, right?"

Maybe not completely, but if she wanted to be with him, she'd have to accept it. "Right. Where'd you get these? Because I'm pretty sure the C-Mart doesn't carry them."

He grinned. "Gotta love online shopping."

"What else did you order to get the free shipping?"

"You'll have to wait and see, won't you." Abe kissed every inch of her breasts, but avoided the nipple area. By the time he said, "On the bed on all fours," the inside of her thighs were completely soaked.

She expected he'd stretch his big, hot body over hers and fuck her from behind. But he slid beneath her until his cock was in her face. "Suck me, Janie, while I suck on you."

The first hot swipe of his tongue on her slit made her gasp. When she didn't move because she was lost in the thrill of Abe's mouth exploring the folds of her sex, he whacked her on the ass.

Janie took the tip of his cock between her lips. No deep throating in this position. Sixty-nine hadn't ever been her favorite. Too hard to concentrate on blowing his mind when he was blowing hers. Even another sharp whack on her ass didn't help her focus. Especially not when Abe's fingers spread her pussy wide, exposing every wet inch to his sucking mouth and eager tongue. Then that wicked tongue snuck back and painted wet swirls around her anus before plunging deep into her channel again. She let Abe's cock slip out of her mouth completely and moaned from the bottom of her lungs.

He stopped playing tease and retreat with her back door and focused all attention on her clit. His tongue rapidly flicked the little nub while his mouth sucked the flesh around it. He kept at it until that moment when the muscles spasmed and she ground her pussy into his face. "Oh, God, yes," as she spiraled into that black hole of pleasure.

When the blood stopped roaring in her ears, she sighed. "Sorry. I'm better at giving blow jobs when I'm not distracted by a tongue on my clit."

He chuckled.

Janie kissed the tip of his cock. "Your turn."

"Nope. Now I've got something else in mind." He rolled

from beneath her and brought them on their knees, back to front on the middle of the bed.

She closed her eyes as he ran those wonderfully callused hands all over her skin. Knowing all the right spots. Hitting them repeatedly. Until she seemed to float outside her own body.

"I love that purring sound you make whenever I touch you like this. It's always driven me crazy." Abe played with her nipples and nuzzled her in the maddeningly erotic manner that turned her brain to mush. "Know one thing I never asked you to try when we were married?"

"Sounds like there were lots of things you never asked me to try with you."

He nipped her shoulder. "Part your knees." A slick digit probed her anus. She relaxed the muscle, allowing his finger to breach the opening. "You're not a virgin to anal sex?"

She shook her head. "I was curious so I've tried it."

"Me too. I like it. A lot. And I don't exactly like it slow and sweet." He licked the shell of her ear. "Grab the headboard."

She angled forward, keeping her stance wide, excited, nervous, half afraid she wasn't ready for this even as her body trembled and she craved it.

After he broke out the lube, he teased her back entrance until he deemed her ready. His hands roughly pulled apart her butt cheeks. The slick cockhead pushed against the pucker, then through the resistance.

She sucked in a sharp breath at the sting. She might not be a stranger to anal intercourse, but she'd never had a cock as big as Abe's filling her ass.

"That's it. Relax. Let me in." He nuzzled the back of her head. "So good, Janie. Just a little more. I'm dying for you to take me. All of me."

He stopped. Waited for her body to adjust.

Her position stabilized them, which freed Abe's hands. He tugged on the nipple stimulators while gently biting the sweep of her shoulder. Whispering how much he loved to feel her shuddering and moaning from his touch.

This verbal side of Abe was new. She liked it. Liked knowing how she affected him. Liked knowing she could tell him exactly what she wanted him to do to her. Even when he already seemed to know.

The man had monumental control. Each flex of his hips sent his cock deep into her bowels, but he kept the pace slow and steady. Never losing his restraint in the retreat as his cock rasped against her tight anal walls. Although she could feel his body shaking and the sweat covering his chest. While she existed in his pleasure and he in his power.

Abe stroked her clit until it swelled. Then he changed tactics and tapped the pillow of nerves. Tapped it to the precise throbbing of the blood in her swollen anal tissues. Tapped it as her entire body twitched, teetering on the brink of the unknown. Tapped it until that rhythm overtook all conscious thought processes.

The change in him was instantaneous when he realized she'd reached that blurry line. No more leisurely, measured thrusts. His cock came completely out of her ass with every withdrawal. Every time he ruthlessly shoved back in, he pulled on her nipples. Hard. The sting in her ass, her nipples, sent her soaring into a blinding abyss where she wanted it all to stop as much as she never wanted it to end. "Wait."

"No. You can take more."

"No."

"Yes," he hissed. He sank his teeth into the magic spot on the side of her neck and she bucked against him. But he held firm, forcing her to let go and feel every twinge of pain. Every sweet pulse of pleasure.

The throbbing synchronized, tightening her back channel around the thick intrusion. An electric current traveled from her neck, to her nipples, to the blood-rich anal tissues and she came undone.

Her orgasm set off his and Abe groaned, the heat of his seed warming her inner walls.

She vaguely remembered him easing her down to the mattress. Tonguing her nipples after removing the clamps. Soothing the sting of her ass with a cool cloth. Whispering to her. Caring for her.

Loving her.

After they'd both settled, Abe gathered her in his arms, keeping her pinned to his chest, as pleased with her total surrender to him, as she was that another barrier between them had fallen. A barrier she hadn't known existed.

Chapter Twenty-two

～

$\mathcal{A}$nnoyed, Tierney snapped, "Come in," at the ten billionth knock on her door. No wonder she had to burn the midnight oil at her cabin after Renner left. She never got anything accomplished here.

Janie burst in and slapped her hands on Tierney's desk. "I'm confused on why you won't hire Tobin Hale permanently. He's local. He's a hard worker. He's got a damn master's degree in reproductive science! All he wants is a chance. Are you so set on the bottom line, on some numbers on a spreadsheet that you don't see Tobin is a great long-term investment?"

Coolly, Tierney said, "My understanding was Tobin applied for jobs at the Forest Service and the Wyoming Department of Natural Resources and his employment here was temporary."

"He received notification from both organizations last week that those positions were filled in house, from current employees, so he's still in the market for a job."

She muttered, "More nepotism at work."

"Which is why I have to ask if you have someone else in mind?"

Tierney blinked at Janie. "Have you been drinking? Because I have absolutely no idea what you're talking about."

"Renner and I discussed this three days ago. He promised he'd talk to you and get back to me. He hasn't. He blows me off when I've asked." Her eyes narrowed. "I assume this issue has come up in all the meetings you've been having lately?"

Shoot. They really had to quit using this office for a quickie. Or for a not so quickie, like yesterday when Renner kept her on the edge for almost an hour. Teasing her with his cunning mouth, then switching it up, using a supercharged vibrator on her until she begged. Only then did he pin her to the floor and fuck her without mercy, wringing two outstanding orgasms from her before he came so wildly he sank his teeth into her breast to keep from roaring like a beast.

Renner had confessed that last part afterward, while he was untying her jaunty little paisley scarf that he'd secured around her wrists. The man had certainly taken his responsibility to further her sexual education to heart.

"Tierney? Are you going to answer me?" Janie asked.

Damn. She couldn't even remember the question.

"I'll answer for you," Renner drawled. He strolled in and sat on the corner of her desk. A desk the wicked man absolutely gloried in bending her over at every opportunity.

Sex on the brain much?

"Well?" Janie demanded, her shrewd gaze zipping between them.

"I haven't talked to Tierney about hiring Tobin, so I do believe you owe her an apology for that ass chewing."

"Sorry, Tierney," Janie said offhandedly and got right in Renner's face. "Why haven't you addressed this with her?"

"I was getting around to it. I've had other things to deal with."

"Things you might not have had to deal with if you'd hired Tobin like I asked."

His spine straightened, a sign Tierney recognized as

Janie striking a nerve. "I wanna know if your *husband* is aware of how hard you're pushing to have this good-looking young stud working for us."

Janie sputtered, "Renner Jackson, you are such an ass-hole. Abe is no longer my husband and you know it."

"Coulda fooled me with the way you're mooning around here all the time. Humming, for God's sake. You're acting like Harper. A newlywed in *lurve*."

"Omigod. I cannot believe you just said that to me." She railed on him, calling him every name in the book while he taunted her with kissing noises.

With irritation, Tierney said, "Break it up or take it outside."

Janie whirled around. "That's turning the tables. You breaking up an argument between me and Renner, not vice versa."

"Funny. But thank you, for bringing the Tobin situation to my attention. Renner and I will discuss it."

"You busy right now?" Renner asked.

"Ah. No."

"Good. Let's do it." He pushed off the edge of her desk, turning to face her, blocking Janie from view. He mouthed, "I want to fuck you."

Her entire body quivered. How Tierney managed not to launch herself across the desk at him made his eyes dance with delight.

"I really appreciate you guys taking care of this," Janie said.

"You're welcome." Renner didn't even turn around when he said, "Shut the door on your way out."

Tierney's body trembled at the ravenous look in his eyes, but she forced herself to discuss business first. "Why didn't you ask me about hiring Tobin?"

"I don't want to talk about Tobin."

The sneering way he said Tobin's name almost sounded like jealousy. "I thought you liked him."

"What's not to like? He's young, good looking, educated,

single, born in a ranching family and he probably knows more about stock breeding than I do."

"You afraid he won't follow orders?"

"No, I'm afraid he'll follow you around like a lovesick calf."

She flattened her palms on the desk. "And because he's . . . what? Single? Young? Educated? Good looking? A cowboy? You think I might encourage him to follow me around? You think I might be attracted to him?"

"He'd be attracted to you, Tierney. Why don't you see that?"

It'd be counterproductive to point out that in her past, men like Tobin were never attracted to her, so she honestly hadn't noticed. "You think I'm the type of woman to switch horses midstream?"

"That's awful folksy comin' from Miz Two Hundred College Degrees, who mocks me for the barnyard references I use."

"Do you think now that I've rid myself of my virginity I'll start searching for other men to conquer?"

"No," he said crossly.

"Why don't you want to hire him?"

The muscle in his jaw flexed. Conflicting emotions flitted through his eyes and she feared he'd pull that incommunicative cowboy bullshit. But he didn't. "I want to hire him, okay? I just don't want you to look at him. Ever. I want you lookin' at me."

You sweet, stupid man. That confession turned her into goo. "You're the only man I've ever looked at like that. I'm with you. Only you. Even though no one else knows it, I know it, you know it, and that should be enough."

"It is." He gave her a wolfish grin. "But an old guy like me ain't opposed to hearin' that kinda sweet talk from his lady once in a while."

Old guy. Right. He had five whole years on her. "Mmm. I suppose to keep our cover after we hire him . . . I could even flirt with Tobin sometimes."

Renner snarled, "Don't make me kill him before you cut his first paycheck."

Tierney put her hands on his cheeks. "This jealous side of you is pretty hot."

"I'll show you hot. Step away from the desk and take off your panties."

That command . . . God. When he turned all growly cave-man on her? She instantly went wet and she didn't argue. Reaching beneath her pleated skirt, she freed herself of the plain white cotton.

He'd moved to rest on his haunches underneath her desk. "Pull up your skirt and sit on the edge of the chair."

"You can't be serious."

"I'm dead-ass serious, Tierney. Do it. Now."

The fabric scraped her bare butt as she shifted her balance forward. "Dammit, Renner, we didn't lock the door."

"I know." He bestowed a depraved grin. "No one will see me under here as long as you keep 'em by the door."

"And what if someone walks in right as I'm about to—"

"Come? Well, sweetness, you'd better come with a straight face, hadn't you?"

"You're impossible," she hissed. "This is a bad idea."

He traced her slit, then showed her the slickness on his thumb. "Oh, I beg to differ. You think this is a great idea. I'll bet your nipples are hard too."

Tierney's face flamed. "No, they're not."

"Will I make a liar out of you if I reach into your bra and check for myself?"

Don't answer.

"That's what I figured. Your body likes this edge of danger, no matter how much your pretty mouth protests. Hold on to the armrests." His mouth skimmed the top of her bikini line. His hands—she loved having those coarse hands on her skin—slipped up the inside of her thighs. He spread her open, exposing every intimate inch to his gaze. To his mouth. To his control.

He swirled the tip of his tongue around the folds of skin hiding her clit, parting his lips to awaken that bit of elusive flesh by sucking on it.

Tierney gnawed her lip and closed her eyes. Damn him. He was a drug. He'd turned her into an oral sex junkie.

Renner's tongue followed the curve of her sex down, past the drenched entrance to her pussy, past the tiny strip of skin that separated the two holes, stopping to lap her back door.

Every lower muscle—pussy, anal, stomach—tightened at that first wet swipe of his tongue. She gasped at the second swipe. Moaned at the third. "My God, you play dirty."

"You like the dirty stuff." The tip of his tongue circled her anus again. "Fair warning, I'll be shoving my cock up this sweet, tight hole one of these days."

She managed to grit out, "You really have time to give me a play-by-play of a future sexual encounter? Can't you focus on this one? Sort of exposed here."

His laughter vibrated against her sensitive tissues and goose bumps zipped up her spine. "You're just impatient for me to do this." He slipped a finger inside her. "And this." He licked her slit from where his finger moved in and out of her pussy to the top of her mound.

Tempting, to let her head fall back and lose herself in pleasure as he gorged on her.

Renner lifted his head. "Tierney, darlin', look at me. Look at yourself. You are so fucking amazing. Is it any wonder I'm obsessed with you?"

She glanced down. Her fingers were white from crushing the armrests. Her chest was actually heaving. Her legs were so tensed they were close to cramping.

"No one's gonna bother us. Janie won't show her face until we show ours, since she wants us in here, uninterrupted, making a decision." He kissed her thighs. Her lower belly. Her white knuckles. "You're sexy as all get-out. Enjoy this. Because I am enjoying the hell out of it. You're like some goddamn addiction." He opened his mouth over her clit and began those light tongue flutters that sent her off like a rocket.

She had to remind herself to breathe. "Renner, please—"

He growled and kept licking.

Three rapid knocks sounded and Janie walked in. "Sorry, but I have one other question—"

The top of Renner's head thunked underneath the desk. Tierney jerked as if she'd made the noise.

"Where's Renner?" Janie asked.

I'm riding his face.

"Tierney?"

"Ah. He's around here someplace."

He licked the crease of her thigh.

She gasped and her whole body writhed like a demented marionette when he blew a stream of air across her wet sex.

Janie started toward her, a look of concern on her face. "What is wrong with you?"

"Nothing! Don't come any closer. I—I think I might be coming . . . down with something."

"Oh. That sucks."

"I'm about to—" Renner settled his mouth over her clit and sucked, and she emitted a sound between a wheeze and a whimper. "Sneeze."

Janie began backing up. "I'll just come back later."

"Shut the door on your way o—oh my God." He did that swirling, suctioning thing with his lips. It felt so damn good she didn't care if the whole compound heard her get off.

About two seconds after the door slammed, Renner cranked up the intensity of his intimate kiss and Tierney flew apart. She didn't bother to keep quiet. She reveled in every throbbing pulse, every rhythmic suck from his eager mouth, every stroke of his rough hands on her bare flesh.

In short, she enjoyed the hell out of it.

Chapter Twenty-three

❧

$\mathcal{S}$now fell in big fluffy clumps outside her window. The holidays officially started next week with Thanksgiving, but this snow had that Christmas vibe. Made her think of eggnog and evergreens and cookies. Which was why Tierney was sneaking into the kitchen for one of Dodie's crispy molasses cookies to satisfy her sugar craving. Maybe she wouldn't be tempted to grab a jumbo bag of M&M's at the C-Mart to stave off her depression because Renner was gone for ten long days.

But as she tiptoed past the metal cooling racks, she heard someone crying. She reversed course and entered the prep area. Another sob sounded and she tracked the source to Dodie, leaning against the wall, unsuccessfully muffling her cries with a towel.

Alarmed, Tierney said, "Dodie? What's wrong? Are you hurt?"

White spots of flour dotted Dodie's blotchy face. "Oh. No. It's just . . ." Tears followed the deep grooves by her mouth and dripped off her chin.

Tierney heard Renner and Janie arguing in the dining room. About Dodie? Must be serious if Renner was still here. As gently as possible, she asked, "Did you burn the pies again?"

She wailed, "Worse. Way, way worse. When Janie hired me, I told her the only time I see my kids is over Thanksgiving. Every year I fly to Texas on the Wednesday before and come home the Monday after. Janie said it wouldn't be a problem. But today when I asked who was cooking the big meal next week and filling in for me the days I'm gone, she got mad. She didn't remember I'd asked for the time off and then said there's no way I can go with a lodge full of people here next week." More tears runneled down Dodie's cheeks. "I already bought my plane ticket. I love this job, but that's my family time. I'm probably gonna hafta quit."

So if they couldn't find a temporary replacement for Dodie, then they'd be looking for a permanent replacement. Tierney patted Dodie's arm. "We'll figure something out. Take a break."

Renner and Janie's argument ended abruptly when Tierney approached. "I'm hoping you're discussing cranberry sauce recipes for next week while Dodie's on vacation."

"Vacation?" Janie repeated derisively. "It'll be the first week of her unemployment, not a vacation."

"You are not gonna fire her to cover your own ass," Renner warned. "Why won't you admit you made a mistake?"

"I didn't make a mistake," she shot back. "Dodie did, thinking she could pull one over on us."

Tierney made the time-out sign. "It'll be a huge problem if we let Dodie walk. We need her. In case you haven't noticed, Muddy Gap doesn't have a huge employment pool to pull from."

Renner said, "Finally. The voice of reason."

Janie's gaze winged between them. "You two actually agree on something? I'd be flipping cartwheels if we weren't so seriously fucked. This just proves my point." Her voice dropped. "Dodie is manipulating us. If we give in this time, what happens at Christmas when she pulls the same crap?"

"You think Dodie, the woman who offered to repay us

for the pies she burned, is a master manipulator?" Tierney snickered. "If that's true, I'll eat my spreadsheet. With relish."

"For the record, I agree with Tierney," Renner said. "Dodie stays. However, we still have the problem of getting fifteen meals cooked while she's gone."

"Okay." Janie blew out a breath. "Maybe I overreacted. It's just everything is going along great and then something happens to throw a wrench into our plans. We've advertised the meal as a traditional dinner with all the trimmings. So I suppose if push came to shove, between me, Harper and Tierney, we could get something together."

Renner looked appalled—and he was looking directly at Tierney.

She poked him in the chest. "Not a word about my lack of culinary abilities, Mr. Jackson. Not. One. Word."

"I wouldn't dream of bringing it up, Miz Pratt," he drawled.

Janie frowned. "How do you know about Tierney's cooking skills?"

"I don't," he lied. "I guessed."

Tierney looked away from the mirth in his eyes. She'd tried to cook for him a few more times, always with disastrous results. But the suggestion about pitching in gave her a great idea. "I have to check on a couple of things, but I think I can get some of the meals for next week handled." This would be a true test of her people skills.

Renner and Janie exchanged a look. "When would you know the details?"

"Later this afternoon. Then we can figure out if we'll need a caterer to fill in the gaps."

"Sounds good to me," Janie said. "Renner? You trust us to handle this while you're gone?" She winked at Tierney. "If I don't allow Tierney in the kitchen?"

He nodded. "You did bring up a good point about Dodie. We need to get someone else in the kitchen working with her. Someone other than her cousin Lou-Lou. Someone who can fill in, if Dodie gets sick or something. So be on the lookout. Now apologize to Dodie, soothe her hurt feelings. Assure her that she'll still have her job when she gets back from her family vacation."

Janie saluted and marched to the kitchen.

As soon as Janie was out of sight, Renner towed Tierney around the corner. "Lookit you. Showing off your mad people management skills." He kissed the curve of her jaw. "It's a serious fuckin' turn-on."

"Everything is a turn-on for you, Renner."

"Definitely everything about you is." His mouth wandered. "Wish I had time to drag you into the closet for a quickie."

"Me too." She rubbed her cheek against his, loving the scratch of his whiskers against her skin. "I'm going to miss you."

Renner eased back and looked at her strangely.

"What?"

"Just surprised to hear that from you."

"Why? Because you think I'm calculating in business that I'd be that way in my personal relationship too?"

"So you're admitting we're in a relationship?"

"Yes." Paranoia made her blurt, "We are, right?"

"Definitely. I understand why we're keepin' it under wraps, but there are times, like now, when I'd really like . . ."

"You'd really like what?"

His eyes were oddly fierce for an instant before he smiled. "Never mind. It'll keep."

"Call me. Or text me. Be safe on the road, cowboy."

"Maybe one of these days I'll convince you to come along with me."

She smoothed a piece of hair from his damp forehead, then ran her finger along the brim of his hat. "Maybe one of these days, I'll surprise you and say yes."

"I'd like that. A whole helluva lot more than you know."

A pan dropped in the kitchen and they broke apart.

She closed her eyes, waiting until his boot steps faded

down the hall and the door slammed before she moved, because she couldn't watch him leave.

∾

Tierney looked forward to her appointment at Bernice's Beauty Barn. The regulars welcomed her like she belonged in Muddy Gap.

Bernice grinned. "You know the drill. Fresh coffee is on. Help yourself."

"Thanks." She poured a cup, adding a generous dollop of cream because Bernice's special brew was wicked strong.

Garnet patted the empty spot beside her. "Take a load off."

Tierney checked out Garnet's getup. A pink skirt resembling a tutu she'd pulled on over lime green leggings and topped off with a black leather shirt covered in chains. "Love the punk rock Tinkerbell look." If Tinkerbell wore orthopedic shoes.

"That's what I said," Pearl exclaimed. "Girl, we think exactly alike."

"Yes, Tierney, if you're always wondering what you've done with your car keys, or if you knock back a handful of pills with every meal, and you are glued to *Wheel of Fortune* every night, I'd agree, you and Pearl could be twins," Maybelle said dryly.

"Oh pooh, you're just pissy because you lost the bet."

Tierney said, "What bet?" the same time Garnet and Vivien said, "Don't ask!"

Pearl confided, "Maybelle bet me ten bucks I didn't have the guts to ask creepy Ralph at the C-Mart to rent a DVD of that porno flick, *Free My Willy.*" She giggled. "I did. She's sore because I got to watch it first last night."

"I only wanted to check it out for research," Maybelle clarified.

Vivien said, "So, Tierney, what's new up at the Split Rock?"

Here's your chance, don't blow it. "We're in a bit of a jam right now, to be honest."

"Anything we can do to help?" Garnet asked.

Bingo. "Yes, actually there is."

Even Bernice stopped snipping Tilda's hair to listen.

Tierney explained the mix-up with Dodie's vacation and needing expert cooks to fix the big Thanksgiving meal and a couple of smaller ones. The silence lingered after she finished speaking—nothing short of begging really—and she wondered if she'd made a judgment error. She didn't know these women. But after the last time she'd fueled their curiosity with stories about the Split Rock, she hoped they'd want a chance to be in the thick of things, instead of on the fringe.

Garnet spoke first. "Sugar, I've probably baked as many pies in my lifetime as Mrs. Smith. I'd love to help out. I have a recipe for maple nut pumpkin pie that'll knock your socks off."

"And Garnet's bourbon caramel bread pudding is heaven in a pan," Tilda said.

"Bob is always carting bird carcasses home," Bernice said. "I can cook six full-size turkeys at one time and not break a sweat. So count me in for the brining and roasting portion of the meal."

"And Bernice's sage, mushroom and bacon stuffing is legendary around here," Tilda announced.

Vivien mused, "I've perfected six holiday side dishes that straddle the line between traditional and gourmet. Pearl onions in a balsamic honey glaze, sweet and sour green beans, a cold broccoli salad with sunflower seeds and dried cranberries, a rice pilaf with roasted vegetables, sweet potato soufflé and gingered carrots."

"I tell ya, Vivien should've had her own restaurant, that's how good she is." Tilda added, "Make sure Dodie makes her cranberry, apple, orange and horseradish relish before she leaves. You've never had anything quite like it."

"I'll handle the mashed potatoes and gravy," Maybelle said.

Everyone looked at Tilda.

"What?"

"We're just waiting for you to brag on Maybelle's spuds," Vivien said.

"The problem with Maybelle's potatoes and gravy is there's never any left over."

Pearl said, "That covers the food. I'm so-so with cooking, but I'm good at cleaning up and I'm an excellent gopher. So that'll be my contribution."

Tierney was truly choked up at their show of generosity. She'd hoped, but she'd never expected total enthusiasm and grace. "You have no idea how much this means."

Garnet rubbed Tierney's back. "It's our pleasure to help out. That's what a community does. Pulls together when someone's in need."

"I—I don't know what to say."

"Never been part of a community before?" Vivien asked.

Tierney shook her head and discreetly dabbed her tears.

"It ain't always sunshine and roses. There are real piles of shit around here, but by and large, we're good folks."

"I see that. Anything I can do, or the Split Rock can do for you all, just let me know."

The pointed, amused and downright hopeful looks they sent one another caused a frisson of concern, but Tierney figured it wasn't anything she couldn't handle.

"Well, funny you should mention that . . . because the girls and I were talking about this very thing, just the other day."

∞

"They want a what?" Janie demanded.

"A community party." Tierney sipped her wine. "In the dining room. It has a sound system for the dance. They'll provide the food. It'll be BYOB. All's we have to provide is the event space and the cowboys."

Janie froze. "No. You did *not* promise them cowboys, did you?"

"I didn't promise them a lot of cowboys, nor did I specify the ages or marital status of said cowboys, but I didn't think it'd be a big deal to track some down. After all, we are in Wyoming."

Groaning, Janie slapped her own forehead. "You weren't at Harper's bachelorette party, were you?"

"No. Why?"

"Because that gang from Bernice's might look like sweet innocent women of a certain age, but my God, they are absolutely wild underneath those pastel twinsets, floral house-dresses and support hose. It's scary, Tierney. They outdrank me, they outdanced me, and they sure as hell outlasted me. I woke up, hungover, with a note pinned to my shirt that said, 'Next time, pace yourself so you don't poop out so early.'"

Tierney laughed. "Buck up because you will be there, smiling that charming dimpled smile of yours, finding them two-step partners all night long if that's what it takes. Because we would've been seriously screwed if not for them volunteering their cooking time last week."

The Thanksgiving Day meal had been a huge hit with the guests, and every couple rebooked their reservations for the following year. The rest of the weekend had been a breeze.

Janie's eyes turned sharp. "Have you spoken to Renner about this community night with the senior set?"

"No. It'll be a surprise when he gets back." She glanced at the clock. Which should be any time now—not that she was anxious. Okay. She was chomping at the bit to see him again. They'd spent hours on the phone every night during his sojourn on the blacktop. She found him easy to talk to, and it really thrilled her they hadn't discussed the Split Rock much at all. In retelling some of his stories, he'd had her laughing so hard she had to clutch her stomach. But they'd also discussed other things, places they'd been, movies, TV, friends. The sweetest thing? He'd picked out a few romance novels from an online bookstore and had them delivered to her, with a suggestion she earmark the good parts for them to try when he got back. So it was ironic that by not seeing him for ten days, Tierney knew him better than she had before he'd left.

"Don't even think about asking me to do your dirty work," Janie warned. "You get to fill him in on all of this."

"I'll shoulder full responsibility. How do you think he'll take the news that the ladies specifically requested him as one of their cowboys?"

"Tierney, you are so dead." Janie's critical gaze swept the room. "Can I have your half of the office after he kills you?"

"Renner's a smart guy. He'll be gracious to the saviors who pulled our asses out of the fire. Besides, I'm putting him in charge of rounding up other cowboys to invite to this soiree, because if he doesn't? His dance card will be full. All night."

Janie shook her head. "I'm formally putting in my request for your shoe collection too. Dead women have no need of Christian Louboutin peep-toe pumps."

"I'm sure Abe will have fun."

"You're asking Abe to come?"

"No. You are."

"Dammit, Tierney, that's not fair."

Obviously Janie didn't want to share Abe even with the senior set. Too bad. Tierney smirked. "If it makes you feel better, I'm making Harper bring Bran."

∞

Renner pulled into the Split Rock at two a.m. He parked behind his trailer and forced himself to drag his suitcase inside. The place was freezing-ass cold so he cranked the heat and showered and shaved quickly. He unearthed a pair of clean jeans from his dresser and pulled on a long-sleeved T-shirt. It'd be torture to put his boots back on after wearing them for the sixteen-hour drive. But with ten plus inches of snow, slipping on a pair of flip-flops to sneak over to Tierney's cabin wasn't an option.

Tierney. He'd missed her. Despite being so damn busy over the last ten days, he'd managed to talk to her every day. It was weird how easily they'd meshed. How much he looked forward to hearing her voice every night. Listening to her opinions and her offbeat way of looking at things.

He'd sent her a few trinkets he thought she'd get a kick out of. Not to mention they'd exchanged some red-hot text messages. But there was nothing like the real thing, having her eager, wet and wrapped around him completely.

He trudged across the moonlit snow to her cabin. The lights were off. He used his key and stepped inside. Even in the darkness a feeling of peace settled over him. He checked the sofa, making sure she hadn't fallen asleep, like she had so many nights after working until the wee hours because her father was a damn slave driver.

At the foot of her bed, he took a second to drink in the sight of her sleeping on her stomach, sheets twined around her naked limbs.

Oh hell yeah. She'd slept nekkid as a welcome home present for him. If he wasn't so goddamn desperate for her, he'd wake her up slowly and sweetly. He stripped and crawled over her, skating his palms up the backs of her arms, threading their fingers together. Burying his face in the spot between her neck and shoulder, bathing his lungs with her scent.

She stirred. Flexed her fingers. Wiggled her ass. "Renner?"

"Were you expectin' someone else?"

"Well, Tobin—"

"Is a dead man if he's ever been in your bedroom," he growled and sank his teeth into the section of skin on her nape that almost brought her to orgasm.

Tierney reared up and her body shuddered beneath his.

Renner canted his hips, sliding his erection up and down the crack of her ass as he used his mouth on her neck. He inhaled the musky sweet fragrance of her hair as he continued to rock into her. He scattered kisses behind her ear. Following the curve with the barest tip of his tongue. Each pass made her writhe and shudder.

In a graceful, catlike move, Tierney slid back, keeping her arms and chest on the bed as she pushed to her knees and allowed enough space for him to slide in behind her.

She'd come to know him so well and loved to anticipate

his needs, even as she verbalized hers. Had he ever had this kind of connection with a woman? Not only in bed, but also out of it?

His cock was in his hand, nudging her pussy and he impaled her.

She expelled a moan and arched.

Gripping her butt cheeks, he watched his cock tunnel in and out of her juicy sex. Mesmerizing as it was, seeing those pink tissues part to take him, he wanted a skin-to-skin connection with her. His hands smoothed over her lower back, her middle back, up her shoulders to circle her wrists.

He flexed his pelvis. Pulled out and slammed back in.

Ten days away from daily sex and his stamina suffered—he was getting close, but evidently so was she. He drove her higher with hot, openmouthed kisses and the slight scrape of his teeth to the side of her neck. Whispering in her ear to give it up, to let go, taking her to that point where her body finally answered the mating call of his. Satisfied their mutual need.

Her hands clenched into fists on the mattress and she released a keening wail. Her pussy squeezed his cock with enough force to stop his thrusting as her orgasm overtook her.

Somehow he kept it together until the last pulse. He pulled out, rolled her onto her back and plowed into her. He craved this closeness, her legs around his waist, her fingers digging into his ass, her scent on his skin and filling his lungs. In that perfect moment, Renner buried his face against her neck, and let go.

Before his dick stopped twitching, his mouth sought hers. He kissed her with the tenderness his body hadn't been able to offer, aware, maybe for the first time, that Tierney gave him something he hadn't known he'd lacked.

Neither seemed eager to break the kiss or the connection of their bodies. But Renner suspected he was crushing her. He lifted his head. Smiled at her. Swept a hank of hair behind her ear. "Hey."

"You sneak in here in the middle of the night, fuck me like a man possessed and all you can say to me is . . . hey?"

"Hey . . . I missed you?"

She smiled sassily. "That's better."

He kissed the corners of her eyes, the bridge of her nose, her cheeks, her chin. "You're beautiful."

"Renner. You don't have to—"

"I want to. Because when I see you every day I take that beauty for granted. When ten days go by without seein' you? I realize I oughta tell you that more often." He kissed the soft set of her mouth. "So I am telling you, Tierney. You're beautiful."

She didn't play coy. She rested her forehead to his and said, "Thank you."

"Now go back to sleep."

"So this was a dream?"

"Dream my ass." He rolled her over and smacked her left butt cheek as he put his mouth on her right cheek and gave her a big hickey.

"Renner! I can't believe you did that."

As his gaze traveled up her curves covered in all that beautifully smooth skin, he had another primal urge to mark her all over. Prove she was his.

So he did just that.

As he stumbled back to his trailer two hours later, he wondered why Tierney never asked him to stay.

Chapter Twenty-four

❧

*A*be had been helping out at the Split Rock, keeping an eye on Tobin, the new hired hand, while Renner was out of town. Although he strolled into the barn early—he didn't beat the kid there. Kid knew how to work, he'd give him that much.

Kid. Right. He wasn't a kid. Which reminded Abe that at Tobin's age, he had already been running a successful ranch operation for a couple of years. He'd already been married. And divorced.

"Hey, Abe. I thought you were Renner."

Abe faced him. "Nope. Although I see his rig is parked in front of his trailer this mornin'."

"He got back late. But I wasn't sure if he'd want me to go ahead and feed the stock like I've been doing, or if there are things he'd rather do himself. I also kept track of everything I did last week, so you can double-check it and see if Renner would rather have me working in another area—"

"Tobin. Slow down. It's early yet and I've barely sucked down my first cup of coffee."

"Sorry. I'm just . . . nervous." Tobin took off his brown and gold University of Wyoming ball cap, ran his hand over his dark head and put the cap back on. "I've been around ranches and cattle my whole life but I feel like a freakin' idiot compared to you and Renner."

That shocked the crap out of Abe. "Yeah? How's that? Because *I* wonder why you're toiling in a barn with a master's degree in reproductive biology."

Tobin mimicked Abe's posture on the opposite side of the support post. "Because I'm the third son of a rancher. My two older brothers were running the ranch by the time I'd started high school. And when I graduated from college, raring to bring my 'new' knowledge back to the ranch, Dad and my brothers saw nothin' wrong with the way they'd been doin' things. So I checked around to see how much education I'd need to get into commercial stockbreeding programs. Or what the state requirements were for ag positions. A master's degree was optional, but it wasn't like I had a job offer to mull over, so I stayed in school. I received my master's in May. I've applied a couple places but the economy is tight around here."

"What about elsewhere?"

He held Abe's gaze. "I never wanted to live anywhere besides Wyoming. It's not like I haven't traveled. I spent part of last year in Brazil learning about their cattle industry. But the bottom line hasn't changed. My family doesn't need or want my help on the ranch. So I'd rather work as a ranch hand, doin' what I love, than get stuck doing something I don't, because my dad thought I'd be better off educated." Tobin sipped his coffee. "Honest enough for you, Abe?"

He laughed. "Yeah."

"What about you?"

"Do I have a college degree?"

"No, I'm curious about the cattle operation you're running with your brother. Rumor is that the Lawson and Turner operations are the successful ones and have been for years when others failed."

Abe shrugged. "We do all right. Why?"

"You're younger than my oldest brother. I wondered if you stick to doin' everything the same way your family did? Or if you're open to new ideas in the ag industry?"

Here was a guy who despite his advanced college degree wants exactly what you've already got: a life as a Wyoming rancher.

"Sorry, man. Forget it. Sometimes I get a little gung ho about stuff."

"It's okay. Just tryin' to . . ." Abe sighed. "Look. I graduate from UWYO next week with a bachelor's in agricultural business."

Tobin's eyes widened. "No shit? That's great! I'll bet you don't have a problem with *your* brother accusing you of thinking you're all hot shit and stuff because of your Ag degree."

"That's the thing. No one knows I've been goin' to school." His eyes flashed a warning. "No one. Not my family. Not my friends."

"Janie?"

"No."

"Why would you keep that a secret?"

"I wasn't sure I'd ever graduate. Some of them classes . . ." He shook his head. "I've been running things my way since I was nineteen. I implemented a few changes while my brother was bullfighting. When Hank came back, he never suggested I was dumb for doin' things differently. Since I've put some of what I've learned in college into practical application, our cattle operation sustains two families, instead of one."

"See? That is the reason you should be touting your degree to your family, Abe. I wish I could use you as an example to my brothers about how progress can work in conjunction with tradition."

Abe had made up his mind to tell his family . . . after the ceremony. After he had the diploma in his hand for sure.

The door slammed. They both glanced at Renner.

"Look what the cat dragged in," Abe drawled.

"Fuck off, Lawson. You can go. Don't let the door hit your ass on the way out."

Abe chuckled. "This is the thanks I get? Fine. Ain't like I don't have plenty of my own shit to do." Renner stopped beside him and Abe gave him a once over. "No offense, but you look like hell."

"That's what life on the road and nights with no sleep will do to ya." Renner swigged from his insulated mug. "Thanks for your help, Abe. I do appreciate it."

"You're welcome. Need anything else, just holler." He pushed away from the post. Tempting to swing by Janie's office, but he had a shitload of stuff to do. Including study.

"Hey, Lawson," Tobin yelled. "Remember what we talked about. Tell her. It's important."

Abe waved him off. But the kid had planted the seed.

∾

"What was that about?" Renner asked testily.

"Just picking his brain about a couple of things. The Lawsons run a top-notch cattle company from what I understand."

"You thinking about jumping ship and goin' to work for Abe and Hank?"

Tobin shook his head. "No, sir. We were just talking. Old-school thinking in ranching versus new-school thinking. I like talking to him. He's not so set in his ways, like my family is. He's a smart man."

"Yes, he is. But in light of your obvious Abe worship, I should tell you, that as much as I need your help around here as a hired hand and bellhop, if you're serious about using your degree, I could use your expertise in setting up a breeding program. 'Course, that'll be down the road a piece. But I wanted you to be aware of my long-term plans."

"No shit?"

"No shit. I've also been thinkin' lately about raising organic beef. Some guys I've known for a while have gotten into it and they swear it's less work and more money." Renner managed a smile. "I'm all about that."

Tobin nodded. "And it's not like you don't have the grazing areas." The kid launched into a long-winded explanation about natural grasses that made Renner's eyes cross. But he wasn't sure that wasn't from being so goddamned tired.

He felt Tobin looking at him expectantly. "Sounds like you've been doin' a little research on the land around Split Rock."

"Here and there. Tierney's been very helpful."

It was all Renner could do not to grab Tobin by the throat and have him define *helpful*.

"Whoa. Boss. I know that look and it's not like that. Not at all. Tierney is hot as hell in that brainy-girl way, and if she wasn't . . . well, I might've been willing to take a crack at her—"

Renner snarled.

"But I'm not the type to poach, okay?" Tobin half cringed. "Jesus, don't tear my limbs off after I've finally found a job I like."

The jealous haze cleared. He bit off, "Explain poach."

Tobin's cheeks colored, but he kept his gaze steady. "I know you and Tierney are involved."

Renner froze. Had she been confiding in Tobin while he was gone?

"Look, I don't need a lot of sleep, so I'm up late. I've seen you goin' to Tierney's, seen you coming back from there in the early morning hours. Seen you shoveling her walkway early every morning."

"Woman would break her neck in them damn high heels she always wears, if I didn't," Renner muttered.

"Last night after you got home that was the first place you went. And man, I don't blame you."

He snarled again.

"No, no, not what I meant," Tobin backtracked. "I meant I don't blame you guys for keeping it under wraps."

"Well, fuck. Doesn't sound like it's under wraps."

"Near as I can tell, no one knows besides me."

"Let's keep it that way."

"Done." Tobin opened his mouth. Closed it.

"For Christsake, what now?"

"Why doesn't Tierney ever come to your place?"

Damn kid brought up the very question he'd been asking himself. Why was he always crawling out of her bed and schlepping himself home? Be nice if she'd spend a few nights at his place. He had to get up a helluva lot earlier than she did.

Does she think she's too good to bang you in a cheap trailer?

"Shit. Sorry I said anything. Never mind."

Renner sighed. "I don't know why. Haven't really thought about it much." *Liar.* "Now that we're done shooting the shit, how about if we get them bulls fed?"

He spent the rest of the day in a foul mood.

He should've been happy that everything had run so smoothly at the Split Rock in his absence.

He should've been happy Wild West Clothiers sales had doubled the projections.

He should've been happy the lodge was full for the next two weeks, but he wasn't.

None of it made him happy.

Renner ate lunch alone at his desk. When Tierney blew in like a wet dream, wearing a skintight black sweater dress, red patent fuck-me heels, and a *do me big daddy* smile, he barely said two words to her before he bailed. He wasn't in the mood for company. He definitely wasn't in the mood to lock the door and have a quickie. He considered hopping in his truck—gee, wouldn't that be a blast, because it wasn't like he hadn't just spent the last ten goddamn days on the road.

Why don't you sneak a pint of ice cream, pop The Proposal *into the DVD player and curl up in your bed like a girl? Because you're sure as fuck acting like one.*

Wrong. He didn't have time to wallow.

Isn't that what's eating at you? You left to check on your stock contracting company and found it's in good hands? Maybe better than when you were running it full-time? And you get back here and find out you're not needed here, either?

Not needed my ass. There was always plenty of shit that needed done. So he returned to the barn, determined to sort through the tack.

The radio provided distraction from his self-pitying thoughts. He nailed up a new section of pegboard and had nearly cleared all the ropes, bridles and halters off the ground when he heard, "Knock, knock."

Renner shot Tierney a look over his shoulder. Yep. She still wore that sexy-assed getup, including the stilettos. "I'da thought you woulda learned your lesson about wearin' them kinda shoes out here."

Tierney blinked at him.

"Something you need?" he asked shortly.

"Have I done something wrong?"

"Doubtful. Why?"

"Seems like you're mad at me."

"Nope."

She tiptoed closer. "I don't believe you."

He shrugged and untwisted a section of rope.

"Renner? Why won't you even look at me?"

Sighing, he faced her. "I have stuff to do after bein' gone for ten fuckin' days, so if you've got something specific to talk to me about, spit it out."

That put starch in her spine. "I wasn't aware I had to make an appointment to talk to you."

"I wasn't aware you had business in the barn. Unless you were here lookin' for Tobin to help him out with some more research."

He was being a dick. He knew it. She knew it. But for some reason Renner couldn't stop it. He just kept working, hoping she'd take the hint.

"Fine. I'll go since you're in a lousy mood. But will I see you later tonight?"

"I'll be at the lodge after supper to meet the guests."

"That's not what I meant. Will you be coming to my place after that?"

Renner shook out a halter from the pile. "Probably not."

Silence. Then, "Why not?"

He whirled around. "Why don't you ever come over to my place, Tierney? Not once in all the times we've been fucking around have you ever offered. I always have to be the one to haul my ass out of your bed and go home in the cold. Did you ever consider that I'd like to be in my own bed sometimes?"

Her stark expression indicated she hadn't considered it, but immediately she rallied with, "No need to snap at me."

"Do you know how nice it would've been to have you waiting for me for a change last night? Especially after I spent sixteen grueling hours on the road? But no. I had to go to you. And then, I got exactly two hours of sleep before I had to get up and start chores this morning. So, yeah, I'm snappy because I'm freakin' tired, okay?"

"You didn't have to come over last night. I knew you'd be tired. I would've understood."

"I'm thrilled you're so understanding. I know my crappy rental isn't as nice as your cabin or what you're used to—"

"Don't go there, Renner."

"Why not? It's obvious *you* won't go there, and by there, I mean you won't lower yourself to cross my humble tin threshold."

"You're being an ass."

He snorted. "Like that's news to you."

Tierney's cell phone trilled. She was torn for two rings. Then she pulled it out and answered angrily, "This is Tierney Pratt," as she walked off.

Chapter Twenty-five

⨯

*P*ompous prick.

How was she supposed to know this stuff about sleeping arrangements? Had the man forgotten she'd been a virgin until recently?

Tierney had no precedent for this and she'd had no clue it bothered Renner so much.

Wouldn't it bother you?

Yes. But the idiot had still hurt her feelings. Reverting to the dick-ish behavior that defined their previous relationship. She'd gotten pissed and walked off. So technically, they'd both regressed.

Fantastic. What was she supposed to do now? Show up on his doorstep wrapped in cellophane with a bow on her freakin' head?

She huddled in her coat against the side of the building. It sucked she didn't have anyone she could talk to. Harlow would ask if she was involved with Renner to spite their father. Her friend Josie's longtime boyfriend had recently dumped her. Sari would encourage her to meditate to find an answer. Celia must've been on a winning streak because she wasn't returning Tierney's calls. Janie . . . nope.

On a whim, she ducked the wind and breezed into Wild West Clothiers. Harper looked up with surprise. "Tierney. What brings you by?"

"Nothing in particular. I, ah . . . to be honest, I needed a mental break, so I might just wander and see what's new."

"Let me know if you have any questions. I'll be unpacking in the back."

From the beginning Tierney questioned the wisdom of a dedicated retail space to sell specialized merchandise. She'd even suggested increasing the size of the art gallery and keeping the Western wear section small.

Which showed she wasn't always right. They'd sold only two pieces out of the art gallery and the retail store flourished. Harper had a great eye for detail, for design, for creating the shabby chic vibe many tried, but few could pull off. Between her and Janie, they'd turned the space into a retro, funky, Western place where both men and women would feel comfortable shopping. Harper had pushed for a men's section, pointing out that not all men came to the Split Rock with a female. Wise suggestion, since Harper had sold a pair of boots to almost every man who'd walked through the door.

Tierney scanned the blouses. Cute or sexy but none her style. As much as she loved the flash of rhinestone belts, not her style either. Harper had amassed an amazing assortment of handbags. Every style from ones fashioned out of old license plates, to ones crafted from old vinyl records, to ones studded with vintage bottle caps, to leather and hide ones dotted with brass nail heads and beads.

"Finding anything?" Harper asked, startling her.

"There's a lot to choose from. You've done a fantastic job setting this place up."

"Thanks. I love my job. But I love my job a little too much sometimes."

Tierney rested her arm on a clothing rack. "And how's that?"

"I have more merchandise packed away because there's

no place to put it on the floor. I intentionally keep some back to rotate in new stock, but I wish I had more room." She pointed to the gallery. "It'd be a better use of space to display the Western art in the hallways, at the lodge and dining area, and expand the retail store."

"You think so?"

Harper nodded, twisting her wedding ring. "I hope this doesn't smack of nepotism, but Bran ties flies." At Tierney's confused look, she explained, "Ties, for fly fishing? He's truly an artist. When I've worn a pair of decorative earrings he's crafted out of funky flies, female customers demand to know where I got them. Then male customers want to know where they can buy real ties like those. Which leads me to believe there's an opportunity to sell handcrafted Wyoming items."

Intrigued, Tierney asked, "What types of items?"

"A woman outside of Laramie makes soy and beeswax candles. They're beautifully packaged in glass jars and the scents are to die for. Another woman in Rawlins designs the most unique wire jewelry I've ever seen. A husband and wife team from Sheridan raises sheep. The wife spins, dyes and weaves stunning decorative items out of the wool. There's a company outside of Moorcroft called Sky Blue that manufactures all-natural beauty products."

When Tierney didn't immediately respond, Harper blurted, "I'm sorry if I've overstepped my boundaries telling you what to do."

"You haven't. I'm happy you've given this so much thought. You're on to something, Harper. Something big."

Her eyes lit up. "You can't possibly know what that means to hear you say that."

"I think I do," she murmured. Just once she'd like to have that same type of "atta girl" from her boss.

"Anyway, what were you looking for when you came in?"

"Something I wouldn't normally wear, but not so far out of the realm of my normal style that I'd feel weird wearing it." She sighed. "Sounds vague, doesn't it?"

"No." Harper looked thoughtful. "I'll be right back." She

was gone maybe two minutes and returned with a wad of red fabric. "I found this last week. It's retro, but not Western, so I wasn't sure what to do with it." She fluffed out the dress and Tierney's breath caught.

The style was a 1940s glam cocktail dress. The upper half was velvet and boasted a keyhole neckline. Long sleeves made from chiffon ended at the wrist with a tiny satin band. A shirred piece of chiffon separated the velvet top from the bottom. The fitted satin skirt ended below the knee, and a ruffle of red netting finished off the dress.

"This is gorgeous. My God. It's—"

"Perfect for you. For the community Christmas party."

Tierney glanced at Harper. "You think so?"

"It's red. It's sexy. It's totally you. And my former clients will be dancing the cha-cha, seeing you in this dress."

"Really? Why?"

"They'll feel you went all out, in every aspect, to make sure the party is a special event. Because make no mistake, this party means the world to them."

"Oh, you're good, Harper. Very good."

"Thank you."

"How much?"

Harper bit her lip.

"No discounts," Tierney warned. "Pretend I walked in off the street, saw this and had to have it. How much?"

When Harper rattled off the amount, Tierney raised her eyebrows. "That's . . . not discounted at all."

"It's vintage Chanel couture. I found it at an estate sale in Colorado in a box of draperies we bought for our house. When I got home I researched it, and wished I was six inches shorter, thirty pounds lighter, and two dress sizes smaller because I would've kept it. But it's ideal for you."

"I love it. I can't wait to try it on."

"I can't wait to see the look on Renner's face when he sees you. He'll be speechless."

How could Harper know about them? Casually, Tierney said, "What makes you think he'll care?"

"Because you annoy him."

She stared at her.

Harper laughed. "No one annoys Renner. Nothing fazes him. But you? You faze him."

She'd certainly done a bang-up job of annoying him today.

Harper headed to the dressing room. "I'll get started on writing up the sale while you're trying this on."

"Give me time to call the bank so I can take out a loan," Tierney said.

"It'll be worth every penny." Harper's eyes were on Tierney's feet. "Do you have the right shoes? Because I have a pair in the back that might work."

"Oh, you are good, Harper. Very good. Bring them into the dressing room."

Chapter Twenty-six

≈

The impromptu shopping trip bolstered Tierney's spirits and vastly improved her mood.

She wasn't sure how to fix the Renner situation. She'd watched him covertly as he'd spent the evening mingling with the guests. Knocking back a drink. Shooting pool. Giving her no chance to talk to him.

Actions speak louder than words anyway.

A lightbulb pinged in her head and she knew exactly what to do. Ten minutes before last call, she snuck into his trailer. His bed was neatly made and she felt no guilt whatsoever about stripping down to the bare essentials and messing it up.

But as she waited in the pitch dark, she wondered if she'd made a mistake. Given what'd been going on with Janie, maybe Renner kept guns strategically located in case of an intruder.

With that thought, Tierney threw back the covers and raced into the living room, just as Renner stepped through the front door.

"Tierney?"

"Hey. Ah . . . surprise! I was in your room, but got a little paranoid you might shoot me. I'm never sure who's packing heat out here. I think even docile Dodie has a pistol in her purse."

Renner snorted and hung up his coat. As he removed his boots, he flicked a glance at the bloodred platform heels on her feet. "You were wearing them shoes in my bed?"

"No."

He rested his hands on his hips. "Okay. I give. Why are you half-nekkid in my house at ten o'clock at night?"

Wasn't it obvious why she was here?

That's when Tierney realized Renner expected she'd take control. If she'd truly come here to seduce him, she'd better prove it.

Despite her nerves, she put on her game face. She permitted a sexy smile, adding an extra swing in her hips as she sashayed to him. "Maybe I'd better show you why I'm here." She fingered his black neckerchief. An idea formed. "This is handy. Untie it."

His too-blue eyes gleamed a challenge. "Whatcha gonna do with it, darlin'?"

She tugged on the knotted end. "Take it off or I will."

An amused smile lifted the corner of his mouth as he untied it and handed it over.

Looping the fabric around his neck, she pulled him into the center of the room. "Stay right here. Don't move."

Tierney felt his hungry gaze eating up her backside. She'd worn a deeply cut push-up bra in bright red, pairing it with red-and-black lace boy-short panties. At his dining room set, she purposely bent over the chair—the panties rode up, giving him a peek of her butt cheeks.

He groaned.

Empowered, she picked up the chair and moved it into the living room. Taking his hands in hers, she placed his palms facing up. She unsnapped his cuffs, following his muscled arms over his broad shoulders to the collar of his Western shirt. *Click* sounded as she released the first pearl snap button. She kissed the exposed section of skin below the hollow of his throat and popped the next button. And the next, rubbing her face against the warm firmness of his chest. When the shirt hung open, she allowed her hands to roam.

God. He was so built. She touched the ridges of his hard abdomen. She curled her fingers over his rib cage, spreading her hands beneath his pectorals to brush her thumbs across his nipples. The hair on his chest was darker than the golden hair on his head. Coarser too. While she kissed his collarbone, she pulled his shirt off and tossed it to the floor.

Gooseflesh dotted Renner's arms and his whole body remained rigid.

Oh, this was fun. She whispered huskily, "Jeans off. Boxers too." Then she stepped away to see if he'd obey.

Renner lifted a brow. "You're serious?"

Tierney lifted a brow right back at him. "Do it now or I leave."

His clothes came off so fast she wanted to check his skin for fabric burns.

My my. He was already hard. A rush of feminine power rolled through her. Strengthened her resolve. She smiled and gave his impressive body a slow inspection. "Nice. Very, very nice. Now. You get to pick. Eyes or hands."

"Eyes or hands what?"

"One word or the other. Choose."

"Fine. Hands."

"Excellent choice." She picked up his neckerchief. "Sit and drop your arms around the back of the chair."

His nostrils flared. "You think you're tyin' my hands?"

"Oh, cowboy, I *know* I'm tying your hands. Unless you want me to leave?"

"Like hell." Renner flopped onto the chair and held his hands at the base of the rungs. Then his eyes lit with mischief and the corner of his sinful mouth quirked.

Tierney tied one end of the neckerchief around his right wrist and wove the fabric through the chair slats before securing the other end around his left wrist with a tight knot. When she stood in front of him, his cocky smirk was gone.

"You think cowboys are the only ones who can tie strong knots?"

"And if I would've said eyes?"

"I would've blindfolded you."

"Dammit, Tierney."

"Don't pout. You'll get to use your hands. Later. For now? I get to use mine." Placing her hands on his shoulders, she swung her leg over his to sit on his lap.

The muscles in Renner's arms flexed as he tried to free himself to touch her.

"Huh-uh. Now be a good boy." She felt his dick twitch against her belly. "Oh and get comfy. Because this might take a while."

Renner muttered.

Tierney threaded her fingers through his hair and kissed the frown lines on his forehead. Lightly placed her lips to his eyebrows. The corners of his eyes. His temples. The small section of flesh in front of his ear. When he shivered, she spent extra time nibbling, sucking and softly blowing on his ears.

The man actually whimpered.

So she gave the other ear the same shiver-inducing treatment.

"Tierney."

"Mmm. This jawline of yours is so strong and sexy." She followed the angular bone from side to side, stopping at the halfway point to tongue the dent in his chin.

Mr. Sneaky dropped his head so their mouths connected. Taking advantage of her surprise by sweeping his tongue into her mouth and scorching her lips with one of his fiery kisses.

She let the kiss go on, because she loved kissing him. But she also wanted Renner to think he'd gotten her so flustered that he was about to wrest control from her.

Wrong.

This seduction was powerful stuff. Electrifying. Maybe even addicting. She craved the crush of his body to hers and the moment when he sent her soaring into pure bliss, but she would not be rushed. By her body's demands or his.

"Tierney," he muttered against her mouth, "baby, untie me. I'm dyin' to touch you."

"Really?"

"Yes."

"Okay."

"Thank God."

She slid back on his thighs, keeping her balance by pushing the arches of the bottom of her shoes into the legs of the chair. She reached behind to unfasten her bra.

His eyes narrowed. "What are you doin'?"

"You said you wanted to touch me. Your mouth on my nipples counts as touching, don't you think?"

"You are gonna be in so much . . ."

Surprise surprise, the man lost his train of thought when her naked breasts were on display. She unhooked her feet from the chair rungs and stood, straddling him.

Tierney gripped his shoulders. She lowered her chest, letting her left nipple brush the seam of his lips. Then changing the angle so the right nipple made the same slow pass. She whispered, "Touch me. Use your tongue."

Renner's teasing licks were fleeting. He sucked her nipple hard; exacting the perfect amount of suction as his tongue rapidly flicked the tip. Tierney's head fell back and she gave herself over to him. To the heat and wetness of his mouth.

He nuzzled the lower curves of her breast. "Untie me. I wanna stick my fingers inside you and see how wet you are." Soft kisses around the outside of her nipple. "I can smell that sweet cream, Tierney. Baby. Let me touch it. Let me taste it."

She pushed back and stepped in front of the chair.

Heat darkened his light blue eyes into flashing pools of pure black.

"You know, I was going to spend a little time playing

with your nipples, but I'll save that for next time since I've got bigger fish to fry."

Renner groaned when she dropped to her knees.

"Just think how long I can drag this out. Taking you to the very edge. Again and again. And you can't use your hands to shove your cock into my throat when you're impatient to come. I can savor you. I'll feel your tension build as you're waiting for me to take you all the way in my mouth." Tierney scraped her nails up the tops of his thighs.

His whole body shuddered.

"You can't grab on to my hair. You can't stop me from doing this." She used the very tip of her tongue to touch the sweet spot below the head of his cock. "Or this."

"Untie me," he said hoarsely.

"No." She locked her gaze to his and suckled the plump head. "You know how hot it was to give you a blow job that first night? Did you know I had no idea what I was doing?"

"No. It was amazing. You're amazing. Beyond amazing."

She tossed out, "Damn sugar mouth. Always gets you what you want," since he loved saying that to her. She drew his shaft in, closing her eyes, losing herself in that wonderful male hardness gliding over her tongue. Making her wet and achy. She sucked until the inside of her cheeks enclosed his cock completely.

"Fuck."

She released a bit of flesh at a time, keeping the suction steady until the tip popped out of her mouth. "I love this. I love everything about this. Mostly the reaction I get out of you." Tierney sucked his cock to the back of her throat and began bobbing her head faster, digging her nails into his quads, bringing him closer to release with each rhythmic suck.

When he swore again and began bumping his pelvis up to meet the downward stroke of her mouth, she pulled off him. Stood and wiped her swollen lips.

"Untie me," he demanded.

"No."

He swore. "Untie me . . . please."

Tierney laughed. "Better. But no."

"Jesus Christ, Tierney. You're killin' me. I want to touch you. I *need* to touch you. Untie me."

"No. But I will do this." She shimmied out of her underwear. "And this." She straddled his groin, rehooking her heels into the bottom chair rungs. "And I'll definitely do this." She circled the base of his cock with her hand and drove it into her slick passage with one downward push.

"Fuck. Fuck. Fuck."

Tierney watched his eyes glaze over. Felt him clenching and unclenching his fists as she curled her hands around his biceps. She rocked her hips forward as she moved up and down in a long delicious slide. As much as she wanted to kiss him, she liked seeing his response. But being a newbie at this seduction game, she wasn't entirely confident it was good for him. She put her mouth on his ear. "Am I doing this right?"

He released a strangled laugh. "I wouldn't survive if you did it any better." He turned his head and dragged a hot openmouthed kiss down the cord in her throat. "Do what feels good for you. Make yourself come. I love it when you come. It gets me hot and gets me off like nothin' else."

She increased the pace. Arching her neck so Renner could lick and suck and kiss wherever he pleased.

Her world became the heat of his body. The sweat-tinged scent of his skin. The continual rasp of his pubic hair against her clit. A buzzing sensation spread down her neck, past her breasts and belly, straight to her core. When that rhythmic pulse teased, just slightly out of reach, she felt a measure of frustration.

"Baby, let me help you." He flexed his pelvis and that movement set her off.

She gasped with each deep throb of pleasure. Her inner muscles tightened and released, the pulses fading until Renner thrust up faster and harder. That extra friction brought her to orgasm again and the muscles squeezing Renner's cock kicked him over the edge too.

He growled against the base of her throat, pushing into her, then going motionless as his cock emptied in a hot rush of liquid.

As Renner panted against her shoulder, Tierney floated her fingertips over the muscles straining in his arms. She feathered light touches down the back of his neck, unintentionally making him shiver and moan. She smiled, feeling . . . satisfied. This had gone beyond power and become a point of pride that she, Tierney Pratt, could have such a potent effect on this strong man.

He lifted his head and snared her mouth in a blistering kiss.

That's when she understood he was taking back the reins.

Renner nuzzled her ear and demanded, "Untie me. Now."

Somehow she eased off him without falling on her face—her legs were decidedly shaky. He'd pulled so hard on the neckerchief the knots were difficult to undo.

Once his arms were free, he moved them briskly to get the blood circulating.

Well, some of his blood had traveled a little farther south than his big biceps and ropy forearms.

"Tierney. Look at me."

"I am."

"At my face."

Her gaze slowly traveled up to meet his eyes. Eyes chock full of heat and male satisfaction.

"You surprised me." He curled his hands around the back of the chair.

"You're not making that sound like a good thing."

"You know how fuckin' hot it was that you tied me up with my own goddamned neckerchief?"

"Ah no." She permitted a small, hopeful smile. "So you're not mad?"

Renner shook his head. "But payback is gonna be mighty interesting."

"You're going to tie me up now?" Why had her voice squeaked? Why did she have the strange compulsion to wave that black neckerchief and surrender to him?

"No. I'll surprise you sometime soon, that way we'll be even." His smoldering eyes searched her face.

He was probably about to say something so blatantly sexual she'd melt into a puddle right in her platform heels. But she needed to clear the air first. "For the record today, you were wrong. Me not coming to your place wasn't an intentional slight. It wasn't because I think I'm too good to step foot in your trailer."

"Look, about that—"

"Let me finish." She pointed at herself. "Recently deflowered virgin here, remember? I don't know any of this 'who stays at whose place how many times' type of stuff. But I do know if you would've said something to me, it wouldn't have come down to this."

"I'm thinkin' you tying me up and havin' your selfish way with me ain't all bad."

She smiled widely. "Really?"

"You are sin in sexy shoes, Tierney. And I know something else."

That twinkle in his eye had become a gleam. A warning. "What?"

"You have about four seconds to get into my bed."

The part of her that hated to be bossed around wanted to retort, "Or what?" The part of her that couldn't wait to be in his bed told the bossy part of her to shut the hell up and she started down the hallway.

At the halfway point when she felt Renner breathing down her neck, she broke into a run. She shrieked when they hit the mattress in a tangle of arms, legs, mouths and need.

And he'd proved to her, twice, just how much he loved having her as his overnight guest.

Chapter Twenty-seven

❦

"Abe? Is everything all right? You seem preoccupied."

He glanced up at Janie from his bowl of chili. "Why do you say that?"

"Because you said you were starved and you've barely eaten a bite." Janie stroked his arm. "I'm worried about you. You haven't been yourself the last week. Locked in your office until all hours. You're exhausted. What can I do?"

He loved this side of Janie. The sweet, caring side. The side that wanted to soothe him with either touches or words. His biggest fear and greatest wish had been one and the same: from the moment she'd shown up in Muddy Gap he'd fall in love with her again.

Again? Did you ever really stop loving her?

No. Abe could admit that now. But he also admitted they'd both needed the separation in order to become the people they were today.

So he decided to tell her about his secret keeping and they'd deal with the fallout. He linked their fingers together. "Is there any chance you can get a couple of hours off on Saturday afternoon?"

"Shouldn't be a problem. Why? What's going on?"

"Well, there's this ... ceremony and it'd mean a lot to me if you were there."

She blinked at him with those long eyelashes and it struck him how beautiful she was to him. Every inch of her. Inside and out. "What kind of ceremony?"

"College graduation."

"Who's graduating?"

Abe's cheeks burned. "Ah. Me, believe it or not."

Her gaze never wavered. "You're serious."

"Completely. In three days I will officially have a bachelor of science in agricultural business from the University of Wyoming."

"Why is this the first I've heard of it? I've been living here with you for weeks." She paused. "Wait. Is that what you've been doing in your office all those nights?"

"Yeah. My classes are all online and I only have time to study at night. So some nights after you fall asleep, I get up and hit the books." He inhaled. Blew out a breath. "The truth is no one in my family knows. Not Hank. Not Celia. No one."

"Why not?"

"Mostly because I didn't want people—my friends and neighbors—askin' me, 'Hey, Abe, did you ever get that college degree?' There were a couple of semesters I wasn't sure if I'd ever graduate."

"When did you go back to school?" When he didn't answer, she figured it out. "After I left."

"I knew that wasn't why you left. But it bothered me. No one ever knew how much I wished I could've gone to college."

She murmured, "I knew."

Of course she did. "One day, I just decided to do it. And I did really well. So I added more classes and let Hank and Celia believe I'd suddenly gotten addicted to Internet porn." He smiled. "Probably I'd've given it up, but with Hank off fighting bulls, and Celia doin' her own thing, I wasn't sure I could keep the ranch goin' by myself. I wanted something to fall back on that wouldn't require me to work as a ranch hand for someone else. But then, Hank married Lainie and returned to ranching full-time. Celia started running the circuits. Which allowed me to increase my credit hours and finish quicker."

Janie didn't say anything.

Abe stirred the chili that'd gone cold.

Then Janie's hands were on his cheeks and she tipped his face up. She kissed him. "Of course I'd be delighted to see you in your cap and gown, waving your diploma. I'm proud of you, Abe. Every day we're together I think I know you so well, and then I learn something like this, which quite frankly shocks the shit outta me."

He laughed.

She kissed him again. "But if I'm taking Saturday afternoon off for you, then I'll need you to stay late at Split Rock Saturday night and help me catch up, okay?"

"Deal." Abe touched the dimple in her right cheek, then her left. "I love your smile. It lights up your whole face. I especially love it when you're smilin' at me." Which seemed to be a lot lately.

"You give me a lot to smile about." She pointed at his food. "Eat up. I have a teacher and student fantasy to fulfill tonight. You never should've used that paddle on me." Janie gifted him with a coquettish look. "Oh, and I'm playing the teacher role, just in case you were curious."

"You're gonna torture me about this, aren't you?"

"Mercilessly."

∞

Late Saturday morning Abe checked his reflection in the bathroom mirror and felt ridiculous. Mostly he felt stupid because he was so damn nervous, and he shouldn't be. Wasn't like he was giving a speech. He adjusted the square hat for the tenth time and the gold tassel swung into his face.

Janie yelled down the hallway, "Abe. Come *on*. I want to

get some pictures of you in your cap and gown before we leave."

Pictures. Like he was ten years old or something.

Quit pretending to complain. You are thrilled Janie's excited about sharing this milestone in your life.

Abe tried not to walk like a cowboy as he crossed the floor. But college degree or not, he was a cowboy. He'd been walking this way his whole damn life. He pushed open the door, grumbling, "Make it fast because I . . ." He stopped in the middle of the deck.

Hank, Lainie and Celia stood beside Janie. His little sister yelled, "Surprise!" and launched herself at him, knocking his damn hat off again.

As soon as Celia was done hugging him, she smacked him on the arm. "You big jerk. I can't believe you didn't tell us." She whapped him again. "And I can't believe I ever felt guilty about keeping barrel racing from you when you were keeping this from us." Then she hugged him. "But damn, bro. A college degree? I'm so freakin' proud of you I could bust."

"Me too," Hank said.

"And to think I was worried that you'd gotten addicted to porn because of your tendency to disappear into your room for hours on end." Lainie gave him a one-armed hug because baby Lawson had grown mightily in the last few weeks.

Abe started to ask, "How did you know?" but realized Janie must've told them, so he amended, "I can't believe you guys came."

"Like we'd miss something so important to you," Hank scoffed.

"To all of us," Lainie said. "I'm just glad *someone* let us know about it."

"Yeah, Janie, we owe you big-time," Celia said.

Janie bowed to Abe. "You're welcome. Now you guys stand together. I want a picture of you with your family."

Three hours later when Abe walked across the stage for

his diploma, he knew when he thought of this day, it wouldn't be receiving the piece of paper he'd remember. He'd remember how Janie had known what would really mark the occasion and make it perfect.

⚮

Janie cried during the ceremony. Twice. She'd practically bawled on the deck step when she truly grasped how much it meant to Abe that she'd told his family of his accomplishment.

They'd had a celebratory steak supper before Celia had to take off. Hank and Lainie headed home with a whispered promise from Hank he'd handle the morning cattle check.

No one was around in the main area of the lodge. She said, "Hang on, I need to check this room," and motioned Abe inside.

When he saw his duffel bag on the bed, he said, "What the hell?"

"I'm not working tonight. I booked us a room to celebrate."

Then Abe got the strangest expression. His gaze moved from the separate alcove for the hot tub, to the sandstone fireplace, to the seating area, to the king-sized bed.

Not that she'd expected he'd whoop and holler, but his stillness bothered her. "If you'd rather go home, that's all right too."

He smiled almost shyly. "No. I wanna spend the night here. You just caught me by surprise. To be honest, I've never stayed anyplace this nice."

"We have billed the Split Rock as a luxury resort. I'm glad you like it. With all the times you've been around you haven't checked out the rooms?"

"No." He wandered to the window. "Are they all like this?"

"This is the only room with a hot tub." Janie smoothed her hands up his broad back and inhaled his familiar scent—starched cotton, warm skin and always, a hint of the outdoors.

"No one has ever done anything like this for me, Janie. Not only renting us a fancy room, but inviting my family . . . I can't believe . . ." He paused and cleared his throat. "Thank you. This is a day I'll never forget."

Janie ducked under his arm to press against the front of his body. "This will be a night you'll never forget either."

Heat flared in his eyes, turning them molten silver. "Yeah?"

"Uh-huh. You know how you always like to be in charge in the bedroom? Well, there's a new kink master in town and her name is Mistress Janie."

"Got big plans for me, Mistress Janie?"

"Mmm-hmm. I even brought a bag of tricks along." She snaked her hand around the back of his neck, pulling his mouth to hers for a kiss. A sweet, slow, wet kiss that she dragged out as long as possible. Then she whispered, "Lose the clothes, cowboy," and slithered out of his grasp.

Abe kept his hot gaze on hers as he kicked off his boots and toed off his socks. Unbuttoned his shirt and carefully draped it across the back of the plush easy chair. Shucked his jeans and underwear, placing them alongside his shirt. He stood in front of her, totally naked, totally hard, and totally at her whim.

She smirked. Circling slowly, she randomly touched him. Tracing the line of his spine down to the cleft of his butt cheeks. Her fingers mapped the dips and grooves of the muscles in his forearms and biceps. She used the back of her knuckles to follow that sexy cut of muscle from his hip to his abdomen. While brushing her thumbs across his nipples, she kissed his chest. One time. Then she challenged, "Suck or fuck?"

"Fuck." Pause. "As long as I get to touch you."

"You don't get to set the parameters, Mr. Lawson. You'll do it my way."

"Oh, you are enjoying the hell outta this, aren't you?"

"Yep. Now hop on in the hot tub and I'll be right there."

Abe removed the hot tub cover while Janie stripped. He

turned on the jets and the water frothed as they immersed themselves.

For several minutes they relaxed in the bubbling water. Her foot connected with his and she inched her toes up his shin. "Do you like this?"

"I'd like it more if you weren't so far away."

She floated over to him, anchoring a knee on either side of his hips. "Is this better?"

"Much." He placed his lips on the side of her neck and sucked, scattering kisses across the slope of her shoulder. Down her chest. Up to her ear. "I'm yours, Janie. Only yours. Do with me what you will."

Even in their most passionate moments, Abe could bowl her over with his pure sweetness. She fisted his cock at the base and rolled back, aligning it so she could join their bodies with a single push.

He groaned. "So good. Every damn time."

As frantic as they always were to get their hands on one another, this time there was no hurry. But there was passion. There was desire. This was the type of lovemaking they hadn't indulged in. Sweet. Long, wet kisses perfectly matched to the leisurely glide of their bodies beneath the cocoon of water. They rocked and touched and tasted, not exchanging words. Letting kisses and caresses speak.

The climb to the peak of pleasure was as unhurried as the descent. When they finally released their tight hold on one another, Janie smooched Abe's forehead. "I'm a little pruny."

"No complaints from me." He nuzzled her cheek. "You'll still be a hot number fifty years from now when you're permanently pruny."

She tossed him a towel and slipped on one of the guest robes. "You want a beer? Or would you rather have champagne to celebrate this momentous occasion?"

"Beer. Definitely."

Abe snagged the other robe and they moved to the sitting area. He raised his bottle to her. "A toast?"

"To what?"

"To you."

That surprised her. "Me? Why?"

"Because you are the perfect woman."

She stilled. "Really? Or are you just saying that because I fucked you and brought you a beer?"

He tipped up the bottle. Drank.

"Abe?"

"I never say something I don't mean, even in jest, Janie. You know that about me."

Ask him if he loves you. Ask him if you two have a future despite your past. Ask him if he wants you to stay in Muddy Gap with him.

But Janie wasn't sure she wanted to hear his answer, especially not tonight when this was his celebration.

After he finished the beer, she grabbed his hand and led him into the sleeping area. She moved a bench a foot from the end of the bed. "Sit."

"You givin' me a lap dance?"

"No. This time it's all about me." Trailing her fingers down his chest, she let her breath whisper across his ear. "But I promise you'll love it."

"I don't doubt that, cupcake." He kissed the line of her jaw to the tip of her chin.

When his hands gripped her ass, she pushed his hands back by his sides. "No-touching rule is in effect."

She crawled across the bed on all fours. She paused, widening her stance and canting her hips so he got an eyeful of the pink flesh between her legs.

Abe muttered something.

Which caused her to stop and peer over her shoulder. "Did you say something?"

"I said you're killin' me."

"And just think. I haven't even gotten to the real show yet."

Grabbing a pillow and her small stash of supplies, she returned to the end of the bed. "I know how much you love to watch me get myself off. So I thought I'd oblige you." The first item out of the bag was her vibrator. Not the small one she used strictly for clit stimulation, but the one with the rotating head and the vibrating tip. Janie flattened her heels on the mattress and shoved the pillow under her ass. "Got a good view?"

"Holy fuck."

She laughed. "I take that as a yes." Holding the vibrator in her left hand, she slowly dragged her middle finger from the entrance to her pussy up through her slippery folds to the top of her pubic bone. "Can you see how wet I am, Abe? I probably won't need any lube when I fuck myself with this. It'll just glide right in. Nice and deep. Do you want to watch me sliding this in?"

He nodded. Vigorously.

"I will. But I need to take the edge off." She flicked on the vibrator and switched it to her right hand, positioning the vibrating head directly on her clit. "This won't take long." She swirled the vibrator head around, searching for the perfect position, every sensation coalesced and her clit spasmed beneath the tip. She gasped, clenching and un-clenching her butt cheeks to the rhythm of the blood pulsing in her sex. After the short, intense orgasm ended, she slumped into the mattress and let the vibrator fall beside her. She sighed and propped herself on her elbows to look at Abe through her splayed legs.

His cheeks were high with color. His jaw rippled from clenching his teeth so hard. His hands were in fists at his sides. And his cock? Fully erect.

"Abe."

He raised his eyes to hers.

"Put your mouth on me. Lick me clean."

Then those big, callused hands were gripping the inside of her thighs. Then his hot, wet mouth was licking, lapping and slurping the juices from every inch of her pussy. His growls vibrated against her flesh, sending goose bumps flowing out. He zeroed in on her clit, driving her back to the ragged edge with the precise flicks of his sinful tongue.

But she didn't want to come again so soon. Janie put her palms on the side of his head and rasped, "Stop."

Abe gave her clitoris a sucking kiss and rubbed her juices that covered his face on the inside of her thighs. He returned to the bench without being asked.

She smiled at him. "Just in case you were curious, you are much better than a vibrator."

He smirked. "Never any doubt in my mind."

"Hand me that towel." She tugged the pillow beneath the small of her back. "Now for part two. This might require some shifting around."

Abe's eyebrows lifted. "My hands are completely free if you need 'em."

"So helpful. For now, we're back to the no touching rule." Janie's heart began to beat faster. She wanted to drive him to the same pinnacle of need that he took her to every time he touched her. No matter how he touched her. She wanted to give him something he'd never expect, but would prove she was up for all kinds of bedroom games. But this? Was over the top.

Her hands shook as she fished out the bottle of lube and the glass dildo. Hooking her heels into the edge of the mattress, she aligned her lower half as she braced her left hand behind her. She uncapped the lube and generously coated her fingers. "Heads up, hold this," and tossed the tube to him.

Bracing her left behind her, she brought her right hand between her legs. Closing her eyes, she swept her slicked-up fingers over the pucker of her ass. Lightly skimming the surface, bringing the nerve endings to attention. When Janie started to insert the tip of her finger into her ass, Abe made a noise she'd never heard before.

But she kept her eyes shut, relaxing her sphincter until her finger was buried to the knuckle. Biting her lip, she began to stroke in and out. Stopping to swirl the tip just inside the opening. A soft moan escaped. It always surprised her how good this felt—the sting of pain blooming into pleasure.

"Are you imagining how hard these muscles clamp down on your shaft when you're buried balls deep in my ass?"

Abe muttered, "Fuck me."

"How about when I do this?" She pushed her thumb into her pussy, which allowed for deeper penetration for her finger into her anal passage. She chanced a look at him and her belly quivered.

His eyes glittered with lust. His nostrils flared. His lips were parted and he was practically panting.

She eased her fingers out and wiped them on the towel before she grabbed the glass dildo. She held it out and murmured, "A little lube please."

Keeping their eyes locked, Abe coated the dildo, fisting his hand around it like he was greasing up his cock.

"That's good." She closed her fingers around the middle and positioned it at the seam of her ass. She whispered, "Watch." One quick push and the cold glass breached the tight ring. She sucked in a sharp breath. This was a lot thicker than her fingers. She kept her gaze on Abe's face as she pushed it in, slowly, letting her body adjust until only the base of the dildo was visible.

Janie began sliding the dildo in and out, moaning against the twin sensations of cold glass and hot friction on those tight tissues.

Abe's grip on the tube increased dramatically and clear lube squirted into the air, as if he'd shot his load on his leg. His embarrassed grin was there and gone. "Premature lubrication."

Janie released a low, throaty laugh.

"Jesus, this is fucking hot as hell."

"Keep watching." Clamping down on her anal muscles, she let go of the dildo base long enough to reach for her vibrator.

"You aren't . . ." Abe swallowed.

"Oh, yes I am." She carefully inserted the vibrator, holding her breath at the immediate feeling of fullness. "Now I could use a hand."

Abe made that possessive growling noise. Using both his hands, he pulled out the vibrator and the dildo at the same speed until only the tips remained inside her. Then he pushed them in simultaneously.

"God." Her back bowed. Her legs shook. Her arms shook. Her belly rippled. She'd never felt anything like that. "Do it again."

But Abe, being Abe, did it his own way. He moved the vibrator and the dildo in opposition. Then in tandem. Teasing again and again.

Janie moaned, "Enough."

"Don't you wanna come?"

She looked at him. "I want to come with you. Always with you. Only with you."

A feral look settled on his face. He removed the vibrator and crowded her until she was in the middle of the bed and he was between her legs. "The dildo stays in." Abe slammed his cock into her. Every thrust of his hips and his groin hit the base of the dildo. It felt as if Abe was fucking her with two cocks. She wrapped her legs around his waist and let herself go.

Abe fucked her like a man possessed. When she couldn't take another second of this raw pleasure, when she teetered so close to the brink, but couldn't seem to reach it, he worked her clit, urging, "Come. Now. Take me with you."

That did the trick. Janie screamed; the orgasm blasted her in waves of ecstasy. Her limbs twitched with each pulse and she finally believed the myth of the whole body orgasm.

Kisses on her cheeks and neck roused her. She blinked her eyes open and Abe smiled. "You have officially blown my mind. That was the sexiest" — he smooched her mouth — "hottest" — another smooch — "did I mention sexiest?" — another kiss — "thing I've ever seen. Thank you. You rocked me."

"My pleasure." She tried to stop her yawn, but failed.

"Tired?"

"A little. Maybe we should rest up before I bring out the next object from my bag of tricks."

Abe trailed his lips along her collarbone. "Should I even ask?"

"No. But a college boy like you is smart enough to know you'll like it."

Chapter Twenty-eight

～

onight was the night.

The lights were dimmed. Someone hung a disco ball on the ceiling; a kaleidoscope of lights bounced across every surface. "Sexy Back" blasted from the speakers. Renner wasn't sure if his eyes were playing tricks on him, or if the ladies, who'd christened themselves the Mud Lilies, had actually brought in a portable stripper pole.

Sweet Jesus, give him strength.

"You ready?" he asked the kid.

Tobin's eyes were enormous. "No. I'm not sure I'll ever be ready."

"That's why we'll hit the bar first. Come on."

Renner inched along the wall. Tobin followed so closely they were practically holding hands. Given the size of the crowd, it was a miracle they reached the bar without enthusiastic revelers accosting them. He signaled to Denise for two beers and handed one to Tobin. "Drink up. Fast. Shit. Too late. Here they come."

Garnet Evans approached first. Her green velvet suit was trimmed with a puffy red boa. Red, white and green-striped stockings stopped at the hem of her skirt, exposing four inches of saggy knee. She wore one red high-topped sneaker, one green high-topped sneaker. She'd also donned a pointed elf hat, to which she'd added a hook with a piece of mistletoe, so the mistletoe dangled in front of her face.

"I thought you boys were gonna chicken out."

"No, ma'am," Renner said. "We had to finish chores before we joined the festivities."

Garnet set her hand on Tobin's arm. "You clean up real good too. Dance with me, cowboy." She plucked the half-empty beer bottle out of his hand and passed it to Renner without looking at him.

Tobin mouthed, "Help me," as Garnet towed him onto the dance floor.

Huh-uh, buddy, you're on your own.

Renner's amusement was short-lived as Pearl Tschetter floated in front of him. Floated being the word, as she'd worn an outfit best described as a psychedelic butterfly run afoul of a metallic paint mixer.

"Mr. Jackson. I've been waiting for you."

"You have?"

"I wanted to thank you allowing your fine resort to be used for hosting a community party. It's a great turnout, don't you think?"

"Yes, it is." He estimated over two hundred people mingled in the dining room. "It's the least I could do. I wanted to personally thank you and the other ladies who filled in over Thanksgiving."

"We were happy to do it. Now as soon as you finish your beer, I expect you'll dance with me."

Not a question. He grinned. "Be my pleasure."

Renner danced with Pearl. Twice. Then he was waylaid by Garnet, who claimed his next two dances. As he'd tried to sneak away to the bar, Tilda O'Toole intercepted him. She also sported an outfit that fell under the costume heading. Dressed like an angel, complete with diaphanous wings. But instead of a halo, red devil horns teetered on her snowy white head.

After Tilda, Maybelle Linberg cornered him. Renner danced with her only once. Poor Maybelle had to keep Garnet from turning the North Pole prop into a stripper pole.

At the bar he ordered another beer and found himself face-to-face with Susan Williams, owner of Buckeye Joe's. Even Susan exuded the holiday spirit in a pair of reindeer antlers.

"Surprised to see me, Jackson?"

"You're always working, Williams. I don't know if I've ever seen you outside of the bar."

"And ain't that a sad state of affairs?"

"It is if you're not happy. So, who's runnin' Buckeye's tonight?"

"No one. I closed it since everyone in town was gonna be here." She toasted him with a drink that appeared to be eggnog. "Cheers. Helluva place you've got. Glad you didn't open a public bar. I couldn't compete."

"Wasn't my intention to compete with the businesses in Muddy Gap. My goal is to become part of the community, not apart from it."

"I'd say so far you're doin' a good job."

"Thanks." He found a spot where he could watch the goings-on, and keep an eye out for Tierney. He hadn't seen the woman yet, but he knew she was here someplace.

The slow song by Keith Urban ended, but Bran and Harper Turner kept dancing, so lost in each other that Renner's heart ached. What would it feel like to have that bone-deep kind of love? And not care who knew you felt that way about the person who filled you with that love?

You're a sentimental fool.

As the next slow song started, more couples joined Harper and Bran. Including Hank and Lainie Lawson, although they weren't dancing close, given Lainie's pregnant state. Abe led Janie onto the dance floor, crushing her against his chest — Renner wondered how Janie could breathe, but Janie's face read joy, not oxygen starvation. Over the last few weeks, things had changed between Janie and Abe. He just hoped Janie was smart enough not to run this time.

Several of Hank, Abe and Bran's buddies were dancing with the Mud Lilies—Ike with Pearl, Fletch with Tilda, and Eli with Maybelle. Tobin was stuck with Garnet again, but he seemed to be enjoying himself.

Everyone was paired up.

Everyone but you.

Since he'd had one beer, he couldn't even blame his melancholy mood on booze.

But he could blame his agitation on the woman who'd set this shindig up, who was MIA.

He wended his way through the crowd on a mission to find her. She wasn't lurking by the buffet tables. She wasn't in line for the bathroom. She wasn't lingering near the bar. For some reason when the song ended, he glanced at the main doorway leading to the dining room and saw her.

Only her.

He stilled.

She stilled.

Everyone and everything faded into the background.

She was a goddess. An angel. A siren in a red dress.

Then he moved toward her without conscious thought.

In that instant, as Tierney was backlit by the glow of the exit sign, Renner knew he loved her. Not because she wore a slinky dress or the sleek way she'd styled her hair, or the sweet smile on her red lips, but because she'd waited for him. She'd seen him and stopped, knowing he'd come to her.

He stood before her, a changed man, a man in love with her for Christsake, and he couldn't seem to make his mouth function.

Smooth.

Tierney, his beautiful brainiac, placed her hand on his chest above his heart, like she did whenever they were alone. "What's wrong?"

I love you.

"Renner?"

"Dance with me."

"What?" Her hand dropped. "No."

"Yes. Now."

"No way. I'm a terrible dancer."

"I'm not. Just follow my lead."

"Are you crazy? People are watching us."

"I don't care."

"People who don't like each other usually don't dance together," she pointed out. "We're not supposed to like each other, remember?"

"So act like you hate that I'm dragging you onto the dance floor with me." Renner snagged her hand.

"I cannot believe you're making me do this," she muttered. "It's unnatural."

"You bein' resistant to my charms in public is natural." He fought the temptation to tuck her against his chest and rest his chin on the top of her head. "But there's no resistance in private, is there, sweet darlin'?"

Tierney was having none of it. She pulled farther away. "What's gotten into you?"

"You." He spun them so no one could see his face. So he could show her the heat in his eyes. "Where'd you get the dress?"

"I bought it from Harper a couple of weeks ago. Why? Don't you like it?"

Renner leaned closer. "I fucking love it. You are so goddamn gorgeous you make it hard for me to fucking breathe."

Her eyes went a soft, liquid brown. "Oh, you suck. Giving me a compliment like that when I can't even kiss you."

He turned his head, allowing his mouth to touch the shell of her ear. Her shudder of pleasure mollified him until he could elicit the real thing when they were alone. "You can kiss me any time you want. But if you need a little prompting, I'm sure Garnet would let you borrow her mistletoe."

"Right. Us. Kissing."

"I'm serious. At least if *you* kissed *me* even with the excuse of mistletoe we might have a chance of keeping it an innocent peck."

"You'd really lay a sloppy, wet one on me? Here in public? In front of our employees and the whole damn town?"

"Yep."

"You're bluffing."

"Any kiss I'd give you would leave no doubt in anyone's mind that we're lovers, Tierney." He spoke by her ear. "What you don't understand? I'd love for every man in this place to know you're *mine*. That I can kiss you any goddamn time I please. I'd happily rub it in their faces that you're goin' home with *me*. And that sexy little fucking dress will be on the floor by *my* bed tonight."

She froze. "The dress did all this?"

"No. You did this."

"How much have you been drinking?" she demanded in a fierce whisper.

He chuckled. "I'm drunk on you. Absolutely intoxicated. Totally wasted on nothin' but you."

A second later, she sighed dreamily. "You are *so* getting some when we get out of here."

"Will you leave them shoes on?"

"As hot as you're making me I'll probably end up leaving the dress on too." She whispered, "Oh. FYI. I'm wearing those thigh highs you like. And a matching thong."

"For God's sake, Tierney, do you have to torture me?"

"You started it."

"And I'm ending it. Right now. Let's go. No one will miss us—"

"Stop." Tierney quit swaying to the beat and repeated, "Just stop."

Janie and Abe danced alongside them. Janie asked, "Is everything all right?"

Renner scowled at her. "Yeah. Why?"

"Looks like you two might come to blows. Need I remind you we don't need a repeat of the drink-tossing episode—"

"We're fine," Tierney snipped. "We're not children."

He didn't need Janie and Tierney getting into it either. "Ladies—"

"No, Renner, let's find out what it'd take to prove to Janie that we're fine. Want me to kiss him?"

Janie's eyes narrowed. "Very funny. I oughta make you two do it just to see you both squirm. In fact, pucker up. Both of you."

"And . . . we're leaving," Abe said, directing Janie to the bar.

"Damn," Renner said. "For a second I thought we'd get a chance to blow our cover."

"Not tonight."

The music stopped.

"I'll see you later." She gracefully disentangled from his embrace and vanished into the crowd.

Took ten minutes to reach the back of the room since people were expressing thanks for the party. Lots of thanks. Renner was pretty bowled over by the amount of good wishes.

Tobin nudged a beer toward him. "Seems folks are heading home."

"Getting to be that time."

"Who's on cleanup duty?"

Renner shrugged. "You volunteering?"

"Given the choice between cleaning up here or bein' the designated driver for Garnet and her Mud Lilies pals? No contest."

"A contest you just won by default." He pointed to Tobin's beer. "Last call for you, buddy."

"Me and my big mouth," he muttered. "If I start gathering them up now, maybe I'll be back before five a.m. when we start chores."

"Ain't no *we* in those chores tomorrow mornin'."

"That sucks."

"Yep."

"What're you gonna be doin' that's so important you'll leave me to my own devices?"

Spending as much time as possible in Tierney's bed.

Tobin sent him a sidelong glance. "Man. Tierney is smokin' tonight. I mean, she always looks fantastic, but she kicked it up a notch or twenty in that slinky dress, didn't she?"

A snarl arose. "If I catch you lookin' at her again I will blacken both your eyes so you can't see nothin' outta them."

Tobin laughed. "Dude. You are so whipped over her."

"No lie."

"So what are you gonna do about it?"

"Need me to draw you a diagram about the birds and the bees, college boy?" Renner taunted.

"With all due respect, boss, fuck off."

∞

The molten stares Renner sent her way were making her nervous.

Don't you mean making you wet?

That too.

Could the man be any sexier? And the heated compliments he'd tossed off in that gruff cowboy way caused her stomach to cartwheel.

The community party had been a huge success. Any attitudes that "highfalutin huntin' place" were too good to mingle with the locals had been laid to rest. Seemed the citizens of Muddy Gap considered the Split Rock a real part of the community.

Tierney organized the cleanup, shooing Janie and Abe out the door, since they had a way to drive and it'd started snowing. Lisa and Denise stuck around, providing a buffer between Tierney and Renner, but as soon as those women clocked out, he'd make good on the hot promises in his eyes.

She couldn't wait.

"Anything else?" Denise asked as she grabbed her coat and stood next to Lisa.

"No. We're done." Tierney couldn't resist poking the antsy man a little. "Renner? Can you think of anything Denise and Lisa need to do before they take off?"

"Nah. I'll walk you ladies out to your cars." He pinned Tierney with a look. "Then I'll be right back to help you lock up."

There was that swooping sense of excitement. She bolted the back door. As she debated on whether to wait for Renner in the dining room or the kitchen, he paused in the doorway. Even duded up in his Western-cut suit he exuded an edge of danger. He was primed. A glorious male animal on the hunt for his mate.

Then his long-legged strides ate up the distance between them. His hands cupped her face and his mouth—God, his mouth—devoured hers.

The heat of his body and his tenacity immediately pushed her to a place where the only thing that mattered was satisfying this yearning for him. Her back met something solid and cold.

And still he kissed her. "First time, fast. Really, really fast," he muttered against her lips. "Need you here. Now. Like this."

With a drawn-out groan, Renner kissed the keyhole playing peekaboo with her cleavage. He traced the cutout with his mouth as his hands followed the silhouette of her body. When his fingers reached the curve of her hips, he slowly and steadily tugged the dress up.

The leisurely slide of the satin lining across her legs was as erotic as the slide of his satiny tongue across her bare skin. Once the fabric bunched around her waist, his lips returned to hers to kiss her hotly. Urgently.

She reached for his belt buckle the same time he did. He gently placed her hand over his racing heart, a gesture that proved beyond a doubt his need, his passion, matched hers.

Fabric whooshed on the front of her knees as his pants hit the floor. He clutched the back of her left thigh and urged, "Wrap your leg around me."

Tierney didn't worry about losing her balance, because as soon as she'd pressed the crease of her knee to his butt, he pulled her thong aside and that thick male hardness was filling her up. Holding her up. Burning her up.

Renner hissed, "So hot. Wet. Tight. Goddamn, you are . . ."

She snaked her arms around his neck and nibbled on his earlobe, absorbing his shudder. "I'm what?"

No immediate answer because Renner was obsessed with bringing them to climax in record time. His hips pistoned with enough force her butt slapped into the metal door. He'd pressed his lips against her temple and his every stuttered breath sent chills rippling across her skin.

The angle of her leg allowed direct contact with her clit. That telltale tingle swelled from the apex of her sex to her nipples. He wound her tighter. And tighter until she was dizzy. "Renner."

"I know, baby, me too." He dragged scorching kisses across her collarbone up to the tender spot below her ear. "You know what you are, Tierney?"

"What?" she panted as he continued to hammer into her.

"Everything. Sweet Jesus, you are everything."

His cock pulsed, hitting her sweet spot and the orgasm consumed her in a throbbing wave of heat. The intensity faded quickly, and Tierney felt him hard and urgent as his seed filled her. Warmed her in more ways than she could fathom.

His body stilled and he murmured her name like a benediction. Before she could speak, his mouth was on hers, letting her know this interlude was more than just a quick fuck against the walk-in refrigerator.

Renner had taken things between them a step further tonight, and Tierney needed to meet him halfway. She eased from his bone-melting kisses to whisper, "Will you spend Christmas with me? Watch sappy holiday movies. String popcorn and cranberries and hang the strands on the tree? Sip mulled wine as we snuggle up on the couch and watch it snow."

He tipped her face up and peered into her eyes. "You aren't leaving to spend Christmas with your family?"

"No. My father isn't a holiday person. Christmas was just

another day." She backtracked. "No big deal if you have plans."

"Tierney. I'd love to spend Christmas with you."

Relief flowed through her. She hugged him. "Thank you. And will you please stay with me tonight?"

"You cooking me breakfast?"

"No."

"Then I'm definitely staying."

Chapter Twenty-nine

❦

What a beautiful, perfect night. Janie stared out the windshield of Abe's truck at the snow flurries shifting across the road in a ballet of white. She might've missed the movement if she hadn't become so rapt watching the shapes and shadows in the stream of headlights. Her fingers tightened around Abe's. "What's that?"

"What?"

"That." She pointed. "See? Right there. Abe, stop the truck."

He hit the brakes

Janie unbuckled and jumped from the cab as soon as he put it in park. The box on the shoulder moved. She hung back for a second, not sure what might be lurking inside.

It sure ain't gonna be a nest of snakes in this weather.

As the box rocked again, a pitiful whimpering echoed to her. All caution fled and she crouched over the open box. "Oh my." A basset hound puppy blinked sad eyes at her and then tried to jump out of the box, yipping and whining.

"Jesus, Janie, what the hell?" Then, "Oh shit. Somebody dumped a dog?"

"It's a puppy. Poor thing. Look at it. Its ribs are showing."

She crooned, "Hey, little guy. It's okay. We won't hurt you. We won't leave you." Leaning closer, she got a whiff of urine. "Think it'll be okay riding in the back of your truck?"

"Gonna hafta be because it sure ain't ridin' inside the truck smelling like that." Abe moved the box flaps and said, "Grab a side."

She blinked at him.

"What? You expected I'd carry it? No dice. If I'm gonna smell like abandoned dog piss, then you are too." Abe dropped the tailgate and they hefted the crying puppy into the truck bed.

"Sure, the one time I'd be happy to see a hay bale poking out of the back of your truck . . . there isn't one."

He slammed the tailgate and peered over the edge. "It'll be fine until we get home."

By the time she climbed into the cab, she'd formulated a plan. "It'll need a bath. And food."

"Which it'll immediately throw up, requiring another bath," Abe said dryly.

"I'll deal with it. I just can't stand the idea of it being outside in the barn."

"Hey." Abe snatched her hand. "I'm not saying we oughta turn the pup out into the wintry night. I just don't want you to ruin that beautiful dress. You looked stunning tonight, if I haven't mentioned it."

She blushed. He had mentioned it. Several times. The extra effort on her appearance had paid off the instant she'd seen the hot look of appreciation in Abe's eyes. "Thanks."

"I had seduction plans." His lips grazed the back of her knuckles. "Good ones like the other night. You really liked that. But I'll save those plans for another time since we'll be puppy sitting."

After reaching the ranch, they left the puppy in the truck bed while they changed clothes. Abe tracked down a cardboard box and Janie tried to prepare the bathroom.

Abe brought in a wiggly bundle wrapped in a ratty horse blanket. "Ready?"

"Yep."

Plop. The stinky thing yipped, attempting to jump out of the tub. The whining increased tenfold when Janie hosed the pup down. Then it bent its furry head and lapped up water. Lots of water. When it finally stopped drinking, the puppy's sides heaved, liquid spraying out the mouth and nose. Poor thing didn't know what was happening and cried like they were killing it. As soon as the vomiting ended, Janie squirted a line of soap and gently scrubbed the fur. Except for the shaking, the dog stayed very still through the bath.

Janie's heart broke at seeing how tiny the puppy was without fur masking his body size. Abe handed her a towel and she fluffed the fur as she dried it. She peered at the spotted underbelly. "It's a boy."

"So it is."

"I'm gonna name him." She braced herself for Abe to tell her not to get attached because they weren't keeping the dog.

A beat of silence passed. "What?"

"George."

"Why George?"

She shrugged. "Just popped into my head." She carried him into the kitchen and set him on a towel. "You think his stomach is settled?"

Abe shook his head. "Give it another hour."

So she and Abe stretched out on the linoleum, watching George explore. The pup was clumsy, as he hadn't grown into his big paws. He was a funny little thing. Curious. Affectionate. Destructive. He ripped the newspaper on the floor to shreds, barking at the pieces that fell around him like confetti.

George yawned and trotted over to Janie's side, snuggling into her leg before he put his jaw on his paw and drifted to sleep.

Janie petted his fur, smitten with the helpless critter. She looked over at Abe and blushed at seeing his amused expression. "What?"

"I never thought you were a dog person."

"Why's that?"

"You barely tolerated Celia's mutt."

She ruffled George's soft coat. "Bringing another dog into Murray's domain wasn't allowed, so I can see where you might've gotten that impression."

Abe reached over and ran his knuckles down Janie's cheek. "Was I really that much of a bastard?"

"No." She paused. "Okay, sometimes. You didn't understand I wanted some things that were ours. Just ours. I know that sounds selfish."

"I'll admit, I thought it was selfish back then. But now? Not so much."

"Did you have any idea how much I wanted a baby?" As soon as she said it, she wished she could take it back.

His hand froze. "You did?"

"Yes. I thought a baby would fix everything between us. I thought it'd give me a reason . . ." Janie angled her face away from his touch.

But Abe, being Abe, wouldn't allow it. He gripped her chin between his thumb and index finger, forcing her to meet his gaze. "You thought it'd give you a reason to stay, didn't you?"

"Yes." *Ask me what it would take to get me to stay now. Prove to me you've really changed.*

Abe's beautiful gray eyes churned with emotion. "How did we end up hurting each other so badly when we loved each other so much?"

"I don't know." It pained her to hear him using love in the past tense. She closed her eyes. She loved him now more than she ever had. But how could she tell him? When she'd repeatedly led him to believe this situation was temporary and he seemed good with that?

"Janie?"

Don't make me look at you. I don't think I can hide the truth from you much longer.

The fur ball against her leg stretched and whimpered. She scooped him up and rubbed her cheek on his soft head.

"What's wrong? You hungry?" She pushed to her feet, grateful to focus on the puppy.

Later, curled up in bed, they listened as George scratched, whimpered and cried in his puppy prison. Janie said, "You think this is what it's like to be parents?"

Abe's hand tenderly traveled the length of her arm from her shoulder to the bend in her elbow. "Maybe. But I'm pretty sure it's against the law to keep a kid in a box."

She lightly elbowed him.

He chuckled. "I imagine it's close. Hearing the baby cry. Getting up with it. Wondering what you're gonna do with the little bugger during the day when you can't take it to work."

"Can George go with you tomorrow? Learn to be a ranch dog?"

"Weren't you the one who brought it home so you could love it and hug it and squeeze it and feed it and call it George?"

She elbowed him again. "Yes, but I can't take a puppy to work with me."

"I can't either. Not when he's so small. We'll have to crate him in the kitchen."

"I hope he's a fast learner."

"I'm a fast learner too. Now I know why you named him George. Because of that Christmas movie you loved so much."

They'd only spent three Christmases together, so she was happy he'd remembered watching *It's a Wonderful Life* with her. "Busted. With the snowy weather, and it being so close to Christmas, the name just seemed to fit."

"Mmm." He kissed her shoulder. "George. The dog who saved my Christmas present."

"What makes you say that?"

"'Cause now I'm hoping you'll think the collar I got you . . . was actually for the dog."

She laughed softly. "I'm glad we're spending Christmas together, Abe."

"Me too."

Chapter Thirty

❧

New Year's Eve was overrated.

Especially when Renner had to pretend to ignore the only person he wanted to be with. The heat and the noise level at Hank and Lainie's first New Year's bash increased, escalating his need to escape.

Renner hadn't seen Tierney for at least ten minutes and he knew where to find her. He cut through the crowd, snagged his coat from the pile in the entryway and snuck out the front door.

Bingo. She leaned against the porch railing. She'd dressed warmly enough for the frigid night: fuzzy tasseled hat, long wool coat, a thick scarf looped around her neck, puffy mittens covering her hands. She looked damn cute. "Hey."

"Hey yourself."

"Had enough of wall-to-wall people?"

"It's a fun party and all, but I needed a minute to clear my head. Then I came out here and it's been hard to pull myself away."

One of his favorite things about Tierney was the city girl had become enamored with this rugged no-man's-land called Wyoming. He secretly loved catching her gazing out their office window. Or sitting on the log behind her cabin. Or sometimes in the mornings she'd wander halfway down the hill to the barns and corral. In those moments when she quietly marveled at nature, she defined serenity. It was a far cry from the uptight Tierney who'd arrived in Muddy Gap four short months ago.

"The view is breathtaking, isn't it?" she murmured.

Renner set his hand on the rail next to hers and drank in the vista. Rocky hills and veiled valleys morphed into snow-capped mountains in the distance. Wispy clouds shuttled by, but didn't mar the majestic black sky. The landscape wasn't all that spectacular compared to the panorama from the rooftop of the barn at the Split Rock. "It's all right, I suppose. I know someplace better."

And just as he expected, she challenged, "Prove it."

"Gladly. But first I've gotta know . . . You afraid of heights?"

Tierney rolled her eyes. "No."

"So let's go."

"Now? Renner. It would be rude not to say thank you to Hank and Lainie for inviting us to their party."

"The booze is flowing. No one will miss us." When she still wasn't convinced, he leaned close enough to get a whiff of her lemon lip balm. "Is it so wrong that I wanna be alone with you on New Year's Eve? I'd like to kiss you at midnight and not give a damn about who's watching."

Those beautiful coffee-colored eyes softened. "Did you practice that line?"

"Nope. Spur of the moment. But it's a damn good one, don't you think?"

"It's all right, I suppose."

"Smarty." He couldn't resist giving her a smacking kiss on the mouth. "Meet me at the barn in about thirty minutes. Dress warm. Wear sensible shoes."

Tierney parted her lips to protest; he kissed her again. "As much as I love them sexy-assed, *do me baby* high heels you prefer, tonight you need to wear shoes with nonskid soles."

Renner waited until Tierney pulled away in her vehicle before he bounded down the steps to his truck.

Half an hour later, as he situated the ladder beneath the hayloft door, he began to wonder if this was a stupid idea. He'd wanted to give her a different way to ring in the New Year. Alone. Just the two of them. The way it oughta be. Hopefully the way it'd play out for years to come.

The main door squeaked and she yelled, "Renner? You in here?"

"Yeah. Come on up to the hayloft."

"You offering to give me a roll in the hay?"

"Maybe after. If you're a good girl."

"But you like me so much better when I'm bad," she purred.

That damn throaty growl always made him hard. "I'm hoping this doesn't freak you out."

Her eyes narrowed on something behind him. "What's the ladder for?"

"To climb on the barn roof for the very best view of this valley and the rock from whence the Split Rock garnered its name." Renner grabbed her hand and tugged her to the ladder. "You'll love it."

"This isn't a trick? Get me up there and push me off?"

"Your concern would've been justified if I'd brought you up here right after you'd first shown up. I'da happily shoved you over the edge." He pressed his lips to her forehead. "It's different now, between you and me. It's ..." *Real.* He released her and squeezed through the trapdoor. The apex of the barn roof was a flat space, four feet wide, before it started to slope down both sides. There wasn't much room to sit; their legs would dangle over the edge. "Give me your hand."

"I'm not sure—"

"Darlin', I promise I won't let anything happen to you."

She climbed up as far as she could; then he grabbed her upper arms and pulled her through the rest of the way.

Tierney clutched him tightly. "Oh God. We're high up."

"I thought you didn't have a fear of heights?"

"I worked on the fiftieth floor of a Chicago high-rise. Of course I don't have a fear of heights as long as I'm encased in glass. Can we please go back down to the ground? I won't even bitch about getting manure on my shoes."

"Tierney. Baby." Renner placed his hands over her cheeks and stared into her eyes. "Breathe."

She did.

When he was fairly certain she wouldn't topple off from dizziness, he said, "Let's sit down."

"Don't let go."

"I won't. Trust me?"

"Yes."

To have this woman's trust was no easy task; he was both humbled and overjoyed. "Do what I do." Renner dropped to his knees. She followed suit. He swung his legs over the edge and kept hold of her the entire time.

"What do you think of the view?"

"I haven't opened my eyes yet."

He chuckled. "Come on. Open them beautiful browns."

"Oh. Wow. This is impressive."

The landscape took center stage and neither spoke.

"That extra story and a half allows you to see over the ridge to the valley below. You don't get this view even on top of the lodge."

"You've been up there?" She paused. "Of course you've been up there."

Renner snorted. "You make it sound like I compete in the X-Games. I'm not exactly a daredevil." He tried several times and several ways to dislodge her death grip on his hand but she wasn't getting the hint. "Tierney, I need my hand back."

"You promised you wouldn't let go."

"I won't." Renner hooked his leg over hers. "There. You can have my hand back in a second. I need to grab something outta my pocket."

"A parachute? In case the wind comes up and we start to slide off the freakin' roof?"

"I wouldn't have brought you up here if there was a chance we'd become kites." He reached in his left pocket and fished out a bottle. "It ain't the traditional champagne, but you want some peppermint schnapps?"

"I've never had that."

He tsk-tsked and uncapped the bottle, sneaking a drink. "You really have led a sheltered life." He held it to her lips and said, "A nip will keep you warm."

Tierney kept her eyes on his as she sipped.

"You like?"

"Mmm-hmm. It's an interesting combination of sweet and warm."

"Reminds me of you." Renner kissed her. The brisk night air had cooled her lips and she tasted sweet from the peppermint. The sweetness vanished in the heat of her mouth as it moved on his, filling him with an underlying tang that wasn't from liquor but was pure Tierney. But he got that same drunken feeling kissing her as he did from too much booze.

He loved her. Loved this woman who was so unlike anyone he'd ever known. She owned him. Heart and soul.

And she didn't know it. When would he muster up the guts to tell her?

Maybe he'd get lucky and in a moment of passion, she'd say it first.

Her tongue darted out to lick away the last remnants of peppermint from his lips. She murmured, "So serious, cowboy. Something on your mind?"

You. I want you in my life like this every damn day. Every damn night. And I don't know what I can offer you to convince you to stay with me.

"Renner? What's wrong?"

"Nothin'. Bet this is a New Year's Eve you won't ever forget."

"I won't." Tierney touched his cheek. "Not ever."

"You don't mind that I dragged you on top of a barn, I'm plying you with cheap booze and you're freezing your ass off?"

"No. I'm glad it's just you and me, checking out the view, sipping schnapps, snuggling up to stay warm."

"It ain't fancy appetizers, Cristal and a black tie gig at a swanky Chicago hotel."

"No. It's much better." She scooted closer to rest her head on his shoulder. "Do you know how I spent last New Year's?"

"No."

"Neither do I."

He didn't laugh because she hadn't meant it to be funny. He passed her the bottle and she took a swig.

"I don't want you to think I'm pathetic, but I've never had the big New Year's date or been invited to a cool party."

"Did that bother you?"

"Some. I'd convinced myself parties were overrated and just an excuse for people to get stinking drunk and take no responsibility for their bad behavior."

"That's what it ends up bein' most of the time. Too much booze, too many promises that are forgotten the next morning in the wake of a wicked hangover."

"What about you? Did you rip it up with your woman du jour?"

Renner trailed his lips down the curve of her jaw. "Once or twice. For the last six years there's been a rodeo in Oklahoma that prides itself on bein' the first rodeo of the New Year, and it always starts at midnight. Which meant me'n Pritchett spent the hours leading up to the rodeo getting ready for it and the hours after it loading up to race to the next rodeo."

"Do you make a New Year's resolution every year?"

"Nope. I made one years ago and I've managed to keep it."

Tierney raised her head and looked at him. "What was it?"

"Guess."

"You swore off marriage?"

He smirked. "That had nothin' to do with a New Year's promise. Try again."

"You decided to work out every day to maintain this slamming body," she cooed.

"Flattery will get you everywhere with me, but you're wrong again. Last chance."

"Shoot." She pushed her glasses up her nose. "You've vowed never to have a job where you can't wear shitkickers to work."

"Wrong." He offered her the bottle but she declined.

"Oh, come on. You can't just say something like that and not tell me."

All of a sudden Renner wished he would've kept his mouth shut. There was a reason he never talked about this stuff.

Her gloved fingers were on his chin, turning his face toward hers. "Tell me. Trust me."

And he found himself doing just that. "In my teens I figured out my dad loved his best friend. He'd probably been in love with the guy his whole life. His best friend felt the same, but they weren't together, not like they wanted to be. It made me sad. Made me realize I'd rather deal with failure than live with regret."

Her eyes filled with tears. She kissed him so gently he had the insane urge to belt out that he loved her. But he closed his eyes and lost himself in the loving touch of this woman who meant more to him than she could ever imagine.

She said, "Thank you for telling me."

"Thanks for not bailing off the roof when you heard my barnyard philosophy." He felt her smile against his neck and whispered, "Your turn. Tell me your resolution."

"Last year around Valentine's Day I decided I wanted a different life. When the contract came across my desk for the Split Rock, I saw it as my chance. It's been the best thing I've ever done, Renner. I want you to know that."

"I believe you. I've been thinkin'. I want you to come to Denver with me next week for the National Western Stock Show. Since there are no guests scheduled, I know you'll just hole up in your cabin all by yourself and work. You deserve a break, so take it with me. It'll be fun."

His request momentarily startled her. Then she casually asked, "What would we do in Denver?"

"My manager will be there and I have meetings scheduled to deal with upcoming stock contracts for various rodeos. When I'm done with that we could do whatever you wanted. Go out to eat. Go to the rodeo. Wander through the vendor stands. Hang out at the sale barns and look at bulls. Or hole up in our hotel room and fuck each other until we can't walk."

She fussed with her glasses. "We'd be alone?"

"With the exception of the thousands of people that flock to the stock show every year. Yeah. It'd just be us."

"Okay. Let's do it."

"Good." His watch beeped, signaling midnight.

He murmured, "Happy New Year, Tierney."

"Happy New Year, Renner."

He slid his hand around the back of her neck, bringing her mouth to his, giving her a kiss she'd never forget. But as the kiss deepened, he knew it was a kiss he'd never forget either.

Chapter Thirty-one

❧

Since Renner had meetings all day, Tierney opted to entertain herself on their last day at the National Western Stock Show. She wandered through the vendor booths at the arena.

She'd watched him in action at the Split Rock and admired his affability with guests and employees. But as Renner Jackson, proprietor of Jackson Stock Contracting, the man oozed charisma. His knowledge of the world of rodeo stock contracting staggered her. Not only did everyone like him; everyone respected him. She also realized the Split Rock's success hinged on him. On his connections. Chances were high the venture would've failed if he wasn't involved on a day-to-day basis.

Tierney wondered how their time away together would change them. She understood sneaking around could heighten the intensity of their feelings. Especially since they'd started out adversaries and wound up in a red-hot love affair. But they'd slipped into couplehood easily. There'd been little adjustment in sharing a hotel room, maybe because they'd been sharing a bed most nights anyway. This trip just cemented the idea she wanted to be "out" as a couple with him all the time.

"Tierney?"

She turned toward Celia and was enveloped in a hug. "Hey!"

"I'm so glad you called me." Celia signaled for Tierney to spin around. "Oh man, look at you. A couple of months in Wyoming and you're rockin' the Western wear."

"I never would've picked this outfit for myself, but Harper has an eye for style."

"With the exception of that hideous turquoise number she chose for me to wear for her wedding. Soon as I saw it I wondered what I'd done to piss her off. God. Talk about a Scarlett O'Hara meets the madam of a whorehouse brides-maid's dress."

Tierney laughed.

Celia started down the long corridor, wall to wall with people. "I imagine Harper is still wearing that well-fucked look of a newlywed?"

"I guess that's one way of putting it."

She waved to someone before focusing on Tierney. "I'll warn ya. I'm not in the finals so I'm feelin' really rude and crude. If you have an aversion to raw language from your drinkin' buddy, maybe we'd best say our good-byes here."

"Bring it on, cowgirl. If I can go toe to toe with Garnet and her gang, I can handle you."

"Hell yeah. That's what I'm talkin' about, letting loose the wild woman lurking beneath the classy business suit."

Several different bars ringed the event center. They paid the cover charge to a makeshift honky-tonk with sawdust on the floor. Metal tubs filled with ice and beer stretched behind the long bar. Women clad in skimpy bikini tops and silver-fringed chaps passed out free samples of chewing to-bacco and posed for pictures. A mix of country and pop music blared from all corners of the room. The cheesy setup seemed to be a caricature of a Western bar, and yet, entirely accurate.

The male bartender didn't look comfortable in a plaid shirt and a straw hat. Funny how after only a few months in Wyoming, Tierney immediately separated real cowboys from poseurs.

"I'll have a Bud Light. Tierney, what about you?"

"Same."

Celia dug in her front jeans pocket and pulled out a roll of bills. "First round is on me. Let's sit there."

They grabbed barstools at a table between the main door and the bar by the dance floor. Celia chinked her bottle to Tierney's. "To cold beer and hot men."

"Amen." Tierney drank and felt curious stares, not all of them aimed at Celia. She caught the eye of a lanky cowboy in a gray hat, boasting a gigantic gold and silver championship belt buckle. He flashed his pearly whites and lifted his bottle to her.

Whoa. Men rarely gifted her with a smoldering once over. Maybe her tight pink shirt had caught his notice.

Or maybe it's your sexual confidence. You're acting like a woman who knows how to please her man between the sheets.

Damn straight. She did please Renner in bed. She pleased him out of it too. And she really felt these last few months she'd come into her own. She finally was figuring out what *she* wanted, not trying to please everyone else.

"How long have you been in Denver?" Celia asked.

"Five days. I didn't call you earlier because I figured you'd be busy." Tierney sipped her beer and wondered how long before Celia asked the question.

The wait wasn't long at all. "So you're here with Renner Jackson? You guys double-teaming the slavering masses to pimp the Split Rock?"

"Not really. He had meetings scheduled with rodeo promoters. Since I've never been to a stock show, I was curious and tagged along."

"Uh-huh. This *is* the man whose handsome face met the business end of your drink at Bran and Harper's wedding reception a few months back?"

"One and the same."

"How long you been screwing around with him?" Celia pointed her bottle. "Don't deny it. I'd think less of you if you weren't nailing him at every opportunity. Jesus. Renner is a fine specimen of manly goodness."

"No argument from me. We've been . . . hooking up for a couple months."

"Is that all it is? Hooking up? Someone to scratch the itch when you need it?"

Tierney sighed. "Honestly? I don't know. At times it feels like more than sex. Most of the time actually. He's just so . . . great. I feel great when I'm with him."

"Does it feel like love?" Celia gently prompted.

"Yes. It does. But it feels one-sided."

"On whose side?"

"Mine. And it doesn't help that we're keeping our involvement on the down low. No one who works at the Split Rock is aware we're involved."

Celia's eyebrows rose. "Not even Janie or Harper?"

She shook her head. "We've been discreet."

"Takin' you to the National Western Stock Show and introducing you to his colleagues ain't exactly discreet, T."

"True. But I don't know what it means." She drained her beer. "I don't have tons of experience with men or relationships so I'm sort of flying blind."

"Before I hit the road, I'd been with one guy. And he didn't even know that I was . . ." An embarrassed look crossed her face. "Needless to say, I was determined to sow my wild oats once I started running the circuit."

"Have you been getting wild?"

"Some. Not as much as people think. Or maybe I oughta say, not as much as I've led people to believe."

The waitress dropped off the beer and Tierney paid. But Celia ordered two shots of whiskey. "I assume both those shots are for you?"

"Nope," Celia answered.

"But I don't drink whiskey."

"You do when you're with me."

Tierney laughed. "And since we're trading off rounds, that means I have to buy shots?"

"Yep." Celia grinned. "We're gonna have some fun tonight."

Tierney managed to knock back the shot without coughing or gagging.

A couple of hot guys moseyed over and chatted with Celia, who flirted shamelessly. After they left, Celia said, "I hope we won't be kicking ourselves for not taking them up on their offer."

"Renner might frown on me sneaking off to a private hot tub party with two cowboys. Wouldn't the guy you're seeing have an issue with it?"

"Breck?" She shrugged. "Nah. We're keeping it casual. That works best for us."

"But didn't this Breck guy whisk you off to an island getaway for Christmas?" Tierney had caught the end of a conversation between Harper, Lainie and Janie at the New Year's party about why Celia hadn't come home for Christmas.

"He took me to Jamaica for two glorious weeks. But Breck is loaded and he didn't wanna go home for Christmas any more than I did." Celia smiled tightly. "I'm sure that sounds horrible. Don't get me wrong. I adore my brothers. But Hank and Lainie were spending their first Christmas in their new house. With Lainie bein' pregnant and all, I didn't want to impose, although both of them would've assured me it wasn't an imposition. And Abe, well, he and Janie need to figure some stuff out. I'd just be in the way again. Harper and Bran have room for me in that huge freakin' house, but it's their first Christmas as a married couple and I'd be a third wheel. So it was better that I packed a half-dozen bikinis and spent my Christmas vacation lounging on the beach drinking mai tais."

"I see your point." The music was cranked a little louder. Trying to hold a conversation without yelling became tough so they drank and watched people pour into the bar.

Time came for Tierney to buy a round of shots. She held her glass to Celia's. "To smooth whiskey and rough men."

Celia tossed back her shot. "I'll have to remember that one."

Another round of beer meant a trip to the ladies' room. When Tierney returned, she was surprised to see a familiar face from Muddy Gap. The man Celia had referred to as the bane of her existence. He'd shoved a barstool at the head of the elevated four-top table right next to Celia—not that she paid any attention to him.

When he noticed her, he stood. "You must be Tierney. I'm Kyle Gilchrist."

"Good to meet you, Kyle."

"Now that you're back to save our table, I'm gonna pop over and say hi to some folks," Celia announced.

"Celia," Kyle said sharply, "you're not listening. I said Breck is lookin' for you."

"And I said *so what*." She drained her beer, signaling the waitress for another. "It's not like it's a secret where I am. I'm where I've been all fuckin' week."

Kyle glanced at Tierney. "How much has she been drinkin'?"

"*She* can answer for herself, and the answer is none of your goddamned business. I'm not drivin', I'm not doin' a striptease on the bar, so fuck off. I don't want you here, Kyle, because you're a buzzkill."

"That right?" He invaded her space and whispered directly in her ear.

Tierney noticed that while Celia's hand on the table curled into an angry fist, she also closed her eyes and went very still when Kyle's mouth was so close.

"There you are, Kyle. Thanks for tracking her down for me." The guy glanced at Tierney and smiled as he sat next to Celia. "You saved us seats." He thrust his hand across the table. "Breck Christianson."

"Tierney Pratt."

"Tierney. A beautiful name." His eyes swept her face and chest with frank male appreciation. "For a beautiful woman."

Talk about good-looking. Breck had curly coal-black hair, which he wore longer than the short cut most cowboys preferred. His dark blue eyes were fringed with thick black eyelashes and his dimpled smile hinted at sinful devilry. Broad across the shoulders and chest, with heavily muscled arms, he resembled a comic book superhero more than a rodeo cowboy. "It's nice to meet you, Breck."

"I'm so very pleased to meet you, Tierney," he drawled seductively.

"Stop dripping testosterone all over her," Celia snapped. "You're a man's man who loves the ladies. We get it."

Breck laughed and curled his hand around Celia's neck, bringing her in for a thorough kiss. "I love it when you get all mouthy on me, sugar pie."

Tierney looked elsewhere and expected her discomfort to be mirrored in Kyle's eyes, but Kyle's entire posture was closed off. His face was a blank mask.

Chairs scraped and the table wobbled.

"Tierney, meet my buddies, Skeeter, Davy and Michael," Breck said. The men dragged over extra chairs and joined them.

She murmured hello and half feared she'd revert to her former wallflower persona. But she'd come a long way in the last few months and there was no awkwardness at all. She found herself engaged in conversation with the guys as Breck and Celia argued in low tones and Kyle drank.

Listening to their rodeo exploits had her laughing so hard she had to rest her forehead on Skeeter's shoulder to catch her breath. Somehow his palm ended up on her lower back.

"Maybe y'all better let me in on the joke, 'cause it looks awful damn funny."

Tierney jumped at hearing Renner's voice. How long had he been standing behind them? "Hey. I wasn't expecting you."

"Obviously." Renner looked pointedly at Skeeter. "Mind getting your hand off her?"

"What?"

"Your hand. Get it off her ass. Now."

"Oh. Oh! Sure. No problem, man." Skeeter pushed away from Tierney, making room for Renner.

Everyone already knew Renner. The conversation turned to rodeo stock, competition, and droned on. After a half hour of mind-numbing shoptalk, Celia mouthed "bathroom" and they slipped away.

Once they were in line, Celia said, "I need a cigarette. Stupid goddamn no-smoking laws."

"Maybe you should track down one of those smokeless tobacco girls to sate your nic fit."

"Ha ha. Smart-ass. Wish I never woulda started smokin." She let her head fall against the wall. "Look. I'm sorry. For the record, I didn't tell Breck my plans because I wanted this to be girl time. I get so sick of his entourage. The man cannot go anywhere without his cowboy posse."

"Renner's been off doing his thing all day too." She frowned. "I didn't tell him my plans. How did he track me down?"

"Fuckin' spies everywhere, that's how. Did you notice the second they parked their Wrangler butts at *our* table it was all about them?"

"I'm used to it. When Renner walks into a room of rodeo contestants, he's swarmed and forgets I'm even there."

"Does it piss you off?"

"Now that I think about it . . . maybe. A little. And what was up with his, *get your hand off her ass now* show of testosterone? And then he ignores me completely?"

"Men suck."

They moved a couple of feet in line and she glanced up to see Celia studying her. "What?"

"I'm thinkin' a little payback is in order." She smiled cheekily. "You up for some fun and games?"

"What kind of fun and games?"

Celia's eyes gleamed. "The kind of fun that'll get us noticed. The kind of games that'll make them sweat and make them hard."

An odd tingle prickled in her belly. The idea of showing Renner she made her own fun . . . really tripped her trigger. "I'm in. What do you have in mind?"

"A little girl-on-girl action." Celia laughed. "You oughta see your expression. We'll get friendly, but ain't like I'm gonna stick my hand down your pants or nothin'."

The lady in line behind them harrumphed and stomped off.

Tierney fought the urge to grin and to cringe—at the same time.

"Just follow my lead. It'll just be a dirtier type of dancin' and drinkin'."

And dirtier said it all.

After fortifying themselves with another shot, Celia dragged Tierney onto the dance floor for Lady Gaga and Beyoncé's duet "Telephone" and taught her more sexy moves—shaking her booty, rolling her hips, swaying her upper torso to the beat—than any of the classes she'd taken.

The DJ kept playing sexy dance tunes. When "Honky Tonk Badonkadonk" came on, Celia playfully slapped her ass. Tierney snatched Celia's long braid, wrapping it around her hand, pulling Celia against her body in a dominant move that caused Celia's eyes to widen . . . just for a second.

Then Celia gyrated her hips with her arms in the air, rolling her shoulders and chest as she used Tierney's body as her personal stripper pole. "Whip My Hair" started, and Celia bent Tierney over and used her braid as a whip on Tierney's butt. After the dance ended, they formed a train with Celia in front and Tierney holding on to Celia's hips. Tierney murmured, "Look at their faces," and Celia let out a throaty laugh.

Skeeter stood up and clapped when they reached the table.

Davy wolf whistled.

Michael toasted them with his beer.

But Renner?

Not so amused.

Kyle?

Not so amused.

Breck? Highly amused. He drawled, "Ladies, you gotta be parched after such a fine display of dancin'. Any drink you want is on me."

Tierney leaned her elbows on the table, zeroing in on Celia's cleavage. "How about a . . . Slippery Nipple?"

"Jesus, Tierney, how much have you been drinkin'?" Renner hissed.

She gave him the cold shoulder.

Celia took the end of her braid and slowly outlined the skin bared by Tierney's sweetheart neckline. "Oh. I don't know. I was thinkin' something more sweet and tangy."

"And a little sticky?" Tierney asked silkily. "I know exactly what you want."

"Because it's what all women want. A long tongue licking that moist section of skin. A greedy-sounding gulp as the thick liquid warms the throat. And finally," she breathed, "a firm bite on the tender flesh until it erupts in sweet juice that flows down your mouth and chin."

None of the guys said a word. Tierney was pretty sure they'd stopped breathing.

"Any of you fellas wanna take a guess on what that is?" Celia asked huskily.

More silence.

Tierney and Celia exchanged a haughty look and simultaneously said, "Tequila shooters!"

Male groans sounded.

Davy piped up, "That's not fair. That's not what you—"

"Shut it," Kyle snapped.

Celia blinked innocently. "What did you guys think I was describing? We were talking about *drinks*, right?"

Tierney swore she heard Renner growl.

Breck waved the waitress over. "Two shots of Patron, limes and salt."

Then Celia and Tierney ignored the men completely. Celia straightened the laces on Tierney's blouse, letting the heels of her hands brush Tierney's nipples. "This is so cute. It's tight enough you could wear it without a bra."

"I considered it until I stepped into a cold room."

Celia laughed. Then she said, "Hang on, you've got something on your face." Celia's finger wiped the corner of Tierney's mouth.

Tierney fought a smile at seeing Celia's smug grin. She knew from the way Celia bent her head it looked as if they were kissing. She casually swept a strand of hair behind Celia's ear. She fingered the long blond plait, wrapped her palm around it and slid her closed hand up and down the length. "Don't ever cut your hair. It's gorgeous. So long. And thick." She stroked a couple more times and squeezed the girth. "So smooth."

Celia said, "You should feel it when it's wet."

"I'll bet it feels amazing."

"It does. Sometimes when I'm alone, I find myself fingering it because it's so soft and damp."

More male groans filled the air.

The waitress dropped off the shots and the accoutrements. Celia placed her mouth on Tierney's ear. "Don't chicken out now. This is the payoff. And for the record? The thing with Renner is not one-sided. He can't keep his eyes off you." Celia eased far enough back that every man at the table could see exactly what she was doing. She picked up a lime. "Open those pretty lips, darlin'."

Tierney held the lime between her teeth, letting her tongue trace the bitter rind.

Celia dipped her index finger into the tequila, painting a line down the side of Tierney's neck. She murmured, "Tilt your head," and sprinkled salt over the wet streak. Celia's hair tickled Tierney's jaw when she put her tongue on Tierney's neck and slowly, oh so very, very slowly, licked away the salt. Celia held up the shot glass and knocked back the booze. As she swallowed, she pressed her lips to Tierney's, sucking the lime from her mouth.

Before Tierney could feel embarrassed, Celia said, "Your turn," switching places with her.

What if she did this wrong? What if she didn't look sexy and free, but awkward and uptight?

Don't think about it. Just do it. Make it hot as sin.

Tierney ran the pulp part of the lime over Celia's lips before placing it between her lips. She swirled her finger into the shot glass, deciding to spread it across Celia's chest. She chanced a look at Celia as she sprinkled on the salt, recognizing her "aren't we bad?" smirk. That spurred Tierney to dip the tip of her tongue beneath the elastic tank top band, flattening it as she lapped up every salt granule.

She tossed back the tequila, leaving her lips against Celia's for a beat before she sucked the lime between her lips and bit down.

This time, she had the guts to gauge the guys' reactions, although her heart raced and she suspected her cheeks were as red as maraschino cherries.

Skeeter rose to his feet for a standing ovation. "Next round is on me."

Kyle's and Celia's gazes were locked in silent battle.

Michael was studying Breck very closely.

Breck said, "Sister's got game," and fist bumped Davy.

She didn't see Renner. Had he left?

Then his strong hand circled her hip. His low voice burned her ear. "We're leaving."

"But—"

"Right. Fuckin'. Now. Do not argue with me."

Holy crap, he was pissed.

She managed to snag her purse off the table and wave good-bye to Celia before Renner clasped her hand in his and hotfooted it out of the bar.

He didn't speak. He didn't slow. He dodged and weaved through the throng until the crowd thinned. Then he cut down a long hallway and opened a door into a big room with metal corrals that denoted a stock containment facility. The barnyard odor lingered beneath the sharp scent of cleaning solution, but no animals were present.

Tierney found her back against those metal rails.

"You like having people watch you get your freak on?"

"Renner, it's not—"

"You put on that raunchy display with Celia to make me horny. Guess what? It worked. Guess what else? I will oblige your exhibitionist tendencies." Renner's impassioned gaze swept over her. "Strip."

"What?" Her eyes scanned the room in a panic. "This is a public place, Renner."

"So was the bar and it didn't seem to bother you. Havin' Celia's hands on you. Havin' Celia's mouth on you." He growled and stalked closer. "I want equal time and I want it right now, so take off your goddamn jeans, Tierney."

Hey, how's that game of "let's do a whole bunch of shots and tease our men out of their dirty minds with girl on girl fantasies" working out for you now?

"I admit we took it a little too far. And I'll make it up to you, however you want, but not here."

"Wrong. Right here, right now."

"Please. This is—"

"Not up for discussion." Renner's blue eyes glittered like sapphires. "And sorry, you're fresh outta tequila and salt, so we're gonna do this my way, without props. So for the last time, take off your jeans or I will cut them off."

"Very funny. Stop kidding around."

He grinned and reached in his pocket to pull out his knife. "Oh, darlin', I ain't even *close* to kiddin' about this. Take. Them. Off."

Was he testing her?

He flicked open the blade. "Now."

Okay. He *wasn't* testing her.

She managed to kick off her boots and peel away her jeans while her hands shook like a junkie's. But as the cold metal bars of the corral dug into the backs of her naked thighs, she admitted she wasn't shaking from fear, but anticipation. He could get her so fired up with just a regal look.

Heat emanated off Renner when he stopped in front of her. "Hold very still."

She did. She couldn't take her eyes off the lust raging in his.

He drawled, "Pity about your panties," a millisecond before he sliced the string by her hip, and then blithely tossed the scrap of lace over his shoulder.

She gasped, "Renner—"

His lips landed on hers in a punishing kiss. As he owned her mouth, he placed her hands on the metal rung beside her head. He broke free to nuzzle her neck. "Hold on tight and step onto the rung behind you." He nipped her earlobe. "Spread your legs."

A dizzy sensation rolled through her when Renner dropped to his knees. He framed her pussy with his rough hands, using his thumbs to hold open the fleshy folds covering her clit. He blew a cool stream of breath across the delicate tissues.

She shuddered.

Renner laughed. "Remind me again what a woman wants? A long tongue to lick that moist section of skin? Would it be *this* section?" He lapped at her slit. Once. Twice. Three times.

"Oh God."

"Or this section?" He flicked just the tip of his tongue below her clit. Not on it. Flicked over and over until she whimpered with frustration. "And I love tasting all this sweet syrup. I love how I can get you so wet, and so hot, that your juice flows down my throat as thick and warm as honey."

Sweat broke out on her belly. Despite the fact half of her body was freakin' naked, her skin was on fire.

"Do I remember something about a firm bite into the flesh until it explodes? Would *this* be the bit of flesh?" He opened his mouth over her clit and sucked. Gently bit.

He teased her until she squirmed, panted and finally yelled, "All right! I'm sorry I taunted you. But right now, I don't care if someone waltzes in while you're going down on me because you've made me so' hot—"

"And that is the answer I was lookin' for." Renner suctioned his mouth like he meant business, like he meant her to come within seconds and she obliged him. The orgasm slammed into her with the force of a freight train, blowing her hair back, shaking her to the rafters; she moaned his name as her clit throbbed beneath his talented tongue.

Then he was on his feet, frantically yanking down his jeans. He hiked her hips up, wrapping her legs around his waist, holding her ass in his hands as he plunged into her. His mouth was wet and hot on the side of her neck as he urged, "Hold on. God, you make me want you." He pulled out and slammed into her. "So ready for me. Every damn time."

She arched her pelvis, rocking into him, lost in his urgency. Her fingers itched to touch him, to rip open his shirt to feel the hard wall of his chest and his heated skin, but she could do nothing but hold on and enjoy the ride.

His strokes speeded up. Renner released a guttural sound against her throat and his whole body quaked with his release.

Before he gifted her with those deliciously sweet and possessive post-orgasmic kisses she craved, a loud clatter sounded from the doorway.

"Shit." Renner set her on her feet, retrieved her pants and tossed them to her.

Tierney dressed in record time and was just slipping on her boots when a security guard walked in. His suspicious gaze moved between them. "What are you two doing in here? This area is off limits to ticket holders."

"I'm not a ticket holder. I'm a stock contractor and I was double-checking the size of this pen before tomorrow."

The security guard remained skeptical. "You need to vacate the premises. Now."

"No problem." Renner held out his hand to Tierney.

It wasn't until they were in the hallway and Renner was hustling her to his truck that she realized she'd left her panties on the floor.

∞

Not that she would've had them on long after they returned to the hotel anyway.

The instant the hotel door shut he'd shoved her to her knees. Impatiently unbuckling his jeans, ramming his cock into her mouth, growling with pleasure as she gave him what he wanted—her immediate and total surrender. She tasted the mix of her juices and his as she brought him off quickly. The room was silent as he came, except for her sucking sounds and the steady beat of his fist on the door that matched the hot ejaculate spurting into her mouth. As soon as she finished swallowing, he hauled her to her feet, dispensed with their clothes and threw her on the bed.

Renner ruthlessly used his fingers and mouth on her pussy, propelling her to the brink, pulling back and pushing her again and again until she begged. Then he let her come.

Before she'd caught her breath from the almost violent, mind-blowing orgasm, he dragged her into the bathroom. He spread her legs wide and pressed her hips into the towel he'd draped over the marble counter.

His warm mouth tickled her ear. "You're mine. Understand? *Mine*. My hands on you. My mouth on you. My cock in you. No one else will ever have you the way I do. No one."

Tierney's mouth dried and her belly roiled watching him uncap the bottle of lube. He'd hinted at wanting this final virginity from her, and she'd demurred, so the fact he was taking it on his terms, and he'd make her enjoy it, ratcheted her lust a thousand degrees.

She attempted to relax as he worked a finger into her ass. Two fingers. Then the slick tip of his cock prodded her anus and slipped past the tight ring of muscle. Moving inch by inch until his cock filled her back channel completely.

His hand clutched her hair, forcing her gaze to meet his in the mirror. The strokes started out slow. The bite of pain was softened by the tingle of pleasure as the nubby fabric of the towel abraded her clit with his every thrust. When he couldn't hold back, when he reamed her ass harder and deeper and faster, without pause, she came, staring into his wild eyes, feeling a connection beyond anything she'd ever experienced.

And when Renner finally reached that point, he sank his teeth into the sensitive sweep of her neck to muffle his cry. The sexy love bite was another sign of his total possession and Tierney climaxed again. Hard.

It was the most intense sexual interlude she could imagine.

But Renner was by no means finished with her. He flipped on the shower, filling the space with damp heat. He carried her into the glass enclosure. Soaping every millimeter of her skin. Kissing her. Caressing her. Muttering sweet nothings against her wet flesh as he reignited their passion. He pinned her to the tile with his strong body and slowly made love to her, creating a dense haze of pleasure that rivaled the fragrant steam enveloping them.

Only then did he dry her off and carry her to bed. Twining their bodies together, his proof that she belonged to him as unassailable as the fact she was completely in love with him.

Chapter Thirty-two

❧

"Tierney? Baby, we're almost home."

She yawned and stretched. "I thought you were going to wake me up so I could drive part of the way."

"You looked so cute and peaceful. Besides, I wore you out last night. You needed to rest up." He smiled cheekily.

Tierney turned her head and kissed Renner's knuckles. She loved the way he always had to touch her, even in sleep. Now that she'd gotten used to constant physical affection, she didn't know how she'd ever live without it. She pushed upright, squinting into the darkness before she reached for her glasses. "How long before you have to hit the road again?"

"Depends on if Pritchett can find any help. If he can't, then I'll be gone soon."

"I'll hold down the fort while you're loadin' them doggies in the chutes." She plucked his hand off the seat and held it between hers. His callused hands were a testament to his hard work. She loved how his hands felt on her body, gentle and teasing. Sometimes rough. But always loving. Every time he touched her or kissed her or made love to her she felt his love. She just wished he could give voice to it.

Maybe you *should give voice to it.*

Right then, Tierney decided to take the first step.

"I hear them gears churning, smart girl. What's on your mind?"

"I don't want you to laugh."

"I won't. Unless you put on a red clown nose and a rainbow wig."

"Now who's trying to make me laugh? But I'm serious." She looked at him in the glow of the dashboard lights. "I don't want to hide our relationship. Not at the Split Rock. Not anywhere else. Not for anyone."

His body went very still.

She wondered if he would've said anything at all if she hadn't prompted him with, "Renner?"

"Sorry. You just caught me off guard."

"Why? Was our time in Denver 'what happens at the National Western Stock Show stays at the National Western Stock Show'?"

After a while he let out a slow breath. "We'd be open about our relationship with everyone for the rest of the time you're at Split Rock?"

Now Tierney understood his hesitation. He believed this was temporary—not that she'd ever led him to believe otherwise. "You think I intend to leave."

"Don't you?"

No. Because I love you. Because I never knew men like you existed. Because we have the start of something real.

It was her turn to stay silent. Grateful for the darkness, she watched the snowy mounds zip by as she gazed out her window.

Evidently Renner needed to finish their conversation. He pulled the truck to the side of the road, threw it in park and shut it off. "Don't start playing games with me now, Tierney."

"I'm not."

"Then look at me and tell me what's goin' on."

"I don't know how to do this."

"Do what?"

She gritted her teeth against the stupid tears that accompanied her dry mouth, sweaty palms and churning stomach.

"Do what?" he repeated.

"I don't know how to tell you I love you, okay?" she blurted. "I don't know how to tell you that I don't ever want to leave the Split Rock. I don't ever want to leave you."

Every bit of air in the cab seemed to vanish.

Tierney was suffocating in her own overheating skin. She fumbled with the door handle. Between the height of Renner's truck cab and the steep incline of the shoulder, she slid gracelessly into the ditch. Snow went down her pants and scraped her palms. She scrambled to her feet and climbed up by the back end of the truck.

Of course Renner was there, grabbing her upper arms and getting right in her face. "Why did you bail out like that?"

"Let me go."

"Like hell. Where were you goin'?"

"To get some air. I can't breathe." She kept her face pointed at the ground and twisted out of his hold. "Just let me breathe."

He let her be. But he didn't leave her.

Tierney wrapped her arms around herself, concentrating on dragging fresh air into her lungs. The icy wind whipped her hair around her face and she welcomed the sting that cooled the burning in her cheeks. She kept her eyes closed and simply breathed.

When she started to shiver, Renner was behind her, tugging her in his coat. He murmured, "Better?" against the whistling wind.

She nodded.

"You ready to get in the truck?"

She shook her head.

"Okay. We'll just . . . stay like this. For as long as you want."

She lifted her chin to look at the sky. Too much reflection

from the snow didn't allow for the night to be pitch black. The stars were silver spatters in a swath of indigo stretching as far as the eye could see. No light. No sound except for the wind. This land was breathtaking in its austerity. Humbling in its magnitude. She loved it here. Even if Renner rejected her, she couldn't return to the life she'd led in Chicago.

Her legs were feeling the effects of the cold. Renner's probably were too, but he hadn't moved or complained. She turned her head into his chest and said, "I'm sorry."

"For what? For saying you love me?"

Her heart raced.

"Are you sorry you love me, Tierney?"

She wiggled until he released her and she spun around to look him in the eye. "No. I'm not sorry I love you."

"Then are you sorry you told me that you love me?"

Why was he pushing her? "I don't know."

"I'm not sorry you told me." He attempted to push her hair out of her face—a losing battle against the never-ending wind. "It just caught me by surprise. But I should've known."

"Known that I love you?"

"No, known that you wouldn't play games. That you'd tell me how you felt about me as soon as you figured it out."

Renner smiled so softly, so wistfully her breath stalled. She feared he was about to tell her that as much as he liked her, he didn't feel the same way.

"You're very straightforward. That's what I love most about you."

A beat passed and then she blurted, "Wait. You love me?"

"Yep. And darlin', you're a lot braver than me, because I've known how I felt about you for a while and didn't have the guts to tell you."

"Define a while."

"Since before Christmas."

They stared at one another.

She said, "Now what?"

"First, this." Renner pressed his cold lips to hers and held them there. "And then this." Their lips moved against each other's. Warmed each other's. Although they kissed for a good long time, the kiss never caught fire. It stayed easy. Sweet. Tender. Loving. Perfect.

Then he rubbed his cold nose into her warm neck and she shrieked. "Omigod, that's cold!"

"Now can we get in the damn truck and go home? I'm freezin' my ass off." Renner took her hand and helped her in the driver's side. As soon as she put her coat on he reached for her hand again. And he didn't let go once on the drive to the Split Rock.

They crested the hill leading to the main lodge and noticed the lights were on. And a Land Cruiser was parked in the front.

He frowned and pulled in behind it. "We weren't supposed to get guests until tomorrow, right?"

"Right."

"Let's see what's going on before we unload the luggage."

Tierney's feeling of unease increased with every footstep. Renner held the door open and they both froze upon seeing the man sitting by a roaring fire, drinking out of a brandy snifter and conversing with Janie.

Hands shaking, she took off her coat and crossed the room. "Hello, Father. What are you doing here?"

"Enjoying the ambiance and the delightful company of Miss Fitzhugh." Gene Pratt stood and held his hand out to Renner. "Good to see you again, Jackson."

"You also, Pratt."

If Renner or Janie was surprised by the lack of affection between father and daughter, neither showed it. Tierney went straight for the bar. She grabbed two bottles of beer, popped the caps, and handed one to Renner.

Her father frowned.

Janie said, "I was just telling Mr. Pratt how lucky it was, Tierney, that Renner was able to give you a ride back from your trip to Denver."

"What were you doing in Denver, Tierney?" her father asked. "Janie was a little vague."

Now she felt guilty keeping Janie in the dark about their relationship. Tierney didn't want to make the woman look incompetent, but not at the expense of maintaining a lie to her father about her relationship with Renner.

She stopped in front of the fireplace. "Actually, I was with Renner the whole time. At the National Western Stock Show."

"Ah. Doing a little word-of-mouth advertising for the resort?"

"No. Renner's livestock contracting company had business meetings set up with rodeo promoters. It was partially a working vacation for him as well as a getaway for us."

Janie's gaze flicked between Tierney and Renner. "Us?" she repeated. "What does that mean?"

"It means that at some point my financial manager has become intimately involved with the man who's borrowed a whole pile of money from me." Her father stared at Renner. "Isn't that right?"

"Yes, sir."

"Involved? As in the two of you are . . . together?"

Tierney nodded.

Janie leapt off the couch and got right in her face. "How long has this been going on?"

"For a while," Renner said.

"Why didn't you tell me?" Janie whirled on Renner. "Either of you?"

"Yes, Tierney, why didn't you share the good news with anyone about your new relationship?" her father taunted.

"Because it's private and has no bearing on our business relationship." She locked her gaze to Janie's. "Since you had no idea that Renner and I were anything but business associates, you can reassure my father that our working hours were solely devoted to business."

Janie looked at Gene Pratt. "Sir. I assure you that I had

no inkling more than a business relationship existed between them."

"I believe you. I see how upset you are by all this, and I don't blame you." He smiled empathetically at Janie. "I'd like to talk to you in more detail about what we spoke of earlier. I'll be here all day tomorrow and I leave on Tuesday morning for Denver."

Another day and night with her father?

"Thank you. There's stuff in the office I need to take home." Janie started up the stairs.

Tierney's father stood. "I'll be in the lounge area. Dodie prepared dinner for us. You'll have to serve, as I've sent her home." He had his BlackBerry in his hand as he wandered away.

Renner mouthed, "Serve?" as they scaled the stairs.

"Yes. God forbid if he ever had to fix himself a plate."

The door to the office was ajar. "Janie?"

"Don't worry, I was just leaving."

"Stay a minute and talk to us," Renner said.

Janie dabbed her eyes with the tissue in her hand. "Why? So you can explain? Save it. I don't want to know." She sniffed. "Jesus. I'm such an idiot. And I'm sure you both got a huge laugh putting one over on me."

Renner touched her arm in a show of support, but Janie flinched like he'd slapped her,

"Don't be nice to me. I trusted you. Both of you. And it hurts like hell that you couldn't be bothered to tell me what was going on between you."

Rather than continue to coddle her, Renner got mad. "Really, Janie? You didn't notice that every time Tierney came near me I couldn't keep my eyes off her? You didn't wonder why we locked ourselves away in this office so often?"

"I thought it was about business," she said petulantly.

"After you moved in with Abe? You never once asked me how I spent my nights. Or who I was with. You didn't question why we went away to Denver together? Don't blame us for *you* bein' oblivious."

"Janie the idiot. It's probably a sign that I should move on," she muttered, slipping on her coat.

"A sign you should move on?" Renner demanded. "What's that mean?"

She gave him a cruel smile. "It's my private business and has nothing to do with you." The door slammed behind her.

He swore.

Tierney walked to the window and watched it snow. Was it really only an hour ago she'd never been happier? That everything she'd ever wanted was finally within reach?

Now she just wanted to cry.

Chapter Thirty-three

❦

Supper, aka dinner in Gene Pratt's world, was a stiffly formal affair. With no table staff, Tierney served the food, poured the wine and acted like the uptight Tierney he'd first met months ago.

Renner didn't like the reversion one bit.

But her father didn't notice because he talked over her. Lectured her in the guise of discussing business. Not once during dinner did Gene Pratt ask a single personal question of his daughter.

As they lounged by the fire, acting ridiculously civilized, Renner topped off Tierney's wineglass. He didn't care if she rebuffed his support; he'd damn well show it in front of her father. Sitting beside her, he draped his arm behind her shoulders. Then he kissed her temple and set his booted feet on the coffee table, like he always did.

Tierney hid her smirk behind her wineglass.

Gene Pratt did nothing so crass as scowl, but disapproval rolled off him. "Where exactly do you see this relationship going?"

"With all due respect, that is between me and Tierney."

"But you aren't so naïve to believe this relationship will continue once Tierney returns to Chicago."

"I'm not returning to Chicago."

It was all Renner could do not to turn and gape at her. Seemed Miz Straightforward hadn't been so forthcoming.

"And I told you I wouldn't accept your resignation. Your six-month sabbatical is nearly up." He swirled the cognac in the snifter. "Besides, you have been doing work for me while you've been on personal leave."

"Freelance work. I billed you accordingly. Your accounts payable department paid me accordingly."

"Are you still in a snit because of Steven?"

"Are you asking if I'm still upset that you promoted Steven instead of me? Not because he was more qualified—I have three advanced degrees in finance to his none—but because he was born with balls?"

Her father gaped. "Tierney. What is wrong with you?"

"What? Women aren't supposed to say balls? Or they aren't supposed to act like they've got them?"

"Is there a point to this crudity?"

"Is there a point to this surprise visit to Wyoming?" she countered. "I'd like to hear it." She held up her hand, warning, "And please don't use a bullshit excuse like you missed me."

"Fine. No bullshit. I came to see how this training opportunity was working. Does your Mr. Jackson know what you're giving up to play cowgirl resort proprietor for a few months?"

Nice. Now the asshole was using his presence to rile Tierney.

"No. But I'm sure you'll tell him." She drained her wine. "Don't forget to put all those dollar signs you're so fond of in front of your answer."

Gene Pratt focused on him. "I'll admit I gave Steven the position in my company Tierney wanted. It wasn't out of spite. It was because I've always had a higher station in mind for her."

Tierney went motionless beside him.

"Awarding the position to Steven was a test for her. If she accepted my decision as what was best for the company and didn't question it at all . . . then I knew I could count on her loyalty—almost to a fault."

He leaned forward. "But Tierney didn't accept it. She forced my hand by invoking the clause that allowed her to choose an oversight position for training purposes. Then she turned in her resignation and set out to prove she doesn't need my company to be successful. That's exactly the type of person I need steering my company. That's why after she's been seasoned a bit, in five years or so, Tierney will take over PFG as CFO."

Her body vibrated with anger. "You're lying."

"No, dearest daughter. I am not."

Silence.

Renner did not want to be dragged into this family drama. Needing a distraction, he frowned and pulled out his phone. "Excuse me. I missed this call and I need to get right back to him." He dialed his voice mail box, waited and said, "Bixby! No, not bad timing." He opened the front door and let it slam, then pressed himself against the inside wall. They wouldn't speak freely with him in the room. Gene Pratt wouldn't stand by and let his brilliant daughter settle for a livestock contractor with shit on his boots in Nowhere, Wyoming. As much as it pained him to admit it, maybe it wouldn't be best for Tierney to settle for it either.

Tierney didn't hold back. "I cannot believe you'd come here and spew such lies. Giving Steven that job was not a test. You did it because you wanted to show me that you control the company. That blood—whether we share it, or whether I spill it to scrape my way to the top of the heap—means nothing to you. I was unhappy. Unhappy working for you, unhappy living the life I thought I wanted."

"I can see why you'd be miserable. Living in a million-dollar condo overlooking Lake Michigan. A hefty stock portfolio. A position in a top company, which you're well

compensated for. And the ability to pick and choose whatever pet project struck your fancy. Like this one."

This was a pet project for her?

"*You* own my condo. I started my own investment portfolio when I was eighteen with my inheritance from my
mother. My salary was twenty-five thousand dollars below
the national average for my educational level. And I wasn't
allowed to pick projects until *after* I handed in my resignation, Dad, so try again."

Pratt sighed. "My point is, you might be happy here
temporarily, enjoying thumbing your nose at me, but you
won't be happy for the long term."

"You don't know what makes me happy."

"And neither do you," he retorted.

"Yes, I do. I found it here."

Renner's heart absolutely turned over in his chest with
love for this woman.

"You've found happiness with him? What will happen
when the cowboy charm wears off?"

"It won't. Renner is the real deal. He loves me in spite of
my privileged background."

"He loves you *because* of your privileged background,"
Pratt said with false sympathy. "You're the gravy train and
he'll ride you into the ground."

"He's not like that. I love him. I love the life I can have
here. There is nothing you can offer me that would change
my mind."

"You sure about that?"

Tierney's laughter held a sour tone. "In fact, you could
offer me the CEO position, your job, right now, with the
multimillion-dollar salary and I'd turn you down. Flat."

Silence.

"You're brainwashed. This is not you talking, Tierney."

"That's where you're wrong. This is me, the real Tierney,
the person I've discovered myself to be when I'm here.
Whether or not I'm with Renner. I love the work I'm doing,
being part of the community. So don't you dare denigrate it.

I don't need your approval, because for the first time in my life, I don't care."

"You're willing to walk away from everything you've known? Everything you've worked for?"

"Yes."

"Forgive me if I don't believe that after you toiled to earn all those advanced finance degrees, you'd give up a chance to put those theories into practical application. You prefer to be in Wyoming, worrying whether the guest in room four has enough clean towels?"

Direct hit. Renner almost heard Tierney deflate from that sharp jab.

"This place won't make you happy for long. We both know it. You need to use your mind, not let it atrophy."

Renner slammed the door and strolled around the corner, shoving his phone into his pocket. "Sorry. What'd I miss?"

Tierney stood and grabbed Renner's hand. "Nothing. We're done talking. I was just telling my father we've still got to unpack."

"Fair enough." Gene Pratt rolled to his feet. "And I'll warn you to tread lightly on ultimatums as I've no patience for them." He smiled at Renner. "Have a good evening, Jackson."

"You too, Pratt."

"Good night, Tierney."

As soon as he shut the door on the room down the hall, Renner said, "Tierney? Baby, are you okay?"

"Not really."

"C'mere."

She willingly went into his arms. His kiss on her forehead became a soft smooch on her eyebrows. The corners of her eyes. The corners of her smile. Then their lips met fully and he ached to see this vulnerable side. He wanted to reassure her that it'd all work out, but he worried they'd just seen the tip of the iceberg where Gene Pratt's determination was concerned. The icy mountain below the surface was always far scarier and able to inflict more damage.

Chapter Thirty-four

≪≫

The front door slammed with enough force it rattled the dishes in the china cabinet.

Abe remained where he was, shoving each carpet sample against the wall, trying to decide which shade of brown looked better when he couldn't tell the fucking difference and didn't really give a shit. Janie should've been home hours ago to help him decide.

He lined up all eight samples in the middle of the empty room.

Thump times twelve echoed to him as Janie stomped down the stairs.

"Where the hell have you been?"

"Working. Why?"

"You could've called. In fact you should've called and I hate that seems to be an option with you lately. I didn't need to sit around and worry about you."

"Who asked you to worry about me?" Her eyes narrowed to slits. "Don't pull this 'where were you' macho bullshit on me, Abe. I didn't like it back then and I sure as hell don't like it any better now."

He bit back his less than flattering retort. His gaze

dropped to her hand, which clutched a very large tumbler of whiskey. "Bad day?"

"You have no fucking idea." She knocked back a big gulp. "So, not only did Gene Pratt of PFG show up out of the blue, but as I was trying to explain why neither his daughter nor Renner was around, guess who strolled in, holding hands, and dropped a fucking bombshell?" She answered her own question. "Renner and Tierney. And get this, they've been secretly screwing around since before Thanksgiving."

Abe said not one word.

"When I got pissy, rightfully so, Renner had the balls to accuse me of being oblivious. He said I was about the only one who hadn't figured out that he and Tierney were involved. Seriously involved. Like in love and shit."

He knew by the gleam in her eye she was about to ask the question he didn't want to answer. But he'd be damned if he'd lie.

"Did you know?" she demanded.

"Officially? No."

"That's not an answer."

"It's not the answer you want. If you're askin' me if I knew they had feelings for each other? Then that answer would be yes."

"How?"

"Jesus, Janie. All's I had to do was look at them. They kept their hands to themselves in public, but they sure as hell couldn't keep their eyes off each other."

She snorted. Knocked back another drink. "So I'm the village idiot. Awesome."

"You're not happy for them?"

"Not at my own expense."

That sounded cold. "Are they firing you?"

"No." She paced to the door to the bathroom and back. "But Mr. Pratt is right. How can I not feel betrayed that they couldn't trust me enough to let me in on their secret? I worked with them. Every damn day. I'm mad as hell."

"Are you mad at them or mad at yourself because you didn't figure it out?"

Janie stopped. Faced him. "How is any of this my fault?"

Abe raised his hands in surrender. "Whoa. It's not your fault. Why does there have to be blame?"

"I blame them because they made me look like a fucking idiot in front of the man who holds my future in his hands."

"I thought I held your future in my hands." He'd attempted a lighthearted tone but didn't pull it off.

"Don't even start with me, Abe. This"—she gestured to the space between them—"was temporary. You knew that."

"Did I? So I should also assume things couldn't change? Just like you assumed things wouldn't ever change with Tierney and Renner?"

She scowled. "Don't be an ass."

"This Pratt guy. Why does he hold your future?"

"Hello? He's head of a corporation that has dozens of properties across the globe. With my interior design work and hospitality training I'd be a great asset to his organization. I'm not tied down, no family, so I can go anywhere at any time."

The "no family" comment stuck in his craw and knocked the hope right out of him. "Did Pratt offer you a job?"

Janie stared into her glass. "I have a preliminary interview with him tomorrow."

"And if you pass the prelim? Then what?"

"Then I fly to Chicago for a final interview with the department head."

His voice was remarkably calm. "That's it then? Does Renner know you're bailing on him?"

"Can you blame me after what he and Tierney did to me?"

"Oh, for Christsake, grow up," he snapped. "Yeah, it hurts when you find out someone you were close to hasn't been completely up front with you. Guess what? That's life. You gonna cut and run every damn time that happens?"

"That's not fair. I never committed—"

"To anything, did you?" He stomped over to her. "Even Tierney, a city girl with no ties whatsoever to Muddy Gap, is more invested in the Split Rock than you are. And I don't mean financially invested. I mean emotionally invested. In the resort and in the community."

Her eyes turned as hard as granite. "You have no right to say that to me."

"I have every right. When we were married, you never deigned to mingle with the townsfolk, did you? The only person you connected with was Bran Turner's grandmother. Oh, and let's not forget about Bran. Bran, who's been *my* friend since we were kids, never said a fucking word to me about any of the stuff you talked to him about. About our marriage, about how freakin' miserable you were with me. How do you think that made me feel, Janie? You wanna talk about feeling betrayed?"

By the way her eyes widened she hadn't even considered that.

George whined upstairs, upset by the loud voices.

Abe saw no reason to back down now. "I made mistakes. But so did you. I freely admitted mine, but you never once took any of the blame. As much as I beat myself up over the years, I'll bet you didn't at all. Boohoo, poor Janie. Your life was so bad with me. You had a man who loved you more than life, who would've done anything to make you happy, who wanted forever with you. Instead of talking to me, helping me figure out how we could improve our relationship, you moped around playing the victim. Because I couldn't read your fucking mind, you ended up making yourself miserable, making me miserable, making my family miserable and rather than stick around and fix it, you bailed. Like you're doin' now. Big surprise."

He was completely out of breath when he finished. They stared at each other, not speaking. Because, really, what else was there to say?

His cell phone rang. Perfect timing. "Hello?"

"Abe. It's Lainie."

A dose of good news would be welcome right about now. "She's finally in labor?"

"No. She collapsed at work. She's bleeding and they rushed her into surgery for an emergency C-section because both she and the baby are in distress."

Fear crawled up his throat. He choked out, "When?"

"They just called. What am I gonna do? I can't lose her. I just . . . can't."

"Hang tight. I'll be there in two minutes." Abe stepped away from Janie, scaling the stairs two at a time.

"I'll be waitin' at the end of the driveway." *Click*.

Abe shoved his feet in his boots, his arms in his shearling coat and his wallet in his back pocket. He'd reached his truck before Janie caught him.

"What's going on?"

"Lainie's had complications of some kind. She's in surgery. I've gotta get Hank to Rawlins."

She stood in front of the driver's door. "I'll come along."

"No. Move."

"Abe. I want to come."

"Why? You don't have any family, remember? You've got nothin' tying you here. I don't even know why the hell you care."

That did the trick. She shrank away from him like he was a monster.

Abe's tires spit gravel as he burned rubber getting to his brother's house. Hank threw himself into the passenger seat with a brusque, "Drive."

"Buckle up. Got the all clear from Sheriff Bullard to get there as fast as possible."

Hank's right hand clutched the handle of a pink and white polka-dotted bag; his left hand squeezed his cell phone so hard Abe feared it might crack. He tapped Hank's wrist. "Ease up or you're gonna break it. Any news?"

"Her friend Vanessa said she'd keep me updated, even when she ain't supposed to. Because Lainie works there, because everybody loves her so much, they're all worried, which makes it worse. Jesus. I can't . . ." His voice cracked.

Abe glanced at the speedometer. Ninety-five.

"Lainie shouldn't have been workin'. She should've been at home with her feet up takin' it easy."

"I'd say it's a damn good thing this happened when she was at work and not at home." He kept his eyes on the road when he said, "Tell me what's eating at you, Hank."

"What if it comes down to saving Lainie's life or the baby's . . . ?"

"It won't come to that. You hear me? They're gonna do everything to save them both."

Hank nodded. But Abe knew he wasn't convinced. Hank's cell phone buzzed and he answered, "How's Lainie? No. I understand. Really? She's okay? What color? I'll be damned. Thanks."

"What?"

"I'm a father. They delivered the baby. It's a girl."

Relief rolled over him. "She's all right?"

"Apparently. She has Lainie's hair color and she's screaming like a banshee. Probably wants her mama. Lainie's still in surgery."

"You know me'n Celia are gonna spoil that baby girl rotten." Abe kept talking the rest of the way to Rawlins.

When they turned onto the street leading to the hospital, Hank said, "Thanks for—"

"No need to thank me. Whatever you need, I'm here."

"I know. You've always been the one constant in my life, Abe. Don't think I don't appreciate it. I don't know what I'd do without you, either." Hank bailed out of the truck and ran in the emergency entrance doors.

Abe parked and considered calling Janie to apologize for his rudeness, but they both needed time to cool off. He just hoped she wouldn't run off.

For the first hour in the waiting room he read magazines. For the second hour he watched TV. At the start of hour three he closed his eyes rather than watch an older man pace back and forth in front of the windows, muttering to himself.

A tap on his shoulder woke him. At first he didn't recognize the blue scrubs. Then he looked up into Hank's face. The frown lines on his forehead had eased somewhat, as had the pinched lines around his mouth. "Lainie?"

"Is fine. She had some kind of placenta rupture. They fixed her up and she's in recovery. She's groggy, but she's fine." Hank closed his eyes and seemed to have trouble swallowing. When he repeated, "She's fine," Abe wondered how many times Hank would say that before he truly believed it.

"Come on. I want you to meet your niece." They cut down a hallway and stopped in front of a window, but the shades were pulled. Hank said, "Be right back."

Abe slumped against the wall, wanting to weep with relief that everything had turned out all right. A door opened and Hank, his rough-and-tumble little brother with the enormous hands and body that took punishment from angry bulls, cradled a tiny pink bundle. When Hank tore his gaze away from his newborn daughter and looked at Abe, with such fierce love and awe on his face, damn if Abe didn't tear up.

"This is Brianna Kate Lawson. Brianna, this is your Uncle Abe. And guess what, baby girl? He's already promised to buy you a pony."

That'd teach Abe to babble under duress. He squinted at the face nearly hidden beneath the pink blanket. "Why's she wearin' a hat?"

"Keeps her tiny head warm." Hank gestured with his chin. "Go ahead and slide it up. Check out her hair. Sweetpea's got a head full of it."

Abe gently edged the hat up and grinned at the coppery curls identical to Lainie's. "She's Lainie's Mini-Me."

"Isn't she beautiful? Just like her mama." Hank lovingly pressed his lips to the baby's forehead, then gave Abe a stern look. "Now cover her head back up like it was so she don't get a chill."

"Sheesh." Abe couldn't help but touch her plump cheek. Marvel at this new addition into all their lives. "Congrats, bro, Miss Brianna is amazing. Has her mama seen her?"

"Briefly. Guess she's makin' a pretty big fuss about wanting her baby, so that's where we're headed now." Hank started down the hallway and stopped.

Happy as he was for his brother and sister-in-law, Abe wanted a family of his own. With Janie. And he understood he might have to make some hard decisions about his future to ensure that would happen. Because he wouldn't live without her ever again.

Abe donned his coat and trudged to the parking lot to his truck. He yawned when he noticed it was one o'clock in the morning.

When he pulled up to the ranch house, Janie's car was gone.

Chapter Thirty-five

❧

$\mathcal{T}$ ierney wasn't surprised by the summons from her father for a breakfast meeting. Right after Renner unloaded her luggage last night, he'd kissed her, urged her to get a full night's rest, and left her alone. Sleep had been the last thing on her mind. Especially since Renner hadn't said a word about anything her father had said.

As usual, her father didn't make small talk. "I had time to think about what you said last night, and I realized you're right."

Sipping her coffee, she watched her father cut up a slice of bacon into perfectly even pieces. "Right about what?"

"About your salary being on the low end." He popped a bacon chunk in his mouth and chewed. "I'm amending my offer; return to Chicago and I'll double your salary. I'll start to train you to take the reins as CFO."

"When?"

"Training would start immediately. You cannot deny the appeal of becoming CFO of a major company before your fortieth birthday."

There was a huge difference between his promise of her becoming CFO in five years like he'd hinted at last night, or

315 WRANGLED AND TANGLED

before her fortieth birthday, which wouldn't happen for another fourteen years. His vague language always tripped people up, in conversations and with contracts.

"I also want to apologize for keeping you stuck in an office, away from the interpersonal workings of the company. I'm pleased to see that your hands-on experience the last few months has vastly improved your people skills. I will feel more comfortable letting you handle some of the face-to-face meetings."

Tierney rested her elbows on the table. "After what's happened here? Really? You aren't afraid that I'll end up in bed with male clients seeking financing from PFG? Or will you strictly have me dealing with female clients?"

He smiled. Delicately wiped his mouth with the cloth napkin. "I trust your moral character. I'm sure being isolated, out of your social element and in constant contact with Jackson played a part in your intimate involvement with him."

The bastard was a master at backhanded compliments.

"But I warn you that Jackson has been married before. Twice. Both short-term liaisons, so I fear his affections are easily earned, easily discarded."

She wasn't surprised her father knew about Renner's marriages—he thoroughly investigated any person he intended to do business with. But why did he think she didn't know? "If multiple marriages are a sign of a lapse in judgment, you'd fall into that same category."

"But there is a difference."

"Which is?"

"I didn't use money, money I hadn't earned, to set me on the path to success."

No. You've just built your success on the backs of people desperate enough to come to you for a loan. "Cut to the chase. What are your terms?"

"You'll inform Mr. Jackson you're returning to Chicago to reclaim your position in the company. But in order to assure there are no ill personal feelings, or any issues with his financial obligation, that PFG is voiding the contract. He'll own the Split Rock, the land, and the buildings free and clear."

"And if he refuses?"

"He won't. If you love him as you say you do, you'll encourage him to take this deal at face value, so he gets the one thing he wants, which, contrary to your belief, isn't you, my dear—but this piece of property. Win-win situation for everyone."

"What if I refuse your terms? For the sake of argument, let's say I stick around to tie up loose ends. During that time, I have a change of heart and decide to stay at Split Rock with Renner. And we'll continue to run the resort as we've been. What then?"

All humor fled his face. His eyes became black chips of ice. "You really don't want to push me on this. I'm being more than generous. To you. And to him."

"That is not an answer."

"Running the resort as you've been won't last long. Renner Jackson is six weeks and two days out from making his first payment on the loan. In the fine print—and yes, daughter, there is always fine print, you'd be wise to check it—is a clause that states I have the right to demand the loan be paid in full, for any reason, before the first payment is made."

"What? That's ridiculous. I've never seen that clause. He has five years to make full restitution for the loan amount."

"No, he does not . . . If I invoke the clause. Nonpayment will put the loan in immediate default, which means PFG would own this property." He flashed his teeth. "I believe some of my less than PC colleagues call this the 'by the short hairs' clause."

Tierney swallowed, hoping the contents of her stomach wouldn't come back up onto the table. "You wouldn't."

"Oh, I would. And trust me, I wouldn't lose a single wink of sleep over enforcing it."

How was she supposed to blithely crush Renner's dream and destroy him financially?

Stay with Renner and he loses the Split Rock.

Leave the Split Rock and the only thing Renner loses is her.

Pretty cut-and-dried decision.

Where would that leave her? Emotionally decimated. She couldn't go back to being the person she'd been before Renner came into her life. She didn't want to.

Why had her father put the decision on her shoulders? Why wouldn't he engage Renner in this? Threaten or bribe him?

That's when Tierney understood this was a game. Gene Pratt excelled at playing one side against the other—especially when two sides started out united. Holding this discussion with her was only half his battle plan. Her decision, her verbal confirmation, would give him the tactical advantage of knowing exactly what type of ammunition to use on Renner.

Not this time. She would not allow him to win. This time she intended to win it all. But first she'd have to level the playing field and become as devious as her father. "I'm sorry, it's just… I'm confused."

"I know this is hard." He softened his tone. "I can see your feelings for Jackson are genuine. But because you don't have much experience with relationships, I believe you're ignoring the possibility this is just a short-term fling for him."

Seething, she looked away.

"I don't enjoy seeing you upset. Which is why I came here. I had to make sure you weren't making a mistake."

Tierney met the phony concern in her father's eyes. "I don't think I can make a decision one way or another right now."

That did not please him. Another of Gene Pratt's strengths? Pushing for a fast decision. But Tierney admitting she was torn seemed to mollify him. "I understand. I'm leaving in the morning, but you can call me anytime. All I've ever wanted was what's best for you."

His idea of love was a twisted array of pride, money and expectation. "Thanks. If you'll excuse me, I have a stack of paperwork to catch up on after being gone."

"I don't have to ask you not to discuss any of this with Jackson, do I?"

"Renner and I are involved. What he wants from me should factor into my final decision."

"On a personal front, talk about it until you're blue in the face." He leaned closer. "But on a business front, you cannot discuss specific contract terms with him, as what we discussed falls under business confidentiality."

Bullshit. Renner signed the contract; he had a right to know what it contained, especially since he'd missed the fine print. So for the first time in her life, Tierney looked her father in the eye and lied. "I understand."

He patted her hand, in a pseudo-fatherly gesture that turned her stomach. "I won't keep you from your work. But I'd like to have dinner, if you're free tonight."

Another bogus offer. Her father seriously underestimated what she knew about his business practices. He had no intention of being here tonight. He'd said his piece to her and set everything in motion. She smiled and lied again. "Of course I'm free. I'll ask Dodie to create something special just for us."

∞

Renner wasn't looking forward to telling Tierney he had to leave again because Pritchett needed his help. Funny, the idea of Pritchett needing help with the business Renner owned. A business he'd sadly neglected in the last year when he'd been building the resort.

Chances were high he wouldn't end up owning the Split Rock when the chips started to fall. The smartest thing he'd done was to keep his stock contracting business out of financial dealings with PFG. So he wouldn't lose everything.

But no doubt in his mind he stood to lose a lot. The worst was the thought of losing Tierney.

Goddammit, he loved her. Loved her in that all-consuming way that scared the living hell out of him because he'd never ever felt that way before. She'd barged into his life, into his bed, into his heart, attaching herself to every part of him and he couldn't fathom being without her.

The door banged open. A shadow solidified. The man strolled into the barn like he wasn't wearing tasseled loafers.

Good thing Renner had a shovel nearby to dig the pile of shit this man was about to unload on him. He smiled, resting his forearm on the top of the corral. "If you're lookin' for me, I'm back here."

"Yes, I was looking for you." Pratt paused. Probably wanting to mimic Renner's posture, but not willing to soil his snappy suit to prove he was the type of guy who hung out in barns.

"You and your daughter have one thing in common."

"What's that?"

"You don't have a freakin' clue about what type of shoes to wear in here. Be mindful of the piles of shit."

Gene's eyes narrowed and he managed a terse, "Thanks for the warning."

"No problem. So, whatcha need?"

"I thought we should touch base. I'm pleased that the revenues are on par with initial expectations."

"That's happy news for you financial types." Renner cocked his head. "But you're not pleased I'm involved with Tierney. You here to warn me off?"

"In a manner of speaking. I don't know how you feel about Tierney—to some extent it doesn't matter."

Wrong. It mattered a whole helluva lot. But he wanted to see where Pratt was going with this.

"My daughter is stubborn. If I said red, she'd say blue. Then she'd change her answer to red. Tierney wants to be an independent thinker. But in the end she always sees things my way."

Renner whistled. "That's harsh. That's also making a pretty broad assumption about her."

Pratt adjusted his tie. "I know her better than she thinks I do."

The cocky statement pissed him off, because it was a total lie. "Well, Daddy-o, I'll go out on a limb to say I know Tierney on a completely different level than you do. A level you ought not discount if this conversation is goin' where I think it is."

"Lust fades. As a man who's been married as many times as you, I know of what I speak."

"You think I'm surprised you know my marital history? Wrong. Ain't something I hide."

"But you did hide that your first wife's daddy paid you off."

"She wanted out of the marriage. Daddy made it happen and decided to compensate me for the hell I endured. I sure didn't argue." Renner allowed the man a once over. "Is that why you're here? To see if I'm still that kind of guy?"

Pratt gave him an equally measured look. "That's the question of the day, isn't it?"

"So be a man about it and get to the fucking point."

"I'm willing to sign over the Split Rock in its entirety to you and stamp the loan paid in full."

"What's the catch?"

Pratt smiled tightly. "Really. You need me to spell it out for you?"

"I'm betting all's I have to do is tell Tierney she was a fling and I want her out of my life for good."

"Simple, but effective."

"Oh, and let me guess. *You* get to tell her that I'd rather have a chunk of dirt than her. That I am the same money-grubbing piece of shit I've always been because I could be bought off. And she's better off without me."

"In a nutshell: yes."

Renner laughed scathingly. "In a nutshell: no. *Fuck* no."

"Did I mention this is not a negotiation?"

"I don't give two shits about your assumption that there's

even room to negotiate when it comes to how I feel about Tierney."

"Is this supposed to prove you love her?" Pratt mocked.

"I do love her. I don't have to prove a goddamned thing to *you*. And that's what gets you, doesn't it? Not only that Tierney loves me enough to walk away from Daddy's purse strings, but she's been done jumping through your hoops since the moment she stepped on this property."

"She's a brilliant girl and she'd be throwing away her life here with you."

Renner pointed at Pratt. "There's your problem. Tierney is not a girl. She's a woman, hell, she's all woman, and she's making an adult decision that you have no part of. She's out of your reach. Done being under your thumb. She's taken control of her own life for a change and I applaud her for that.

"You only see her as another asset. Another thing you own. I know she's smart. Yeah, she's probably too smart for the likes of me. But her brain ain't the best part of her. Her heart is the best part of her. And I can't believe I'm the lucky guy she's decided to give it to."

"Pretty words," Pratt sneered. "Think she'll stick with you when all you've got to offer her is your twice-divorced heart?"

"At least it's honest. And I ain't putting conditions on it."

"You'll lose. You'll both lose." It appeared Daddy-o was losing his cool. He bit off, "Take the offer, Jackson."

"Take your offer and shove it, Pratt. We're done."

"We're not done. Not by a long shot. You'll be hearing from me." He turned and walked out.

Renner was half tempted to shout something juvenile like, *bring it on, motherfucker*. He'd let that bastard fore-close on the Split Rock before he'd ever turn on Tierney. But the bastard was her father. Although Gene Pratt didn't have an issue making Tierney choose between Renner and him, Renner would not do the same thing to her.

This was all kinds of fucked up. But what sucked the most? He couldn't stick around and hash it out. He needed to be on the road in an hour. He walked to his truck so he could talk to Tierney before he left.

∞

Ten minutes later Renner burst into the office, demanding, "Did you know?"

Tierney's hands froze on the keyboard. "Know what?"

He threw the sheaf of papers at her. "That PFG has a clause in the contract that can force me to pay back one hundred percent of the loan before the year is up? Or I default on everything?"

By the guilty look on Tierney's face, she'd known. Maybe she'd even put the damn clause in.

Fuck.

Had he been played for the fool again?

"How did you find out?" she asked quietly.

"After your father"—he started to say, *used you as the currency to buy me off*, but amended—"had a chat with me, he oh-so-thoughtfully left a copy of the contract on the seat of my truck with the clause in question circled." Renner clenched his hands into fists. Gritted his teeth so hard his jaw ached.

"What did my father say to you?"

Renner laughed bitterly. "As if you don't know."

"I don't. I swear." Tierney came around to rest her backside on the front edge of her desk.

"I've let you deal with all the financials regarding the Split Rock. I didn't question you. Not like you questioned *me* on every goddamned thing about this place." Anger burned up his throat and heated his face. "Did you get a big fuckin' chuckle out of that? The dumb cowboy so desperate that he'd believe everything you told him?"

"It wasn't like that, Renner, not at all."

"So when I came to you needing more cash, where did that money come from?"

Tierney averted her eyes.

Not good. "Answer me, dammit."

"From my personal account."

Renner's mouth dropped open. "What? Why? Just to maintain the fucking lie? Or to have something to hold over my head? So you could own me too?"

"No. I did it because I believe in this place. I expected it'd be successful given the chance. But I also knew unforeseen expenses in the first year of operation for a new business can wipe out any financial reserves. So I covered it and kept track of the cash outlay."

"Yeah? You've gotta have a lot of cash outlay available to 'cover' those expenses. Since I know little about your personal financial situation, I wanna know where you got the money."

"I earned it."

"How?"

Tierney dropped her gaze again and he recognized she was still keeping something from him.

"Tell me."

"When you saw me working after I first arrived? Ninety-nine point nine percent of what I was doing had nothing to do with the Split Rock. Ninety-nine point nine percent of it was . . . killing time."

"That's why you could piss with me endlessly about every aspect of it? You had nothin' better to do?"

She nodded.

"Jesus. When did that change?"

"When you needed money from the escrow account and that account was already empty. I lent my available cash reserve to the Split Rock general fund. Then I was broke. I have stocks and other investments, but no ready cash. So I did freelance work for PFG. But I earned it. Every penny of it."

"Not willing to ask PFG for a loan because the price of selling your soul is a little high?" Cheap shot, but he took it anyway.

Tierney's back snapped straight. "I absolutely do not ask my father for money. Ever."

"It ain't like he doesn't have enough to go around," Renner pointed out.

"True. But if you think he treats me any differently because I'm his daughter? Then you've underestimated him. You overestimated his faith in me too." She closed her eyes. "That stung whenever you called me a spoiled daddy's girl. You even assumed he paid for my cabin. He didn't. I did. He didn't give me a dime for my education. What I didn't earn in academic scholarships, I paid for out of my own pocket. The only thing my father has ever provided is a rent-free place to live in Chicago. That's only because the condo is in the office building he owns and he expects me to work damn near twenty-four hours a day for the privilege of living there."

Renner stared at her with absolute incredulity. His head spinning, his stomach in knots. His heart aching.

"What?"

"I feel like I don't even know you."

"You know me better than anyone ever has, Renner."

"Wrong. The Tierney I thought I knew didn't play games. She was straightforward. This"—he gestured to nothing in particular—"is far from honest."

"Would you have taken the money from me if you'd known you didn't have an open line of credit from PFG?"

"Fuck no," he spat.

"You needed that money. Without it—"

"I'd be exactly in the same position I'm in now. Seriously screwed and no way out."

Tierney shook her head. "Listen, it might seem bad right now, but I know we can come up with a plan."

"There is no *we* anymore, understand? I trusted you. And I . . . There's no way I can come up with that kind of money to pay you back or your father back. If I'da been able to snap my fingers and conjure that much cash last year, I sure as shit wouldn't have borrowed from PFG." Frustrated, behind schedule and absolutely heartsick, he stomped to the door.

"Renner. Wait. Where are you going?"

"I still have another business to run, and thank God for that."

"When will you be back?"

"I don't know."

Tears spilled down her cheeks. "Please. Don't leave like this. I love you."

Damn her show of vulnerability. The woman was always rock solid. The fact she was crying tied him up in knots. "I have to leave. I don't have a choice."

Chapter Thirty-six

❦

*G*athering her meager things from Abe's place hadn't been a monumental undertaking last night.

Always ready to leave at a moment's notice, aren't you?

Nothing wrong with that. But her motto, no fuss, no muss—move out and move on, seemed a little hollow.

Janie hadn't expected Abe to coddle her after she'd shared her craptastic day, but his anger had been totally unexpected.

Not unwarranted though.

Her cheeks heated when she considered the words she'd carelessly tossed off. She realized she must've come across as a cold unfeeling bitch in both matters of the head and matters of the heart.

The night had been filled with many revelations. Not all of which she'd shared with Abe, especially after he'd demanded to know why she hadn't noticed Tierney and Renner were in love.

Duh, cowboy. You want to talk about piss-poor powers of observation? How come you haven't noticed I'm head over heels in love with you?

She was so lost in thought she literally ran into an infuriated Renner after she left Gene Pratt's room.

He put his hands on his hips and said, "He got to you too, Janie?"

A million excuses and explanations bounced around in her head, but none exited her mouth.

Renner stared at her. Hard. Then Renner, the most even-keeled person she'd ever known, latched on to her bicep and hauled her down the hallway into the laundry room. His eyes, usually a calm, serene blue, were snapping fire. "What did that bastard promise you?"

"What do you mean?"

"Don't play coy with me, Janie. Gene Pratt. He offered you a job with PFG, didn't he?" When she didn't immediately respond, he laughed bitterly. "That's just awesome."

"Ren, I—"

"Don't give me your 'this was a temporary gig' reminder. I honestly don't think I can take another piece of bad news today."

"What other bad news?" Her stomach clenched at Renner's expression of defeat.

"Nothin' that concerns you anymore. And I wouldn't want to say anything against your new boss." He walked past her.

But Janie hooked her finger in his belt loop and dug her heels in to stop him. "Oh, no, you don't. Get back here and talk to me."

"I'm talked out, to be honest." He sighed with weight-of-the-world weariness. "Look. Things run their course. I get that. But I'd hoped since you'd been with me on this project from the start, that maybe you'd stick around longer than a few months."

"That's not fair."

Whiny much? And didn't you use the same excuse last night with Abe?

Renner's hands gripped the doorframe. He wouldn't turn around and look at her. "I know it ain't, but I can't help the way I feel. I'm sure our paths will cross again someday."

"Why does it sound like you're leaving?"

"Because I am."

"Where are you going?"

"Back to what I know. Back where I belong." Renner said, "Good luck with your new job, Janie."

She was so stunned she let go of his belt loop. Those long legs and determined stride carried him out the door. Her response, "But I turned it down," was lost in the whir of the washing machine.

∞

Hours later, when the resort was completely quiet, Janie tracked Tierney to Renner's trailer.

She sat on Renner's unsightly mint green and turquoise sofa, with a box of tissues on one side and a bottle of peppermint schnapps on the other.

Janie took the chair opposite the couch. "We need to talk."

Although Tierney's eyes were red and puffy beneath her glasses, she wore a look of defiance. "I'm not in the mood to hear anything you've got to say." She swigged directly from the bottle. "Save your breath if you plan to wax poetic about the wonderful job opportunity Daddy dearest offered you. The man's a slimy liar, a cheat, and . . . I'm out of other names but I'm sure more will come to me."

Janie rested her forearms on her thighs. "Why does everyone think I jumped at the chance to work for PFG?"

"Didn't you?"

"No. I'll admit I interviewed with him today. I wanted to see what breaking my loyalty to Renner was worth to him."

"And?" Tierney asked dully.

"First off, he changed his mind and made it a formal interview rather than preliminary. His offer was to triple my current salary, immediate relocation for a three-year hospitality training position with the Grand Gateway Hotel in Muskrat Cove, Wisconsin."

"That's the crappiest property PFG owns. The manager is a troll and the employee turnover is close to ninety percent." Tierney tipped the bottle again. "What was his response when you declined the offer?"

"He seemed smug. Especially after I told him I loved working for Renner. And you. He told me to enjoy it while it lasted." Janie watched Tierney squirm. "Wanna tell me what that means?"

"Renner's contract contains a fucked-up payment clause even I didn't catch. My father will forgive Renner's debt entirely, turn ownership of the Split Rock over to him completely, if I return to my previous position with the company in Chicago."

Janie frowned. "Weren't you always planning to return?"

Tierney shook her head. "No. I resigned. Everything I've done here has been on my own. Including lending the resort money out of my personal account, which naturally I hadn't told Renner and when he found out . . . he wasn't pleased."

"And I thought I was fucked," Janie muttered. "So what are you going to do?"

"What are my choices? Take everything from Renner because he was stupid enough to fall in love with me? And if I love him as much as I say I do, then shouldn't I make the ultimate sacrifice and walk away so he can have what he worked so hard for?"

"Did Renner tell you that's what he wants?"

"No." Tears slid down Tierney's cheeks. "It would've been easier—smarter certainly—for us to fall in love with someone else. But we didn't. It's so screwed up. Renner is . . . everything. Now I can't imagine my life without him. I'm still pinching myself that a man like him would want me. Love me. But he does, I know in my heart he does. And we're both in a helluva mess because of it." She sniffed. "So if you've got any advice, Janie, I'd love to hear it."

Janie stood and grabbed a glass from the kitchen. She held it out so Tierney could share the schnapps. After a slow sip, she plopped down, propping her feet on the coffee table. "Tit for tat, girlfriend. Here's my fucked-up situation. I'm so in love with my ex-husband it ain't funny."

"Does Abe know?"

"Who knows? When I was complaining to Abe about

not knowing you and Renner were in love, he got a little pissy and said it was obvious. I'm thinking to myself, if he could see that with you guys, how could he *not* pick up on the fact I'm goofy in love with him? So that made *me* pissy. And then I reverted to the bratty behavior I pulled when we were married." She scowled at her drink and drained it. "Which went over well, especially when I hinted I was ready to pack up and leave Muddy Gap, I had nothing tying me here, yada yada yada."

"Did you mean it?"

"No." She bit the inside of her lip to keep from breaking down. "Now I think I've screwed up any chance of convincing him I love him, and everything I tried so hard to get away from years ago is exactly what I want now, because it's better now. We're both better. Frankly, even with all that weird shit that went down, I've never been happier in my life than the last few months."

"Tell him that." Tierney reached across the table and refilled Janie's cup. "If it's not about your pride, if you want a life with him, then you're going to have to make the first move and prove it."

"I don't know if he trusts me."

Tierney lifted her glass. "Well, there you go. Get him to trust you. Then your problem is solved."

"Sounds simplistic."

"The best things often are. So . . . now that I've helped solve your crisis, how about returning the favor?"

"Me? You're the financial whiz." Janie shoved a hand through her hair. "There's got to be a way to keep this place out of your father's hands. Except for writing him a check so you take ownership of the Split Rock, then turn it over to Renner, because he will see you bailing him out as charity. Trust me on this."

"Just like he assumed my father handed me the job," she murmured.

"Exactly. I know life is not supposed to be about keeping up appearances, but out here in the West? It is. Renner won't be able to hold his head up in the community if locals assume you're his sugar mama."

When Tierney slowly straightened, Janie saw the wheels spinning. "What? You already came up with something, didn't you?"

"Maybe. I need a couple days to see if it's feasible."

Janie took that as her cue to leave. "At the risk of sounding self-centered, do I still have a job?"

"Of course. I know why my father wanted to snap you up, Janie. You're very good at what you do."

"Except for my inability to sniff out office romances," she said dryly.

"We were discreet."

"Well, discretion sucks. Maybe if we toss it to the wind, we'll both get lucky with what we want."

Tierney flashed a decidedly sharklike smile. "Not luck. Skill. We both have the skills to get what we want. We just have to be smart enough to use them."

∞

Janie rolled out of bed at four a.m. She muttered as she dressed in her warmest clothes, including the ugly neon orange winter cap Abe had purchased for her at the feed store. She shivered as she climbed in her car in the pitch black and drove out to the ranch. The lights were still off in the house, but she knew he'd be up soon.

Abe hadn't bothered to lock the door. She snuck into the kitchen and started coffee, listening to George whimpering in his crate. She whispered, "You have a lot to learn about being a ranch guard dog, pup."

As the pot brewed, she dug in the front coat closet for an old pair of Celia's coveralls and a small jacket.

Shoot. She eyed her athletic shoes. They'd have to do until she found time to buy a new pair of boots.

She pulled out two insulated mugs from the cupboard. When she turned and saw Abe leaning against the counter, his muscled arms folded over his chest, his dark hair rumpled from sleep and even darker whiskers covering his strong jaw, her heart swelled, flipped over in her chest, and clogged her throat. She couldn't leave this man—this beautiful, stubborn, wonderful man she loved so much—and she hated she'd led him to believe she could.

"Janie? What the devil are you doin' here this early?"

Vocal cords, don't fail me now. "Making coffee before we start chores."

Abe's eyebrows lifted. "We?"

"Uh-huh." *Eloquent, Janie.* She squared her shoulders. "I realized something the last two nights I spent alone. Since I've lived here with you, I never once got up and helped with chores. Granted, you didn't ask. Nor did you poke me in the ribs until I rolled out of bed, grumbling, like you used to do when we were married."

"You always hated that."

"But I never realized why you woke me up. Now I understand it was your way of showing me you wanted to start the day with me by your side."

Abe's gunmetal gray eyes stayed on hers.

"I didn't understand a lot of things back then that I do now. I'm here because I need to apologize for the childish way I acted the other night. I was looking for a reason to fight. It was easy falling back into old familiar patterns. We'd fight. I'd retreat. Or I'd storm off. And I expected you to find me or follow me. I expected you to coax me back." As much as she wanted to look away, she forced herself to hold Abe's eyes. "Did you know that's one of the things that hurt the most when I left? You didn't come after me. At the time I believed it was a sign it was over between us because you didn't care enough to chase me down. Now when I see myself reverting to that woman-child who expected you to make all the effort, I'm embarrassed. I'm ashamed. I don't want to be her. I'm *not* her anymore.

"So you should know . . . I lied. I had no intention of taking Gene Pratt's job offer. I thought by taunting you with the possibility, you'd beg me not to leave. You'd convince me that although we'd both changed in the past eight years, we still belonged together. I wanted that sweet coaxing from you so badly that I picked a fight to get it. But you didn't give it to me. I spent all night stewing in my own stupidity. I spent all yesterday wondering how I could have my pride and have you. But know what I figured out?"

"What?"

"I don't want pride when it comes to you. I want honesty. So here's the whole truth, Abe. I love you. I want to stay in Muddy Gap with you here on the ranch. I want you to take a chance on me. On us. Starting fresh."

Abe pushed off the counter and wandered to the coffeepot. He took his own sweet time filling both mugs. Janie had to bite her tongue to keep from yelling at him to hurry up and tell her if they had a future.

When several long minutes passed and Abe didn't move, didn't speak, Janie had a bone-deep fear that she might be too late.

Finally he cleared his throat. "I'll give you the chance. But there will be conditions."

Sweet relief nearly knocked her to her knees. "Anything."

Abe turned around. "This time when you marry me, you will take my last name."

Her jaw dropped.

Then he was right there, his rough fingers under her chin. His mouth covered hers in a warm and gentle kiss. A kiss packed with promise and forgiveness. And love.

Love that he confessed the instant he broke the seal of their lips. "Janie. I love you. So much." He kissed her softly. "Wanna hear something crazy? In the hours I laid in bed missing you, I decided if you left, I'd follow you. No matter where you went."

"What?"

"I figured since I have a college degree, I could find a job doin' something besides ranching."

Her confused eyes searched his. "But you love the ranch."

"Yeah, I do. But I love you too. Last time I picked this place over you. I should've chased you down and I didn't because of my pride. I never thought I'd get another chance and I ain't dumb enough to blow it. So if you've really got your heart set on livin' someplace else—"

She shook her head and didn't bother to hide her tears.

"Hey, now." Abe's thumbs wiped the dampness from beneath her eyes. "None of this. Your cheeks will freeze when we get outside. Can't have my bride-to-be wearing permanent tear tracks, now can I?"

Janie stared at him. "You really want to marry me again?"

"Yep. Right away, too. But like I said, there are a couple of conditions."

"Change my name. Check. What else?"

"No running away for you or clamming up for me if we hit a rough patch. We talk it out, figure it out, and if we can't do it on our own, then we find a professional to help us sort it out. Though I doubt it'll come to that this time, I wanna make sure we're on the same page."

"Deal."

"Also, I want kids."

There was that catch in her heart again. "Soon?"

"As soon as you're ready. I'm ready now. I know your career is important to you and that's fine by me."

"How much did Hank and Lainie's baby have to do with this need to reproduce?"

"Some. Not a jealousy thing, or a competition thing, but a you thing."

She peered up at him. "A *me* thing?"

"When I see you, Janie, I see a future, our future, and that future includes kids. And you and me bein' pruny together in fifty years." Abe smiled. "Now that's out of the way, we've got cattle to feed. I'm grateful for your help since Hank is too busy admiring his baby girl and fussing over his wife."

"Harper told us all about Lainie's close call. I'm relieved

everything turned out so well." She bit her lip. "Do you think your family can ever forgive me for leaving you? Let me be part of the family again?"

"It don't matter what they think, Janie, because I forgive you. And you and I are already a family. We've been building it since the moment you moved in."

She buried her face in his chest and held him tightly, grateful for the love of this amazing man and second chances.

As they grabbed the mugs and headed out the door, Janie knew they had more to discuss. Lots more. Not everything would get solved today. But they had a damn good start on it.

Chapter Thirty-seven

/❦

Two weeks later . . .

"*C*all me back, dammit." Tierney angrily punched the END CALL button on her phone.

Janie glanced up from where she sat at Renner's desk. "He's still not taking your calls?"

"No. What is wrong with him? What if the Split Rock burned down and I needed to get ahold of him?"

"At the risk of pissing you off, he'd probably be happy because the insurance money would cover the damages and then he could afford to pay back the PFG loan."

Tierney crumpled up a sheet of paper and lobbed it at Janie. "Not funny."

"If it makes you feel any better, he's not returning my calls either."

"Actually, that doesn't make me feel better. It makes me feel . . ." *Lost. Alone. Unsure whether I've done the right thing.*

Then Janie's hands were flat on her desk as she stuck her nose in Tierney's face. But Tierney's gaze automatically focused on the brand-new two-carat diamond, centered in a white gold wedding band, surrounded by square-cut amethysts. Thrilled as she was that Janie and Abe worked out their differences and had gotten remarried last week, she still felt a pang of jealousy.

"Renner is always incommunicative when he's on the road this time of the rodeo season. The truth is he's too busy during the day with back-to-back events. At night, he's too exhausted. The cycle starts anew each day."

"But I don't have the luxury of time. We need to move on this now. I can't do anything until I hear from him." She'd come up with a plan to pry the resort from her father's clutches that was so perfect, bordering on sheer brilliance, that she couldn't wait to get Renner's approval and input.

"How much time before the note is due?"

"Three weeks." She held up her hand to stop Janie's rebuttal. "Don't say plenty of time. I need a full week for the money to clear all channels. So I'm desperate to get in touch with the elusive man."

"Well, there's nothing you can do beyond tracking him down and kidnapping him."

Tierney stilled. Kidnap. Huh. What a great idea.

"Oh, Miz Pratt, I do not like the look in your eye."

"I imagine Renner will like it even less, Mrs. Lawson." She smirked and pushed her chair away from her desk. At the door she grabbed her coat, her mind already racing a million miles an hour.

"Where are you going?"

"To the barn."

"For what?"

"Kidnapping supplies."

❧

Renner's phone vibrated at five thirty in the morning. He'd been asleep exactly two hours. He blindly reached for the buzzing object on the nightstand and rolled over on the lumpy mattress. "This'd better be good."

Hugh Pritchett released a stream of gibberish that instantly jolted Renner awake. "Whoa whoa whoa. Slow down. Start over from the beginning 'cause I didn't understand a word you said."

"BB is gone."

"What the fuck are you talking about, Pritchett? BB, our bull, is gone? As in . . . ?" His heart nearly stopped. "Dead?"

"No. Gone. As in vanished. As in stolen."

Renner scrambled upright. "What? How could that've happened?"

"No clue. But here's the damndest thing." Pritchett laughed awkwardly. "It's gonna sound stupid."

"Tell me."

"BB left a note."

"If this is some kinda big fucking joke, Hugh, I ain't laughing. At all."

"I swear, boss, I'm not kiddin'. I hadn't checked on him in two days. So this morning when I went to check he was gone from his pen. And there was a note tacked to the fence post."

"A note. From BB," Renner repeated dully. Jesus. He felt like an idiot asking, but he did anyway. "What did the note from BB say?"

"It said, and I quote: Headed to my new home, where the heifers are hotter, the view is better and the mountain air is sweeter." Hugh was quiet for a couple of breaths. "Does that make any sense to you?"

"Yeah, believe it or not, it does."

Tierney. Damn her hide. She'd stolen his damn bull.

How?

Why?

Her last voice mail warned, *Losing my patience with you, cowboy. Desperate times call for desperate measures.*

He should've taken her warning seriously.

"So do you want me to call the sheriff and report stolen livestock?" Pritchett asked.

Renner sighed. "No. I know exactly where BB is."

"You do?"

"He's been hauled to the Split Rock."

"Shit." Then, "Wait. Was this planned?"

"By me? Hell no."

"What're you gonna do?"

"Hit the road. Guess it's a good thing I was already on my way to Wyoming."

∞

Renner thought about giving Tierney a heads-up that he was on his way. He'd also considered scaring the crap outta her by having one of his buddies from Kansas call her, pretending to be an investigator with the CRA regarding the recent rash of livestock thefts.

But ultimately, he'd just decided to show up.

He'd been thinking about her nonstop for the last twenty-two and a half days. He missed her. God, did he ever miss her. He wondered how he'd survived the loneliness on the road before she'd come into his life. It'd killed him, not texting her a hundred times a day. Not talking to her for an hour before his head hit the pillow every night. The woman had wormed her way into his heart. She owned his soul. As much as he'd loved what he'd built at the Split Rock, he loved what he'd begun to build with her more.

As Renner passed between the twin stone pillars marking the entrance to the ranch, his pride was tinged with sadness. Although he'd thought of little else except her on the six-hundred-mile drive, he needed time to get his bearings before they met face-to-face. He drove down to the barn. Snow was several feet deep and he found himself looking at the pens. No sign of BB.

Renner parked and entered the barn from the side door.

Tobin poked his head around the corner. His eyes widened, but so did his grin. "Looking for something?"

"You'd better have my goddamned bull in here, Tobin. BB better be getting daily damn massages and the best fresh mountain hay money can buy."

"He's in the big stall."

"I can't believe she roped you in—"

"For the record, Tierney gave me no choice but to help her temporarily liberate BB."

"She threaten to fire you?"

"Ah. No. She threatened to grab BB on her own. I knew she'd hitch up a cattle trailer and try to coax a two-thousand-pound bull into the trailer by herself. I figured it'd be better for me to be with her, helping her, even when I didn't agree with what she was doin'." Tobin beamed. "Although she was right in knowing exactly what it'd take to get you to come home. I had August Fletcher check BB out as soon as we unloaded him. Mean SOB is perfectly fine."

"Good thing. I was worried."

Tobin looked confused. "Tierney didn't assure you everything went okay when you talked to her?"

When Renner didn't answer, Tobin swore.

"Please tell me you didn't come down here and check on your bull before you saw Tierney? Dude. What is wrong with you?"

He threw up his hands. "I'm an idiot, all right?"

"Damn right you are. You've been gone three weeks. Three weeks in which she's been so damn miserable—"

At the word *miserable*, Renner booked it out the door.

He tried to think where she'd be this time of day, but he had no freakin' clue what time it was. Or what day it was. Too many long hours on the road with limited sleep. Too many hours filled with thoughts of her. Too many hours trying to figure a way out of this mess.

Renner hoofed it up the path that led from the barn to the lodge. He heard a noise and glanced up at the parka-clad woman at the top of the path. Her cheeks were rosy. Her brown eyes were enormous behind her glasses. Her lips were parted with an O of surprise.

"Renner? Is that really you?"

"Yep."

Brilliant answer.

Then Tierney did the most un-Tierney-like thing. She shrieked, raced down the hill and threw herself into his arms.

He closed his eyes, held her close and breathed her in.

This was where he belonged. With this woman. No matter what happened, no matter where they ended up, as long as they ended up together, everything would be all right. He trapped her face in his hands and gazed at her adoringly. "I'm sorry I left like I did. I love you. God, I love you so damn much that it's been killin' me to be away from you."

"When I didn't hear from you—"

"You grabbed the bull by the horns?" he said dryly. "Or should I say, you got pissy and took the whole damn bull? BB is a dangerous animal, Tierney. Makes me crazy to think you'd pull a stunt like that. You could've gotten hurt."

"But I didn't." Tierney poked him in the sternum. "You forced me to get creative to capture your attention since you wouldn't return my calls."

"I . . . I needed . . ." He rested his forehead to hers. "Hell, I don't know what I was thinkin'. I hoped I could come up with the money, turn this situation around, but nothin's changed."

"Wrong. Everything has changed." Her gaze dropped to his mouth. "I want to kiss you. I've imagined what I'd do when I saw you again. Most of the scenarios were X-rated."

He laughed. "I really love that about you too."

"But I know once I start kissing you I won't want to quit." Tierney stepped away from him, but she grabbed his hand. "Come on. I need to show you something." She led him up the path to the back door of the lodge and up the staircase into their office. When he tried to tug her into his arms for a full body-on-body kiss, she ducked. "No way. Once you put your hands on me, I'm toast. I need a clear head for this." She pointed to the couch. "Sit. I'll get the paperwork."

"What? No PowerPoint?"

"It's not quite done," she tossed over her shoulder as she pawed through files on her desk.

"I was kiddin'."

Tierney peered at him over the top of her glasses. "Never kid about PowerPoint."

Damn, he loved this woman.

She wandered over, file folder clutched to her chest. "Umm. Would you like coffee?"

"No."

"How about a soda?"

"No."

"Maybe you want something stronger?"

Why was she so nervous? Her nervousness set him on edge. "If I wanted something to drink, I'd get it myself. Now get on with it."

His snappish answer had the intended effect. She squared her shoulders and took the chair to his left. "While you were gone, PFG sent a certified letter, invoking the clause from the initial contract, which required payment in full. Although not required to do so, the official reasoning for the change in the contract terms is 'questionable financial judgment that could result in possible loan default.'"

Renner muttered, "Total bullshit."

"I concur. I broke down the payoff amount and realized PFG had not figured the price of the land and the improvements you'd made *before* your loan application into that payoff amount. So as your self-appointed financial overseer, I requested an immediate reconfiguration of the total due, which they are required to complete as quickly as possible because of their change in contract terms."

He understood Tierney's need to explain every minute detail, but it was damn difficult not to urge her to get to the point.

"You with me so far?" she asked.

"Yeah. Keep goin' but I wouldn't mind if you just hit the high points. Or the low points."

"When I received the revised loan payoff amount, I was surprised to see it wasn't as much as I'd projected." When he started to ask a question, she held up her hand. "No, I did not secretly use some of my own money to buy off a chunk of the loan to lower the total amount due."

"Okay. Show me the number."

"But don't you want to know about—"

"No. I wanna know exactly how much money it'll take to pay off the note."

Tierney turned the paper and tapped her pen on the number at the bottom of the page.

Renner whistled. "That's . . . still a shitload of cash."

"Yes, but when you break it down, the amount of collateral you have in the land is sixty percent. So you probably could find a traditional financial institution to lend you the money. But I'm expecting in this economy the terms would be less than ideal and the payments would be steep."

"But doable if I could shave a couple hundred thousand off the bottom line."

"How would you do that?" she demanded.

He didn't look at her. "I've been talking to a couple of other stock contractors and they're willing to buy BB outright. Cash."

"No way. That is not in the plan. BB could be the center of a great breeding program, because you could earn more by selling his semen than selling him outright."

"Now you're officially scaring me. How the hell do you know the value of bull semen?" Renner sighed. "Tobin."

"He's smart and he's got some great ideas. But explaining that part of Plan B will have to wait until we're through this Plan A."

Renner grabbed her hand to force her attention. "What? You have two plans?" He sighed again. "Of course you have two plans."

"Plan A or Plan B. You have two choices." Tierney linked their fingers. "I need you to listen to me very carefully. I may have not offered full disclosure on why I was in Wyoming, but that didn't make anything that happened here, or between us, any less real. I love you. I want to be with you, in this community I've grown attached to. But if that's not what you want, I'll walk away. From you. From everything."

His heart almost stopped. "Walk away? Why?"

"My father presented me with another option. I haven't

given him an answer because you left and I wasn't sure what you wanted. But I'm offering full disclosure now. PFG will mark your loan paid in full and you will retain sole ownership of the Split Rock if I return to Chicago and my position with Pratt Financial Group."

His anger resurfaced and a displeased growl escaped. "No. Fucking. Way. I will never ever let you be used as a bargaining chip again. Never. You understand me? I wouldn't take the deal when that bastard tried to bribe me a few weeks ago and I sure as hell won't let you take it either."

Tierney's eyes clouded. "What deal?"

"Part of the reason I was so pissed off that day I got wind of the contract clause? Wasn't because of the contract, Tierney. It was because your father had the balls to use you against me. He promised to forgive every penny of the loan, transfer full ownership of Split Rock back to me if I broke it off with you permanently."

"Happy to see I'm worth so much to him," she said bitterly.

"You're worth everything to me. I didn't wait to give him my answer. I told him no. Period. My feelings for you weren't for sale." He frowned. "Which is why I was so surprised that he left a copy of the contract in my truck."

She fidgeted. "Ah. He didn't do that. I did. I swear I had no idea about that stupid clause until he got all cocky and told me. Then he warned I couldn't legally disclose it to you. So I had Tobin make a copy of the contract—your original from your desk—he circled the pertinent section and put it in your truck. So technically *I* didn't do it."

He kissed the back of her hand. "Have I mentioned how much I love this steel-trap mind of yours?" He let his lips move up the inside of her wrist. "And your other parts. Want me to refresh your memory on which parts?"

"Later. But first you need to hear the other option."

"Fine. Hit me."

"Shareholders. I've rounded up enough shareholders to

buy into the Split Rock to pay off the loan. Plus, we'd have enough operating funds for two years. And before you ask, it was not fully funded by me."

"Then who?"

"Ever since we hosted that community party, people in Muddy Gap have been asking how they can show support for the Split Rock. After talking it over with Janie and Harper, we decided to pitch the idea to locals—a chance to buy in and invest in the community. We wanted a mix of business owners and individual investors." Her eyes sparkled. "The best part? We had enough financial backing to pay off the loan . . . within three days."

Renner found himself picking his jaw off the floor. "Seriously? Who kicked in?"

"Well, the Mud Lilies pooled their resources. Bernice. Susan Williams. Dodie and her family members. Janie and Abe. Harper." She grinned. "Besides you and me, Harper would own the largest chunk. Bran will do anything to support Harper's career and make her happy. He probably would've fronted all the money if no one had come forward."

Beyond stunned, he just gawked at her. "Seriously? This is perfect. This is better than perfect, better than me being solely responsible for taking on the challenge of running it or PFG taking over. I—I . . ." A lump clogged his throat. "How did you ever come up with this idea?"

She pressed her lips to his. "Because this is our home. Here we have what we've both wanted. A place to belong. A sense of community. A chance to give back and be part of something permanent. We both want to set down roots."

"God. Tierney." He rested his forehead to hers and tried not to feel dizzy with hope.

"It's a little overwhelming. But it's a good thing, right?"

"It's an amazing thing. I can scarcely wrap my head around it." He stared at her for a beat. "What was Plan B?"

"If you would've sent me packing back to Chicago, the shareholders would've used the money to invest in a semen collection facility for stock breeding programs. Seems Abe Lawson recently earned some kind of ag degree. He, Tobin, Hank, Bran, Fletch and Eli were going to approach you about tying their idea in with the Jackson Stock Contracting Company. Even if it wasn't associated with the Split Rock."

"I'm interested. I guess Pritchett will be moving to Wyoming or looking for another job."

An anxious look darkened her eyes. "You all right with this? I worried that you'd accuse me of overstepping my boundaries again."

"No more boundaries between us. Ever." He kissed her. And kept kissing her until she began to make those low-throated sexy moans. He broke the seal of their mouths to whisper, "You have no idea how much I missed you."

"Not as much as I missed you. Wanna hear something funny? I snuck into your trailer and slept in your bed a couple of nights because the sheets smelled like you."

Overwhelmed by her, by everything, wanting to take everything she offered before she changed her mind and snatched it back, Renner blurted, "Tierney. Marry me."

Her eyes went wide. "You want to marry me? Not just live together?"

"Despite evidence to the contrary, I believe in marriage. Besides, third time's a charm, right?"

She whapped him on the arm.

"Kiddin'. I want to spend every moment of the rest of my life with you as my wife. As soon as possible. Please marry me, Tierney Pratt."

"Yes. God, yes." She kissed him so sweetly that he didn't realize she was crying until he felt his cheeks were wet. "But we're not getting hitched in Vegas."

Epilogue

～

Four weeks later ...

The party was in full swing. The new Split Rock Ranch and Resort shareholders had invited everyone in the community to the celebration and grand reopening. Also, Willie had lined up a tribal elder to perform a Crow cleansing rite to put restless spirits at peace, not only around the structures, but also across the area that'd long been considered bad luck land. Tierney wasn't sure she believed in that type of woo-woo Indian stuff, but she agreed it couldn't hurt.

The Mud Lilies had turned the party into Tierney and Renner's belated wedding reception. Bets were placed whether the happy couple would smash cake in each other's faces, given the drink Tierney had thrown in Renner's face that had started their romance ball rolling. It was funny now, to hear the comments from locals, that they "knew" Renner and Tierney were meant for each other from the start.

Two weeks ago, after a quick trip to the county courthouse to officially tie the knot, they drove to Chicago to pick up the rest of Tierney's belongings from storage. They'd spent the weekend in the city, visiting Tierney's old haunts. She'd introduced her husband to her friends Sari and Josie, which led to the inevitable question: did Renner have any hot-looking single cowboy friends in Wyoming?

The most important thing they'd done in Chicago was pay off the note in person. Tierney wanted to leave after that, but Renner insisted they meet with her father.

Gene Pratt was strangely subdued when his secretary ushered Renner and Tierney Jackson into his office. Renner gave him a copy of the paid-in-full loan receipt. Then he'd shaken her father's hand, thanking him for the loan because it'd brought Tierney into his life and she was worth more than any amount of money.

Class act, her husband.

"So are you pregnant yet?" Garnet demanded, pulling Tierney from her thoughts.

Maybelle looked like she wanted to throttle Garnet. "Do you remember our discussions about boundaries?"

"Yeah, yeah, yeah. I suppose that means as a part owner of the Split Rock I can't demand the cowboys workin' for us always wear hats, unbuttoned white shirts, tight Wranglers and spurs at public events?"

"No."

"Shoot. I guess I'd better apologize to Tobin. I chewed him out for bein' out of uniform."

Tierney bit back a laugh.

Maybelle whipped out her notebook after Garnet left. "For the record, as one of the new owners, will you be involved in the day-to-day operations of the Split Rock in your previous position?"

"I'll be involved, since I'm a majority shareholder. Janie Lawson is general manager of the facility. Harper Turner is handling retail—in fact she's expanding the entire store. Tobin Hale is heading up the new livestock breeding program. I'm focusing on building an independent financial consulting business, as well as supporting my husband"—she got such a thrill saying *my husband* — "in his endeavors to move his base of operations for Jackson Stock Contracting to Muddy Gap."

"That's lovely, Tierney. We're happy for you two. We're glad you're sticking around."

Tierney watched Maybelle lumber away.

His warm, hard chest pressed into her back and his mouth grazed her ear. "I couldn't help but overhear . . . Are you pregnant, Mrs. Jackson?"

"No."

"Do you wanna be?"

She turned into his arms. "We've been married less than a month and you're already talking about babies?"

"Must be Hank and Lainie's darlin' little Brianna that's putting thoughts in my head." Renner kissed her. Seemed he was always kissing her in public just because he could. "I give Abe and Janie two months before she's knocked up. So I'm just following the Lawson boys' lead and giving you a heads-up that I wanna have babies with you, Tierney. Lots of them."

"Where would we put all these babies? We live in a small cabin, remember?"

His brow furrowed. "I wish you'd let me build you a real house."

"Some day. But for now, can't we just be happy with what we've got? Being with you every night makes it more than a house; it makes it a real home. Our home."

"And to think I never wanted to get tangled up with you." Renner gave her the smile that was hers alone. "I love you."

She toyed with the neckerchief he'd looped around his neck. "Oh yeah? The sooner we cut the cake, the sooner you can take me home and prove your undying love for me."

"Such a tyrant. Come on, I bribed Garnet into putting extra sprinkles on the cake just for you. Because I have it on good authority that everything in life is better with sprinkles."

"I used to think that. But now I know everything in life is better with . . . you."

"Damn sugar mouth. Gets you whatever you want."

"And everything I've ever wanted is right in front of me." Tierney kissed him.

Keep reading for a preview of the new release
in Lorelei James's bestselling Mastered Series,

Unraveled

Available now from New American Library.

*S*hiori Hirano wanted to beat the fuck out of someone.
And by "someone" she meant that smarmy asswipe
Knox Lofgren.

Ob-Knox-ious had been in rare form today, harping on
safety protocols until the newly earned black belt class looked
ready to commit hara-kiri just so they wouldn't have to listen
to their Shihan drone on and on.

And there was another point of contention. Everyone
else in Black Arts dojo called Knox "Shihan" since he was
the highest-ranking belt after Master Black.

Or he was until *she'd* arrived.

Since Shiori outranked him by one belt level, she called
him Godan, one step down in the ranking system—which
really got his goat. Then he retaliated by refusing to refer to
her by any official title at all, calling her She-Cat or Shitake.

Yes, they were shining examples of leadership.

Her brother, Ronin Black, had left Knox in charge of his

martial-arts dojo while he took a ten-week sabbatical to Japan with his wife. While Shiori agreed Ronin deserved the break, she wasn't sure she'd survive working eighty days with Knox.

"Are there any questions before you're dismissed?" Knox asked the class.

Jesus. Loaded question.

And of course the biggest pain-in-the-ass student raised her hand. "Shihan, I'm a little fuzzy on that sit-up guard and sweep. Could you demonstrate?"

The silly chit expected Shihan would beckon her up to demonstrate? And he'd press his big body to hers as he relayed directions in his deep bedroom voice? No. He'd want her to observe and that meant . . .

"Shiori, I need your assistance."

Right-o, Captain Asshat. And I need a gin and tonic. Jumbo-sized. Pronto.

Refusing wasn't an option, so she rolled to her feet and moved to the center of the mat.

"Gather 'round so you can all see this." As soon as the students had formed a circle, he sat and placed his right foot above her left knee.

She went to grab his left leg for the sweep, and he grabbed her white gi top by the lapels and shoved her to the mat, rolling her onto her shoulder and pinning her arm down with his knee on her gi sleeve.

When Knox went into side mount, it took every ounce of restraint not to immediately counter his move.

Little Miss Ten Million Questions asked to see the move one more time. And of course Shihan obliged her.

Finally he dismissed the class. She was about to bail when two hands landed on her shoulders.

So tempting to give in to her instinct and do a sweep and roll and jam her knee into his balls, but she refrained. She deserved a fucking cookie for that.

"Mandatory meeting with ABC instructors in five minutes in the second-floor training room."

"Yippee." She shook off his hands and started walking away.

"Great attitude. I saw some of that in class tonight. Curb it before next class."

"No problem. As long as you curb your tendency to over-explain a simple technique for the benefit of jiggly tits, who'd just love for you to show her every mount technique in your arsenal."

Knox stopped and latched onto her arm. "Jillian? She asked a valid question."

"No, she asked for a demonstration. And I'm pretty sure her nipples pouted when you didn't demonstrate on her. You demonstrated on me again."

"Which is your job."

"No. My job would've been to show the class how stupid that move is in the first place and the best way to counter it."

His eyes cooled. "But you didn't do that . . . in deference to me?"

"Yes, sir."

"There aren't any students around now, She-Cat. So let's take this to the mat."

"That offer is so freakin' hard to refuse, but—"

Knox crowded her against the elevator door. "That wasn't an offer."

Shit. "You're pulling rank on me?"

"Damn straight. You and me. Upstairs. Now." He lowered his head and whispered, "Put your money where your mouth is, Rokudan. Put me in my place."

Shiori balled her hands into fists against his sarcastic use of her sixth-degree black belt rank, Rokudan. What really rankled were the goose bumps flowing down the left side of her body from the rumble of his voice in her ear.

Knox walked off without looking back.

What the hell was wrong with her? She hadn't uttered a peep, hadn't tossed out an insult, hadn't even created silent cutting remarks in her head when he'd made the challenge.

Because Knox affects you in ways you're scared to admit.

When she entered the training room, Deacon looked at her, then at Knox, and said, "Jesus. This again?"

Shiori ignored him.

Knox waited for her on the mat. No hint of smile on his face; just the determined set of his jaw.

"How do you want me?"

That seemed to fluster him for a second before he barked, "Standing sweep."

Knox grabbed onto her and tried to drive her into the floor.

She turned her upper body but kept her feet planted—tricky to execute without ending up with torn ligaments in her knee—and pushed on his center of gravity.

It knocked him back a step, as she'd intended, but his balance recovery was quick. So instead of her dog piling him, he crushed her back to his chest in a bear hug and at the same time he swept her feet out from under her.

They hit the mat hard.

Shiori threw her leg on the outside of his and pushed off with her other foot, which allowed her to control the direction they rolled.

Somehow she'd telegraphed her intent, because Knox countered and shoved her face-first into the mat—after he'd clipped her in the mouth with his elbow.

So he had her pinned down in the most humiliating position—with him lying on top of her, both of her arms trapped.

Then his warm lips were against her ear. "Come on, She-Cat. Put me in my place. Show me how stupid that move was."

"Get the fuck off of me."

"I'm game anytime you wanna teach me another lesson," he murmured again, and then he was gone.

Shiori rolled onto her back. Fuck. Was she losing her touch? She pushed up into a sitting position and wrapped her arms around her calves.

That's when she noticed the blood.

And the crowd that'd gathered around them.

Sophia "Fee" Curacao snatched a towel and doused it in water before she crouched beside Shiori. "You okay?"

Shiori nodded and held the towel to her mouth, where the wound was starting to sting.

Fee stood and glared at Knox. "I cannot believe you drew blood on her the first fucking day you're running the dojo, Shihan."

"It's all right, Fee," Shiori said softly. "I should've been paying better attention."

The sight of blood had changed Knox's taunting mood. "You're damn right you should've been."

Not an apology—not that she deserved one. Annoyed by the guys staring at her and the fucked-up way Knox was studying her mouth, she pushed to her feet. "I'm fine. Let's get this meeting over with."

Knox said, "Not you. Take off. You bleed, you leave."

Shiori rolled her eyes. "That is a shitty rhyme and a shitty rule, so I'm not going anywhere."

"Suit yourself." Knox clapped his hands for attention. "Gather 'round."

Deacon, Ito, Zach, and Jon moved in on Knox's left. Blue, Fee, Terrel, and Gil moved in on his right.

Knox ran through the list of weekly events and changes twice as fast as Ronin would have done, and they were finished with the meeting in ten minutes. New record.

"Anything to add, Shiori?"

"No, sir."

"Then we're done. See you all tomorrow." Knox left immediately. Maybe he had a hot date.

She punched in the number to the car service and requested a pickup. She didn't bother going to the locker room to change since she'd have to soak her gi to get the bloodstains out.

On the way out the front door she realized she had twisted her knee in that scuffle with Knox.

But all in all, a limp and a little blood—not bad for the first day.

∞

The next morning Shiori was in the conference room on her laptop, answering questions from her account managers at Okada, the family business, when Knox shuffled in.

He hadn't shaved, and she hated that the dark bristle accentuating his angular jaw looked so good on him. He wore wrinkled gi pants and his gi top wasn't closed, so she had a peek at his sculpted chest and muscular abs. She glanced up and caught Deacon staring at her from behind his laptop.

She couldn't help but snap, "You're late, Godan."

"Long night. I had to drive to Golden after class—"

"Not interested in where you go for your booty calls. Deacon and I—"

"Don't you drag me into this, darlin'," Deacon drawled.

Those two stuck together on everything. These next two and a half months might be the most combative of her life—and she'd worked in her grandfather's office, where every day was a battleground.

Knox glared at her as he turned over a coffee cup. "Not a booty call—not that it's any of your damn business if it were—but I had a family thing to deal with."

Deacon said, "Everything all right?"

"Now it is. But I'm fucking tired and need a gallon of coffee to wake up."

He started to pour a cup and Shiori said, "That's not—"

"Jesus, She-Cat. Give me two goddamn minutes before you start in on me."

Fine. Don't say I didn't try to warn you.

Knox took a drink from his cup. A grimace twisted his mouth, and he turned and spewed the liquid into the sink. "What the motherfuck is *that* shit?"

"Tea."

"Why? That's a coffeepot, not a teapot." His eyes narrowed. "You did that on purpose."

"I was the first one here, so I made tea. When you're the

first one here, you can make coffee." She smiled and sipped her tea.

Knox looked at Deacon for support.

"Don't you drag me into this either. She tried to tell you, but as usual, y'all prefer to snap and snarl at each other instead of listening."

"Are you drinking tea?" Knox demanded.

Deacon grinned at Shiori. "It ain't bad if you dump half a cup of sugar in it."

Knox snagged a Coke out of the fridge. "For the record, I'm buying one of those one-cup coffeemakers so this never happens again."

"Or you could be on time?" Shiori said sweetly.

∞

"I didn't have to sit through this many meetings in the army," Knox complained the next afternoon when they were gathered in the conference room.

"Sorry to inconvenience you when you were so *busy* upstairs playing footsie with Katie, but I don't have the backstory on this situation," Shiori retorted.

"Jealous, She-Cat?" he purred. " 'Cause I could talk Katie into letting you play footsie with us sometime."

"Stop bein' an ass, Knox, or she'll put you in charge of answering Ronin's e-mail," Deacon warned.

Not so much with the "I got your back, bro" between these two today.

"This e-mail came in last night." She picked up the printout and read, " 'Greetings, Sensei Black. I've recently had a philosophical difference with the leaders of the Cherry Creek Martial Arts Studio and have opted to stop training with them. This leaves me in a bind because the only other dojo I'd consider training in would be ABC, which is now part of Black Arts. I was part of the group of students who stormed into your dojo several years ago when Steve Atwood threw down the fight challenge.' " She glanced up. "What the hell is that about?"

"Steve Atwood is a cocky prick, and our students were

beating his students in tournaments. So he showed up here one night with thirty of his highest-ranking students and challenged Ronin to a public fight."

"Of course Ronin accepted," Shiori said.

Knox nodded. "He might've beaten him to death if I hadn't stepped in. Anyway, Atwood lost some students"— he grinned—"to us when the parents realized what a fucking tool bag Atwood had become. But as far as I know, we haven't taken on any new students from that martial-arts club since that time."

"That incident is why we have hard-core security before anyone can even enter the dojo," Deacon pointed out. "In hindsight that ended up being a good thing."

"This guy is a third-degree black belt. And he doesn't want to join our program but Blue's." Right after Shiori had come to the United States, Alvares "Blue" Curacao's Brazilian jujitsu dojo, ABC, had become part of Black Arts. "So before we bring this up with Blue and ABC, Black Arts needs to have a united decision."

"Tell him we aren't interested in further discussion," Knox stated.

"No. Set up a meeting. With me," Deacon said. "That way he'll see our updated security and that we don't fuck around. I'm a good judge of sincerity."

Knox snorted. "You? Come on, D. You hate fucking everybody. You are the only instructor who actively tries to get students to drop from your classes."

"Better he sees that than the milk and fucking cookies you've been serving the students in your classes recently."

Anger emanated from Knox, distorting the casual atmosphere like a poisonous cloud. He remained deadly still. Several long moments ticked by before he said, "Your opinion is noted, Yondan. You arc excused from this discussion."

Deacon pushed to his feet. He paused at the door and seemed to struggle with whether or not to speak. But he left without saying a word.

And how fucking awesome was it that Knox had learned the "I'm your sensei; my word is law" attitude from Ronin?

When Shiori felt Knox's ire directed at her, as if she'd contradict him, it took her a breath or two to look at him.

"Is that how you'd like me to respond to the e-mail? That we're not interested in him training in our facility in any capacity?" she asked.

"Forward the e-mail to me and I'll respond, but yes, that is my intent."

"Of course."

Shiori slid her laptop closer and started opening screens. Her fingers fumbled on the keys beneath Knox's penetrating stare. "Done."

"Do you disagree with my decision?" he asked coolly.

She met his gaze. "No, Shihan, I don't."

His eyes darkened. "That's the first time you've called me Shihan."

She closed her laptop and stood. "That's the first time you've acted like you deserve the title."

∞

Thursday night classes were always crazy. Still, it surprised her to hear, "Shihan needs you in practice room one."

Shiori glanced up at Deacon and moved toward him, standing in the open doorway. "What's going on?"

"I was filling in for Zach in the yellow belt class, and uh, well, now there are a couple of students who are cryin'."

"You made kids cry?"

"The fuck if I know what I did wrong. But you can hear those two girls bawlin'—"

"You made little *girls* cry?"

Deacon looked away. "Just go help Knox."

She passed through the open training areas. The wails assaulted her ears before she reached the room.

Knox had two little girls, age seven or so, up at the front of the class. With the way the building echoed, the girls' cries were actually louder outside the room. She shot a quick glance to the other students, a dozen boys and girls, who were watching Shihan with wide eyes.

Shiori set her hand on Knox's shoulder. For the briefest moment she thought he might act instinctively and put her in a wrist lock.

But he cranked his head around and gave her a surprised look. "What are you doing here?"

"Deacon said you needed help. What's going on?"

"Near as I can figure, that one"—Knox pointed to the dark-haired girl sobbing with her forehead on her knees—"attempted a wheel kick and her foot caught *her*"—he gestured to another dark-haired girl sobbing with her forehead on her knees—"in the face. Then girl number two pushed her down and tried to choke her out."

"Is either one hurt?"

He shook his head. "Go back to your class. I've got this handled."

Right. "What set off the waterworks?"

"Deacon put them in time-out for the rest of class and said he'd talk to their parents about banning them from watching MMA TV shows."

Seemed reasonable. MMA was great for showcasing high ability levels for different styles of martial arts, but kids didn't grasp that they shouldn't try those moves until they'd been trained properly. "What are their names?"

"No clue."

"Mind if I try to talk to them?"

"Have at it."

Shiori tapped girl number one on the foot. "Hey. You need to stop crying and get a grip."

Knox snorted. "Great help. And believe it or not, they *are* calmer than they were a few minutes ago."

"Don't you just have the magic touch?" she said sarcastically.

"No, but I do have two little sisters."

He did? Why hadn't she known that?

Knox touched girl number two on the arm. "Can you talk to me, sweetheart?"

Girl number two raised her head. Her sobs had faded into hiccupping sniffles. "Addy is mean. She said she's gonna get her orange belt before me so she doesn't have to be in the same class as me because I suck."

Girl number one looked up. Holy shit. They were identical twins. She retorted, "Abby is just mad because I'm better at jujitsu than she is."

"Are not!" Abby yelled.

"Am too!" Addy yelled back.

"Are not!" Abby yelled louder.

"Am too, and I don't want anyone thinking that you're me, because I *am* better!" Addy shouted.

"Girls," Shiori warned.

A warning that didn't stop the escalating screaming match.

Knox rolled his eyes. Then he sat between the two warring girls. "Enough."

"She started it," Abby said sullenly.

Addy tried to kick her.

Knox put his hand on Addy's leg. "Ms. Hirano, there's another class in room two. Since Addy thinks she's ready to move belt levels, will you please escort her into that class?"

"Right now?"

"Yep. Abby, say goodbye to your sister."

"Come on, Addy," Shiori said.

Addy didn't budge. Abby gasped. "You can't do that! We have to be in the same class."

Shiori shrugged. "No, you don't. My brother and I didn't even go to the same martial-arts school. Plus, the crying and carrying on makes me wonder if you even like taking jujitsu classes."

Another gasp—from Addy this time. "But it's our favorite thing!"

"Then maybe you should act like it. Come on, Addy. Let's get you settled in the other class."

"Please don't put me in a different class," Addy pleaded with Knox.

"I didn't mean what I said," Abby added. "Addy is helping me learn better. Please let her stay."

"You're both sure this is what you want?" Knox asked. They both nodded.

"Fine. But your actions do have consequences. You will sit out the remainder of class, and if I see any grappling, hitting, or kicking, I will have words with your parents."

"We'll be good, Shihan. We promise," Addy said. She mimed zipping her lips, and Abby did the same.

Knox patted them each on the leg and stood. "Pay attention because I may test you after class."

"I'm impressed," Shiori admitted to him grudgingly.

"My sisters yelled and screamed at each other, but the second Mom tried to separate them, they were best buddies again. I thought I'd give it a shot."

"Smart."

"All right," Knox said, standing in front of the class. "Get up. Take off your belts. At the count of ten, we'll have a belt-tying contest." He inclined his head to Shiori. "Ms. Hirano? Will you lead the countdown in Japanese?"

"Ready? *Ichi, ni, san, shi, go, roku, shichi, hachi, kyu, ju!*"

A flurry of belt tying ensued.

"I've always wondered. Did you and Ronin ever take jujitsu classes together?" Knox asked.

"No. He was always way more advanced than me. Our dad didn't feel the same need to push me into it like he did Ronin. Our mother is the one who insisted I train—probably preparing me to spar with my grandfather." She paused. "But once when I was about five I asked Ronin to practice with me."

"What happened?"

"He kicked me so hard—by accident—that he broke two of my ribs. He felt horrible. So horrible that he agreed to play dolls with me every day until I was better." Shiori shot him a sideways glance. "And no, you cannot tell Sensei Black you know that story."

Knox grinned. "No worries. I played dolls with my sisters, too, and I was a helluva lot older than eight."

"Done!" a towheaded boy in the front row yelled.

"Good job, Dylan. Now you get to come up front and pick what we do next." Knox leaned down and whispered in his ear.

His ease with younger kids didn't surprise her, since the man got along with everyone.

Including you?

Yes. They'd forged an unspoken truce yesterday after Knox had knocked Deacon down a peg, proving he could lead.

Now if they could just get through the last day of the week without incident, she might believe—just might—they'd survive the next nine weeks.

FROM *NEW YORK TIMES*
BESTSELLING AUTHOR

LORELEI JAMES

THE BLACKTOP COWBOYS SERIES

Corralled
Saddled and Spurred
Wrangled and Tangled
One Night Rodeo
Turn and Burn
Hillbilly Rockstar

Praise for the series:

"Her sexy cowboys are to die for!"
—*New York Times* bestselling author Maya Banks

"Lorelei James knows how to write
one hot, sexy cowboy."
—*New York Times* bestselling author Jaci Burton

Available wherever books are sold or at
penguin.com

facebook.com/LoveAlwaysBooks

S0534